The DEADLY Glade

Jeri Bolliger

Disclaimer
This is a work of fiction. Names, characters, places and events are either the product of the author's imagination or are used fictitiously. Any resemblance to actual persons, living or dead, incidents, or locales is entirely coincidental.

Author photograph by Ann Hoffelder

Contact the author:
Anza Press
P.O. Box 8676
Newport Beach, CA 92658

E-mail: JeriBolliger@hotmail.com

For Will

CHAPTER 1

Wesley County
Southern Oregon
1875

Creeping up behind the blacksmith and smashing his head with a rock was almost too simple. A bottle of moonshine fell from Daniel Nolan's hand and shattered, intensifying the stench that reeked from his grimy buckskin jacket. Then his body sagged like a half-filled sack of flour and rolled sideways off the log where he'd been sitting.

When they met by chance last week, he'd known the blacksmith at once. There was no mistaking the hawkish nose or narrow-set blue eyes that now stared sightlessly. Had there been a flicker of recognition in Nolan's eyes as well? He couldn't be sure, but he'd killed before with less reason. Now he needn't worry about anything those eyes had seen.

Years of shoeing half-wild horses and repairing broken wagon wheels had added muscle to Nolan's lanky frame, and dragging the corpse feet-first across the rutted wagon track and into a shallow ravine required considerable effort. No wonder they called it dead weight. He slumped against the trunk of a yellow-bark pine and waited for his ragged breathing to return to normal.

The forest glade was dim and quiet except for the reassuring chirp of crickets and the occasional call of a warbler. A chill wind stirred fallen leaves and sent others floating down from the branches of a nearby sycamore. Moving away from the pine tree, he gathered dead branches and covered the body, leaving the head exposed.

He unsheathed a knife from his belt and cut a patch of skin from Nolan's scalp above the hairline. Odd. He'd expected more blood. There'd been plenty when the rock caved in the back of the blacksmith's head. Maybe that was why there was less now. He'd never scalped anybody before, so he couldn't be sure. He tucked the scalplock into his belt, cleaned the knife by rubbing it in the dirt, and returned it to its leather sheath.

After covering the corpse with leaves and berry brambles, he stepped back and surveyed the scene. Satisfied the body was well hidden, he broke a low branch off the pine. He backed away from the ravine, using the needles at the end of the branch to erase his tracks and obliterate the bloody path the body had made when he'd dragged it to its hiding place. When he reached the road he listened again, but his keen sense of hearing told him no other humans were nearby—at least none who were alive.

Everyone in Oakfield knew Nolan was a drinker who disappeared periodically. The blacksmith's squaw and half-breed boy wouldn't start looking for him until tomorrow, if then. The woman didn't speak English, and the stiff-necked Methodist settlers weren't likely to pay any attention to a redskin anyway.

The Indians in the area had long since been removed to reservations, but there were rumors of renegade bands hiding out in the mountains that ringed the valley. The Modoc war was fresh in everyone's memory. If someone discovered the body, the settlers in Oakfield would know where to put the blame.

He headed into the woods, glanced at the darkening sky and shivered. Black clouds rolled across the Cascade Mountains to the east. Days were getting shorter. An unseasonable frost had already headed most of the waterfowl south. The weather in this part of Oregon was unpredictable, but all the signs pointed to a bad winter. Maybe they'd have snow before October. Maybe nobody would find Daniel Nolan until spring.

CHAPTER 2

Bianca Stratton guided the hand of her youngest nephew, Jorgen, as he placed a wild rose on the plain oak casket. Then she stepped back and averted her eyes as her older sister, Viola, the only mother she'd ever known, was lowered into the ground.

September sun filtered through branches of Douglas fir, casting late afternoon shadows on three small granite blocks that marked the graves of the infants who had died since Jorgen was born. Nearby, the names of Bianca's parents were engraved on a rose-colored marble slab. Her frail mother had barely survived the covered wagon journey that brought the Strattons to Oregon. Two years later she died giving birth to Bianca. When Bianca was six, her father succumbed to pneumonia.

Now the stonecarver would make another headstone. Viola Knudsen. 1848 — 1875. She'd lived only twenty-seven years.

Bianca bowed her head and stared at the frayed cuffs of her black silk mourning dress. Too many deaths, she thought. Too many funerals.

"Dear Father," the preacher was saying, "receive our beloved Viola, a devout Christian wife and mother. You've called her home, Lord, together with her precious baby girl. We know they both rest safely in Thy care and are especially blessed in Thy sight."

Eight births in twelve years. Four infants stillborn. Four boys now motherless. How could the preacher say Viola was blessed? Bianca pushed Jorgen gently toward his father.

Rolf Knudsen placed a clump of red Oregon soil in the hands of each of his four sons. Bianca watched in dry-eyed anguish as her nephews, husky blond replicas of Rolf, dropped the dirt into the grave.

Four-year-old Jorgen's voice broke the silence. "Aunt Banky, why isn't Mama here?"

Bianca pulled him close. "She's up in heaven, Jorgen."

"I want her to come back home."

Bianca looked down and saw her hands, which felt somehow detached from the rest of her body, tearing her worn handkerchief to shreds. She stared at the dark splotches on her skirt and realized she was crying.

Neighbors bringing covered dishes dropped by the farmhouse all afternoon and evening. The aroma of cinnamon buns, meatloaf and chowder lingered in the air, adding to the queasiness in Bianca's stomach.

At nightfall she settled the boys in their beds, drying their eyes and comforting them as best she could while she heard their prayers. Then she tidied the parlor, stored the leftover food in the springhouse, and sank into her accustomed chair at the kitchen table.

Rolf poured a cup of coffee and joined her, the blond hair on his freckled arms still damp from scrubbing at the backyard pump after winding up his evening chores.

"We'd better talk," he said.

Bianca waited. Idle conversation was not in Rolf's nature.

"Hilda's worried about how things will look."

All the Knudsens were worriers. Rolf's sister, with her husband and brood of eight fretful children, had hitched up their wagon right after the funeral, concerned that they might not get home before dark.

"Hilda stews a lot," Bianca said.

"Well, she's right. You're seventeen, Bianca, a woman grown. While Viola was alive, your living here on the farm was a natural thing. But now people will talk. I spoke to the preacher this afternoon. He agreed to marry us tomorrow." His calloused hand touched her shoulder.

"Marry? Tomorrow?" Bianca cringed from Rolf's awkward caress. Surely she'd misunderstood.

"It's the only way. I know it's soon, but—"

"Soon? The flowers are fresh on Viola's grave. Are you out of your mind?"

"She'd want me to take care of you, and I thought—"

"You thought you had the right to plan the rest of my life without as much as a word to me? Well, Rolf, you were wrong. I watched Viola grieve for each of the babies that lie buried in the graveyard. I saw her eyes lose their sparkle as childbearing stole her strength. My own mother died giving me life. Even if I loved you, I wouldn't marry you."

"So what will you do?" He stirred a spoonful of sugar into his coffee and frowned.

"I'll . . . I'll leave."

"It's not as if you have money of your own or relatives to take you in."

"I'll get a job." She willed herself to ignore the pounding in her temples. "You know I've qualified for a teaching certificate."

"They're looking for schoolmasters. Nobody around here will hire a young girl just out of school." The line between his eyebrows deepened.

"So now I'm a young girl." An angry flush heated her chest and neck. "A minute ago I was a woman grown."

"I told Viola it was a mistake to send you to that academy. Taught you nothing useful, used up the money that should have been your dowry, and made you uppity to boot."

"Not too uppity to care for your sons and tend Viola while she bled to death birthing your babies. And now it's my turn, is that it? Well, not if I have to move from orchard to orchard picking apples to earn my keep!"

"Don't be hasty, Bianca."

"Hasty? Viola's body is barely in her grave and you're talking marriage. Now, that's what I call hasty. Not that it matters, Rolf. I'll never marry. Not you, not anybody. Not ever!"

Chin high, she marched to her bedroom and slammed the door. Then she lurched to the bed, reached underneath and slid out the earthenware chamber pot. Spasms wracked her body as bile welled up from deep inside her. When the waves of nausea subsided, she sank onto the goosedown comforter and buried her head in her hands.

Exhaustion granted Bianca a few hours of sleep, after which she tossed, restless and wide-eyed. It was still dark when she rose, lit a candle, dressed, and packed her meager wardrobe into the cedar chest under the dormer window. Her hope chest had been a Christmas present from Viola the year she turned eleven. She was expected to fill it with dainty embroidered linens and lace-edged pillowcases, but her attempts at fine handiwork were a disaster. The chest became her favorite nook for reading, and until this morning it held nothing but the precious books that had belonged to her father.

When the first rays of sun edged over the Cascades, she blew out the candle and sat down on the edge of her bed. She could almost hear her sister's voice.

"Don't be so impulsive, Bianca. How many times do I have to tell you?"

But caution didn't come easily. She should have learned her lesson a year ago when she'd urged Patches, her docile mare, to jump a fast-moving stream. The horse balked, and Bianca plummeted onto the rocky bank, a searing pain in her head the last thing she remembered before her world went dark. She still had nightmares of hearing whispered voices, opening her eyes and staring blindly at the murky grayness that clouded her vision. She despaired of ever being able to read or continue attending the academy, but after several weeks her eyesight, blurred at first, returned. She tried repeatedly to get back in the saddle, but nausea and dizziness overwhelmed her before her foot touched the stirrup. Finally she admitted that her riding days were over.

Now she'd packed herself up without any notion of where to go or how to get there. She couldn't move the wooden chest out of her room without help. And even if she left her belongings behind, saddling the mare and riding away was out of the question. Still, she thought, she could walk to the county seat as she had every morning to get to school.

She put on her bonnet, stowed her precious academy records in a crocheted satchel, and tiptoed through the silent kitchen and out the back door. The Wesley County courthouse was only a short distance past the academy, and her brisk walk covered the three miles in less than an hour. It would be another hour before anything was open.

She sat on the courthouse steps wishing she'd remembered to stop by the springhouse for an apple and a cinnamon bun, but, of course, she hadn't. Just as she hadn't thought to curb her tongue the night before. Rolf and the boys were the only family she knew. It wouldn't be easy, but she'd have to make peace with Rolf somehow.

She reached inside her satchel and fingered the diploma she'd been given when she completed her studies. An early Methodist mission school had prospered and grown into Wesley Academy, one of the few institutions of higher learning in Oregon. Bianca's father, Charles Stratton, had been one of its founders. A scholar and a dreamer, enchanted with his vision of Oregon, the golden land on the shores of the far Pacific, he had neither the hardy constitution nor the practical skills needed to survive the reality of the wilderness. When Emily, his wife, died giving birth to Bianca, Charles retreated even farther into the small library of leather-bound volumes that had been shipped around the Horn.

Viola, only eight when their mother died, had been a practical child, mature beyond her years. She took control of her father's general store, making sure necessities such as flour, vinegar and salt were always in stock. The customers welcomed her cheerful bantering, and the store became the town gathering place. Charles was only too happy to travel to Scott's Landing or Oregon City to buy the items on Viola's list as long as he could pick up a new book or two at the same time.

Returning from one such trip, he was caught in an early snowstorm and died of pneumonia a week later. Six-year-old Bianca was devastated. Fourteen-year-old Viola sold the thriving business to a Swiss immigrant and happily married Rolf Knudsen, the serious Norwegian farmer who had been courting her for over a year. Since then the Knudsen farm had been Bianca's home, and Viola and Rolf her surrogate parents.

When Bianca was thirteen, Viola insisted that Bianca's share of the proceeds from the sale of the store be used to send Bianca to the nearby Wesley Academy. Rolf, who always looked on the dark side but rarely questioned Viola's wisdom on any topic, objected strenuously.

But Viola, as usual, prevailed. Each day Bianca rose at dawn to help with the chores and feed and dress her four nephews before walking the three miles to school. Still, she managed to be near the top of her class all four years. Although her studies and responsibilities at the farm left little time for socializing, Bianca treasured the opportunity to learn from professors who shared their knowledge of the world.

Rolf said nobody would hire her to teach, but Dr. Freeman, her favorite professor, had told her teachers were in short supply. She was better educated than many. At least she could try.

When the courthouse doors finally opened, Bianca went inside and wandered the dim corridors until she found a door marked Office of Education. A scrawny-necked boy about her own age looked up from an oak desk.

Bianca handed over her records. "I've graduated from Wesley Academy. I'm here to apply for a teaching position."

"I'm just a clerk. The commissioner won't be in for a while." He leafed through her papers. "Most places want schoolmasters."

"I know, but—"

"If you want a job, you'll need to meet with the commissioner and pass the oral examination. He should be in soon if you care to wait."

The oral examination, which Bianca awaited with trepidation, consisted of little more than a cursory perusal of her academy records. The commissioner, a portly man with a ruff of white chin whiskers and a bemused air, made out a certificate and handed it to her with a flourish.

"Well, young lady," he said, "your academic record is outstanding, and Professor Freeman recommends you highly. That's good enough for me. Now, let's see what we have for you."

Bianca held her breath as the Commissioner leafed through a stack of papers on his cluttered desk.

"Ah, here's something. The settlers at Oakfield have built a schoolhouse and taken up a collection for a three-month school. They requested a man, but it's been nearly a year and nobody has applied. I see they're now willing, reluctantly, to consider a woman."

"Oakfield?"

"It's small. Pretty isolated. About eighteen miles south of here. Not even a village, really, which is probably why nobody wants to go there."

Bianca breathed a small, hopeful sigh. "And you think perhaps I could—"

"The pay is board, room and twenty-five dollars a month, plus an account at the store for teaching supplies. You'll board with the minister's family. Of course, for a schoolmaster the pay would be more, especially if he had a family and needed a place of his own."

"Of course."

We'll put you down for the school in Oakfield and send a wire to the general store so folks will know you're coming. If you head out there tomorrow you can be settled and ready to commence class on Monday. When you come back you'll be an old hand. By then we may have something better."

She walked out of the courthouse dazed and astonished. It had been almost too easy. Now all she had to do was figure out how to get to Oakfield.

CHAPTER 3

Bianca awoke with a queasy sense of disorientation. Rough muslin sheets chafed her neck. Peering through the early half-light, she took in the unfamiliar whitewashed walls of the tiny room. She stretched, trying to persuade her cramped legs it was time to get moving. Then the challenge of a new place, a new occupation—a new life—flooded her consciousness. She threw back the covers and sprang out of bed.

She poured water from an enamel pitcher into the chipped bowl on the bedside table. As she splashed sleep from her eyes, the shock of the icy water brought her fully awake. Sounds assailed her ears—doors slamming, kettles clattering, and the shrill voices of the four Pangston girls she'd met briefly the night before.

Recalling that she'd displaced ten-year-old Cora by moving into the garret above the parlor, Bianca felt a guilty pang. Now the eldest Pangston daughter would be sharing a crowded bedroom with her three younger sisters, but Bianca would have a room of her own. Last night Mrs. Pangston had said providing a degree of privacy was the least they could do for the new schoolteacher.

Schoolteacher. Schoolmarm. It sounded so settled, so proper, so—old! Well, she would have to face the fact that at seventeen she was practically an old maid. Picking up her silver-framed looking-glass, she regarded her image with detachment. She was no beauty, surely. Not that her looks mattered.

She ran her hand lovingly over the mirror's frame. It had been her mother's treasure, carried across the plains in the cramped covered wagon on a journey she was ill-equipped to withstand. Then the mirror had belonged to Viola, for whom the stonecutter was even now working on a grave marker.

Again the events of the past few days came rushing back. Everything had happened so fast. Rolf seemed distraught with grief, and then had come his insensitive proposal of marriage. On reflection, Bianca realized he must have been desperate to have someone to look after the boys. She did love them dearly, especially little Jorgen, who seemed almost as if he were her own. But Rolf—as a husband—it was unthinkable.

She was determined never to marry, but if—just if—she ever did, it would have to be to someone who was bright and artic-ulate, someone who knew more of the world than milk-cows, chickens and alfalfa.

An uneasy truce had prevailed once Rolf accepted the fact that she was actually leaving. He'd grumbled, but in the end he'd loaded up her chest along with a box of books and a few supplies she'd picked up in town the day before. On Friday morning he'd hitched up his surrey and driven her to Oakfield. Now she was about to start her career—not that she intended to spend the rest of her life teaching in a small backwater like Oakfield. But it was a start.

Hearing a wail from below, Bianca laid the mirror aside and dressed in a simple gingham skirt and blouse. She hurried down-stairs to the crowded kitchen where Mrs. Pangston, apparently undismayed by the chaos around her, stirred a kettle of mush that bubbled atop the cast-iron stove.

A chubby, blonde toddler, whose name Bianca couldn't recall, lay flat on the floor, flailing her arms and screaming. Eight-year-old Katie sat at the rectangular table, making faces and squealing with feigned outrage as her older sister, Cora, braided Katie's unruly red hair into two tight pigtails. Six-year-old Gertrude was setting the table, arranging the flatware and napkins with mathematical precision.

"Mother, I think you should do something about the baby." Gertrude pursed her narrow lips in disapproval. "Her face is getting all red, and she's going to get her dress dirty, too."

Cora stepped over the screaming toddler and dipped her comb into a glass of water. "Katie, hold still. The more you wiggle, the more it pulls. Gertrude, go out to the springhouse and get some milk for the mush."

"I don't know why you think you're entitled to order everybody around." Gertrude scowled.

"Girls, that will do," their mother said, but her words seemed to have little effect.

"I'll go get the milk and call Papa," Gertrude said. "You know I always try to be a help to you, Mama."

Katie stuck out her tongue at her departing sister. The toddler kept wailing, and Bianca wondered how she could tolerate three months of living with the minister's family. She was accustomed to the roughhousing of her nephews, but she'd never been around a houseful of little girls before. Still, living here was better than boarding around as many teachers were forced to do. At least she had a room of her own, and the minister's wife seemed pleasant enough. Perhaps the Pangstons were just having a bad morning.

"Miss Stratton, I hope you won't judge us hastily." Mrs. Pangston seemed to be reading Bianca's thoughts. "The girls didn't sleep too well last night. It will take a little time for them to get used to all sharing a room. We moved Tina out of our bedroom only a week ago. I think it's a good idea to have the cradle empty for a while." She looked down and patted the bulge beneath her apron."

"Oh, I'm really sorry—" Bianca began.

"No, no. You mustn't feel that way. We need a teacher so badly here in Oakfield. My husband worked hard to take up the collection for a three-month school, and we want it to succeed.

I'm afraid not everyone in Oakfield appreciates the importance of education as much as Cushing and I do, Miss Stratton."

"Please call me Bianca. I hope you won't treat me like a guest. I always helped my sister with the chores. I won't feel comfortable unless you allow me to help here, too."

The young woman smiled. "As you can see, Bianca, I need all the help I can get. And you must call me Mattie."

"We've never been to a real school, but Mama says we'll like it," Cora said. "I already know how to read a little."

"Bianca—what a funny name." Katie's green eyes twinkled. "Can I call you Bianca?"

"She's your teacher, and you will call her Miss Stratton." Mattie's reproof was firm. "And I think Bianca's a lovely name."

"My father was a great admirer of Mr. Shakespeare's plays," Bianca said. "He used to read them aloud to me when I was very small. Bianca comes from a play called *The Taming of the Shrew*."

"What's a shrew?" asked Katie.

"It's a woman with a bad temper," Bianca explained. "In the play Katherine and Bianca were sisters. Katherine behaved very badly, so they called her a shrew."

"Katie's real name is Katherine," Gertrude said. "She's mean sometimes, too."

Katie dipped her fingers in the water glass and flicked a few drops at Gertrude.

"I thought a shrew was some kind of little animal." Cora gave Katie's pigtail a tug and secured it with a piece of twine.

"You're right," said Bianca. "But those little animals are said to be cranky, so I think that must be how an ornery person came to be called a shrew."

"Well, anyway, Tina's the shrew in this family," said Katie.

"Am not!" the toddler wailed.

The screen door opened and Cushing Pangston came in, wearing worn overalls and looking more like a farmer than a preacher. Tina's screams stopped as if by magic. She scrambled to her feet and climbed into her father's lap almost before he was seated at the table.

16

When everyone had found a place at the table, heads were bowed and Cushing Pangston commenced a lengthy blessing punctuated with many stammers and clearings of his throat. Bianca found herself hoping the preacher's Sunday sermons would prove more articulate. The prayer finally ended, and Bianca raised her head to find Katie, seated directly opposite her, grinning wickedly behind her napkin.

The thin, lumpy cereal had grown cold during the lengthy blessing. Adding watery milk didn't help, and there was no sign of a sugar bowl on the table. The first spoonful congealed in her throat, reminding her of the homemade laxative paste which was Viola's all-purpose remedy. Bianca washed it down with a sip of tasteless liquid from the coffeepot and hoped this breakfast wasn't a fair sample of Mattie's cooking.

Back upstairs she hung her clothes on wooden pages protruding from the wall and finished unpacking. The hand-embroidered dresser scarf Viola had given her at Christmas brightened the room and hid the scars on the small dressing table. She placed the mirror on the scarf and carefully unwrapped her parents' framed marriage certificate, which was embellished with scrolls and flowers. Oval tintypes of her father and mother, looking very young and serious, were centered near the top. The images were the only pictures she had of her parents, and she hung the certificate carefully on a nail above her bed.

Her undergarments and a few mementoes from the academy remained in the chest. She shoved it under the paned window and tidied the bedclothes. Then she surveyed the small room. There was nothing else to be done here, she thought, so why was she idling when she should be making the schoolhouse ready?

So much had happened so quickly she hadn't been able to sort it all out. But there was no question that on Monday she would be facing a dozen or more students who expected to see a teacher and not a nervous young girl.

She took a deep breath, put on her bonnet, and headed downstairs. There were books to unpack and lessons to plan. Mattie provided a broom, a bucket, a tin of soft lye soap, and muslin flour sacks to use as cleaning rags. Bianca loaded the box of books she'd brought with her into a rickety wheelbarrow and piled the supplies on top.

She pushed the squeaking wheelbarrow down the narrow dirt road, certain something important was waiting for her if only she had the courage to look for it. There was a big world to see, for one thing. At the academy she'd been fascinated by the map of the world in her classroom. She'd moved her finger across the oceans, visualizing distant cities and exotic lands. Then she'd found Massachusetts, where her father was born, and New York, where her parents were married.

Her professors were always talking about the cities "back east" with their colleges and theaters and opera houses. Bianca couldn't imagine why anyone would leave such places for the wilderness of Oregon. She'd often wondered why her own parents had made their ill-fated journey.

"They had their reasons," was Viola's tight-lipped response whenever Bianca asked.

She stopped asking, but she never stopped dreaming. She wouldn't have many expenses here in Oakfield, so she should be able to save most of her salary. In time she could save enough for fare on one of the packet ships that would take her to San Francisco and the railroad leading east. Now, as the unpainted schoolhouse came into view, she knew it was time to start making those dreams come true.

The school stood in the center of a clearing. In the far corner an outhouse backed up to a thickly wooded knoll. To the east an enormous oak tree sheltered a well and pump. A split rail fence enclosed the spacious yard.

Light from the open door revealed a cloakroom which ran the width of the building. The place had the vacant odor of stale sawdust. Past the cloakroom Bianca surveyed the large room which would be the center of her life for the next three months. Six rough-hewn tables and benches crowded the rear of the room. A pot-bellied stove stood in a front corner, a supply of wood stacked neatly beside it. Centered at the front of the classroom, a substantial desk faced the tables and benches. Sturdy bookshelves flanked a slate blackboard.

Four double-hung windows would let in a good amount of light, she thought, once the grime had been scrubbed from the small glass panes. A quick inspection revealed that most of the dirt was on the outside of the glass, and she was sure the uppermost panes were too high to reach from the ground outdoors.

She unpacked the box of precious books and arranged them on the bookshelf. Her earliest memories were of being cradled in the crook of her father's arm while he paced back and forth, a book in his free hand. While other babies listened to lullabies, Bianca had dropped off to sleep to the sound of her father's sonorous bass voice, reading aloud from Shakespeare, Scott, Tennyson or whatever else was at hand. Now she forced herself to concentrate on the tasks before her rather than the flood of memories each leather-bound volume evoked.

Once the sturdy, wooden box was empty, she carried it outside along with the cleaning supplies. The pump needed only a little priming before her bucket was full of water. Standing on the box she was able to reach even the highest windows easily. Being tall did have some advantages, she thought. She worked her way around the building and found herself humming the cheerful tune Viola had often sung when she was tidying up the farmhouse.

While she was polishing the streaks from the last window, Bianca felt a tingling sensation between her shoulder blades, not quite a chill, but the uncomfortable feeling that someone was watching. She turned and scanned the dark woods at the edge of the clearing, sensing a rustling movement in the undergrowth in the shadows behind the outhouse.

"Hello?" she called, but the sharp cry of a willow flycatcher was her only answer. Shaking her head at her own foolishness, she reminded herself that being in strange surroundings had a way of kindling her imagination. Of course there were noises in the woods, and if she was being watched by anything larger than a bird, it was probably a fox or a deer.

Back in the classroom she cleaned the inside of the window-panes and smiled with satisfaction as light streamed in. Finally she unrolled the large map of the world Professor Freeman had given her in recognition of qualifying for a teaching certificate. She propped it up on top of the shelf and stood back to admire her handiwork. The people of Oakfield had built a good little schoolhouse. She would strive to be a good teacher, too.

A muffled sound interrupted her reverie, and she whirled around. A pair of huge, dark eyes peered through the bottom pane of the back window. The face vanished so quickly she wondered for a moment if her own eyes were playing tricks. She stepped to the window in time to see a barefoot child with a thatch of black hair disappear into the woods.

Of course, she thought with a smile. One of my pupils getting a peek at the new schoolteacher. She sat down, filled her inkwell, opened a lined tablet, and began thinking about Monday. Many of the students, like the Pangston girls, would be attending school for the first time although they might have learned some letters and numbers at home. Some of the younger children would be frightened, and the older pupils would likely be embarrassed to find themselves in class with those who were little more than babies.

Realizing she'd better plan carefully, she dipped her pen in the inkwell and began writing.

CHAPTER 4

Cushing Pangston primed the pump in the lean-to behind the manse. He liked to think of it as the manse, even though it might be years before a proper church could be built on the adjacent land. When the water began to flow he dipped a stiff brush into a pail of Mattie's lye soap and scrubbed his grimy hands. He repeated the process until his knuckles were nearly raw.

He'd been up before daybreak, and except for the brief time the family had spent together at the breakfast table, he hadn't sat down. Now it was well past noon. His back ached, and his shirt was damp with sweat. His hands were clean, but a film of dust seemed to be a permanent part of his skin and his clothing. He hated farming. Mattie could talk as much as she wanted about good, rich soil, but he firmly believed cleanliness was next to Godliness. At times it seemed impossible to be a good minister and a good farmer at the same time.

After graduating from the seminary Cushing had waited for a call to a church in some tidy New England town. He occasionally filled in for an ailing pastor, but was never asked to return. Nearly two years later the call came from Oakfield. Being uprooted from the civilization of Connecticut seemed out of the question, but Mattie said it must be the Lord's plan for them to start a new life in Oregon. She didn't point out that this might be his only chance, but he knew it was so.

Now Oakfield had been home for more than four years. He visited the sick, baptized babies, and officiated at occasional weddings and too-frequent funerals. Unless he was under stress, his hesitant speech was at least coherent in a small group, but he realized his sermons were disastrous. And this morning, with the presence of the young schoolmarm at the breakfast table, he'd stammered even while giving the blessing in his own kitchen.

He hadn't expected Bianca Stratton to be so young or so pretty—well, not pretty, exactly. Her wide-spaced brown eyes had looked down at him with an air that made him uncomfortable. She looked down at him—that was it! The young woman was simply too tall. Cushing dried his hands, knocked the mud off his boots, and went into the house.

In the kitchen Mattie was up to her elbows in bread dough, a smudge of flour dusting her nose. Squeals and footsteps overhead told him the girls were upstairs. He took a seat at the table and sighed.

"Mattie, I've been praying about it, but I have misgivings about hiring that young woman."

"It's a bit late for second thoughts," Mattie pointed out.

"She's not at all what I expected." Cushing's stammer rarely appeared when he was talking to Mattie or the girls. "For one thing, the wire from the commissioner described her as a maiden lady. I pictured someone older—more settled. Instead we get this—this great towering girl."

"She is tall, but I'd hardly call her towering."

"Mattie, I feel it in my bones. This young woman is going to be trouble."

Mattie shaped the dough into a loaf and covered it with a damp cloth. "Her references were excellent."

"I still wish we'd hired a schoolmaster."

Mattie shaped another loaf of bread. "Nobody else applied," she reminded him. "I think I'll take some leftover baked beans and biscuits to the schoolhouse and see how she's getting along.

I can show her how to get to Fowler's store in case she needs supplies."

"I've got a sermon to prepare for tomorrow," Cushing said. "I can't be interrupted constantly if the girls start squabbling."

"They'll be fine," Mattie assured him. "Gertrude and Katie still have chores to do. Cora's primping in front of the mirror as usual, but she promised to keep an eye on Tina."

Bianca glanced out the window, saw Mattie heading toward the schoolhouse, and jumped up to open the door.

"What a nice surprise," she said. "Come inside and tell me what you think of my morning's work."

"I see you've been busy," Mattie said approvingly. "I thought you might be ready for a bite to eat."

Bianca sat at her desk and unpacked the lunch Mattie had provided. "This is really kind of you," she said. "Won't you share it with me? There's much more food here than I can possibly manage."

Mattie perched on an empty wooden box by the corner of the desk. "Well, I can always find room for a biscuit or two," she said. "You know, it's really nice to have someone to talk to—another woman, I mean. I don't know how to explain it, but there seems to be something about being the minister's wife. It's as if the womenfolk around here feel they have to be terribly proper when I'm around. You seem—well, different."

"I'll take that as a compliment," Bianca said with a laugh. "Being around you and the girls feels like the time I spent at the farm with my sister and her boys. You remind me of Viola—she was always so organized. She seemed to take everything in stride." Bianca stopped and blinked back sudden tears.

"I know you're grieving her loss. And you must miss your nephews, too." Mattie reached across the desk and placed a comforting hand on Bianca's arm.

After a moment Mattie broke the silence. "Well, it looks like you have everything ready for Monday. I thought you might want to walk to the store with me when you've finished eating. There's an account for school supplies at Fowler's store. It's also the post office, and now Ed even runs the telegraph."

"Sounds like a busy place."

"I'll introduce you to Ed's wife, Agnes, and Edna and Edwina, the twins who help their parents in the store. They're thirteen, and Ed thinks they'll be more use if they learn to read and do sums better than they can now. They're going to be in your class along with the three younger Fowler boys. We probably won't see much of Ed Fowler. He usually keeps busy in back."

"I think I have most of the books and supplies I'll need," Bianca said. "Of course, most of the pupils will bring their own slates, and I picked up some copybooks while I was in Wesleyville getting my certificate. But I forgot about chalk."

"Then the walk to Fowler's is an even better idea." Mattie helped herself to the last remaining biscuit. "This good autumn weather may not last long, and going to the store won't be nearly so pleasant once the cold sets in."

Bianca closed the door and followed Mattie down the road. "I noticed the schoolhouse was open when I got here. Should I get a lock for the door?"

"I don't think there's a locked door anywhere in Oakfield," Mattie said. "Things are pretty safe around here."

"Once in a while we had chickens go missing at the farm," Bianca said. "My brother-in-law said Indians were taking them, but Viola said foxes and hawks were to blame. Still, she always kept everything locked, so I guess it became a habit with me too."

"The Indians are on reservations so we rarely see them unless they're hired out to do work. None of the farmers around here has a spread big enough to need extra help except at harvest time. Mostly we all pitch in and help each other."

"My brother-in-law says there are quite a few Indians who never got put on the reservations or who escaped."

"I guess that's true. Anyway, I don't think anyone around here would hire an Indian even if he had a pass from the reservation.

They have a reputation for stealing anything that's not nailed down. I can't honestly say we've ever had any real problems, although apples and pumpkins do disappear at harvest time. I guess, being savages, they don't consider that stealing."

"One of my professors said Indians don't understand the whole idea of owning property. He said they believe the land and everything growing on it is there for the nourishment of whoever needs it."

"Well, those are heathen ideas," Mattie said, "but I guess savages can't help being ignorant of the ways of the Lord."

Around a bend in the road Bianca saw a large clapboard building. A painted sign above the door identified it as Fowlers General Store. An outside stairway on the south side led to the second floor.

"The Fowlers live upstairs," Mattie explained. "Agnes has been after Ed to build a real house separate from the store, but Ed's a cautious man with a dollar. Besides, I think Agnes really likes to be able to keep an eye on everything."

As they drew closer, Bianca saw two grizzled men sprawled comfortably on a bench in front of the store. One man's gray beard was stained with tobacco juice and an accumulation of grime. The brim of a tattered hat shaded his eyes, and one hand rested on the rifle propped beside him. His companion sported a black moustache with waxed tips curling forward. Both men nodded in greeting as Bianca and Mattie approached.

"Good afternoon, Cap, Frenchy." There was a distinctly chilly tone in Mattie's voice, and Bianca found herself quickly ushered inside.

Mingled aromas of tobacco, pickles, fresh-ground coffee, leather, linseed oil, peppermint, bacon and sharp cheese sent Bianca's senses reeling with childhood memories of her father's store. But her first glance quickly dispelled any nostalgic feelings. Her father's store had been bright and tidy, with a potbellied stove and straight-backed chairs in the center where everybody gathered to tell stories, play checkers and share tidbits of news.

Fowler's store was dim, cold and cavernous. Boots, kettles, bridles and farming implements hung from the rafters, casting ominous shadows over the shelves on either side. A partition separated the front of the store from what apparently was a fairly large room in the back. Above the partition a chimney pipe disappeared through the ceiling. A swinging door led to the rear of the store.

The stove must be back there, Bianca thought. No wonder it's so cold here in front.

"Agnes, this is our new schoolteacher, Bianca Stratton." At Mattie's introduction the storekeeper's wife emerged from the shadows behind the dry-goods counter. She was a tiny birdlike woman whose beaky nose eclipsed her other features.

"Miss Stratton." Agnes Fowler bobbed her head in welcome. "We're very glad to finally have a teacher in Oakfield. If there are supplies you need, I think you'll find we've got practically everything here, and anything we don't have we can get. Of course, special orders take a while. Ed goes to Scott's Landing regularly to meet the packet ships that come up from San Francisco, and he makes the trip to Oregon City every month, too. Which reminds me, Mattie, that calico you wanted is finally here. I'll pop into the back and get it for you."

Still talking, the tiny woman fluttered toward the swinging door, her high-pitched voice echoing in the dark recesses of the store. "Ed, where did you put that calico Mattie Pangston ordered? Aren't you done unpacking those crates? Edna, you and Edwina finish candling the eggs and get them put away. And where are the boys? I thought they were supposed to be back here helping you."

"Agnes likes to keep everybody busy," Mattie said. "She also likes to talk. Cushing says we don't need a newspaper in Oakfield as long as we have Agnes."

Then the rear door swung open and two pretty girls wearing identical sprigged muslin dresses appeared, each carrying a large wooden bowl piled high with eggs. They were small like their mother but had been spared her nose. Their long brown hair was tied back with identical blue ribbons. Bianca wondered how she'd ever tell them apart.

"I'm your teacher, Miss Stratton," she said with a smile. "And you must be Edna and Edwina, though I must admit I haven't the slightest idea which is which."

The twins giggled and quickly disappeared behind the grocery counter where a crudely printed sign read, "Frsh beef livr."

Agnes Fowler emerged through the swinging door carrying a bolt of calico, a tape measure and a large pair of scissors. "Now, how much did you want, Mattie? It's all right if you don't take the whole bolt. Edwina already has her eye on this for her new quilt."

After Mattie's transaction was completed, accompanied by a lengthy monolog by Agnes on the unreliability of help in general and the failings of Ed Fowler in particular, Bianca bought her chalk. Edna and Edwina remained out of sight, but Bianca could still hear them giggling as she and Mattie left the store.

Outside, Mattie glanced at the now empty bench and sniffed, "Good riddance!"

"Oh, you mean the men who were here before?" Bianca asked. "Do they live here in Oakfield?"

"Well, yes, unfortunately." Mattie sighed. "I can't seem to look on those two with proper Christian charity. The one with the long whiskers claims to have been a soldier in the Indian wars. He says he left the army with the rank of Captain, and maybe he did. His name is Henry Mackay but everybody calls him Cap, and there's nobody around here who can dispute any of the bloody war stories he tells."

"And the other man?"

"He has some name nobody can pronounce, so he's known as Frenchy. He lives in a cabin in the woods north of here, and I understand he used to do some trapping for the Hudson Bay Company. I don't know what he does these days except hang around with Cap in the back room here at Fowler's store. Neither he nor Cap attends church, but then the French are known for loose morals, aren't they?"

"Well, I guess they don't have any school-age children, so I needn't worry about them," Bianca said. But she couldn't help wondering exactly what went on behind that swinging door.

CHAPTER 5

Bianca squirmed in the hard wooden chair as Cushing Pangston's tedious sermon limped on. Four rows of chairs had been set up in the parlor, and Bianca sat at the back with two Pangston girls on either side. Shortly after the opening hymn, she gave up trying to listen and let her gaze travel around the small congregation.

The Fowlers took up the whole row in front of her, and the elaborate bonnets Agnes and the twins were wearing blocked most of Bianca's view of the next two rows. Ed Fowler, a wiry little man with bushy gray sideburns, sat next to his tiny wife. Two of the sandy-haired Fowler boys were already as tall as their parents, but Bianca's height enabled her to see over their heads. The lectern where Cushing Pangston stood shuffling his notes was centered at the front of the room. Mattie, hair arranged in side puffs and wearing a maroon silk dress, perched at the small melodeon in the left corner. In the front row a tall, blond couple sat with two tow-headed children sandwiched between them.

Mattie had said there would be around a dozen students in her class, and the four Pangstons, five Fowlers and two little blonds in the front row accounted for eleven. Bianca wondered about the dark-eyed child who had peered into the schoolhouse window. I really should try to listen to the sermon, she thought. There'll be plenty of time to take roll tomorrow morning.

In spite of herself, Bianca found her gaze returning to the second row, in front of the Fowlers, where a tall, dark-haired man kept shifting in his chair. She had tried not to stare when he came in late. As he walked past she noted shiny cowboy boots and a ten-gallon hat which made him seem even taller than his more than six feet. Once seated, he removed the hat to reveal a thatch of hair as dark as Bianca's own. He wasn't young—probably nearly as old as Rolf—but there was an unmistakable aura of vitality about him.

At the sound of the melodeon striking the first chords of *O for a Thousand Tongues to Sing*, Bianca dropped her eyes, fumbled for the hymnal she was sharing with Katie, and rose for the singing.

Ed Fowler stood with his family for the final hymn. If past Sundays were any indication, he figured they'd have to wade their way through all the verses. He'd never been a church-goer until Agnes got religion after they were married, and he dreaded Sunday mornings. It was bad enough having to get all dressed up in his Sunday shirt. Agnes starched it so stiff he could hardly move his arms. But the worst part was sitting through the sermons. Cushing Pangston was a self-righteous jackass who couldn't string six words together without clearing his throat.

At least Ed was getting a gander at the new schoolmarm this morning. Cap and Frenchy had told him she was too tall but otherwise a looker, and he had to agree. He wondered what was wrong with her. There were lots more men than women in Oregon, and every gal he knew of had plenty of chances before her sixteenth birthday. When several of the hands at Donovan's ranch began sniffing around the twins, he got rid of them soon enough. He planned to see his girls safely married by the time they were fifteen, but what he needed was a couple of steady workers who would help out at the store. Of course, if Oren

Donovan took a shine to one of his girls, having a rich rancher for a son-in-law wouldn't be too bad either.

Ed was sure Oakfield would boom when the railroad went through, and he was in a perfect spot to expand. He could see it in his mind—first Fowler's Hotel, then Fowler's Saloon. Of course, Agnes would object to the saloon, but he knew how to get around Agnes.

A sharp poke in the ribs brought him back to the present. He closed the hymnal and bowed his head for the benediction.

Jesse Landry didn't attend Sunday services regularly, but it was good to get away from the ranch for a while, even if it meant sitting on the spindly chairs in the preacher's parlor. Saturday night in Fowler's back room the new schoolteacher had been the main topic of conversation while cards were shuffled and whiskey poured. Jesse liked to keep tabs on things, and there hadn't been any new blood in Oakfield for some time.

She'd noticed him when he came in, he could tell. Women usually did. Although he didn't see anything special when he looked in the cracked mirror and shaved his leathery skin, there seemed to be something about his looks women admired. Not that he was complaining.

Large for his age, he'd left home at thirteen and known his share of women in the years he'd spent lumberjacking, mining, fur trading and riding the range. But he'd never found one he was willing to settle down with. Settling down had never much appealed to him anyway until a couple of years ago when he'd landed the job of foreman at Donovan's ranch. Now the thought of staying in one place didn't seem so bad. Maybe, he thought wryly, I'm getting old.

The benediction finally ended. Jesse stood, turned, and found himself looking directly into a pair of large, almond-shaped brown eyes. His slow, appraising glance took in a small straight nose, full sensual mouth and determined chin. It gave him an odd feeling to have a woman looking at him almost straight on, and he glanced down. Her severe black dress couldn't hide the tantalizing curve of her breasts and the slim, girlish waist. Cap and Frenchy had been right. The new schoolmarm was a lot of woman.

"Allow me to present myself, Ma'am," he said. "My name's Jesse Landry. I'm the foreman at Donovan's ranch."

"Bianca Stratton," she said, extending her hand. "I'm the—"

"I guess everybody in Oakfield knows who you are, Miss Stratton. Not much happens around here that folks don't hear about, and we've needed a school for some time. I'll be bringing a couple of boys myself tomorrow morning."

"I'll look forward to seeing them," she said, "and to meeting your wife, too."

"Oh, no, ma'am. The boys aren't mine. Oren Donovan is Mrs. Donovan's nephew, though she raised him like her own, and Hank Mollers is an orphan too. His uncle is one of the hands at the ranch. I try to keep an eye on them. Hank, he's more of a follower, but Oren can be a real handful."

"Until tomorrow, then," Bianca said. His eyes followed as she moved forward to greet Agnes Fowler and her brood.

CHAPTER 6

Rolf Knudsen's surrey pulled into Oakfield early Sunday afternoon. He knew the boxes he'd brought were really an excuse to see Bianca again. He was surprised how empty the farmhouse seemed without her, even though his widowed sister, Berta, had come down from Salem to keep house and look after the boys. He hoped Bianca didn't think he wanted to marry her to get a free housekeeper. Actually, that was probably what she did think. It had been thoughtless of him to propose so soon after Viola's death. He'd never been good with words anyway.

He hadn't been able to explain how he really cared about Bianca and was worried about what people would say. With Viola gone, people would look at him and Bianca and think the worst. The townsfolk and farmers around Wesleyville were straight-laced, and some of them were mean-spirited too. Bianca was clever about bookish things but not so smart about people. She didn't realize some folks were plain evil. He'd tried to warn her about trusting people, but she wouldn't listen. She never had.

He hitched the surrey to the fence outside the preacher's house, stepped up on the porch and knocked.

"Now who can that be?" Mattie was stirring up dumplings to add to a pot of stewed chicken simmering on the stove. "Probably somebody left something in the parlor after the service."

"I'll get it, Mama." Gertrude was already at the door.

Bianca, looking out the kitchen window, recognized the rig and couldn't imagine why Rolf had come back so soon. She hurried through the parlor and met him as he stepped inside.

"Rolf, what are you doing here? Are the boys all right?"

"They're fine. Berta's with them," he said. "She helped me go through the cupboards, and I brought some of Viola's things."

"I can help carry them up to Cora's—I mean Miss Stratton's—room," Gertrude offered.

"Thank you, Gertrude, but I believe I can manage. You go help your mother." Bianca headed out to the surrey with Rolf trailing behind her.

"I knew Viola's clothes wouldn't fit you, but Berta found some things I didn't even think about—a lace-edged handkerchief, that brooch she liked so much, a heavy shawl, and her two Sunday bonnets." He paused awkwardly. "Of course, I knew Viola would want you to have them, so I thought I'd bring them by."

"That was very thoughtful of you, Rolf." She waited. Driving a rig over eighteen miles of bad road was hardly something one did as a casual drop-in visit.

"Bianca, I—well, I guess bringing things was really an excuse. I don't want you to think badly of me. I was wrong to ask for your hand so soon. But you must know how much the boys love you, and I—well, I care about you."

"I really miss the boys," Bianca said. "And I care about you, too, Rolf, but only as a big brother. I could never—"

"Please don't say never, Bianca. If only you would leave this place and come back home—"

"I have no intention of leaving. I'm looking forward to teaching and being on my own."

"But I worry about you. We don't know anything about these people. Oakfield isn't even a real town—just a crossroads with a few farms scattered around. I don't feel good about it at all."

"Rolf, I'll be fine. You always expect the worst."

"I believe in being realistic."

"Then be realistic about me, please." She picked up the hat-box and the shawl. Then she turned to see Mattie coming down the path.

"Mr. Knudsen, you're welcome to stay for Sunday supper," Mattie called.

"Thank you, Mattie," Bianca answered before Rolf could accept, "but it will take my brother-in-law several hours to get home. His sister is expecting him at the farm, and she'll be worried if he's not back before dusk."

Rolf scowled, jumped in the rig and drove off without so much as a wave.

Bianca sighed. Rolf and the boys were the only family she knew. In time Rolf would go back to thinking of her only as a sister, but until then it was best if she simply kept her distance.

That night as she brushed her unruly hair into submission and reviewed the events of the day, Bianca couldn't help thinking about Jesse Landry. He was even taller than Rolf. It was an unnerving experience to have to look up at a man. She wasn't sure she liked feeling almost fragile, but her heart gave a totally uncharacteristic lurch as she remembered Jesse was coming to the schoolhouse in the morning.

The hatbox and shawl lay on the bed where she'd dropped them before supper. Viola had been her compass, her mentor, and her best friend. Bianca knew she'd been holding her grief inside, afraid to allow herself to really accept her loss. She knew Rolf meant to be thoughtful, but she wasn't ready to wear Viola's clothes and claim them as her own.

She fingered the crocheted burgundy shawl, recalling the care her sister had taken spinning and dying the yarn. She lifted the lid of the large hatbox, and the scent of lavender, Viola's favorite flower, brought a fresh rush of memories. She started to replace the lid when she recalled Rolf mentioning a brooch. The only jewelry Viola had ever worn was her plain gold wedding band.

The bonnets in the hatbox were nested together, swathed in yellowing tissue paper. She lifted them out and fingered the lace-edged linen handkerchief Viola habitually tucked into the sleeve of her black silk Sunday dress. A small velvet pouch lay in the tissue at the bottom of the box. Bianca loosened the drawstring and removed the brooch—a circle of delicate gold leaves, flowers and tendrils surrounding a deep purple amethyst.

She held it close to the flickering candle, marveling at the intricate workmanship and the brilliance of the gemstone. She shook her head, wondering where it had come from and why Viola had never worn it. Bianca was sure she'd never seen it before.

It was too much to think about right now, she decided. She slid the brooch back into its velvet pouch and placed it in the hatbox. She picked up the bonnets, reached inside to smooth the crumpled paper, and felt something hard buried under the tissue.

She recognized her father's leather-bound ledger as soon as it was in her hand. Turning the yellowed pages, she scanned the lists of items he'd purchased along with the dates and amount paid. Not much of a memento, she thought. Still, the fading entries were in her father's hand. She could picture him at his desk, dipping his quill into the inkwell, and she cherished the memory.

She flipped through the last few blank pages and glimpsed something written on the flyleaf at the very back of the book. A name and address. Leandra Stratton, Beacon Hill, Boston, Massachusetts.

CHAPTER 7

Bianca arrived at the schoolhouse shortly after seven. Class would commence at eight, and she wanted to be there before any of her pupils arrived. Even so, the fair-haired couple she'd seen at church service was waiting, two children clinging tightly to their mother's skirts.

Bianca greeted them as she opened the door. "I'm sorry we didn't have a chance to talk yesterday morning after service," she said.

"Lars Larson." The man took off his cap and nodded. "Sorry, English not good."

"Your English is fine," Bianca said with a smile. "Please come inside."

"We wait here, thank you. My boy, Bjorn, he has eight years. Elke, she has six. They talk Swedish. No English."

"I'm sure they'll learn English quickly." Bianca hoped her tone was reassuring. How could she hope to teach children who wouldn't understand a word she was saying?

"Maybe they can't be in school—I mean, with no English. Is all right they come?"

"Of course it's all right." Bianca bent to look directly at the two clinging youngsters. "I'm your teacher, Miss Stratton," she said. "Can you say Miss Stratton?"

Two pairs of unblinking blue eyes looked back at her.

Lars Larson turned and spoke rapidly to his wife in Swedish, and she smiled broadly.

"I tell her you say Bjorn and Elke come to school," he said. "Everybody happy."

Bianca went inside and put her shawl and lunch basket on the coatroom shelf. Then she tacked up the map. She looked out the window and saw the schoolyard rapidly filling. The Fowler boys were chasing the Pangston girls around the oak tree at the edge of the clearing, and there was a good deal of squealing and shouting. She stepped to the door, and as if by magic the running and yelling stopped.

The children stared at her. Then somebody hollered, "Last one's a rotten egg!" A stampede of small bodies hurtled toward the back fence. Bjorn and Elke Larson, hand in hand, stared forlornly as their parents headed down the road. Then Elke began to wail, a series of piercing screams. The Fowler twins, Edna and Edwina, watched disdainfully from the well.

"Come now, children. It's time for class to start." Bianca tried to sound authoritative, but her voice was drowned by Elke's howls. She stepped off the porch and bent to pat Elke's shoulder, but the little girl cringed and cried even louder. Tears of frustration filmed Bianca's eyes. A fine teacher she was going to be. What good were all her careful lesson plans when she couldn't even corral the children into the schoolhouse or comfort a frightened little girl?

She clapped her hands. Then she moved to the schoolyard and yelled at the top of her lungs, "Come to the door. Right now."

Her voice carried cross the yard, and a welter of children raced toward her, pushing and shoving to be first in line. Finally they settled down and arranged themselves haphazardly by the door. Elke's sobs diminished as Bianca explained they were to walk—not run—into the schoolhouse, hang their wraps on a hook in the coatroom and place their lunch baskets on the shelf.

"After your things are put away, you will go into the class-room and sit down quietly. The smallest children will sit at the front tables and the oldest pupils at the back of the room. Later I will assign seats."

As the last straggler went inside, she looked up to see Jesse Landry standing by the gate. She'd been so intent on finally managing to get things under control she hadn't noticed his buggy on the road. Two boys came up the path. The taller one, with a mop of curly brown hair and a pair of shiny calfskin boots, walked with a self-assured swagger.

"Good morning, Ma'am," he said, taking the steps two at a time. "I'm Oren Donovan."

The other boy, a wiry youngster with a rash of adolescent pimples across his forehead, bobbed his head and looked at his dusty, bare feet.

"Good morning," she said. "Please remove your caps and put them in the coatroom along with your coats and lunch baskets."

"I'm sure you'll be able to keep 'em in line before long." There was undisguised amusement in Jesse Landry's voice.

"Keeping order is not a problem when young minds are well occupied," she said, covering her embarrassment with her best schoolmarm tone.

"If you say so, Ma'am." He grinned and executed a mock salute.

Bianca hurried inside, shut the door and paused in the coatroom to wait for the flush on her cheeks to subside. Of course, she didn't care a fig about Jesse Landry's opinion. But the way news traveled around Oakfield, everybody in the settlement would be laughing at her before lunchtime.

Inside the classroom Bianca introduced herself and then had the pupils stand, one at a time, and tell the class a little about themselves.

"We already know each other," Cora objected.

"That's true," Bianca said. "But I don't know any of you very well. And maybe you would like to tell something special—something everyone here doesn't know. For example, although I've lived on a farm most of my life, I don't ride horseback. The truth is, I had a bad fall a while back, and now I'm too afraid. Now, Cora, it's your turn. Say your name, your age, and tell us one special thing about yourself."

"My name is Cora Pangston. I'm ten years old, and I had my very own room until the teacher came to live at our house."

The twins giggled in unison. Bianca sighed and called on Oren.

"I'm Oren Donovan. I'm fourteen. I'm a better shot than anybody else at the ranch, and I don't know why anybody'd be scared of a horse."

Bianca discovered six-year-old Lenny Fowler liked to draw pictures and had recently lost a tooth. Nine-year-old Lloyd Fowler said Katie Pangston was all right for a girl. Katie announced that she was a princess who was only living in Oakfield until her ninth birthday in November when her real parents, the king and queen, would come and take her back to the castle.

"Katie, I'm going to tell Papa you're telling fibs at school," Gertrude said.

"I'll be nine in November. That wasn't a fib." Katie and Lloyd exchanged conspiratorial grins, and Bianca quickly called on the next child.

When she got to the Larson children, Bianca explained that Elke and Bjorn were born in a country called Sweden and hadn't learned to speak English.

"You mean they don't know how to talk?" Junior, the oldest Fowler boy, shook his head in amazement.

"Of course they can talk, dummy."

Bianca wasn't sure which Fowler twin had spoken, but they both looked scathingly at Junior.

"They will learn English very quickly, especially if we all help them. And I expect you to treat everyone with respect." Bianca looked pointedly at the twins. "That includes your brothers and sisters."

The twins appeared mildly contrite and lapsed into silence.

Bianca indicated the map and explained that it was a picture of the whole world. "Our country is the United States of

America." She swept her hand across from the Pacific to the Atlantic. "But, as you see, there are many other countries in the world." She was surprised to see Bjorn's hand waving tentatively. "Yes, Bjorn?"

The sturdy little boy moved hesitantly to the map and pointed. "Sweden," he said clearly. Then he pointed to an area in the northeastern portion of the United States. "Minnesota," he announced. Rapidly his hand moved toward the Pacific coast. "Oregon!" Smiling broadly, he returned to his seat.

"Very good, Bjorn! You must have a map at home." She pointed again. "Map."

Bjorn nodded. "Map," he echoed.

The spontaneous geography lesson continued as questions flew. "Where's California? My uncle went there to look for gold."

"My Pa was there, too."

"Jesse went to some place called Frazier River. There's gold there, too, but I don't know if he found any."

"My grandmother lives in Missouri."

"Show me Connecticut where Mama was born."

Few of the children had been born in Oakfield, and all of them seemed to have relatives who lived somewhere else. Bianca set them writing alphabet samples in their copybooks, pleased the map activity had gone well.

Since the weather was still warm, she suggested her pupils take their lunch baskets outside at noon, and she joined the group in the shade of the oak tree. Mattie had insisted on packing Bianca's lunch. At breakfast Bianca had been too nervous to do more than pick at Mattie's greasy bacon and hominy, but now she ate cheese, apples and hard-boiled eggs with real enjoyment. Although the eggs were tough and chewy, she noted with satisfaction that not even Mattie could ruin an Oregon apple.

Except for the initial confusion about lining up, the morning hadn't gone badly. She looked around at her pupils and was pleased she could recall each one's name and age. Already she was beginning to get a sense of who would learn quickly and who would require extra help. She scanned the faces again with a sense of something amiss.

"When I was getting the classroom ready on Saturday," she said, "I caught sight of a small boy with black hair and big brown eyes. I think he was about your size, Lenny. Is somebody sick?"

One of the twins spoke up. "Nobody's ailing. Mama would have told us."

Bianca smiled, recalling what Mattie had said about Agnes Fowler being the local equivalent of a newspaper.

"Everybody's here," Cora said with authority.

Lenny Fowler spoke with a noticeable lisp due, Bianca assumed, to the recent loss of his front tooth. "Well," he said, "There's Aiden Nolan."

"Who?" Junior wore a look of puzzlement, which, Bianca realized, was pretty much his habitual expression.

"You know," Lenny said. "The blacksmith's boy."

"Oh, him." Junior wolfed down an apple turnover. "His Ma's a squaw."

Lloyd Fowler spoke up. "Injuns have no call for book learning."

"Uncle Charlie says they can't learn to read or write anyway," Hank added.

"I'm afraid your uncle is mistaken," Bianca said. "There was a girl named Sarah at the academy when I was there. Her father was a missionary, and her mother was one of the Indians he converted to Christianity. Sarah was the best student in our class."

"Papa would never allow us to go to school with Injuns." The twin who spoke tossed her long braid.

"That's right," her sister echoed. "Mama won't even let us talk to that squaw when she comes into the store."

"Aiden's only half Injun," Lenny pointed out.

Bianca stood and brushed the crumbs from her skirt. "Lunchtime is over," she said. "If you need to use the outhouse, please do so before you come inside. Ladies first."

"I always pee outside," Junior said.

"Well, then, please walk to the edge of the clearing." Bianca picked up her lunch basket and retreated to the steps. She didn't want to get into an extended discussion of outhouse habits, and

42

the topic of educating Indians was also best left alone, at least for the moment.

As the day progressed, Bianca's confidence rose. She noted with amusement that Edna had maneuvered herself onto a bench near Oren Donovan and seemed to hang on his every word. The twins were dressed identically in pale blue shirtwaists and dark blue overskirts made in the latest style with side puffs and bustles. Edna seemed to take the lead while Edwina followed along. When Bianca commented on the rows of fine tucks on their blouses, she learned both girls were talented seamstresses. The elaborate bonnets they'd worn to Sunday service were their own handiwork.

Quiet, sensitive little Lenny Fowler finished everything quickly and then moved to sit beside the two Swedish children. Bianca watched as he pointed to his eye.

"Eye," he whispered. "Eye."

Bjorn and Elke grinned and pointed to their eyes. "Eye," they whispered back.

"Nose." Lenny pointed and whispered.

"Nose," Bjorn and Elke echoed.

When Bianca approached, Lenny looked up guiltily.

"I'm sorry, Miss Stratton. I'll be quiet." he said.

Bianca gave his shoulder a reassuring pat. "You're not bothering anybody as far as I can tell," she said.

"Nose," said Bjorn, pointing by way of explanation.

"Yes, I see," said Bianca. "Lenny, how did you learn to teach English?"

"Aiden Nolan showed me. Me and him are friends, sort of. He learned me how to talk Injun, and I learned him some English. He already talks English real good, though."

"Why don't you and Elke and Bjorn go to the empty bench by the coatroom door? Whenever you're done with your work you can give them an English lesson."

The three youngsters gathered up their slates and copybooks and moved to the rear of the room.

The afternoon sun heated the classroom, and everyone began to yawn and fidget. Oren and Hank seemed more interested in shoving one another off the bench than in doing sums. When she moved them to different sides of the classroom they grumbled but complied. She breathed a sigh of relief. Both boys were nearly as large as she with muscles toughened from riding and chores. She hoped they'd never defy her.

Class was dismissed at two-thirty in order to give everybody time to get home well before dark. Homework could be accomplished by the light of kerosene lamps, but chopping wood and tending kitchen gardens required daylight.

Bianca heard a noise in the coatroom and moved to the front of the building. Junior Fowler stood, eyes averted, holding the broom.

"Why, Junior, I thought everyone had gone."

Junior turned red to the roots of his sun-streaked hair. "I thought maybe I could help you some," he mumbled. "I'm real good at cleaning and such."

"That's very thoughtful of you," Bianca said. "But aren't you needed at home?"

"I sweep out the store in the morning. Pa don't want me around too much after that."

"Well, I can always use help. Let's see how handy you are with that broom. Then you can erase the blackboard."

When the cleaning was finished, Bianca thanked Junior and told him it was time for him to head for home. He seemed to take real pride in making the classroom tidy and attractive. She practically had to push him out the door to get him to leave.

"You work on those numbers this evening," she called as he finally headed up the path toward the road.

"All right, Miss Stratton. Goodbye, Miss Stratton. See you tomorrow, Miss Stratton."

Bianca sighed and returned to her desk. Junior was a slow learner, big for his years, and he apparently was developing a crush on her. She'd have to deal with him carefully.

But it was the face of a small, dark-haired child Bianca couldn't get out of her mind. Aiden Nolan, the blacksmith's half-breed son. Aiden, who wasn't considered worthy of an education because his mother was a squaw.

Was it possible that his exclusion from her class was merely an oversight? It seemed unlikely after hearing the children's comments which, she was certain, reflected the attitude of their parents.

At the academy she'd had to copy a quotation from the blackboard every morning and then memorize and recite it the following day. She'd hated the activity at the time, but lately some of those quotations popped into her head at opportune moments. She was learning to treasure the grains of wisdom they provided.

Now a line from James Russell Lowell seemed to come directly from her own conscience: "They are slaves who fear to speak for the fallen and the weak."

She knew what she had to do.

CHAPTER 8

Bianca was relieved to find Reverend Pangston seated at the kitchen table while Mattie and the girls were outside finishing up their afternoon chores. It would be easier to talk to him alone.

"I want to ask you about the blacksmith's boy. The children told me his name is Aiden. He wasn't at school today, and I wondered why."

"If they told you . . . ahem . . . I'm sure they also mentioned . . . the child is a half-breed, you know."

"Yes, but since he doesn't live on the reservation, he belongs in school."

"The blacksmith didn't . . .well, there was no financial contribution . . . I mean . . . "

"Are you saying his parents don't want Aiden to attend school?"

"Well, I assumed . . . uh . . . that is, we thought it would be better if—"

"But, Reverend Pangston—"

"The blacksmith is new to Oakfield. He may not have the funds to pay for the education of a child who probably can't even learn the most rudimentary—"

"I don't mean to be difficult." Bianca sat down at the table and leaned across to look directly into the preacher's eyes. "But you must know from your study of history that the first school west of the Rocky Mountains consisted of two dozen half-breed Indian boys."

"I'm afraid my studies at the seminary didn't include the education of half-breeds."

"Their teacher, a Mr. John Ball, reported they were docile, attentive, and made good progress."

"Which has nothing whatever to do with our school here in Oakfield. Don't you already have enough students to keep you busy?"

"It just seems so wrong."

"You've been hired to teach, not to meddle in . . . matters which don't concern you."

"A child who's not in school concerns me very much."

"There are other considerations, Miss Stratton. The feelings of the community are strong. It hasn't been so long since the Rogue Indian . . . uprising."

"More than twenty years! How can you deny an education to a small boy who had no say in determining who his parents were?"

"Miss Stratton, you go too far!" Cushing Pangston's neck turned an alarming shade of crimson, and his stammer disappeared.

"I'm sorry if I've upset you, but I simply cannot teach here if a child who deserves instruction is denied the right." She stood and headed toward the door.

"Miss Stratton, let's not be hasty."

Bianca turned, stared down at the minister, and waited.

"Our original request was for a schoolmaster who would prove a steadying influence. I hope the community won't feel hiring you was a mistake. For your own sake, you'd best let this matter drop." He stood and banged his empty coffee cup on the table for emphasis.

"I don't see how, in good conscience, I can do that. At least I can speak to the family and find out what their wishes are. I understand the Nolan place is south by the river."

The preacher moved closer and wagged his forefinger. "There are those who are not as filled with Christian charity as I might wish. You have youngsters in your class who are almost as old as you are. A rumor of impropriety between you and those boys from the ranch would be hard to stop once it got going."

Bianca shook her head in disbelief. "You can't seriously think—"

"What I think is not the issue. I can't order you to stay away from that squaw and her half-breed whelp. I can only warn you. And, Miss Stratton, you've been warned!" He marched out, slamming the screen door behind him.

Bianca headed for the parlor and stepped onto the front porch. She needed to put as much space as possible between herself and Cushing Pangston. She paced the porch in a rush of indignation as his poisonous diatribe echoed in her mind. A warning, he'd called it. Well, there'd been no hesitations or throat clearings in his final speech, and she knew a threat when she heard one.

Then, as she recalled his words, anger gave way to foreboding. Cushing Pangston was a tedious man—small in stature and small-minded as well. But that didn't mean she shouldn't take him seriously. Going against him—and probably most of the other parents as well—could cost her the job she needed so desperately. How could she take such a risk for one small boy who, quite possibly, would be happier running free in the woods?

Even as her head urged caution, Bianca's heart directed her feet toward the blacksmith's house. Meadows sprinkled with thickets of blueberries and Oregon grape gradually gave way to lush vegetation. Then the road narrowed and the forest seemed to enfold her, the scent of pine, cedar and fir almost overpowering in its pungency. A late afternoon breeze freshened the air, and she became aware of the sound of water.

The road curved and climbed to the top of a knoll where Bianca could see the slow-moving river ahead. Cottonwoods edged the riverbank, almost obscuring a bend in the stream. Before she reached the river she found a narrow track leading off to the east. A sign nailed to a fencepost read "D. Nolan, Blacksmith." After a few minutes Bianca could see a small clapboard house with smoke wisping from its stone chimney.

A family orchard, branches nearly bare now, stood north of the house. On the south side, sloping down toward the river, well-tended rows of peas, beans, squash and sweet corn had been planted. Beyond the nearby chicken house and shed, almost on the banks of the river, stood an assortment of rough-hewn structures where she assumed the blacksmith did his work. Seeing no sign of activity and no smoke coming from the forge, she went directly to the front door of the house and knocked.

After several minutes, during which Bianca could hear muffled voices inside, the door opened a crack, and she looked down into the same huge, dark eyes she'd seen outside the schoolhouse.

"Good afternoon," she said. "I'm Miss Stratton, the schoolteacher. And you must be Aiden."

"Yes, Ma'am." He quickly averted his eyes, and the door remained nearly closed.

"I'd like to speak to your parents, please."

"My pa ain't here, and my ma, she—" He interrupted himself to duck back inside. Bianca heard a rapid exchange of words in a language she didn't recognize. Then Aiden was back. "My ma, she's ailing right now."

"I'm sorry," Bianca said. "Is there something I can do to help?"

"No, Ma'am, but my ma says if you want Pa to do some smithing for you, you need to come back later—maybe tomorrow or the day after."

"I don't have any work for your father, Aiden. I came about you."

"Me, Ma'am?"

"Today was the first day of school. When I asked Reverend Pangston why you weren't there, he said nobody had remembered to speak to your parents. That's why I'm here."

The boy disappeared inside the house again, and there was more conversation inside. The door opened a little wider when he returned.

"You mean I can come to school?" There was a spark of hope in his voice. "My ma knows it costs money, but she says we can pay."

"Your father can talk to Reverend Pangston or Ed Fowler about the money. School starts at eight in the morning. I'll be looking for you."

Bianca headed away from the Nolan's farm feeling she'd at least done what her conscience dictated. She wondered what had prompted the blacksmith to leave his forge unattended with only his young son to care for his ailing wife. At any rate, she'd done her best. If Aiden's father failed to approve his attending school, the matter was out of her hands.

The walk back seemed shorter, even though the stretch from the river to the South road was mostly uphill. However, as she neared home her sense of accomplishment faded as she reflected on the implications of her actions. Even some of her professors at the academy characterized all Indians as ruthless and deceitful. Half-breeds such as Aiden were generally believed to be even more dangerous and untrustworthy due to their tainted blood.

Reverend Pangston, an educated man, apparently regarded Indians, even converted ones, as little better than savages. She thought his words were the empty threat of an ineffectual man who would avoid controversy at all costs—but what if she was mistaken? Bianca squared her shoulders and entered the Pangston's house. If Aiden Nolan did show up at the schoolhouse door, she suspected the real battle was just beginning.

The Pangston girls chattered through supper. Bianca skipped dessert and escaped to her room as soon as she'd helped Mattie clear the table. Passing up Mattie's lumpy rice pudding was no hardship, and Bianca had no desire to cross swords with Cushing again.

Upstairs she laid out a fresh skirt and shirtwaist to wear the next day. Aside from her black silk Sunday dress, her entire wardrobe consisted of the few plain clothes Viola had made to see her through her years at the academy. Now she also had Viola's shawl and bonnets. And the brooch. Not that she was likely to have any occasion to wear it.

She picked up her father's ledger and opened it to the last page—the page with the mysterious name and address. It had been a long, tiring day filled with unexpected challenges. Leandra Stratton, whoever she was, hadn't crossed Bianca's mind aside from a fleeting thought when she'd pointed out New England on the map this morning. Now she stared at the name and address. Leandra Stratton—related to her father. A cousin? An aunt? A sister?

Bianca's memories of her father were like the tissue in the hatbox—fragile and yellowed with age. She'd only been six when he died. If he'd ever talked to her about his family, she had no recollection of it. The entry in the ledger had been written more than a decade ago. Leandra Stratton might well have died or moved away from Boston. Still, Bianca saw a possibility, no matter how slight, of contacting her kinfolk.

She opened her wooden chest and took out an ink bottle, quill pen, and a precious sheet of pale blue writing paper which folded to make its own envelope. Then she sat at her small dressing table, staring at the blank page, wondering what to say, where to begin.

Dear Miss Stratton? No, that wouldn't do. Leandra Stratton might be a married lady. Bianca nibbled her thumbnail in frustration and shoved the blue stationery aside. She took out the tablet she'd been using to jot down lesson-plans. Nearly an hour later, after countless cross-outs and new beginnings, she stood and paced back and forth in front of the small window. Essays and compositions had always come easily at the academy. Why was a simple letter so hard?

She sat down, smoothed the blue writing paper. Dipping the quill in the ink, wiping it carefully, and concentrating on using her best penmanship, she wrote.

Dear Leandra Stratton,

I discovered your name and address written at the back of a ledger that belonged to my father, Charles Stratton. My father loved books and read to me a great deal, but I have no recollection of his ever talking about his family. I hope you will not think it impertinent of me to write to you in this manner, but I long for any scraps of information you might be able to provide.

Father died eleven years ago when I was six. My mother, Emily Bowen Stratton, died when I was born. My older sister, Viola, married young. She and her husband made a home for me on their farm. My beloved Viola died in childbirth this September. I am now teaching school in the small settlement of Oakfield, which is seventeen miles from the county seat of Wesleyville in the Southern part of the state of Oregon.

Aside from my four small nephews, Viola's sons, who remain on the farm with their father, I had no knowledge of any kinfolk until I discovered my father's ledger among some of Viola's belongings.

I have often wondered what led my parents to embark on their perilous journey to Oregon. I know my mother must have been frail. I believe she gave birth to several children, but only Viola and I survived. All through my years at school I envied my classmates who shared letters from their relatives in the East. If, indeed, you are kin to my father, I will cherish any information you can give me about the Stratton family.

Yours truly,
Bianca Stratton.

She blotted the letter carefully, folded it and sealed it with a bit of wax from her candle. She'd post it at Fowler's store tomorrow after class.

CHAPTER 9

"You're here early," Bianca called.

"Good morning, Ma'am." Aiden, wearing a starched white shirt and faded blue overalls, sat on the stoop outside the school-house door. At Bianca's approach he jumped to his feet.

"School doesn't start for over an hour. Are you sure you're not needed at home?"

"My pa's still gone, and my ma said I could come but I shouldn't be in the way. Am I in the way?"

"Of course not," Bianca replied with a smile. She pumped a bucket full of drinking water, and he insisted on carrying it inside.

"That's pretty heavy," she protested as he followed her through the door.

"I'm stronger than I look. Every morning I fetch water from the river and carry it to the forge for my pa. His bucket is big—bigger than this one. Now where do I set it?"

"Put it on the floor right here." Bianca pointed out the dipper hanging from a nail inside the classroom. "Lenny Fowler said you taught him to speak Injun."

"Yes, Ma'am. It's the kind of talk folks use when they can't understand each other too good. My pa calls it jargon. My ma talks jargon good."

"I see," said Bianca. "But the language you and your mother speak—that's different, isn't it?"

Aiden nodded. "Jargon's good for trading, but not for telling stories or singing songs. My ma knows lots of stories. I tried to tell some to Lenny, but they don't sound the same in English."

"It's nice that you and Lenny are friends," Bianca said.

"Lenny's not mean like some that comes with their folks to wait while my pa mends their wagon wheels."

"Nobody will be mean to you here at school. I won't allow it," Bianca said, hoping she was equal to the task.

Bianca glanced out the window at the children straggling into the schoolyard. She wondered if Jesse Landry would bring Oren and Hank again today. She'd learned the Donovan ranch was more than five miles up river, a long walk even for two strong boys. Of course, a busy ranch foreman had better things to do than cart them to school every day. Still, she felt pang of disappointment when a chestnut horse came down the road with the two boys riding bareback.

Although the children weren't as well-behaved as they had been the day before, lessons went smoothly, and Bianca felt things settling into a routine. She introduced Aiden to the class and promptly silenced Oren and Hank's muttered remarks.

Lenny made space on the back bench, and Aiden scurried to take a seat by his friend. Bjorn and Elke, who apparently had no preconceived notions about the education of half-breeds, greeted Aiden with welcoming smiles. The rest of the class ignored him. Considering the sentiments the children had expressed the day before, Bianca counted herself fortunate Aiden's presence caused so little commotion.

During lunch she mentioned her letter, and the twins offered to add it to the mail bag at the store when they got home. She knew it would be weeks before the letter reached Leandra Stratton and even longer before she could dare hope for a reply.

Still, she'd done what she could. Any news would be welcome, no matter how long she had to wait for it.

"Just wait till I get hold of that mealy-mouthed minister." Ed Fowler slammed barrels and boxes from one place to another. "He knows I won't have my young 'uns at school with no half-breed trash."

Frenchy and Cap sat at the table in Fowler's back room listening to Ed cuss. His brother had been killed in the Rogue Indian wars, and Ed had no use for any Indian or for any white man who married a squaw. Frenchy reported he'd seen the school-teacher leaving the Nolan place yesterday when he'd been fishing at the river. Early this morning Cap had spotted the Nolan's half-breed boy carrying his lunch basket and heading for the schoolhouse.

"Calm down, Ed. Join us in a small drink, yes?" Frenchy suggested.

"Good idea," Cap agreed. "I could use a nip."

"You can always use a nip." Ed's voice was tinged with irritation, but he brought a bottle and three glasses to the table, sat down and poured a couple of fingers of bran mash liquor into each glass. "It's a little early for me, but what the hell." He cradled the glass in his small hands and sipped appreciatively.

Frenchy said, "I don't know why you're upset with the preacher."

"Me neither." Cap downed his drink in one gulp. "It seems to me it's the schoolmarm who's causing the trouble."

"She wouldn't dare tell that squaw to send the boy to school on her own hook," Ed said.

"But you know Pangston," Cap countered. "He ain't never done nothing less'n somebody was behind pushing."

"Cushing Pangston's to blame, and he'll answer to me," Ed said. "I've got the most young'uns, and I put up the biggest share of the money. Without me we wouldn't have no school."

"You're right, Ed," Cap said. "This whole school thing is womenfolk's doing. I never had no schooling to speak of and I can't say it hurt me none."

"I don't want my girls hobnobbing with no half-breeds, and that's final." Ed refilled the glasses.

"Well," Frenchy said, "I've run into Aiden—that's his name, Aiden—fishing down at the river. A bright little fellow."

"Take it from me, the smarter they are the sneakier they are," Cap said. "And half-breeds is the worst of the lot"

"What I can't figure is how Daniel Nolan let this happen." Frenchy swirled the amber liquid in his glass. He knows this town wasn't keen on having a squaw-man here. I spoke to him about it. He said he'd keep his family out of everybody's way for a few months until folks got used to the idea."

"I bet Dan'l don't even know what's going on," Cap said. "I ain't seen him for a couple of days."

"More likely he's off on one of them drinking sprees of his," Ed said. "He's a queer one, that Daniel. Don't even come by here for a sociable drink like normal folks. Buys two or three bottles and disappears into the woods."

"He's a lone drinker for sure," Cap said. "He's gone off on one of them sprees more'n once in the three months he's been here."

"But he's a damn good blacksmith," Frenchy said. "And we sure need a blacksmith."

"True enough." Ed put the bottle away. "All the same, I'm going to talk some sense into Daniel Nolan when he turns up."

That evening Bianca took her place at the supper table, bowed her head, and made a silent prayer that Cushing Pangston's evening blessing would be mercifully brief. As if in answer, a loud knocking on the door sent Gertrude scurrying from the table. Minutes later Jesse Landry, hat in hand, appeared in the doorway.

"I'm sorry to interrupt your supper," he said, "but Mrs. Donovan asked me to ride around and let everybody know what's happened."

"What is it? What's going on?" The Pangston girls were a chorus of questions.

"Now, girls, mind your manners," said Mattie. "Please come in, Mr. Landry. You're more than welcome to join us for supper. Gertrude, take Mr. Landry's hat."

"Thank you Ma'am, but I need to get to the other settlers as quick as I can. And it might be a good idea if the girls left the room for a few minutes."

Jesse waited while Cushing, showing a rare flash of decisiveness, said, "Girls, go back to the kitchen and finish your supper. The rest of us will remove ourselves to the parlor."

Bianca followed Cushing to the parlor wondering what in the world could have brought Jesse here. But the tingle spreading clear down to her toes at Jesse's nearness almost overshadowed her curiosity.

"I'm sorry to upset you folks, but it seems we've got ourselves a renegade Indian in the area. Oren and Hank were out hunting rabbits around dusk and they came upon the blacksmith—his body, that is."

"Oh, dear." Mattie wrung her hands. "What should we do?"

"Lock up good and keep the girls close to home. That's about all you can do."

"But . . . uh . . . an Indian." Cushing Pangston's face went white. "How did you . . . er . . . ascertain this was the work of a renegade?"

"Well, Reverend, that's why I thought it best the youngsters not hear this part. It seems the blacksmith was robbed and murdered. And he'd been scalped."

Cushing turned even paler.

"But the Indians are on reservations," Mattie said.

"Well, yes. But there's been problems from the start with three or four different tribes all on the same land. Troublemakers keep escaping. They head south and hide out in the hills."

"Poor Aiden," Bianca murmured, as the reality of the black-smith's death began to sink in.

"Yes, that poor little boy." Mattie chimed in. "Do he and his mother know what's happened?"

"Yes, Ma'am. A couple of hands from the ranch took the body to the Nolan's place straightaway. Lars Larson's making a coffin. He's done some carpentering for us out at the ranch." He turned to Cushing. "Mrs. Donovan thought you might go see what kind of arrangements the widow wants to make."

"Well, I don't know . . . She isn't, you know, I mean she isn't really a . . . well, he didn't attend services, and—" Cushing's stammer was back in full force.

"Of course Cushing will go," Mattie said. "But I don't believe the woman speaks English, so arranging for the burial may be difficult. I wonder if Mr. Nolan has family we should notify."

"I don't believe . . . It seems nobody really knows anything about the Nolans. I mean . . . I don't see how I can . . . " Cushing was nearly incoherent.

"Aiden speaks his mother's language," Bianca said, "and his English is as good as any of my other pupils. I'm sure he can help."

"The ranch hands who delivered the body told me the boy never spoke a word," Jesse said. "They figured he only talked Injun lingo like his ma."

"The poor child was probably in shock." Bianca's blinked back tears at the thought of what Aiden must be feeling.

"I'll pay a call on the . . . bereaved in the morning." Cushing stood and rubbed his hands together nervously. "I hope the . . . uh . . . the lad will talk to me."

Bianca stole a sidelong glance at Jesse and was mortified to discover him looking at her at exactly the same moment. She turned away as soon as their eyes met, but there was no way she could control the flush of embarrassment on her neck and face.

Mattie, Cushing and Bianca returned to the supper table after Jesse left. Cushing told the girls the blacksmith had died, and refused to elaborate despite their questions. Bianca thought it was foolish to try to spare the children from the truth. When Oren and Hank got to school in the morning, Bianca was sure everybody would hear the story with many more gory details than Jesse had supplied.

Later in her attic room, her head buzzed with questions. Aiden had said his father was away, and at the time she'd had no reason to question him further. When had Daniel Nolan left, and where had he gone? She hadn't even asked Jesse where the body had been found. The boys had been hunting rabbits, he said. There were woods all along the riverfront near the Nolan's place.

Again her thoughts turned to Aiden and his mother. What would they do now? Apparently the Nolans had only been in the area a few months. If their land had been a homestead, would it revert to the government because they hadn't been there long enough to prove up on their claim? She recalled the neat little house with its family orchard. The house wasn't new, and the trees were well established. Daniel Nolan had probably purchased the property from a previous settler, which meant it now belonged to his widow.

Or did it? Were the Nolans properly and legally married? Did an Indian woman married to a white man inherit his property if he died? And what about Aiden's rights? She'd never thought about such things before and felt embarrassed by her ignorance.

At Wesleyville she had always been able to turn to the professors at the academy with her questions, but now she felt completely at a loss. She tried to tell herself it was really none of her business, but she couldn't dismiss Aiden from her mind now any more than she'd been able to when she'd found he wasn't to be allowed to attend school.

Sleep, when it finally came, was accompanied by a jumble of dreams. Aiden running barefoot through the woods away from the schoolhouse. Jesse, leaning against an oak tree, smiling. Cushing, in the front of the classroom, his speech unaccountably clear, delivering a diatribe about the wages of sin while the children cringed in terror. Then Rolf was there, telling her it was time to go home. She followed him to the surrey where Viola was waiting with the boys. Joyously she threw herself into Viola's comforting arms. But then Viola was gone and it was Rolf's arms holding her while the surrey raced through the dark woods, low branches brushing across her face and Rolf's voice telling her this was a dangerous place. She was struggling to free herself when she awoke to a gray dawn, her covers tangled and her body shivering.

CHAPTER 10

Bianca was surprised to see Aiden waiting by the door when she arrived at the schoolhouse early Wednesday morning.

"I can't come to school today," he said. "Ma needs me at home."

Bianca patted his shoulder. "I heard what happened to your father, and I'm so very sorry. Of course your mother needs you."

"Yes, Ma'am, she does."

"Is there anything I can do to help?"

Aiden shook his head. "I guess not, Ma'am. They're burying Pa tomorrow. Mr. Larson's bringing the coffin today. Ma says the sheriff might stop by, too. She understands most everything white folks say, but she don't think she speaks good enough to talk to them. That's why she wants me there."

"I think Reverend Pangston is going to see your mother as soon as he finishes his morning chores. You'd you better go on home now so you'll be there when he comes."

"I don't think Ma likes the Reverend much," Aiden said. "She's a Christian woman, my Ma. The missionaries even gave her a Christian name—Joanna. She knows more about the Bible than my Pa. She tells me the Bible stories, but I think I like her other stories better."

"Reverend Pangston means well," she said.

"When we first moved here, Pa spoke to the preacher about Ma and me going to church. Reverend Pangston never did say we'd be, you know, welcome like, so we never went. Ma don't like to go where she ain't wanted."

"I certainly understand," Bianca said. "Run along, and don't worry about the lessons you're missing. You can stay after class next week and get caught up."

Aiden was obviously reluctant to leave. "They say an Indian killed my Pa," he said.

"That's what Mr. Landry told us."

"Well, Ma don't believe it. She says she knows no Indian done it."

Of course his mother would want to shield Aiden. Still, facts were facts. "I hope you'll help your mother tell the sheriff everything she knows," Bianca said.

"He won't listen." Aiden's tone was resigned. "Ma says lawmen never listen to anything our people tell them."

Bianca couldn't think of anything to say to that. Aiden was probably right. She didn't know anything about the sheriff, but she suspected it would never occur to him that an Indian might have worthwhile information.

"I can fill the water bucket for you before I go," Aiden offered.

"No, thank you. Your mother really needs you right now. You hurry on home."

Bianca turned to open the door and then looked back to see Aiden running down the road. He stopped and waved, and her eyes filled with tears. Something about that little boy in his faded overalls and dusty moccasins touched her deeply even though she'd only known him a few days.

From the way he took to his lessons she knew he was very bright, but there was something more in those dark eyes. It was as if he had seen too much of the world in his eight short years, understood he would probably be treated badly, but still had the courage to reach out to people he might be able to trust. She was flattered that he seemed to count her in that number.

As she filled inkwells and wrote the daily assignments on the blackboard, Bianca couldn't help reflecting on Aiden's apparent lack of grief at his father's death. What sort of man had Daniel Nolan been? Where had he come from? How had he happened to marry a native woman? What had led him to Oakfield? And did Joanna Nolan have a valid reason for believing someone other than an Indian had killed him?

The children were full of talk as they streamed into the classroom and settled in their seats.

"An Injun killed the blacksmith," Junior announced.

"Miss Stratton knows that already," Gertrude said. "Mr. Landry came to our house right off."

"Did he say he was scalped?" Junior wasn't to be deterred from giving Bianca the news.

"Oren and Hank found the body," Katie said. "If Miss Stratton wants to know about it, she should ask them."

"All right, everyone," Bianca said, "settle down. I know you want to talk about what happened, so we'll take ten minutes discussing it. Then we'll proceed with our lessons, and I'll hear no further mention of Mr. Nolan's death. Is that understood?"

Hank and Oren described in chilling detail how they'd been in the woods north of the ranch hunting rabbits when their dog began barking and acting up.

"If it hadn't been for old Brownie we'd have never found him," Oren said.

"He smelt him. Dogs can smell better'n we can," Hank amplified.

"The body—it was down in this gully all covered with dead branches and leaves," Oren continued.

"We tried to get old Brownie to come away, but he kept yipping, so we went and had ourselves a look." Hank seemed determined not to let Oren monopolize the limelight.

"Was there lots of blood?" Lloyd asked.

"I'm telling it the way it happened," Oren said. "At first all we could see was a boot sticking out from where old Brownie dug the leaves away."

"Then we pulled off the branches and saw some buckskin britches. We thought maybe we'd found us a dead Injun," Hank said.

Oren glared. "Quit interrupting, Hank. I'm telling this."

"I was there as much as you was."

"Well, then, you tell it." Oren clamped his lips together.

"Naw, you go on. You tell it better than me."

"We didn't know who it was until we uncovered his face. I recognized the blacksmith because I was over there last week with Jesse getting a new shoe on one of the wagon horses. When we saw he'd been scalped, we hightailed it back to the ranch and told Aunt Nora."

"Did he—the blacksmith, I mean—did he have his rifle?" Lenny spoke up.

"Didn't see no rifle," said Hank.

"Well, if he was out in the woods, why didn't he have a rifle?" Lenny persisted.

"I guess the Injun stole it," said Oren. "All Injuns steal, and they'll do most anything to get their hands on a rifle."

"I don't believe all Indians steal," said Bianca. "And we don't know if Mr. Nolan had gone hunting, so we have no way of knowing whether or not he had his rifle with him." Then, remembering what Aiden had said, she added, "We don't really know he was killed by an Indian."

"He was scalped, Miss Stratton," one of the twins reminded her.

"Scalped!" The echo, in case Bianca had missed the point the first time, came from the other twin—Edwina, no doubt.

"My Pa said an Injun killed him," Junior said stoutly.

"Well, I understand the sheriff is coming over from the county seat. I'm sure he'll be able to determine what happened. Now, take out your copybooks, and let's get on with our lessons."

At dismissal time Bianca cautioned the older children to stay close to their younger brothers and sisters and go straight home. Bianca completed her janitorial duties hastily. She hurried back to the house and offered to help Mattie with supper preparations, hoping she could somehow salvage something edible from Mattie's disastrous cooking.

Mattie refused assistance but welcomed the opportunity to talk. She said Cushing's visit to the widow Nolan had been brief. He hadn't been invited in but had been forced to stand on the front stoop while he offered his condolences. Aiden had spoken to his mother in her own language. However, Aiden's translations were much shorter than Cushing's words, so he questioned whether or not the boy had really tried to convey his meaning.

"Aiden told me his mother understands English fairly well," Bianca said.

"I've heard lots of savages pretend not to understand. It helps them avoid responsibility."

"Aiden also told me his mother had been converted to Christianity," Bianca said. "So I don't think it's fair to refer to her as a savage."

"I'm not one of your pupils who needs correcting," Mattie snapped. "I've heard about these so-called Christians who still keep to their old ways and worship their heathen gods in secret."

"I'm sorry, Mattie. But Aiden says his mother is self-conscious about speaking to strangers. She thinks her grammar isn't good enough."

"Well, Cushing suggested a simple graveside service for tomorrow afternoon, and I gather she understood well enough to agree." Mattie tossed a pinch of salt into the simmering kettle of watery soup. "Now all we have to do is hope the sheriff catches the renegade before the rest of us are murdered in our beds."

"There are still several hours of daylight left," Bianca said, glancing out the window. "I brought some work home for Aiden. I think I'll walk there before supper. I'm really worried about him."

"Really, Bianca. You'd best be worried about the rest of us."

"I know, but if any of my other students had lost a parent I'd feel the same." Bianca knew this wasn't, strictly speaking, the truth.

"Well, since you're bound to go, you might as well take one of the pound cakes I baked this afternoon." Mattie wrapped the still warm cake in a clean flour sack, and handed it to Bianca.

"Thank you, Mattie," Bianca said with a smile, wondering how anyone who skimped on ingredients the way Mattie did would even try to bake a pound cake. "I'll tell the widow you sent your condolences."

At she neared the Nolans' gate, Bianca saw a sleek, bay horse feasting on fallen fruit from a nearby apple tree. Then the front door flew open, and Aiden ran to meet her.

"Miss Stratton! Ma saw you coming. She wants you to come in, please, Ma'am."

CHAPTER II

Sheriff Tyler Wells had stopped at Fowler's store to get directions to the blacksmith's house, and the twins assured him the boy spoke English as well as his mother's lingo. Now he paced in front of the Nolans' stone fireplace, feeling totally frustrated. The youngster seemed terrified, and the Indian woman wasn't talking. Tyler spoke the trading jargon common to all the tribes, but he wasn't able to get anywhere.

A well-made cedar coffin rested on two straight-backed pine chairs. When Tyler explained he wanted to lift the lid and examine the body, the woman planted herself in front of the coffin and raised a ruckus.

Tyler had a renegade Indian in custody at the county jail awaiting the arrival of the circuit judge who'd hold court the first week in October. The previous Sunday morning the Indian, Joe Red Deer, had been caught stealing chickens on a farm near Wesleyville. The farmer and his wife left church services early because their colicky baby wouldn't stop crying. As their wagon rounded a bend in the road near their farm, they spotted the Indian leaving the henhouse hanging onto a chicken in each hand. The farmer shot him in the foot, tied him up and brought him back to town.

If Joe Red Deer had murdered Nolan, Tyler knew his job would get a lot easier. However, when Frenchy Blauchet came to town and reported the blacksmith's murder, the Indian repeatedly denied any knowledge of the crime. He claimed he'd never been as far south as Oakfield. He insisted he'd been picking apples up north near Yoncalla until the morning the farmer shot him. Unless someone had seen him in the vicinity of Oakfield, there was no way to tie him to the blacksmith's murder.

Tyler tried to get the Nolan woman to look through the meager belongings he'd taken from Joe Red Deer. She just jabbered, and the boy hightailed it out the door. Tyler'd been up before dawn, and he had no stomach for riding all the way back to Wesleyville in the middle of the night. He figured he'd best call it a day, ride on over to the Donovan ranch and talk to the boys who found the body. He'd been told Widow Donovan would give him a hot supper and let him bed down in the bunkhouse for the night.

He jammed his worn Stetson on his head and started out the door, almost colliding with a woman on the front stoop. He guessed some neighbor lady had decided to pay a visit and bring a basket of comfort food to the widow. The blacksmith's boy was holding her hand and talking up a storm, but as soon as he saw Tyler he clammed up.

"I'm Bianca Stratton, the schoolteacher here at Oakfield," the woman said.

Tyler had heard Oakfield had finally hired a teacher, but he'd assumed they'd found a schoolmaster. Now he looked at the visitor appraisingly, wondering how such a handsome young woman ended up being a schoolmarm in this backwater spot.

"And Aiden tells me you're the sheriff."

"Tyler Wells, Ma'am."

"I hope you're here because you're really going to conduct an investigation."

The edge in her voice annoyed him. "That's my job, and I'd best get on with it."

He brushed past her, mounted his horse, and rode away.

70

Bianca stared after the sheriff for several minutes.

"What a strange man," she murmured.

"I know you told me to talk to him," Aiden said, "but Ma thinks he's going to make us go live on the reservation."

"You didn't answer his questions?"

"I didn't say nothing. He wanted to open up the coffin, but Ma wouldn't let him."

"Well, maybe I need to speak with your mother," Bianca said. "Will she talk to me, do you think?"

Before Bianca had a time to knock, Joanna Nolan opened the door and motioned her inside. The woman's most striking features were her large, expressive eyes, which, like Aiden's, were so dark it was hard to tell where the iris stopped and the pupil began. Her hair was parted in the center, pulled severely back from her face and plaited into two thick braids that fell almost to her waist. An assortment of colorful beads and shells had been woven into the end of each braid. Her skin, almost a match for the red-brown Oregon earth, was smooth and unblemished except for a purplish bruise spreading from her left cheekbone to the line of her black hair.

As Bianca averted her eyes from the bruise, Joanna spoke rapidly, and Aiden translated. "My ma says she believes you're a friend because you fixed it so I could go to school. She don't want to talk English because you're a teacher and you'll see how wrong she talks."

"I think you and your mother are both very smart," Bianca said. "You both know two languages, and I only speak one."

"Please sit, Miss Stratton," Joanna Nolan's smile illuminated her round face as she gestured toward a straight-backed chair with a laced rawhide seat.

After only a few minutes Joanna apparently felt comfortable enough to abandon the awkward process of speaking wholly in her native tongue and waiting for Aiden to translate.

"Tomorrow Aiden not go school." Joanna said. "Very sorry not go school today, but ..." She glanced meaningfully at the coffin."

71

"I understand," Bianca said.

"I put prayer sand in cedar box with Daniel. Tomorrow preacher say white people prayers." The woman's hand brushed the discolored area on her face almost reflexively. "Daniel, my husband, need many prayers."

Bianca nodded sympathetically as Joanna, with Aiden's help, recounted what she knew of Daniel's life. He'd gone to a gold strike in the north and returned six months later with high hopes and a small fortune only to find that his first wife and their three small children had been carried away by a virulent measles epidemic. For several years he wandered aimlessly, drinking heavily, squandering most of his money in the process. At a mission church near the reservation he'd been taken in, sobered up, and encouraged to work at his old blacksmithing trade.

It was there he met Joanna, who served as a cook and housekeeper for a missionary's family. Daniel took the pledge, and for the first few years of their marriage he remained sober and hardworking, but the Nolans never stayed in one place for long.

Then Daniel began drinking again, sometimes disappearing for weeks at a time. When they bought the house and set up the blacksmith shop in Oakfield, Joanna hoped things would be better. Instead, Daniel's periods of sobriety became briefer. He grew hostile and abusive with her, and she even began to fear for Aiden's safety.

At the end of the telling, Joanna's large eyes filled with tears. "But he is good man when drink not in him," she said. "I not want him dead. I not know what to do. I want Aiden learn white people ways. No want go reservation. But Daniel gone, and I not want be alone from my people."

Bianca hurried home in the gathering dusk, reflecting on her conversation with Joanna Nolan. How lonely and isolated her life had been. And now, what did the future hold for her and the small boy Bianca had come to care about so deeply?

CHAPTER 12

The gathering in the back room of Fowler's store was larger than usual when Jesse Landry arrived. Speculations about the blacksmith's murder opened the door for lengthy war stories from Cap.

"They tell us they rounded all them red devils up back in '54 and put them on reservations, but it ain't so," Cap was saying. "Redskins on the reservations get passes to work on the outside, and they take off for the woods. We shoulda finished the job and shot the lot of them. Then we wouldn't have no renegade Injuns prowling around stealing and killing and God knows what else."

"Well, Cap," Jesse drawled from the doorway, "if you've killed half as many redskins as you say you have, there shouldn't be any left in the whole state of Oregon."

Jesse pulled up a wooden box, pushed his Stetson back from his face and ordered a drink. "And give the rest of the boys another round, too, Ed," he added.

"What bank did you rob, Jesse?" Ed asked jovially as he uncorked the jug. "I can't recall the last time you stood the house for drinks."

"Thought I'd let you know you can stop worrying about being massacred in your beds. Sheriff Wells is out at the ranch spending the night, and he's already got that murdering Indian put away in the Wesleyville jail. Some farmer caught him stealing chickens and shot him in the foot."

"I guess the sheriff's next job will be to hustle the squaw and the boy back to the reservation where they belong," said Cap." Good riddance, too."

"Amen to that," said Ed. "That'll put an end to my having to help pay for that little half-breed's schooling."

"And maybe now that busybody schoolmarm will stop meddling in what don't concern her," Cap added.

"Well, I don't know about that," said Jesse. "Sheriff Wells said she turned up at the Nolan place as he was leaving."

"Wait until Agnes hears that," said Ed. "No respectable woman, especially an unmarried one, goes calling on a squaw. Even that mealy-mouthed preacher wouldn't allow Mattie to go near there. When word gets around, the womenfolk will see to it that Bianca Stratton never finishes her three-month stay in Oakfield. She'll be lucky to last three weeks!"

"Nolan had a nice piece of land down by the river—good, solid little house, too," Cap said.

"I thought you were going to buy that land when the Bransons moved back East." Frenchy said.

"I gave it some thought, but I figured Branson would come down some on the price, anxious as he was to get back to Vermont and what he called civilized society. Then, before I could even make an offer, Nolan turned up and paid full asking price." Cap emptied his glass and waited expectantly for someone to offer him a refill.

"Paid cash, too, I understand," Ed said. "I always wondered where a feller like Nolan would get hold of that kind of money."

"I heard he had a lucky strike in the gold fields," Cap said.

"Pour Cap another drink before he dies of thirst," Jesse said. "And I'm ready for another shot, too."

"Have you still got your eye on that land, Cap?" Frenchy asked. "I never figured on you going into the blacksmithing trade."

"Hell, I'm no blacksmith," Cap said, "but that land's the only place the railroad can build a bridge across the river."

"You really think the railroad will get this far?" Jesse asked.

"No question about it," said Ed. "Them Southern Pacific fellers have been nosing around here ever since the line from the East connected up with San Francisco. Oakfield's in a direct line to the pass through the Siskyous where Dollarhyde runs his toll road. We already got telegraph wires in. Next we'll get the stage running regular through here, and then the railroad will come too. No other route makes any sense."

"That would open up some new markets for our cattle," said Jesse.

"I thought them cattle belonged to Nora Donovan," said Cap. "Have you got something going on down there that makes you more than a foreman?"

Jesse joined in the general laughter. "Mrs. Donovan's a fine woman, but she's a little long in the tooth for my taste."

"Well, there ain't much to choose from around here," Cap said, "unless you fancy the squaw widow,"

"How about the new schoolmarm?" Frenchy winked and tweaked his moustache.

"She's too damn tall," Ed said.

"I always fancied a gal big enough I could find her in the dark," Jesse said with a grin.

"Well, tall or short, that one's nothing but trouble," said Cap. "I can spot them busybody do-gooders a mile off. When there's no Injuns around fer her to cozy up to she'll most likely start fillin' the young'uns' heads with notions about women getting the vote."

"Anybody who gets mixed up with that Stratton woman is plumb crazy." Ed agreed.

"You may be right." Jesse finished his drink and stood up "But then, I always did think a challenge made things more interesting. See you boys later."

The road to the ranch wound through the hills where the scent of wild honeysuckle hung heavy in the cool night air. A three-quarter moon drifted low in the sky, one minute lighting the road and then half-hidden by clouds wafting across its face.

Like a teasing woman, Jesse thought. One minute she's giving you a look that sets your blood on fire, and then she disappears behind a cloud of Methodist propriety. He wondered if Bianca Stratton had any idea how much he'd thought about her, dreamed about her, since that first Sunday after services when their eyes met.

Despite the long hours he'd been putting in at the ranch, sometimes falling bone weary into his bunk, the dreams persisted. She was always there, just out of reach. Well, he'd change that. He knew she felt at least some of the same attraction. He could tell when a woman took a shine to him. Bianca Stratton was different, though. Maybe all that book learning had made her wary and standoffish. He'd have to take it slow, like taming a wild horse. He'd always had a way with horses.

Before turning in, Jesse stopped by the ranch house. He was the foreman, but Nora Donovan was a hands-on manager who kept track of everything. She knew exactly how many head of cattle were on each section of the range, how much feed had been put by, what it cost to feed and house the hands, and, it seemed, a million and one other details. She wrote everything down in her leather-bound ledger, and the nightly review of the events of the day and plans for tomorrow was part of her routine.

Now, sitting across the massive oak trestle table Nora used as her desk, Jesse recalled Cap's taunt and admitted to himself that a man could do a lot worse than team up with Nora Donovan. She was a small, wiry woman whose thick, black hair was parted in the center and pulled back into a coil on the back of her neck. Her dark eyes missed nothing. But below her aquiline nose, a generous mouth with laugh lines at the corners belied the severity.

Jesse accepted the glass of port, which had become part of their evening ritual, and responded respectfully to her questions about progress on the replacement of rotted fence posts in the bottomland along the river. Then he waited for what he thought of as tomorrow's orders of the day.

"I've been thinking about the blacksmith," she said.

"Oh? What about him?"

"His equipment. I was planning to set up a forge here on the ranch before Nolan opened his shop. The new hand you hired last week told me he'd worked for a while as a smith's apprentice. He could probably handle the kind of work we have here. I want you to go over to Nolan's place tomorrow after the funeral and make the widow an offer on the forge and other tools. I think three hundred would be a fair price."

"I bet if you talked to her yourself at the cemetery you could get it all for two-fifty—maybe even less. Then later I could send a couple of the men over with the wagon to load everything up."

"No, Jesse." Nora Donovan took a sip from her crystal wine-glass and dabbed a linen napkin to her lips. "I wouldn't want the word to get around that I was taking advantage of a widow woman before her man was hardly in the ground."

"Well, I don't think anybody in these parts is too concerned about the Nolan woman. Squaws don't rate very high with most of the folks in Oakfield."

"Mexicans don't either," Nora snapped. "I know what it's like to be an outsider in my own country."

"I'm sorry, Nora. I didn't think—I mean—you're Spanish. It's not the same at all."

Nora smiled. "California was part of Mexico for a lot of years before it became a state. Nearly all native Californians are mixed Indian and Spanish blood. My father, proud man that he is, likes to boast about his Spanish heritage and the land grant his grandfather received from the king of Spain.

"But I remember my Toltec great-grandmother. And I remember how our family was treated after California became a state. Gradually we, who had grazed our cattle on the same range for untold years, became foreigners in our own homeland.

"I will go to the service for Mr. Nolan tomorrow, and I will offer my sympathy to his poor widow. And later tomorrow you will go and inquire, respectfully, if she wishes to sell the black-smith equipment for three hundred dollars. Is that clear?"

"Of course, Nora. You're the boss." Jesse tried for a lighter tone, wishing he'd kept his mouth shut earlier. He'd worked for Nora Donovan for nearly three years, but this was a side of her he'd never seen before. He wasn't sure how to deal with it.

CHAPTER 13

Cap Mackay stood at the edge of the clearing where rough headstones and wooden crosses spelled out Oakfield's meager history. Cap had been in the area off and on for more than a dozen years and knew first-hand about most of the folks who had come and gone. He'd been among the early prospectors who hadn't struck it rich in California and hurried to the Rogue River Valley when gold was discovered there in the early fifties. It turned out there wasn't all that much gold in southern Oregon, but the mild climate and fertile soil persuaded some to remain as settlers. However, after hearing tales about the hostile Rogue and Klamath Indians, others moved on.

Cap's first foray into Oakfield had been during the Rogue wars, and after that he'd helped put down Injun uprisings all over the northwest. A couple of years ago he decided he'd had a bellyful of sleeping on the ground and eating bad grub. Truth was, he was plain too old for soldiering. Cap had regretfully rejected the call to serve with Lindsay Applegate and his kinfolk at the new garrison at Fort Klamath. Instead, he'd settled down in a little cabin he'd bought for back taxes.

Cap made no pretense of listening to Cushing Pangston's awkward attempts at a eulogy for a man nobody in these parts had really known. Instead he looked down and surveyed the panoramic view the hilltop afforded. The valley was a pretty spot with more shades of green than a body could imagine. The river, slow-moving this time of year, reflected the deep blue of the sky as it snaked its way in a southwesterly direction.

Looking at the river, Cap smiled and then quickly sobered and bowed his head, hoping nobody had noticed. He didn't want anybody to think he was happy about the blacksmith's death, even though it was beginning to look like things were finally beginning to go his way. The river would make his fortune. The only question in his mind was how to go about getting hold of the blacksmith's land. If the sheriff did his job and moved the squaw and her little half-breed to the reservation where they belonged, he should be able to snap up the place.

On the other hand, he'd lost one chance at the land by trying to pinch pennies, so maybe he ought to make an offer while the squaw was still here. That is, if she really owned the spread. Cap had never given much thought to land laws, but he reckoned a lot depended on whether or not Daniel and the squaw had ever been legally hitched, and if they had, whether she could furnish proof the knot had been tied right and proper. Still, one way or another, he'd get his hands on that prime piece of riverfront.

Summer heat and drought had taken the fight out of the river, but after the winter and spring rains it would be another story. The bend in the river where Nolan had his blacksmith hut slowed the raging torrent even when the banks were overflowing. It was the only possible place to build a railroad bridge. And everybody knew the railroads paid top dollar when they had to.

But now, with the prize in sight, Cap wasn't sure what to do next. Maybe he ought to ride over to Wesleyville and talk to the lawyer fellow who'd hung his shingle in the same block as the bank and the land office. Still, it might be better not to say any more, the way rumors spread. Somebody else might get ideas if they hadn't already.

Cap sensed that Pangston was winding up the service and looked around at the small group gathered around to pay their respects. The coffin sat at the head of the grave, with the preacher behind it. Mattie Pangston stood on her husband's left, with a toddler hanging onto her heavy black skirt and the rest of the Pangston bunch huddled together behind her. The nosy schoolmarm towered over the Pangston brood, the wind catching unruly strands of dark hair that escaped from her black bonnet.

On the other side of the grave the squaw woman stood straight as an arrow, with the half-breed boy beside her. Except for the buckskin moccasins and long black braids, the squaw didn't seem much different from the other women. Which went to show you couldn't always pick out a savage by looking.

Lars Larson and his yellow-haired wife and brats stood behind the squaw woman. Nora Donovan and Jesse Landry, along with several ranch hands and the two wild whippersnappers who found the body, made another little group at the foot of the open grave. The young sheriff, Tyler Wells, had arrived late, tethered his horse and stood behind the ranch hands. Cap wondered why he was hanging around.

None of the Fowlers turned out for the service, which didn't surprise Cap considering Ed Fowler's feelings about Injuns. He did think it was strange Frenchy hadn't come to pay his respects. Aside from being as close to a friend as Daniel Nolan had in these parts, Frenchy liked to be in on whatever was going on. He wasn't a gossip like Agnes Fowler, but he knew pretty much everything about everybody. It wasn't like him to miss a burying.

After a chorus of amens two of the ranch hands lowered the casket into the ground and began shoveling dirt into the hole. The Larsons and Pangstons started down the hill. Nora Donovan spoke briefly to the squaw woman and then, with a hand from Jesse, hoisted herself into the farm wagon.

Cap watched from the shade of one of the ancient fir trees, wondering if speaking to the squaw now would help his chances of making a deal when the time was right. He'd made no secret of his belief that the only good Injun was a dead one, so talking to the woman now might start folks wondering what he was up to. He sure didn't want that snoop of a schoolmarm getting any ideas. She seemed to be sticking to the squaw and the boy like glue. He turned and headed down the gravel trail. He'd drop by the Nolan place later when he was sure the coast was clear.

After the last shovelful of soil had been added to the mound of earth marking Daniel Nolan's grave, Bianca watched Jesse ride away beside the attractive dark-haired woman everyone called Aunt Nora. Bianca had pictured Nora Donovan as a plump, gray-haired matronly sort. Now that image had been jarred considerably. The real Nora Donovan was much younger than she had expected. And Jesse Landry seemed to treat her with great deference. Not that it mattered a bit how he treated her. He was Mrs. Donovan's employee, after all. And if he was more than that, it certainly didn't make any difference to Bianca.

She'd dismissed school early so the children could join their families at the service. Joanna and Aiden were still standing beside the grave. Then Joanna put a packet of some kind of twigs on the grave and bowed her head.

Aiden moved silently to Bianca's side. "My ma wants you to please come to our house." His dark eyes seemed even more somber than usual. "There's something she wants to show you."

"I can walk home with you and your mother now if it's all right with her." Bianca looked up and met the Indian woman's eyes. Joanna Nolan gave an almost imperceptible nod, turned away from the grave and disappeared into the circle of fir trees.

"Ma don't like roads. She knows paths through the woods. Sometimes she shows me places where special plants grow. She'll be home before we get there."

Impulsively, Bianca reached out and took Aiden's hand in hers, half expecting him to pull away and follow his mother. When he squeezed her hand and moved close beside her, she swallowed and blinked back tears. Cushing Pangston's pedestrian eulogy hadn't moved her in the least, but Aiden seemed able to tug at her heart without saying a word. Whatever was to become of him?

Joanna Nolan glided down the forest path, her moccasins making no sound and leaving scant trace of her passing. She plucked an occasional sprig of hyssop or madder and tucked it into the doeskin pouch at her waist. Gathering herbs for cooking, healing and communicating with the Great Spirit was as automatic as breathing, but her mind was a confused jumble of grief, questions, and doubts.

Her concerns were about Aiden's future. Did he belong with her people or his father's people? Was the Great Spirit who would direct his life the Christian God the missionaries had told her was loving and powerful, or the Spirit who had guided her parents as they taught her the rituals and stories of her own people?

Sometimes Joanna was certain there was but one God who spoke to all people and didn't care whether they addressed Him on their knees in church or through the scented smoke rising from a village campfire.

But then she recalled pictures the missionaries had shown her of people burning in Hell because they hadn't embraced the true faith. She wondered if poor Daniel was burning in Hell. She was certain the Devil took hold of his soul when he had drink in him. But when he was sober he read the Bible and prayed earnestly for forgiveness.

Whatever the future held for Aiden, Joanna sensed that learning the white man's ways was critical. He finally had a chance to learn to read and write, but how could he become an educated man if the sheriff sent them away? On the reservation those who escaped the deadly illnesses were no better than slaves sent out to work for the white men. But shouldn't Aiden learn to know and love the only family he had? What was left of her family was at the reservation—an aging uncle and two cousins.

Then there was Joanna's brother, Running Fox, who, along with a few others, had eluded the soldiers when her people had been rounded up. Now they were hiding out and defying the white men in the great mountains to the south. Only a few years ago it would have been unthinkable for peaceable tribes like her own or the haughty Klamaths to join forces with the unpredictable Modocs. For some of those the white men called renegades, the threat of a common enemy proved stronger than tribal taboos and distrust.

Distrust, she reflected sadly, seemed to be a lesson she kept learning. She had nobody to whom she could turn except the brother who disapproved of her marriage, or perhaps the Stratton woman who had taken it upon herself to let Aiden attend school.

Joanna didn't know how to get in touch with Running Fox. He turned up at her house from time to time, always when Daniel was away. She realized she couldn't deal with the white men's laws by herself. She had to trust someone. The tall teacher seemed kind, and Aiden said she treated all her pupils fairly. Aiden trusted her, and Aiden was wise beyond his years.

CHAPTER 14

When Bianca and Aiden reached the Nolan place, Joanna was waiting in the doorway. Aided by Aiden's translations when her English faltered, Joanna told of her concerns about the future. A square oak box sat on the table. Its lid was hinged with leather straps, and the top and sides were intricately carved with leaves and flowers. Bianca hadn't noticed it on her previous visit. Probably Joanna usually kept it tucked away.

"Papers of my husband stay in box," Joanna said, lifting the lid almost reverently. "Some papers important. Some only for remembering. I not read. Aiden not yet learn enough."

"How can I help?" Bianca asked.

"Sit, please. Read." Joanna moved the box toward Bianca, who took a seat in the straight-backed chair flanking the table. Joanna sat beside her while Aiden stood solemnly beside his mother.

Bianca pointed out that reading everything in the box would take hours. "Maybe I should tell you what they are, and then you can decide which ones you want me to read all the way through," she suggested. Joanna nodded in agreement.

Even so, it was more than an hour before the entire contents of the box had been sorted. There were receipts for blacksmith tools and supplies as well as for clothing and household items. Dozens of letters from Rachel, Daniel's first wife, testified to the time he had spent prospecting.

A number of yellowed newspaper clippings shared a theme Bianca knew all too well. One obituary told how Daniel's first wife and their three children had been taken with diphtheria. There were other death notices—names Joanna said she didn't know but assumed were either relatives or friends. A baby stillborn, a young woman killed in a fall from a horse, a miner killed in squabble over a claim, another miner killed in a barroom fight, a family who perished when their cabin caught fire.

At the bottom of the box, under a few fading tintypes, were the items Bianca hoped she would find. She read them aloud, word for word. A wedding certificate, a will, and a deed.

The wedding certificate proved Daniel and Joanna had indeed been legally married, and the will left everything to Joanna. The will, dated the day after the wedding certificate, was witnessed by the same missionary who had performed the ceremony. Bianca silently thanked the thoughtful minister who must have known first-hand what problems could arise from a mixed marriage, even a legal one.

"You think is all right, then, for Aiden?" Joanna asked. "They not make us go to reservation?"

Bianca's words of reassurance were interrupted by the sound of footsteps on the wooden porch outside and three authoritative knocks on the front door. Aiden looked at his mother anxiously.

"See who knock, Aiden." Joanna's voice was calm.

Bianca followed Aiden to the door and found herself facing Sheriff Tyler Wells. He shifted his weight from one foot to the other and hastily removed his gray Stetson when he saw her.

"Good afternoon, Sheriff," Bianca said. "If you've come to pay your respects to Mrs. Nolan, I might suggest that the graveside services might have been a more appropriate time and place."

"Good afternoon, Miss Stratton," he said, adopting Bianca's tone of cold formality. "I'm sorry to intrude on the grieving widow's privacy, but I'm afraid my business here is of an official nature."

"Come in, Sheriff," said Joanna.

"I hope you have information on who is responsible for Mr. Nolan's untimely death," Bianca said, following him to the table where Joanna remained seated beside the oaken box.

"There's nothing new I can tell you about that, Ma'am. What I came for is—"

"Isn't that what sheriffs are supposed to do? Apprehend criminals and see justice done?" Bianca asked.

The sheriff's eyes narrowed, and Bianca noted that their color had changed from hazel to a pale, cloudy gray. That and the set of his square, determined jaw persuaded her she'd better not push Tyler Wells too far.

"Sometimes justice involves duties I would rather not have to perform," he said. "I've received a complaint about Indians inhabiting these premises. I'm sure you know the law requires natives to be removed to reservations."

"We do not go," said Joanna.

"It will take me several days to get word to the Federal Marshall," Tyler Wells explained. "I wanted to give you some time."

"Please sit down, Sheriff Wells," Bianca said. "I think we can save you the trouble of notifying the Marshall."

After carefully reading the wedding certificate, and will and the deed, the sheriff turned to Joanna and smiled. "This does make my job a lot easier, Mrs. Nolan," he said. "There seems to be no legal question. It appears you and Aiden have the right to remain here as long as you wish, or to dispose of the property as you see fit."

Tyler Wells turned to Bianca. "I'm not sure where you fit into all this, Miss Stratton," he said. "But as you seem to have befriended Mrs. Nolan you might want to suggest she see a lawyer at the county seat to be sure everything is handled properly."

"You're right, of course." Bianca realized she hadn't given any thought to the necessity for Daniel Nolan's will to be entered into probate. Perhaps she'd been hasty in her assessment of the sheriff's capabilities.

"Since Mr. and Mrs. Nolan were legally married, she and Aiden should have the same rights as a white family would have." The sheriff smiled again, and Bianca realized Tyler Wells was actually quite an attractive man. "I don't anticipate any problems," he added, "but in cases like this it pays to take extra care."

"About this so-called complaint," Bianca said. "Who filed it?"

"I don't really think that's important now."

"Maybe not. But finding out who murdered Daniel Nolan— you must agree that's important," Bianca persisted.

"Of course. But when we're dealing with renegade Indians and random acts of theft and violence we aren't always able to come up with solutions."

"Joanna—Mrs. Nolan—doesn't think Daniel was killed by an Indian," Bianca said.

"Naturally she'd want to believe someone else was responsible."

"No," Bianca insisted. "Please, listen to her." She turned to Joanna. "Won't you talk to the sheriff? I don't think he wants to harm you, and it's his job to find out who really killed Daniel."

Joanna explained, with Aiden supplying the English words when she hesitated and reverted to her own language.

"Is the scalping," she said. "The tribes I know— people who lived on these lands—they cut off enemy's head. They not scalp."

Bianca noticed that the sheriff was listening carefully.

"Maybe your husband met up with an Indian from another part of the country—one from a tribe that did take scalps," he said.

Joanna explained that a scalp would be a trophy taken after raid or battle. "My husband, he has no battle. His gun still here. His head smash, like someone hit with big rock."

Tyler Wells turned to Bianca. "I wish she had let me look at the body before he was buried," he said.

"I sprinkle herbs. I say words to help spirit leave for great journey," Joanna said quietly. "My people believe nobody must look on body after journey begins. I Christian woman, but I not go against ways of my people."

"I understand what you're saying." Tyler Wells appeared to be mulling things over. "But I'm not convinced. Maybe it wasn't a renegade. Maybe it was an Indian with some kind of personal grudge against your husband."

Joanna blanched. "But I am sure . . ." Her voice faltered and she cast a significant glance at Aiden. Then she folded her hands in her lap, pursed her lips, and lapsed into silence.

Inwardly Bianca cursed her own insensitivity. Of course Joanna didn't want to go into the bloody details of Daniel's terrible death in front of Aiden. He was such a stalwart little person that it was easy to forget he was still a very young child who had just lost his father.

Glancing out the window, Bianca improvised. "Aiden, I noticed when we came up the path that your vegetable patch looks a bit droopy," she said. "We haven't had rain the last few days, and you've had a lot on your mind. Maybe this would be a good time to see to the garden."

Joanna's eyes met Bianca's in silent understanding. "Yes, Aiden. I too saw dry earth. Get pail. Make two, three trips to well. Water beets and carrots."

Aiden nodded obediently and went outside.

As the door closed behind Aiden, Tyler Wells turned to Joanna, "That's a pretty bright youngster, Mrs. Nolan. Now, I'd like to know—"

"Is about scalping. Is not right," Joanna said.

Bianca tried to clarify, but without Aiden to translate, the communication was awkward. Joanna seemed to be saying she'd seen bodies where scalps had been taken. She was a young girl, and Apaches attacked their tribe. But what was done to Daniel was somehow different. Her English wasn't adequate to explain in detail why she knew this was so, but she was totally convinced no Indian had killed her husband.

Tyler Wells remained skeptical. "Let's say I accept what you're telling me, Mrs. Nolan. I'm not saying I do accept it, you understand, but for the sake of argument, let's assume someone other than an Indian killed Daniel Nolan. I've talked to Ed and Agnes Fowler, and they've neither seen nor heard of any strangers in the area. And Mrs. Donovan and the people at the ranch haven't seen anyone out of the ordinary either. Oakfield's a small place. Strangers get noticed."

Bianca had to admit there was logic in what the sheriff was saying. Agnes Fowler certainly kept close tabs on everybody and everything. But if Joanna was right and Daniel's murder hadn't been at the hands of an Indian, and there hadn't been any strangers around, the alternative was even more horrifying. Could someone who wasn't a stranger, someone everyone in Oakfield knew, have killed Daniel Nolan?

CHAPTER 15

After the sheriff rode away, Joanna stood for a moment at the door, watching as Aiden accompanied the teacher to the gate. Then she sat in front of the oaken box, fingering the papers it held and trying to remember what Miss Stratton had told her about each one.

She wondered if it had been a mistake to show Daniel's private papers to Miss Stratton and then to the sheriff. Confiding in strangers gave them power over you, which could be a very bad thing. She'd been careful not to speak of her troubles with Daniel. The sheriff didn't need to know how violent he became when he was full of drink. At least he had never harmed Aiden, although the night before he was killed he'd raised an angry fist when Aiden tried to protect her. She and Aiden were probably better off without Daniel if what the sheriff had said about the will and marriage paper was really so.

And nobody, not even Aiden, knew about the gold in the brown leather pouch. Joanna wasn't supposed to know, either. Daniel kept it hidden in his secret place, but she'd spied on him as he lifted the loose board in the corner of the bedroom floor.

When she first heard of Daniel's death she'd feared he might have taken the pouch with him as he did sometimes, but it was still there. Maybe someone had seen it when Daniel was out drinking. If the killer had been after Daniel's gold and didn't find it, would he come looking for it now?

She hoped the sheriff was right and that she and Aiden wouldn't have to go to the reservation, but she was filled with fear and uncertainty about the future. She might be able to hire someone to work the forge, but she didn't really understand how to go about it. Besides, that would mean letting another stranger into her life.

Neither the missionaries nor Daniel had taught her how to survive alone in the white man's world. Most of the people in Oakfield either treated her badly or looked through her as if she didn't exist. She believed Miss Stratton was kind, but she, too, was an outsider who might only stay a short time and then move on. If Joanna sold the house and land and went back to the reservation, could she use the money to make a better life for her people, or would she end up losing everything?

She knew it was only a matter of days until Running Fox would learn of Daniel's death if he hadn't heard the news already. That was another thing she hadn't told Miss Stratton or the sheriff—about her brother and his hatred for Daniel. Her brother suspected her bruises were not, as she claimed, the result of her own clumsiness.

For a moment she wondered where Running Fox had been when Daniel was killed, but she quickly banished the thought from her mind. Her brother had a violent temper, and if he'd encountered Daniel in the woods he might have fought with him. But never would he have hit him from behind with something heavy and deadly. Never would he have cut on his scalp. Never.

Even the sheriff acted as if he now believed someone other than an Indian might have killed Daniel. But would he think so if he knew about Running Fox?

Tyler Wells left the Nolan house feeling disturbed. It was a relief to discover that ousting the Nolans from their home was something he didn't have to face. But the woman's insistence that an Indian could not have murdered her husband was unsettling.

The blacksmith was a periodic drinker who became mean and quarrelsome when he was under the influence. The Indian woman hadn't said so, but everybody he'd talked to at Fowler's store and out at the ranch seemed to know about his drinking. As far as Tyler could tell, that was pretty much all anybody did know about Daniel Nolan.

Tyler had noticed the bruises on the widow's face the first time he'd come to talk to her. Maybe Daniel Nolan had hurt her one time too many, or maybe he'd gone after the boy. The squaw could have followed her husband into the woods, sneaked up behind him and bashed his head in.

But that didn't explain the scalping. The scalping—now that was a real puzzle. Had Nolan been killed by an Indian who wanted everybody to know it? Or a squaw who was skilled at misdirecting the facts? Or, had somebody who wanted Nolan dead tried to make it look like a renegade Indian was responsible?

It wasn't a bad scheme, when he stopped to think about it. Everybody he'd talked to accepted the blacksmith's death as a renegade's act of violence or revenge. Tyler had to admit he'd still be acting on that assumption if the schoolteacher hadn't persuaded the boy and his mother to talk to him.

The young schoolmarm was another puzzle. How did an educated woman like Miss Stratton get mixed up with a squaw and her half-breed? Hobnobbing with an Indian woman wasn't likely to win the teacher many friends. Not that she seemed to care about making friends. She'd been more than a little sharp-tongued with him, that was for sure.

She was a nice-looking woman, though she didn't seem to pay much heed to appearances. He'd noted her drab clothes and hair flying off in every direction. No wonder she hadn't married. Women were scarce in these parts, but brainy, sharp-tongued women were another matter. A man didn't want to marry a woman who knew more—or thought she did—than her husband. And Bianca Stratton was tall, with a way of looking you straight in the eyes. No fluttering eyelashes for her.

She was a puzzle, but of course he was partial to puzzles. Solving puzzles was one of the reasons he'd agreed to run for sheriff instead of assisting in his Uncle Clayton's law practice. As sheriff most of Tyler's duties were pretty routine—drunken brawls at the saloon, missing cattle and horses, squabbles over property lines.

Death, even violent death, was no stranger to these parts, but this particular murder was a different matter. Which led him back to the same question—why would anybody kill a drunken blacksmith who probably had little of value with him?

Tyler was hungry. His horse needed to be fed and watered. He'd stop by Fowler's store, ask a few more questions, spend another night at the Donovan ranch, and head back to the county seat in the morning.

CHAPTER 16

Walking home in the fading afternoon light, Bianca was hardly aware of her surroundings. She moved quickly, as if adopting a purposeful stride could force her mind to sort out the conflicting thoughts and feelings swirling inside her head. It had been a long, confusing day, and she'd left the schoolhouse without making any preparations for tomorrow's lessons.

At least Joanna and Aiden's immediate problems were no longer a matter of concern. Daniel Nolan couldn't have been such a bad sort if he had cared enough about Joanna to be sure they were legally married. He'd even provided for her in his will.

Her relief that Aiden and Joanna's future seemed no longer in imminent danger gave way to the realization that her own reputation was probably on shaky ground indeed. Leaving the cemetery with Aiden and having the whole community watch her head toward the Nolan's house had been foolish. It was one thing to intercede on behalf of a child's schooling, but by openly befriending Joanna she'd probably crossed the line in the eyes of most of the settlers around Oakfield.

The young sheriff seemed sincere, but he was more likely than not at this very minute in the back room of Fowler's store regaling the other menfolk with a story about the nosy schoolteacher and the squaw. The sheriff had been right, though, to suggest Joanna obtain legal advice.

Perhaps she'd been unfair in her first assessment of the sheriff. He did seem to listen to Joanna. Maybe he was at Fowler's store asking questions and conducting an honest-to-goodness investigation. She should have tried to find out more about his plans. On second thought, that would have probably only given him further evidence she was simply a busybody.

Well, a pox on all of them, she thought, paraphrasing one of her father's favorite lines from Shakespeare. She'd done what she needed to do, and that was the end of it. She had a contract for three months. If they wanted to get rid of her, they'd have to pay her anyway. She'd go back to Wesleyville and apply for another school. Of course, the lack of a recommendation from her first and only teaching position would be a terrible drawback, but teachers were in short supply. She'd manage somehow.

A chill gust of wind sent a shower of brown leaves around her ankles, and she pulled Viola's shawl more snugly around her shoulders. It was nearly dark, and she shivered, realizing she should have started back sooner.

She was almost home when the crack of a gunshot shattered the evening calm. A shell whizzed over her head, splitting the bark of the pine tree on her left. Bianca froze. Then she turned and stared at the empty road behind her. There was no other sound. Even the wind was momentarily still.

Fighting her terror, she gathered her skirts and ran toward the minister's house. As the dark shape of the house came into view another shadow appeared ahead of her. She stopped short, gasping for breath.

"Where in the world have you been?"

At the sound of Cushing Pangston's voice, Bianca's heartbeat slowed to something approximating its normal rhythm. Then she realized he was blocking the road, shotgun in hand. For a horrifying moment she wondered if he'd been responsible for the shot she heard.

"Thank the Lord you're all right! Supper's waiting, and we were all worried. Mattie sent me to look for you."

"I'm afraid I lost track of the time, and then—the shot—did you hear the shot?" She tried to keep her voice from quavering as she drew near enough to see the minister's scowling face.

"Of course I heard it. Twilight's the best time for rabbit hunting, but those fool boys oughtn't to be allowed to run wild. Comes from having no man of the house. Nora Donovan should keep closer track of them. And you've no business gallivanting around the countryside at this hour, even if the Sheriff has locked up that renegade."

He hurried her back toward the house, lecturing her about being out alone at dusk, and she couldn't help noticing that once again he was speaking without a stammer.

Bianca wondered if Oren and Hank had really been hunting rabbits so far from the ranch. Surely they knew better than to fire close to the road. She looked down at her trembling hands. Cushing was right about her needing to be more careful.

"I'm sorry you were worried."

"You should have more sense than to be keeping company with a squaw and then running around alone after dark. We've got enough trouble around here without having hunting accidents, too."

He looked down at his shotgun, and the scowl turned to a frown of consternation. "Oh, no. You . . . you didn't think . . . of course, I didn't fire the . . . it was a rifle shot . . . "

His words, which had been without hesitation when he was angry, now seemed to dissolve into incoherence. She followed him into the house and took her place at the table where Mattie and the girls were waiting.

"I think funerals are awful." Katie' broke the awkward silence that always seemed to follow the saying of Grace. "But I guess it would be worse to plunk somebody in the ground without at least a few words—even somebody like Daniel Nolan nobody even knew or cared about."

"I'm sure Mrs. Nolan and Aiden cared a great deal." Bianca shot Katie a look of disapproval and unfolded her napkin.

"Well, I'm praying for poor Mr. Nolan's soul," Gertrude announced.

"He didn't go to church, but of course I shall pray for him too," Cora said.

"You better ask the Lord to forgive him for drinking whiskey, then." Katie rolled her eyes and helped herself to a biscuit.

"Why would you say such a thing?" Mattie's shocked expression seemed a bit forced. "No spirits are sold in these parts."

Katie was not to be put off so easily. "Lloyd Fowler says Daniel Nolan bought whiskey all the time, and when the store was out of real whiskey, he bought something called moonshine Frenchy makes up in the hills."

"Rot gut is what Junior calls it," Gertrude added. "I think that's disgusting."

"Rot-gut, rot-gut. Got-rut, got-rut," Tina chanted, pleased with the sound of some unfamiliar words.

"Drinking whiskey is a sin, isn't it?" Clearly Gertrude enjoyed pointing out moral lapses.

"That will do, girls." Mattie said.

Cushing shifted in his chair, and Bianca got the distinct impression that Katie's pronouncements about Fowler's store were not news to the preacher. Mattie was saying they certainly could not continue to patronize the store if Ed Fowler was selling whiskey, and Cushing pointed out there was really no alternative.

"Well, if whiskey is being sold, I'm sure Agnes has no idea of it," Mattie insisted. "She's one of the most outspoken members of our ladies' temperance group."

"I don't know about that." Katie seemed to relish conflict. "Lloyd knows. He helps Junior unload the wagon when his pa comes back from Scott's Landing with supplies. And if Junior and Lloyd know, I bet Edna and Edwina do, too. And if Edna and Edwina know, I bet—"

"That will do, Katie." Mattie's tone was firm. "Cora, pass the potatoes to your father."

"Well, Mrs. Fowler does seem to know everything about everybody around here," Cora said. "The twins told me their mother said old Mrs. Donovan used to—"

"That will do!" Cushing scowled. "We do not indulge in gossip in this house."

Bianca was startled at the vehemence in Cushing Pangston's tone as the girls lapsed into stunned silence. She reflected on how foolish it was for parents to keep things from their children in a misguided attempt to shield them. After only a few days, Bianca had learned her young charges missed very little that went on around them and had no qualms about pooling their information.

Although nothing more was said about Daniel Nolan or the back room of Fowler's store, Cushing looked very uncomfortable. He took a piece of bread, mopped the last of the gravy from his plate, and began talking about next Sunday's sermon. Prudence and keeping one's own counsel seemed to be at the top of his list of possible topics.

Later, while the girls were clearing the supper table, Cushing said he'd be glad to have things get back to normal now that Daniel Nolan had been laid to rest and the criminal incarcerated.

"I suppose that poor woman and her child will be going north to the reservation," Mattie added.

Bianca told them about the marriage certificate and Daniel Nolan's will. "The sheriff says Mrs. Nolan should check with a lawyer in Wesleyville, but he doesn't think there will be any problem if she wants to stay here."

Cushing frowned. "Well, I think it would be better for all concerned if the woman went back to . . . to her own kind."

Bianca noticed that Cushing's stammer seemed to return whenever he spoke of anything that might be the least bit controversial.

"And, Miss Stratton, I'm sure you will be relieved to be able to concentrate on your duties now that it is no longer necessary for you to involve yourself in the widow's affairs."

"We'll all be glad to settle back into a routine," she said.

"You may find that maintaining a proper atmosphere of attentiveness will be a problem after all the distractions that have occurred. I understand you don't even have a hickory stick in the schoolroom. Those boys from the Donovan ranch. They're a pair of unruly youngsters who are allowed entirely too much freedom. I'm afraid they're up to no good. Why, they were even whispering and snickering during my eulogy."

Bianca managed to remain silent, inwardly commending herself for her growing self-control.

"And then shooting off a rifle when they know they shouldn't be hunting so close to the road. It's clear that you'll need to—"

"Rifle?" Mattie interrupted. "What's this about shooting off a rifle?"

After relating her frightening experience, Bianca escaped as quickly as she could to her attic room. She was glad the talk had moved away from Joanna and Aiden. She hadn't said anything about Joanna's certainty that Daniel's death had been at the hands of someone other than an Indian. The Pangstons felt the matter was resolved, which was probably just as well. If the sheriff really continued his investigation everyone would know it soon enough. There didn't seem to be any secrets in Oakfield.

Of course, that wasn't really true. Underneath the surface, secrets lurked everywhere. And if someone from Oakfield had killed the blacksmith, there was one terrible secret someone would do anything to keep. She wondered if the shot she heard could have been from Cushing's gun. He said it was a rifle shot, but that was only his word. One gunshot was like another to her ears.

Had Mattie really sent him to find her or was he quietly tracking her as she made her way home? No, that was ridiculous. What reason would Cushing Pangston have to hurt her—or even to frighten her?

She dismissed that notion and vowed to keep rein on her imagination. Cushing had been right to reprimand her for being on the road alone as darkness fell. Of course there had been a hunter in the woods. Still, she would talk to Oren and Hank tomorrow. She was sure she'd be able to find out whether or not they were responsible.

Rolf's past admonitions seemed to ring in her ears. "What do you know about any of these people?" Everyone came here for a reason. And the reasons? For many it had been the dream of a golden land of opportunity. And for some, no doubt, it had been to escape from an unsavory past.

Recalling Cushing's comment about not having a hickory stick, she bristled. As far as she knew, Cushing Pangston had never set foot inside the school since she came. Possibly he had had been quizzing Mattie or the girls. More likely, she'd been the topic of discussion at Fowler's store. If so, they'd undoubtedly talked about more than her lack of a hickory stick. Championing Aiden's right to an education had been an unpopular and headstrong act, but she didn't regret it. Befriending Joanna would subject her to even more criticism.

As she drifted into sleep she reflected that most of the people in Oakfield would be happier if she went away. Well, she wouldn't give them that satisfaction. Besides, where would she go? Certainly not back to Rolf's house.

CHAPTER 17

Tyler Wells helped himself to a seat, propped his boots on an empty keg and surveyed the gathering in Fowler's back room. The ranch hands who'd lowered the coffin into the ground were there, along with Jesse Landry. Ed Fowler was dispensing booze and opinions, though only the opinions came free of charge.

"If you ask me, we'd better get rid of that nosy schoolmarm before she stirs up any more trouble." Ed gave the makeshift counter a halfhearted swipe with a damp rag. "Did you see how she stuck to the squaw and her little half-breed after the burying?"

Heads turned as a newcomer made his way through the swinging door.

"Evening, Frenchy." Ed poured a drink and pushed it across the counter. "Missed you at the graveyard this afternoon. Thought you and Nolan was friends."

Eyes, dark and shiny as creek pebbles, appraised the group. "Damn molar kept me up all night. Got so bad I rode over to Wesleyville and had the barber yank it out." He downed the drink in one gulp and sank into a cane-backed rocker near the stove.

Tyler regarded the man with interest. Brown curly hair streaked with gray brushed the shoulders of a beaver collar. His luxurious waxed moustache was much too dark. Probably he colored it with lamp black.

Tyler extended his hand. "Tyler Wells. I'm the new sheriff."

"Etienne Blauchet, but folks call me Frenchy. Heard you were looking into Daniel's death. Sorry to miss the funeral. A stubby index finger brushed his swollen jaw. "Still hurts like hell. Pour me another drink, Ed. The good stuff."

"You didn't miss much," Jesse Landry said. "The best thing about Pangston's funeral talks is they're shorter than his Sunday sermons."

"Well, this one was even shorter than usual," Charlie Mollers, a bandy-legged ranch hand, spoke up. "From the sound of it, the preacher never even met the feller he was burying."

"Hell, nobody knew him." Ed refilled Frenchy's glass. "I don't even know how he come to settle in Oakfield. He shoulda knowed we don't want no squaw-man here."

Frenchy swirled the glass and stared into the liquor like he was reading tea leaves. "I fished with Daniel some, him and his boy. Kept to himself, Daniel did. Can't think why anybody'd kill him."

"Crazy Injuns don't need no excuse where massacring a white man's concerned." Jesse pulled the makings out of his pocket and rolled a smoke.

"When soldiers kill Indians it's a raid, but when they fight back, it's a massacre. Why is that?" Tyler noted a trace of an accent in Frenchy's speech.

Ed scowled across the bar. "Now don't tell me we got us another Injun lover, Frenchy."

"I trapped and traded with quite a few redskins up north." Frenchy sipped his drink, rolling the whiskey around in his mouth before swallowing it. "I've met good Indians and bad ones, like I've known good and bad white folks. Same goes for the yellow and black, I guess."

"Too bad my brother and his family never heard about good redskins before them murdering devils burned down their cabin," Ed said.

Tyler ordered a round and waited. He'd learned he could usually find out more by listening than conducting anything folks might consider a formal investigation.

After a while Frenchy broke the silence. "What did you mean by *another* Injun lover, Ed?"

"Before you turned up we was talking about the funeral and how that new teacher woman cozied up to the squaw." Ed seemed relieved to switch the direction the talk was taking.

"She even headed down the road with the half-breed hanging onto her skirt." Charlie Mollers added. "My nephew, Hank, he says she's making a real pet of that little brat."

"The boy—his name's Aiden." Frenchy massaged his jaw gingerly.

"Well, the Stratton woman oughta stick to her ABC's since that's what we're paying her for." Ed put on his friendly host face and raised his glass to thank Tyler for the drink.

"Cap and I saw her when she came into the store last Saturday," Frenchy said. "Not a bad-looking woman."

"Too bad she's such a troublemaker," Charlie said, "what with women in such short supply in these parts."

"Awfully tall, though." Frenchy observed.

"Nothing wrong with a tall gal—especially a handsome one." Jesse Landry said. "Of course, it'd take a big man to handle a woman that size."

"If you're applying for the job, you'd better move fast." Ed said. "You mark my words, we'll be getting rid of that school-teacher any day now."

From there the talk veered off to politics and whether or not Grant drank as much whiskey after he'd got himself elected President as he did when he was a general.

After another round Tyler decided it was time to head for the bunkhouse at the Donovan ranch. On his way out he nearly ran headlong into Cap Mackay, who staggered through the door, rifle in hand. For a moment Tyler considered going back inside, but Cap's wobbly gait and rheumy eyes convinced him the old man was in no condition to shed much light on anything.

As he rode toward the ranch, Tyler reflected that his visit to Fowler's back room hadn't netted anything much in the way of new information, although it sounded like Landry had taken a shine to the new schoolmarm. A person didn't have to look far for Indian haters in this part of the country with the Modoc war still fresh in people's minds. Still, he'd been surprised by Ed Fowler's bitterness.

The old trapper, Frenchy Blauchet, was an interesting cuss. Tyler knew many of the early fur traders had taken native wives. Maybe Frenchy's experiences in the north had given him a point of view different from that of the settlers who came later. He'd mentioned fishing with Nolan and the boy. Despite his accent, Blauchet didn't murder the King's English the way Cap did. Tyler decided he'd better pay a visit to Frenchy. Maybe when he wasn't nursing an aching jaw he'd be able provide a clearer picture of what had made Daniel Nolan tick.

CHAPTER 18

The ride from Donovan's ranch back to Tyler's office at the county seat was an easy one this time of year when the air was crisp and the road was firm. Friday morning as his bay gelding settled into a loping gait, Tyler reflected that both he and the horse would be glad to return to familiar surroundings. The bunkhouse at Donovan's ranch was reasonably comfortable, but his own cot in the modest frame house he shared with his uncle was a whole lot better.

Both bunkhouse and cot were a far cry from the comfort of the featherbedded four-poster of his childhood in Savannah, but those days were long gone. His two older brothers had died in the war, one at Antietam and one at Gettysburg. His older sister, Jennilee, had married a New Orleans merchant whose wealth was derived from smuggling and other nefarious operations. His father, devastated by the loss of his sons and the ruin of his plantation, died of a heart attack shortly after Lee's surrender at Appomattox.

Tyler and his mother went to Atlanta to live with her brother, Tyler's uncle Clayton, who took them in despite the meager living his struggling law practice afforded in the turbulent times the Yankees called Reconstruction. Before long Tyler's mother moved to New Orleans to be with Jennilee. Tyler remained with his uncle Clayton in Atlanta and attended college while serving as a part-time deputy sheriff.

Prospects for the future were bleak all over the South, while the great West beckoned as a land of optimism and unlimited opportunity. A paddle wheeler up Mississippi and the newly completed railroad connection to San Francisco made Tyler and Clayton's trip west an easy one. However, San Francisco was more than adequately supplied with legal expertise. After an unproductive visit to the California gold fields, they took a packet ship north to Oregon.

Clayton hung out his shingle in Wesleyville with modest success. Most of the Oregon settlers were vehement abolitionists, so Tyler followed his uncle's lead and stifled any expression of pro-Confederate sentiments. Tyler's inner feelings about the South were an ambiguous mix of sorrow, anger and resignation, but he was determined not to dwell on the past. Even his southern drawl began to disappear.

When Wesley County suddenly found itself needing a sheriff, Tyler was appointed on an interim basis and duly elected the following November. It wasn't the career he envisioned, but he discovered that he actually enjoyed the job. No two days were the same, and as long as he didn't alienate too many people he had the luxury of carrying out his duties pretty much as he saw fit.

Right now those duties included resolving the fate of Joe Red Deer and winding up the investigation of Daniel Nolan's murder. He'd come to Oakfield fairly certain the two incidents were related. He could make short work of the whole business by simply charging the redskin. An Indian's protestations of innocence wouldn't carry any weight. Hell, he'd lie if he were in that poor devil's moccasins. Still, there was more than a trace of nagging doubt, and Tyler had a feeling there was something he'd missed.

This morning at the ranch he'd talked with Mrs. Donovan. She asked a lot of questions about Nolan's widow and child and seemed genuinely concerned about their welfare. He also spoke again to Oren Donovan and Hank Mollers. He was particularly interested in having them describe the wound to the blacksmith's scalp. They complied eagerly, but since Tyler had no experience with scalping, the information wasn't especially useful.

The Nolan widow's unwillingness to attribute the scalping to an Indian bothered him more than a little. Everyone agreed that lying was second nature to Indians, but Joanna Nolan had no reason to lie—unless, of course, she was protecting herself or someone else. Still, the Indian woman had seemed forthright and sincere once the schoolteacher arrived and persuaded her to talk to him.

His thoughts returned to the young schoolmarm, and he found himself wondering why everyone seemed so anxious to be rid of her. True, she'd been outspoken to the point of rudeness when they'd first met. And he guessed she wouldn't win any friends in this part of the country by taking up with a squaw.

Still, he couldn't help being touched by the teacher's concern for the little half-breed boy. He wondered if she was as caring and protective of all her pupils. But the men at Fowler's had been right about one thing—Bianca Stratton was a fine-looking woman.

Taking orders from a woman was something Jesse Landry had never quite gotten used to, but Nora Donovan was a fair employer who rarely interfered in his supervision of the hands. Even though he wasn't looking forward to dropping in on Joanna Nolan, he figured he might as well get the business of making an offer for the smith's equipment over with.

Since it was on the way, he left early enough on Friday to drop Hank and Oren off at the schoolhouse and spend a few minutes with Bianca before she started class. He ran his hand over his chin, glad he'd taken the time to shave close and trim his moustache.

The schoolyard was empty except for the Larson children chasing each other around the oak tree and hollering something that sounded like "Muley Bright." Jesse tossed the reins to Oren and jumped down from the wagon.

"You and Hank tie up the rig," he said. "Gather all your belongings, too."

The schoolhouse door swung open, and the little half-breed, empty bucket in hand, scampered toward the well. Bianca stood in the doorway, smiling.

"Good morning, Mr. Landry. I hope you're not neglecting your duties at the ranch just to bring Hank and Oren to school."

"Matter of fact, ranch duties brought me out this way. I'm heading over to see Widow Nolan." He waited to see if she would mention her visit to the Nolan's, but she stood there looking cool and unruffled. Even her hair was fastened neatly into a bun on the back of her neck with only a few stubborn strands curling around her ears.

"I'll be coming back this way later this afternoon," he said. "Maybe you'd like to ride out to the ranch. Mrs. Donovan said she'd like to meet you. She was going to speak to you yesterday at the funeral, but you left before she had a chance to say anything."

Nora hadn't said anything of the kind, and the ranch wagon left the cemetery before Bianca. What was it about this woman that got him all flustered? Women, even uncommonly fine-looking ones, didn't usually affect him this way.

"I'm afraid I promised the twins I'd give them some extra help with their reading after class." She tilted her head to one side, met his glance, and quickly looked away.

"Well, we'll have to make it another day. Speaking of extra help, maybe you can give me a hand, too."

"Oh, I think you're a little old for a reading lesson, Mr. Landry."

Jesse grinned. "You're right, Ma'am. It's help with the Nolan woman I'm after. Mrs. Donovan sent me to make her an offer on Daniel's forge and tools—a very generous offer."

"I don't see how I can be of any assistance there. I have no idea what her plans are now that she knows she and Aiden have legal right to the property."

"Legal right?"

Bianca nodded. "Daniel Nolan left a will. Mrs. Nolan has a marriage certificate and a deed to the property, too. That's why I went home with Aiden yesterday after the funeral. She doesn't read English, and she wanted me to go through Daniel's papers."

Jesse removed his Stetson and twirled it thoughtfully. "Well, I don't see how that will have any effect on Mrs. Donovan buying the blacksmith's equipment. Some extra cash might help her make ends meet for a while."

"There's certainly no harm in making the offer," Bianca agreed.

"Well, now, here's my problem. I understand the woman's wary of strangers, and I don't know whether she'll understand what I'm doing there. Does she talk any English at all?"

"She's self-conscious about speaking, but she understands English quite well. I'm sure you'll have no trouble. Or, you could go when Aiden is home. He speaks his mother's language, and his English is very good."

Jesse noticed the schoolyard filling up. The Fowlers had arrived along with the Pangston brood. Bianca would be disappearing into the schoolroom with her charges in a matter of minutes, and it might be days before he'd have a good excuse for stopping by the schoolhouse again.

"Maybe you could help the twins tomorrow." He climbed the steps to stand beside her. I sure hate to disappoint Mrs. Donovan." He looked down at her and smiled so she'd know exactly who'd be disappointed if she said no.

"I'm really sorry." She turned, clapped her hands, and the children headed for the door.

The Fowler twins, trailed closely by Oren and Hank, reached the steps before any of the younger children.

"Good morning, Mr. Landry," Edna and Edwina chorused.

"We're so excited about the fall fiesta." Edna looked up at Jesse and fluttered her eyelashes.

"We've been waiting to dance with you again. It seems like so long since the Fourth of July picnic," Edwina added.

Jesse suppressed a smile. The twins were even identical in the way they flirted.

"Aunt Nora's got everything planned," said Oren, "and we're—".

"Well," Gertrude interrupted, "I'll bet your aunt Nora will be having a talk with you after she hears you nearly shot Miss Stratton last night when you were out hunting rabbits."

"No such thing," Oren protested. "We never left the ranch last night, did we Hank?"

"That's right. We were—we were right there—uh—doing chores right up to suppertime."

"What's this about somebody shooting at you?" Jesse's voice lost its bantering tone as he turned again to Bianca.

"I'm sure nobody was shooting at me. I was on my way home, and I heard a shot. That's all there was to it." Bianca motioned at the young ones still running around the oak tree. "Come inside right now, children," she called.

"Wandering around those woods alone is a damnfool thing—pardon me, ma'am—a foolish thing to do." Jesse's eyebrows furrowed.

"I wasn't wandering around the woods. I was on the road almost home, and Reverend Pangston was right there."

"Well, ma'am, I'm afraid the preacher wouldn't provide much protection against a renegade Indian. But I'd be proud to offer my services whenever you need them."

"That's very kind of you, Mr. Landry."

Jesse was pleased to see the color rise on Bianca's cheeks as she herded the last of her charges inside and closed the door behind her. He wondered who had fired the shot. Hank and Oren said they never left the ranch last night, but Jesse couldn't be sure where they were from the time they got back from the funeral until they turned up for supper. They weren't supposed to leave ranch property without permission, but neither of the boys was known for obeying orders or having much common sense.

Then he recalled how Cap had come into Fowler's late, reeling with drink. He'd been carrying his rifle. Drunk or sober, Cap was a crack shot. Cap rarely went anywhere without "Sweet Betsy," but he wouldn't fire near a roadway unless he did it on purpose, to scare Bianca.

The more Jesse thought about it, the more it sounded like the kind of damnfool thing the old man would do. But why would he want to frighten her? Not that Cap Mackay needed a reason for acting crazy when he'd had a few drinks, and he'd had more than a few last night. Jesse shook his head and turned the wagon toward the Nolan's place.

Bianca decided to postpone the day's routine. Until everyone had an opportunity to talk about the shot fired in the woods she'd never be able to settle them down to grammar or geography.

"I think we'll take a few minutes this morning to talk," she announced. "I'll give everyone a chance to say something, and then we'll get to our regular schoolwork. Who'd like to begin?"

Several hands shot up at once. Bianca called on Junior Fowler first.

"I think we better find out who's trying to hurt you, Miss Stratton. I don't want anything bad to happen to you, and—well, that's all I have to say." Junior's chubby cheeks were red with embarrassment.

"Thank you, Junior." Bianca noted Oren's hand waving furiously. "Yes, Oren?"

"Honest, Miss Stratton. Cross my heart and hope to die. Honest! Me and Hank never went out shooting yesterday. And Aunt Nora would have my hide if I ever shot where any folks were around."

"My uncle would lock up my rifle if he ever figured I wasn't fit to be trusted with it," Hank said. "I had to pitch hay for two summers to earn the money to buy it in the first place, and I've always been right careful I can tell you."

"Well," Lenny Fowler said, "if Hank and Oren weren't out shooting, somebody else was on the road. Did you see anybody, Aiden?"

Aiden shook his head. "I never looked outside after Miss Stratton left."

"Larson people all in house," Bjorn announced. Elke nodded in agreement.

"Thank you, Bjorn. Your English is improving every day!" Bianca smiled in encouragement, wondering if she would ever hear Elke's voice. She had seen the little girl whispering with Aiden and Lenny, but so far Elke had never spoken aloud.

"Well, I don't know where anybody was," Edna said, "and I'd rather talk about the fiesta than some shot in the woods where nobody got hurt."

"Me, too," agreed Edwina. "I need to get started making a new dress. I think wine red would be good. Papa got some real pretty taffeta the last time he was in Oregon City."

"I don't want to talk about no dance," Junior said emphatically.

"And I don't want to talk about sewing, neither," said Lenny. "Next you'll want us to look at pictures in the giddy lady's book."

"It's Godey's Lady's Book," said Gertrude. "Everyone knows that. And I'd like to talk about the funeral. After all, it isn't every day that we have a funeral."

Katie glared at her younger sister. "Aiden," she said, "we're all sorry about what happened to your pa."

"I think we've had enough conversation for this morning." Bianca moved to the front of the classroom. "Take out your copybooks and begin your penmanship practice."

CHAPTER 19

Joanna Nolan had always found pleasure in preparing and cooking food. As a child she'd picked the wild blueberries and huckleberries that grew in abundance in the woods. In the swales she'd gathered roots of blue camas lilies as her people had always done. The missionary's wife had taught her to bake the sourdough biscuits, cakes and fruit pies white men favored, a skill that had pleased Daniel greatly. But now as she chopped carrots and cabbage fresh from her kitchen garden, she found little enjoyment in these tasks that usually brought her comfort.

She had not accepted the offer the tall, fine-looking Mr. Landry had made yesterday for Daniel's forge and tools, although she believed it was probably a fair offer. Mr. Landry had smiled and spoken in a friendly manner, but she could tell he was not pleased to return to Mrs. Donovan without an answer. She sensed that Mr. Landry thought she didn't understand what he was saying.

Sometimes it was useful to let white people think their language was too confusing for her. Actually, he had been quite clear, but she wasn't ready to make any decisions until she was sure the house and land were truly hers to keep. She hoped she and Aiden could stay here if they chose to.

She added fresh parsley and stirred the stew simmering in the iron pot which hung in the fireplace. Although there was a wood-burning stove in the kitchen, she preferred slow-cooking her soups and stews in the keeping room.

She had heard white people call it a parlor, but that didn't seem like the right description of the cozy room where she and Aiden spent most of their time. The parlor in the missionaries' house had been a cold, formal place which required a great deal of dusting and polishing of dark furniture.

Joanna thought it was foolish to have a room that nobody used. Probably keeping unused blacksmith tools was just as foolish, but until she talked to someone she trusted, she was reluctant to part with anything of value.

Mentally recounting the meager assets she and Daniel had accumulated in their years together, she went to the bedroom, lifted the loose floorboard, and reached for the leather pouch. She'd never touched it before, and its weight surprised her. Daniel considered it of great value, but she knew nothing of its real worth. She sensed without opening the drawstring that it contained gold.

She was sorry Daniel had felt he needed to keep secrets from her, but she would have no secrets from her son. There were many things about which she needed advice, and there was nobody she could really trust except Aiden. He had a right to know about the leather pouch. They would talk about it this evening. She carried the pouch back into the keeping room and placed it carefully on top of the important papers in the wooden box.

She knew it was likely Running Fox had heard the news of Daniel's death by now. Although she and her brother were at odds on many things, she had implicit trust in his devotion to her and to Aiden. It would be good to talk things over with him. Still, she hoped he would not risk coming to Oakfield. If he were caught, he would probably be taken to the reservation and hung as a trouble-making renegade. That is, if his terrible temper didn't provoke his captors into killing him outright.

The slam of the back door jarred her back to the present, and Aiden hurried in carrying a basket of fresh eggs.

"Three large brown ones today," he said, speaking in their native tongue, "and five white ones. The hens are doing a good job."

"Did you remember to feed the chickens as well as gather the eggs?"

"Of course, Mama. I'm very responsible. That's what Miss Stratton says—that I'm very responsible."

"She's right. You're a good boy, Aiden. I could never manage without you."

Aiden trotted back to the kitchen only to return minutes later. "I put the eggs away," he said. "Now, when are we going to go to Wesleyville to talk to the lawyer man?"

Joanna sighed. "It's not that simple, Aiden. Wesleyville is too far to walk."

"I can ask Lenny to find out from his ma if somebody's going. I bet we could get a ride easy."

"We do not impose ourselves or ask for favors, Aiden."

"If you took the money from Mrs. Donovan, we could buy ourselves a horse and wagon. Then we could go anyplace we wanted without asking for help from anybody, and I could ride the horse every day. I'd take care of him, too, and feed him and brush him and—"

"I know, Aiden." Joanna smiled. Daniel had promised Aiden a horse as soon as the blacksmith shop was showing a profit. Even without selling the forge, there was probably enough gold in the pouch to buy a horse and cart, but she was resolved not to use the gold unless a dire emergency faced them. Aiden was too young to understand the feelings of insecurity that haunted her.

"I bet Miss Stratton would go to Wesleyville with us if we asked her," Aiden said. "I bet the preacher would let her use his wagon, too."

"Miss Stratton has done too much for us already, Aiden, and I'll hear no more talk of horses today. We will wait until we hear from the sheriff."

"But when is he coming back? Did he say he was coming back?"

"You must learn patience, Aiden. We have a roof over our heads and we have plenty of food. You are going to school and learning what you need to know to live in the white people's world. Everything else will happen in its own time."

Aiden walked to the cot in the corner of the room, reached underneath the bed frame, pulled out his school bag and opened a book. Joanna watched him, feeling both proud and anxious. She prayed the Great Spirit would grant her the wisdom to make the right decisions and keep him safe in the days ahead.

Saturday morning Bianca helped Mattie and the girls with the chores. In the afternoon she did her own laundry. She scrubbed the white linen collars and cuffs that relieved the drabness of her everyday cotton dresses and reflected that it was hard to believe that she'd been in Oakfield only a week.

As she hung her cambric shirtwaist on the line, she saw a cloud of dust down the road. Even before the dust cleared she recognized the surrey and Rolf's one extravagance, a matched pair of chestnut trotters. She was in no mood to deal with Rolf, but there was nothing she could do. She finished hanging up her clothes and, still carrying the willow clothesbasket, walked toward the gate.

Rolf climbed down, unhitched the horses and let them graze on the grass along the fence posts. "Now, don't start scolding me as if I'm one of your pupils," he said. "I know you don't want me turning up all the time to check on you, but the boys and I are all the family you have. With what I heard about renegade Indians murdering settlers around here, I couldn't rest easy until I was sure you were all right."

Bianca couldn't help smiling. Rolf meant well, even if his view of the world was depressingly bleak. "As you can see, I'm perfectly fine. It's true that the blacksmith was killed, but the sheriff already has someone in custody." There was no need to mention the shot in the woods. "Now, tell me about the boys."

"They miss you terribly, Bianca. Every night Jorgen finishes his prayers by asking God to bless his mama up in heaven and to send his Aunt Banky home soon."

The sound of her nickname brought tears to Bianca's eyes. "I miss them, too," she said.

"Then come home with me. Berta will stay on and look after the boys, so you needn't worry about your reputation. You could probably get a school right in the neighborhood if you are determined to teach. I want you to be safe, and I know that's what Viola would want, too."

"I've made a commitment, Rolf. Please try to understand. I wouldn't break my contract even if I wanted to. I'm only beginning to see how I can help my pupils, and I look forward to each new day."

"It's your safety I'm concerned about."

"I never want to lose touch with you and the boys, Rolf, but you simply mustn't keep worrying about me and fussing over me."

"I know you're right, Bianca," Rolf admitted, but the worried frown that had etched an indelible vertical line between his pale eyebrows remained. "I only wish—"

"Oh, Mr. Knudsen. How nice to see you," Mattie's voice was a welcome interruption, but her hospitable insistence that Rolf come inside and stay for supper was the last thing Bianca needed.

"I'm sure my brother-in-law wants to start back soon in order to get home before dark," Bianca said.

"Actually, I'm delighted to accept your invitation." Rolf slipped past Bianca and greeted Mattie on the front stoop. "You see, I was hoping I could persuade Bianca to come home with me, and I knew packing up her belongings would take some time, so I made arrangements to spend the night. When I stopped at Fowler's place the storekeeper said I'd have no problem bunking at the Donovan ranch."

Bianca followed Mattie and Rolf into the parlor where they were instantly engulfed by the four Pangston girls all talking at once, as usual.

Cora managed to make herself heard above the clamor. "You can't leave us, Miss Stratton. We all need you."

"I have no intention of going anywhere—not for the next few months at least," Bianca said. "Now let's all head for the kitchen and see what we can do to help your mother."

Bianca noted with amusement that Rolf, whose appetite was normally prodigious, only picked at Mattie's stringy chicken and soggy dumplings. Perhaps he'd think twice before accepting Mattie's hospitality in the future.

Throughout the meal Rolf and Cushing talked about Bianca as if she weren't present, and most of the conversation revolved around plans for her future. She kept her silence, but it wasn't easy to listen to Rolf's assurances that she would soon come to her senses and return home where she belonged.

Only the chatter of the four girls, delighted at having company, kept Bianca from feeling the meal was a complete disaster. Rolf was refusing a second helping of curdled cobbler when a pounding on the door sent Gertrude running to see who was there.

"Fire! Over at the blacksmith's place!"

On hearing Lars Larson's alarm, Rolf and Cushing dashed out the door. Bianca watched helplessly as the men hitched up Rolf's surrey and disappeared into the gathering dusk.

CHAPTER 20

Aiden drifted in and out of consciousness, reassured by his mother's voice and the touch of her cool hand on his forehead. He opened his eyes and saw his mother and another woman with shining dark hair, and he wondered how he came to be in this strange, large bed with its soft sheets that smelled of lavender.

Blurred images filled his head. Sitting at the supper table. The smell of rabbit stew. His mother's voice saying, "Smoke. I smell smoke." A crackling sound. Dashing outside to see orange flames eating the shingles off the roof.

Then he remembered the precious wooden box and the important papers they had to take to the lawyer in Wesleyville. He'd pulled free of his mother's hand and raced into the house. The last thing he remembered was smoke—great clouds of smoke stinging his throat.

He wanted to ask his mother if the box was safe, but he couldn't make a sound, and his throat felt raw and burned.

"Don't try to talk, Aiden. You're safe now." He relaxed at the sound of his mother's voice and her words spoken softly in their own language. "You're at Mrs. Donovan's. You have a bad lump on your head and burns on your hands, but you're going to be all right."

"Your mother has been very worried about you," the dark-haired lady said.

Aiden remembered seeing her at the funeral. Mrs. Donovan, Oren's aunt. He wanted to ask how he came to be at her house. Had his own house burned to the ground? It was awful to be so full of questions and not be able to say a word.

Miss Stratton sometimes called him a little chatterbox. He wondered if he'd ever be able to talk again. There was so much he wanted to say. He needed to tell his mother what he'd seen, but he couldn't seem to keep his eyes open a second longer.

The Fowler clan arrived first for Sunday service, and Junior hurried to Bianca's side. "I got to be on the bucket brigade last night right alongside my dad," he announced proudly.

"Did you see Aiden and his mother?" Bianca asked. "Are they all right?"

"Aiden was lyin' there by the gate with his head in his ma's lap when I got there. Then some ranch hands loaded him and his ma into a wagon and took them to Donovan's."

Rolf's surrey pulled up, and Bianca rushed to meet him. "Tell me about Aiden, Rolf. How badly is he hurt? How did it happen? Who's looking after him?"

"Hold on there, Bianca. One thing at a time." Rolf scanned the arriving worshippers. "I think the little fella's going to be all right. Looks like he inhaled a lot of smoke. He hasn't been able to talk, so nobody knows exactly what happened to him. Near as I can figure they were inside, smelled smoke and got out in good time. The roof was on fire. Probably started from some sparks from the chimney. You know how dry things are right now. For some reason, the boy ran back into the house. Anyway, his mother and Nora Donovan are taking good care of him."

"Oh, I hope he's going to be all right. Are you staying for the service?"

"I think I'd better be getting on. I expect the Lord will forgive me if I skip Cushing's sermon." An uncharacteristic grin accompanied Rolf's rare attempt at humor. Then his sober expression returned. "I see you're determined to stay here in spite of everything."

"You're such a worrier, Rolf."

"A murder, somebody shooting at you—oh, yes, I heard about it last night on the bucket brigade-—and now a fire." The frown lines deepened on Rolf's forehead. "Way too many catastrophes around here to suit me."

"But the fire was an accident—some sparks from the chimney, like you said."

"Too many coincidences for a place as small as Oakfield." Rolf shook his head. "I don't like it, Bianca. I don't like it at all."

More people arrived for the service as Rolf drove off. Bianca went inside and sat in the parlor next to the Pangston girls. Mattie was launching into the first chorus of *Jesus, Lover of My Soul* when Jesse Landry, hat in hand, brushed past and took the only remaining seat in the front row beside the Larsons.

Bianca guessed Jesse was about the same age as Rolf, but everything about Rolf seemed old, sour and settled. Jesse sizzled with vitality and humor. Even the lock of dark hair that fell across his forehead seemed to have a will of its own. Bianca knew Rolf's slicked down blond hair wouldn't dare get out of place. She suppressed a smile and tried to concentrate on Cushing's sermon.

After the service Bianca lingered outside. She gave Elke and Bjorn a hug, told the twins how nice they looked in their new bonnets, and moved to join Mattie and Agnes Fowler.

"It was a good thing Lars Larson was out in his east forty and spotted the smoke," Agnes said. "Ed told me the men got there in time to save the house. Of course, they'll have to replace a good part of the roof. There's a lot of smoke and water mess inside, but the kitchen and bedroom are pretty much all right."

"I understand Mr. Larson and some of the hands from the ranch are going over this afternoon to fix the roof and clean things up," Mattie said.

Agnes nodded. "Ed and Junior are going too."

"How kind!" Bianca knew settlers banded together when adversity struck, but she was surprised at Oakfield's apparent change of heart where Joanna Nolan and Aiden were concerned.

As if reading her thoughts, Agnes said, "I think everyone feels poor Mrs. Nolan has had more than her share of trouble, even if she is an ignorant squaw woman. Of course, if she'd been cooking on that perfectly good stove she's got in the kitchen instead of stewing things up Injun style in the fireplace, the fire probably wouldn't have started in the first place."

Mattie nodded. "Savages don't take to civilized ways, do they? Cushing told me they have a heathen custom of burning all the clothing and possessions of the dead. Maybe that's what caused the fire."

With great difficulty, Bianca managed to hold her tongue during this exchange. She hated to find herself agreeing with Rolf about anything, but she was afraid the fire had been caused by something much more sinister than a spark from the chimney.

Jesse Landry drove away from the preacher's house wondering why he'd bothered to come to church in the first place. He wanted to talk to Bianca, but he'd been held up by a broken section of corral and a couple of loose horses. After the service she was surrounded by youngsters and womenfolk. Going over to her might have caused talk, and no way did he want to be part of the Oakfield gossip grapevine.

Jesse hadn't been able to figure out what was going on between Bianca and her brother-in-law. He'd met Knudsen briefly at the ranch last night and looked him over during breakfast this morning. A sober cuss, but clearly concerned about his sister-in-law. Knudsen asked a lot of questions about the blacksmith's death and about the shot in the woods. He seemed to think the fire was part of some kind of pattern—too many coincidences, he'd said.

Jesse wondered if the boy, Aiden, would be able to tell more about the fire when he got his voice back. The blaze at Nolan's house had Cap's handiwork written all over it. Anybody else who wished the widow harm would have done a better job, but Cap was always hatching some crazy scheme and too full of white lightning to follow through without making a mess of it.

Jesse thought he might drop by Fowler's this evening and wait for the booze to loosen Cap's tongue. Meanwhile there were chores at the ranch. Even though Nora Donovan considered Sunday a day of rest, he'd have to put a couple of men on that broken corral right away. As for a visit with Bianca Stratton, he'd have to come up with another excuse to stop by the schoolhouse.

CHAPTER 21

The long drive back to the farm provided Rolf time for some serious reflection. Somehow, he'd kept going during Viola's final days, and at the graveyard he knew he had to be strong for the sake of the boys. Since then he'd run around like a crazy fool, working twelve hours a day and then chasing over to Oakfield on one pretext or another.

His sister, Berta, did a good job taking care of the household chores and looking after the children. But the farmhouse was filled with Viola—her crocheted doilies in the parlor, her appliquéd Tree of Life quilt on the bed, the lavender scent that lingered whenever he opened a bureau drawer or a linen cupboard. He could hardly bear to be there.

His eyes filled with tears, and wrenching sobs welled up in his throat. Alone with the rhythmic clip-clop of the horses' hooves as a somber accompaniment, he cried his loss to the cloudy autumn sky.

After his outburst subsided, he realized he'd been shutting his boys out because they, too, filled him with reminders of the void Viola's death had created. He shook his head in self-reproach. The boys were grieving, too. Berta was kind, but she wasn't their mother. He resolved to let go of his hopeless obsession with Bianca and spend more time with his sons.

It was obvious Bianca didn't care for him except as an older brother. Still, he needn't feel doomed to a life of celibacy. He might be ancient in Bianca's eyes, but thirty-six wasn't really so old. He had a lot of life ahead, and if he hung onto his notions of replacing Viola with Bianca, there was a good chance he would drive her away for good. Did he really want to add the loss of their beloved Aunt Banky to the grief his boys were already feeling?

This morning at the breakfast table, after the hired hands left, he'd visited for a few minutes with Nora Donovan. She'd spoken about the death of her husband. Kirk Donovan had been a semi-invalid after being thrown from his horse and trampled. Nora thought she was prepared for his passing, but still she'd been devastated at the loss. Afterwards, she'd thrown herself into running the ranch. Her open manner, so foreign to Rolf's life-long pattern of constraint, made him uncomfortable, but she took no notice.

"I guess there's no way you can prepare to lose the most important person in your life," she had said. "You have to feel your grief and pray the Lord will give you the strength to go on."

As the Knudsen farmhouse appeared on the horizon, the trotters picked up their pace. Rolf reflected that maybe his brief conversation with Mrs. Donovan had triggered his uncharacteristic flood of feeling. Perhaps there was something to be said for such expressions of emotion. He had to admit he felt more like himself than he had since Viola's last illness.

Still, his newfound objectivity regarding Bianca didn't lessen his concern. There was something strange going on in that isolated little community, and Bianca had landed right in the middle of it. She was, after all, very young. Her sheltered life had given her no experience in dealing with evil, unscrupulous people. Cushing Pangston and his wife seemed like solid, upright folks. Rolf could only hope they would prevent Bianca's headstrong ways from involving her too deeply in whatever was amiss in Oakfield.

Nora Donovan hovered near the stove where an elderly Chinese gentleman presided over a kettle of gently simmering chicken broth. "Now, don't spice up the soup, Chang," she said. "Aiden needs something warm and soothing."

"My chicken soup cured your croup, and your little sister's too." His left hand shooed her away. "So don't you tell me how to cook, Missy. It's bad enough you keep bringing home more mouths for me to feed."

Nora laughed. "You're a fraud, Chang. You'd like nothing better than to stir up grub for the whole state of Oregon if we could fit them around the table."

"What I'd like is for you to clear out of my kitchen. Sunday's supposed to be a day of rest, but there's no rest for poor old Chang."

"Poor old Chang, indeed! Every time I try to pry you out of the kitchen, you pucker up like somebody stuffed a lemon in your mouth." Nora poured a cup of coffee. The enormous kitchen with its stone ovens and tantalizing aromas was her favorite room, even though Chang considered it his private domain.

Joanna Nolan peeked tentatively through a side door, and Nora motioned her into an empty chair.

"Aiden sleeps now." Dark circles ringed Joanna's eyes, and worry lines etched her mouth.

"I'm making my special soup for your little boy," Chang said. "It cures everything. Fever, chills, everything. Here, you try some, too." He ladled steaming broth into a large bowl and placed it in front of Joanna.

"Oh, I can't—"

"You need to keep your strength up," Nora said. "Besides, there's no use arguing with Chang."

Joanna tasted the soup. "Mmm. Onion. Celery." She inhaled the aroma and licked her lips. "Also dill. Very good."

Chang beamed.

Joanna said she needed to be home when the neighbors arrived to repair the fire damage, but she was worried about Aiden. After many assurances that Aiden was in good hands and looking after him wasn't an imposition, Nora persuaded Joanna it was all right for her leave.

"Don't worry, Missy. I'll take soup to the young fellow myself. I'll see he drinks it, too."

Seeing Joanna's puzzled frown, Nora explained. "Chang calls every woman under sixty Missy. That way he doesn't have to remember their names."

"That's not true." Chang ladled more soup into Joanna's bowl despite her protests. "Missy is a term of respect."

Nora laughed. "Don't pay attention to anything Chang says. He was second cook at my father's rancho in California, and he still treats me like a child."

"I'm first cook in this house, and don't you forget it."

"Not much chance of that!" Nora was pleased that the good-natured banter brought the trace of a smile to Joanna's face.

Joanna carried her empty soup bowl to the oak counter and stared at the tiled sink with its indoor pump. "Very fine kitchen. Water right here." She examined the stone ovens with obvious approval and turned to Chang. "You lucky cook."

"Missy has to keep me happy so I won't go cook in some fancy San Francisco restaurant."

Nora rolled her eyes, and was rewarded with a laugh from Joanna.

"I go now," Joanna said.

"Don't worry about Aiden," Nora said. "We'll take good care of him. I'll have one of the hands saddle up a gentle buckskin mare for you to ride."

A short while later Nora looked out the kitchen window and watched Joanna mount the horse and disappear among the oak trees.

"That's a good woman," Chang observed. "She doesn't waste time on foolish talk like some people I know. That farmer who was here last night—he's not much of a talker either."

"Oh, you mean Mr. Knudsen. He was visiting Miss Stratton, the teacher. He pitched right in to help put out the fire."

"That farmer's about the right age for you, Missy."

"Don't talk nonsense, Chang."

"You can't fool old Chang, Missy. That farmer's not as handsome as Mr. Jesse, but you had roses in your cheeks at breakfast this morning."

"Stick to your pots and pans, old man." Nora clattered her empty cup into the sink. "I've got a sick child to take care of."

But as she walked across the veranda Nora couldn't help but reflect on the young teacher and her brother-in-law. A seventeen-year-old would naturally be attracted by Jesse Landry's dash and charm. Bianca was obviously too immature to appreciate the solid, quiet attributes of a man like Rolf Knudsen.

"Hold up, there!" Cap waved his arms and stared at the heavily loaded wagon. "Where in blazes are you off to?"

Ed Fowler scowled and reined the draft horse. The wagon creaked to a halt. "Some people have to work, even on Sunday."

Frenchy sat next to Ed, staring straight ahead.

"Hey, Frenchy, I was just fixin' to go over to your place."

Frenchy's eyes darted from side to side. "You'll have to catch me later," he said.

Ed cleared his throat and fiddled with the reins. "We've gotta get moving."

"Where you headed? I ain't real busy. Mebbe you could use a little extra company." Cap moved closer to the wagon and tried to get a look at what was under the tarp.

"This here's a heavy load, Cap, and there ain't no more room in the wagon." Ed flicked the reins and the wagon inched forward.

Cap moved to Frenchy's side of the wagon. "I was hoping you'd go with me to talk to the squaw woman, seeing as how you was sort of a friend of her husband."

"I knew him some, but I wouldn't say we were friends." Frenchy mumbled.

The wagon moved faster, and Cap had to trot to keep up. "Well, when you gonna get back?"

"Can't rightly say. Anyway, the Nolan woman's out at Donovan's. If you ever went to church, you might be able to keep up with what's going on." Ed's whip cracked over the horse's flank, and the wagon lurched forward.

Dust clouded Cap's eyes and choked his throat. He swore, moved to the side of the road and reached for his flask. After a few swigs his breathing was pretty much back to normal. Which was more than he could say for the way Ed and Frenchy were acting. Ed never went for supplies on a Sunday. If he was on a buying trip, he'd be starting out with an empty wagon, not a full one. What was under the tarp? And what was eating Frenchy?

Cap stroked his beard and tried to figure it out. He knew Frenchy was real smart and had some kind of fancy schooling when he was young, but Cap always thought they were friends. Now Frenchy couldn't be bothered to give him the time of day. Come to think of it, Frenchy wouldn't even look him in the eye. And Ed—talking down to him like he was nobody instead of one of his best customers. Cap had felt right chipper when he headed over to Frenchy's, but now his head was starting to ache and his hands were none too steady.

He trudged back to his cabin and circled around to the shed behind the house. An old gray horse with milky eyes whinnied at his approach, and Cap shook down some fresh hay. The Donovan ranch was too far to walk, and it had been months since he'd put a saddle on poor old Smoky. He'd hoped for Frenchy's help, too, which went to prove you couldn't count on nobody.

He retrieved a worn brush from a pile of harness at one side of the stall and groomed the animal's bony haunches. He and Smoky had soldiered together for nearly twenty years, and the pair of them had been put out to pasture together. Smoky had never let him down. Which was more than he could say for any of his so-called human pals.

CHAPTER 22

Getting her students to concentrate on their lessons was no easy task when school convened on Monday morning. Everyone wanted to talk about the fire. Junior, by virtue of having actually been on the bucket brigade, was regarded as something of a hero. He basked in the unaccustomed glow of attention.

Bjorn Larson had gone with his father Sunday afternoon to help repair the damage to the Nolan house, but his limited English prevented him from keeping anyone's attention for long.

All the youngsters seemed to be genuinely concerned about Aiden, especially Lenny Fowler, who was visibly upset. "My Pa heard some of the men from the ranch talking. Aiden can't talk, Miss Stratton. The smoke burned the inside of his throat, and he can't say nothing."

"I'm sure he'll get his voice back soon." Bianca tried to sound reassuring, although she'd heard damage to the vocal chords could be serious. "He's a strong boy, and Mrs. Donovan and Aiden's mother are taking good care of him."

"Aunt Nora put him up in my room. I had to sleep in the bunkhouse last night." Oren Donovan swaggered with the importance of being the person with the most recent news of the tragedy. "Aiden's mom went back to their place this morning, but

Aiden's going to stay at the ranch until he's better. This morning Aunt Nora sent Jesse to Wesleyville to fetch Doc Schneider."

"I'm sorry you had to give up your room, Oren," Cora said. "I know how you feel 'cause I had to move in with all my sisters when Miss Stratton came."

"It's not bad sleeping in the bunkhouse. Aunt Nora likes to keep her men comfortable."

Oren favored Cora with a broad smile, and Bianca thought Cora was going to swoon on the spot. Edna had been flirting with Oren since the first day of school, but Bianca hadn't realized Cora was also smitten.

"I sleep in the bunkhouse all the time," said Hank. You always know what's going on 'cause ranch hands hear everything. My uncle says it's like the important folks sort of forget the hands are around."

"Sometimes grownups forget kids are around, too. I hear lots of stuff at my Dad's store." Lloyd grinned and crossed his eyes.

Katie giggled.

"You better stop that, Lloyd," Gertrude cautioned. "Your eyes will get stuck"

"That's just one of the things grownups tell you when you're getting their dander up." Katie glared at Gertrude.

"We get lots of visitors at the ranch, too." Hank wasn't about to give up being the focus of attention. "Aunt Nora puts up anybody riding through who needs a place to sleep. The sheriff stayed there last week, and last night there was some farmer, and—"

"He's Miss Stratton's brother-in-law." A scornful glance at Hank accompanied Edna's interruption. "He was here to see Miss Stratton. Then the fire broke out, and—"

"I think we've had enough talk about the fire for now. Open your readers and review last Friday's lesson. Lenny, bring your book and I'll hear you read *The Ant and the Dove* aloud."

As she watched the youngest Fowler child make his way to her desk, Bianca reflected that Agnes Fowler had nothing on a schoolteacher when it came to keeping up on local gossip.

She was certain most of the settlers in Oakfield had no idea of what goldmines of information their children were.

During the day Bianca passed around a fresh copybook and gave each student time to write a message to Aiden. "Spelling doesn't count," she said, "and you don't have to write anything unless you want to."

"Can I do a sketch?" Edwina asked.

"I'm sure Aiden would like that very much," Bianca answered.

"Oh, I'll draw something, too!" Lenny exclaimed.

While lessons were progressing, Bianca watched the copybook move around the classroom. She recalled the initial reaction when she'd announced that Aiden would be joining the class. Although she made it clear nobody was required to send a message, everyone did. She smiled as she watched Elke Larson draw a stick figure carefully labeled "Aiden" propped up in bed with a bandage wrapped around his neck. Another stick figure with huge tears running down her face was labeled "Elke."

Although Hank and Oren offered to deliver the copybook, Bianca said she'd visit Aiden this afternoon and take him some schoolwork as well. As soon as the words were out of her mouth she wondered if she was using Aiden's misfortune as an excuse to go to the ranch and perhaps see Jesse.

She'd had no chance to talk with him after yesterday's service without being terribly obvious. Rolf's appearance probably set enough tongues wagging, and she didn't intend to provide Oakfield's busybodies with more gossip. After all, it wasn't as if she had any real interest in Jesse Landry. If she needed further proof marriage only led to trouble and unhappiness, Joanna Nolan's pathetic situation was evidence enough.

CHAPTER 23

Bianca dismissed class, convinced Junior she didn't need extra help, and headed briskly home. Mattie was more than willing to hitch up the wagon and accompany her to Donovan's ranch. As the wagon passed the schoolyard and headed southeast toward the river, Bianca marveled at the countless shades of green spread before her. She wondered if even an artist like Edwina could capture them all.

Mattie, apparently glad for a break in her routine, chattered amiably.

"Nora Donovan is an interesting woman," she said. "People say she's Spanish, but she's really Mexican——you know—part Indian. You'd never guess it, though. I mean, her skin's not much darker than yours, and she's quite cultured and all."

"It's very kind of her to look after Aiden," Bianca said.

"She's attractive too—for an older woman, I mean. There she is on that ranch with all those men—especially that handsome Jesse—and yet there's never been any gossip about her. At least, none I've heard."

"In a place as small as Oakfield, I'm sure if there were any rumors you would have heard them."

"Not necessarily, Bianca. You'd be surprised how people censor their remarks whenever the minister's wife is in earshot. I declare, if it weren't for the girls I'd probably never hear anything at all."

"They do like to talk," Bianca said with a smile.

"Over the next rise you'll have a good view of the Donovan spread. I don't know exactly how many acres the ranch takes up, but I've heard it's in the thousands."

Bianca gasped as the ranch came into view. "Why, it's a whole village! There are some pretty large farms around Wesleyville, but I've never even imagined anything like this."

"The ranch house is over there to the east where the trees are. You can't really see it until we get closer. Those buildings off to the right are the stables and bunkhouse, and you can see the main barn and some of the corrals back closer to the woods."

Mattie reined the horse. Bianca got down, shoved the heavy board aside, and opened the wooden gate that marked the entrance to the ranch. She waited until Mattie drove the wagon inside and then closed the gate behind them.

A hard-packed road curved through a double row of oak trees. Through the trees Bianca caught tantalizing glimpses of the ranch house, a sprawling one-story building constructed of wood and stone. A wide porch, shaded by low eaves, extended across the front.

As the wagon emerged from the arcade of oaks Bianca exclaimed, "What a beautiful house! I've never seen so many windows. It must have cost a fortune to bring all that glass around the Horn."

"The original house was the big log cabin where Jesse Landry lives now. I guess by the time Kirk Donovan got around to building this place, he could pretty much afford anything he wanted."

Even before Bianca and Mattie climbed the wide, stone steps, the oak door swung open and Nora Donovan moved outside to greet them.

"Mrs. Pangston, what a nice surprise."

Mattie took Nora Donovan's outstretched hand and turned to Bianca. "And this is Bianca Stratton, our new schoolmistress."

"Of course. I remember seeing you at the funeral." Nora Donovan stepped inside and gestured for Mattie and Bianca to follow. "You've come to see Aiden. He'll be delighted."

"How is he?" Bianca couldn't prevent the note of anxiety in her voice.

"He's not feverish, and the burns seem to be healing well. He still can't talk, and of course that bothers him a lot."

"He's a regular chatterbox," Bianca said. "Not to be able to speak must be the worst punishment imaginable."

"I sent my foreman for the doctor, so we should know more soon."

The size and opulence of the house was unlike anything Bianca had ever experienced. The front door led to a parlor at least three times the size of the schoolhouse. The great room boasted a floor of shining planked oak, a soaring beamed ceiling, and a stone fireplace large enough to roast an elk.

Following Mrs. Donovan to a wide veranda, Bianca realized the view from the front of the ranch house only revealed a small part of what was actually there. The house was shaped like a "U." A covered porch served as a corridor and made it possible to go to any room of the house without going through any other part. Cobblestone pathways wound through the central open space to a fountain covered with brightly colored tiles.

Inside a sunny room near the end of the corridor, Aiden lay propped up amid a pile of down pillows. His normally ruddy face was pale, and his tousled thatch of hair appeared darker than usual in contrast to the white lace-edged pillowcases. Bianca bent over him, arms outstretched. Her impulsive hug was rewarded with a lopsided smile that brought tears to her eyes. When she gave him the copybook the children made, he seemed delighted and tried to thank her.

"Don't try to talk, Aiden," Mrs. Donovan said. "Just remember all the things you want to say and save them inside your head until your throat feels better."

Bianca nodded in agreement and perched on the edge of the featherbed. She read the pages in the copybook aloud while Aiden traced the words with his fingers. When the last page had been turned Aiden mouthed the word, "More," and flipped the pages back to the beginning. After the third reading Bianca shook her head and patted Aiden's hand.

"That's enough for now, Aiden. Mrs. Pangston and I need to get back home before dark, and you mustn't tire yourself."

"Your teacher's right," Mrs. Donovan agreed. "You need to rest until the doctor gets here."

Bianca bent down to give Aiden a goodbye hug, but he pushed her away and gestured anxiously, mouthing words she couldn't make out.

"What is it, Aiden? Is there something you want to tell me?"

His eyes darted at Mattie and Mrs. Donovan, and he shook his head slowly. But then he took her hand and squeezed it hard.

"It's all right, Aiden." Bianca's voice sounded reassuring, but she squeezed the small brown hand to let him know she understood that everything wasn't really all right. "I'll go see your mother tomorrow and ask if there's something I can do to help her. Would you like that?"

Aiden nodded.

"Now, your job is to rest and get better. And I'll leave the copybook here on your bed. Why, I bet you can read it all by yourself by now."

Bianca gave Aiden a final hug. She and Mattie followed Mrs. Donovan back down the open corridor to the main part of the house.

"I must tell you, Miss Stratton, I really had to bully Oren into going to school at first. But, although he'd never admit it, he seems to be really taking to it now."

"I'm happy to hear it," Bianca said. "Maybe the pretty Fowler twins have something to do with his change of heart."

Mrs. Donovan laughed. "That may be part of it, but I've even found him reading outside in the garden. I never thought I'd see him with a book in his hand instead of a rifle or a slingshot. Last night he actually gave his favorite slingshot to Aiden."

A door on the far side of the room swung open and Jesse Landry appeared, hat in hand.

"Well, good afternoon, ladies. I saw the preacher's wagon outside and figured Aiden had rated a visit."

He tossed his hat onto an ornate library table, and Bianca took a deep breath and waited for her unruly pulse to slow to its normal rhythm.

"Oh, Jesse, I'm glad you're back. Did you see Doc Schneider?" Mrs. Donovan moved swiftly to intercept Jesse midway across the room.

"I'm sorry, Nora, but they've had some cholera up north. Doc's wife doesn't know how soon he'll get home, but she promised to send him on down as soon as she claps eyes on him."

"Thank you for taking the time to ride over to Wesleyville, Jesse."

"No problem. But now I've got some cattle to see to. I'll check in with you this evening as usual."

Jesse retrieved his hat. Then, at the door, he turned and his eyes met Bianca's before he left.

"My goodness," said Mattie. "Every time I see that man I can't help staring. Do you think he knows how flat-out fine looking he is?"

"Oh, yes," Nora Donovan said. "He knows."

"Mrs. Donovan, about Aiden. I think it's—well, it's wonderfully kind—-all you've done for him." Bianca, rarely at a loss for words, found herself stammering. She was puzzled about the relationship between Jesse and Mrs. Donovan, not that it was any of her business. Still, the dark-haired woman seemed so self-assured, so competent, so intimidating that Bianca felt like an awkward child.

"Call me Nora. Everyone does. And now, please join me for a cup of tea. It's not often I have ladies come to call."

"That's very kind," said Mattie, heading briskly for the door, "but we really do need to get back to the manse before dark."

"Of course." Nora Donovan turned away, but not before Bianca saw the flicker of hurt in her eyes. At the door she said, "Miss Stratton, I hope you'll come back to see Aiden again soon. Your visit was the best medicine he could have."

As the wagon rolled away from the ranch house, Bianca found herself thinking of all the things she should have said and done while they were there. Why hadn't she been able to find out what was troubling Aiden? Why hadn't she asked Mrs. Donovan how soon Aiden would be going home? Why had she felt like a silly schoolgirl as soon as Jesse Landry turned up? Why hadn't she accepted the invitation to tea before Mattie had a chance to refuse so brusquely? What was wrong with Mattie, anyway?

"She's Catholic, you know." Mattie answered Bianca's unspoken question. "They even have a chapel right there on the ranch, and a traveling priest comes by every month or so to say Mass."

"Of course," said Bianca. "I was wondering why I hadn't seen her at Sunday service."

"Cushing says Catholics believe the so-called sacramental wine they drink at mass is really Christ's blood. Not a symbol of his blood, but really his blood! And all those candles and chanting in Latin, why it's nothing more than voodoo if you ask me."

As they neared the schoolhouse Bianca said, "Drop me off here, Mattie, if you don't mind. It's still early and I left this afternoon without tidying things up."

As she watched the wagon lumber away, Bianca wondered again how someone as warm-hearted and caring as Mattie could be so narrow-minded. Well, Nora Donovan had invited Bianca to come back, and Bianca was determined to make her next visit without Mattie.

Nora Donovan watched her departing guests with mixed feelings. After all these years it still hurt and angered her when people like the apple-cheeked minister's wife treated her as if she were an outsider. She'd been in this valley longer than most of the other settlers. She opened her home to strangers. She extended help whenever and wherever it was needed, but nothing seemed to make her acceptable. She was of mixed Spanish and Indian blood. She was Catholic. For this, her proud heritage, they looked down on her. How dare they!

The young teacher, though, was a different matter. Nora sensed no prejudice there. She'd heard and silently applauded when Bianca bullied the minister into allowing Aiden to receive an education. Getting Oren and Hank to go to school had required threats and bribery, but now they attended with only the obligatory grumbling young folks seemed to require as part of growing-up. And today, when Bianca impulsively embraced young Aiden, Nora saw the joy in his eyes. She had also noted the long look that passed between Bianca and Jesse.

Keeping a huge ranch running smoothly and profitably was a daunting task for anyone, and even more difficult for a woman. As long as Kirk Donovan was alive, even after his fall, his presence served as a shield. She made the decisions, but in the eyes of the ranch hands and cattlemen Kirk was still the boss.

As a widow, she needed someone who could deal with the men, and she could find no fault with the way Jesse handled the job. They had a good, easy relationship, and she would be a fool to change it.

Still, a man like Jesse, capable and young, would want more. A spread of his own, for one thing. She couldn't fault him for being ambitious, and Lord knows, aside from Kirk Donovan, Jesse Landry was the most attractive man she'd ever met. She'd miss her husband every day of her life, but no number of feather quilts could warm the bed the way a man's strong arms could. But if she married Jesse Landry, she'd know in her heart it was really the ranch he wanted.

Her thoughts returned to the long look that passed between Jesse and Bianca. There was chemistry there, no doubt about it. She wondered why the schoolteacher hadn't married before now. Expediency and a shortage of marriageable women had given rise to the custom of a widower marrying the old-maid sister of his departed spouse. Nora had been madly in love with Kirk Donovan since he first rode into the courtyard of the family hacienda, so the custom had suited her well despite her genuine grief at her sister's death.

Bianca Stratton, however, though nearing old-maid status in pioneer country where girls routinely married at thirteen, was hardly a typical spinster. Maybe, Nora reflected, too much time with books left a girl with little understanding of what it meant to be a woman. But Bianca certainly wasn't oblivious to Jesse Landry's charms. He had seemed a little distracted lately, but now she realized he'd taken a shine to Bianca, and that was ample explanation. She knew Bianca could provide Jesse with something most men would consider more valuable than land—a young wife and, eventually, sons to carry on his name. She remembered how Kirk Donovan's face would light up when Oren came into the room.

Thinking of Oren brought Nora's mind back to the recent series of events. Oren and Hank stoutly denied knowing anything about the shot that had narrowly missed the schoolteacher. Still, those two were a handful who'd been known to bend the truth if they thought punishment was in the offing. And they had been out that evening. She'd better have another talk with them.

CHAPTER 24

Cap Mackay sat up, wondering groggily if the pounding was inside his head.

"C'mon, Cap. I know you're home."

Cap reached for his rifle, trying to remember whether or not it was loaded. Somebody was beating on the door, and he didn't recognize the voice. Nobody but Frenchy ever came to his cabin. If the room would stop rocking like a leaky rowboat, maybe he could figure out what was going on.

"Open up, Cap. It's Sheriff Wells. I need to talk to you."

Sheriff Wells. That would be the young feller who'd been around asking questions about the blacksmith.

"All right, now. Stop your banging. I'm coming."

As the door creaked open, the glare of the morning sun blinded him and sent stabs of pain through his already throbbing head. He motioned the sheriff inside, tossed a couple of dirty shirts off the only chair, and tottered back to sit on the side of the bed.

"Have a seat, Sheriff," he said.

"I stopped by Fowler's store this morning."

Wells was talking friendly like, but Cap knew there was no such critter as a friendly sheriff.

"Ed was kind enough to give me directions to your place."

"Ed needs to learn to keep his mouth shut," Cap mumbled. "So what are you doing back here? I thought you caught that Injun that killed that blacksmith feller."

"I'm pretty sure the man we have in custody hasn't ever been as far south as Oakfield, so I have to consider that Dan Nolan's murderer is still out there."

"Is that right?" Cap sized up the sheriff with a long look. "A young feller like you probably hasn't had all that much experience with the ways of them red devils."

"Not near as much as you've had, from what I hear."

"Well, you heard right." Cap relaxed. "I put my share of Injuns in the ground when I was in the Army. If you need a hand, I'm still a pretty fair shot."

"That's what I wanted to see you about. I understand that the schoolteacher was badly frightened by a shot that narrowly missed her."

"I heard some youngsters was out shooting rabbits, and she got spooked." Cap tried to keep up his bantering tone, but he hadn't expected any questions to take this direction. Still, he wasn't about to let some upstart sheriff get him rattled. "Seems like with a murderer on the loose you'd have more important things to look into."

"True enough, but for a place the size of Oakfield there's been way too much going on lately. The murder. That shot. And then the fire. All connected somehow with the Nolans. It's got to make a person stop and think."

The sheriff tilted back in the chair and sat there looking relaxed. Cap wished he had a cup of strong coffee to help clear the fuzz out of his head, but he'd let the stove go clean out and hadn't even brought in a fresh supply of kindling. Still, if there was one thing he'd learned in the Army, it was you never told nobody nothing if you could help it. You didn't volunteer for damnfool missions, and you didn't volunteer no information neither. If the sheriff wanted to sit there like he was having a nap, Cap could play the waiting game all winter.

Then the sheriff leveled the chair with a thump that felt like thunder inside Cap's aching head. "So where were you when that shot was fired?"

"Well, now, it'd be right hard to say where I was seeing as how I got no idea when—"

"I'll make it easy. Where were you Thursday about dusk?"

"Thursday. The day of the funeral, as I recall."

"You'll also recall that I almost ran into you as I was leaving Fowler's store. You had your gun with you."

"Have to be some kind of damn fool to go out without his rifle when there's murderin' redskins on the loose."

"Mrs. Nolan seems pretty well convinced that it wasn't an Indian who murdered her husband."

"You ain't putting stock in some squaw's view of things?" Cap shook his head in disbelief.

"I'm trying to get to the truth."

"Sheriff, I had more than a bellyful of them red devils over the years. Injuns is trouble, and half-breeds is worse. And if you been asking around, you know everybody in these parts feels the same way, 'cept maybe for the nosy teacher woman. I hear she's took a real shine to that youngster, and I know she's been over to the Nolan's place to see the squaw more'n once. Maybe she's the one you oughta be talking to."

Tyler Wells got up and went to the door.

"You're right about one thing. I've got more important things to do than jaw with you. But, if anything else happens to the teacher or Mrs. Nolan or her son, I'll be back on your doorstep faster than you can down a swig of Frenchy's white lightning."

Tyler climbed into the saddle and took deep breaths of the fresh, pine-scented air to clear the fetid stench of Cap's cabin from his nostrils. He shook his head in disgust and wondered how anybody could live in such filth. He'd noticed a hunting knife lying on the table next to the rotting remains of a half-eaten boiled rabbit. A knife like that could have made short work of scalping the blacksmith, but every male in Oakfield over the age of ten probably had some kind of hunting knife. Even the spineless excuse for a preacher probably had one.

Cap might be a drunken old sot, but he was no fool. Whatever he was up to, he wasn't about to give a straight answer. Still, Cap was right about one thing. The schoolteacher seemed to have stuck herself right in the middle of everything. He couldn't figure her for having any part in the murder or the fire, but maybe she could throw some light on the whole situation. It was still early afternoon. Her pupils would be long gone, but there was a chance she'd still be at the schoolhouse.

"The door was open, so I walked in. Hope you don't mind."

Bianca turned from erasing the blackboard to see Tyler Wells, hat in hand, looking strangely uncomfortable.

"I didn't even know you were still in Oakfield, Sheriff Wells. Shouldn't you be off somewhere rounding up cattle rustlers or harassing Indians?"

The sheriff moved to the front of the classroom and leaned his lanky frame against Bianca's desk. "Miss Stratton, I don't know what I did to get you all riled up, but whatever it was, I'd like to start out fresh. I'm really a pretty decent sort and a passably competent sheriff, or so I've been told."

Bianca turned back to the blackboard, hoping the sheriff wouldn't notice the flush coloring her neck and face. She wasn't sure why caustic remarks simply popped out of her mouth whenever Tyler Wells appeared. She finished removing the last traces of the morning's arithmetic problems, put down the eraser and turned slowly to face him.

"I don't know what gets into me sometimes," she admitted. "I guess we got started off on the wrong foot because I was afraid something bad was going to happen to Aiden."

"And now something bad has happened." Tyler spoke softly. "I don't know exactly what's going on here, but I aim to find out. I don't think you're responsible for any of this trouble, but you're right in the middle of it."

"It does seem so. If I hadn't stirred things up by insisting Aiden be allowed to attend school—"

"Then a bright little boy would be missing out on something important for his future."

"But I needn't have traipsed over to the blacksmith's place and stirred up talk by making friends with Joanna Nolan."

"True enough. And I'd probably have hustled the widow and her son off to the reservation."

Bianca smiled in spite of herself. Tyler Wells had a disarming manner, and he might even be a good sheriff. She found herself wondering about his background. There was the slightest trace of a drawl, and he talked more like a gentleman than a country lawman.

"So," Tyler continued, "I think it's time we buried the hatchet—uh—poor choice of words there. Anyway, I've talked to just about everybody in Oakfield. Everything I hear points me right back at you."

"You can't believe I—"

"I believe somebody murdered Daniel Nolan. If Joanna Nolan is right and that somebody is no redskin, then I probably don't need to look any farther than right here in Oakfield to find the killer."

"But what reason would anyone have? The Nolans have only been here a few months."

"Well, there's the blacksmith's fine piece of land. The word is Cap wanted to buy it but was dickering over the deal when Nolan turned up and paid full price."

"That hardly seems like a motive for murder. I mean, land around here is plentiful. Good land, too."

"That's true, but I understand that in the spring that particular piece of land is the only place you can ford the river for forty miles in either direction, so if somebody wanted to build a bridge—"

"Or a trestle if the railroad comes through!" Bianca nodded. "Of course! Then that land would be really valuable."

"Still, I don't see how killing Daniel Nolan would ensure Cap—if it is Cap we're talking about—-of getting the land. Of course, if Nolan's widow and child were sent packing to the reservation, that would put things pretty much up for grabs."

"And nobody would expect a nosy schoolmarm to befriend a squaw and unearth a marriage certificate, a will and a deed from a pile of old papers." Bianca recalled how protective Joanna had been of her precious wooden box. "Oh, Sheriff Wells, what if those papers were burned in the fire?"

"I'm afraid that might cause a real problem. You and I can both swear we saw a will and a marriage certificate, and there ought to be a copy of the deed on file at the courthouse. But when I was reading for the law I discovered that lots of records get lost in the shuffle over the years, and records about Indians seem to have a special way of disappearing."

"You're a lawyer? Why in the world are you wearing a badge when you could be practicing a real profession?"

"I know quite a few people who'd give you an argument about the law being a real profession." Tyler Wells grinned, and Bianca found herself noticing the way the corners of his gray-blue eyes crinkled when he smiled. "Let's say I think a sheriff probably does more to help folks in trouble than most lawyers do. How I got here is a long story, but I find I kind of like the job. But we were talking about legal documents, so I guess I better find out whether or not they were destroyed in the fire."

"I went to Donovan's ranch and saw Aiden this afternoon. I promised him I'd go and see Joanna. I can ask about her papers."

"Then I'll leave it up to you. I've got to get back to Wesleyville to see when the circuit judge will be turning up, but I'll be back this way late tomorrow afternoon."

"I'll go see Joanna right after I dismiss class tomorrow. You might stop by there when you head back to Oakfield."

"Good idea. Of course, none of this necessarily gets me any closer to solving Nolan's murder. Maybe the land doesn't have anything to do with it. Maybe somebody didn't hold with a white man and a squaw living in the community. Maybe it's something else entirely, something out of Daniel Nolan's past none of us knows anything about. Or maybe Joanna Nolan is wrong, and I really am looking for a renegade Indian who hated white people and wanted to be sure everybody knew it. Maybe Daniel Nolan happened to be in the wrong place at the wrong time."

"Any of those things is possible."

"Possible, yes. But I paid a visit to Cap Mackay this morning. From what Ed Fowler tells me, Cap's a pretty steady drinker. Even so, he must have really got himself a snootful yesterday to be in the bad shape he was in when I woke him up."

"If he's a murderer, maybe his conscience is hurting."

"Well, it was his head hurting this morning, but he still wasn't about to give me a straight answer on anything. He's up to something, but I'm not sure what."

"So, you've really been investigating! I guess I was afraid you would write poor Mr. Nolan off as another casualty in the bloody struggle between the settlers and the Indians."

"Like I said, Miss Stratton, I am a pretty good sheriff. I'm sorry I couldn't examine the body. Sometimes a victim can tell you things, even though he's no longer alive. I had Hank and Oren take me to the forest glade where they found Nolan. I located a good-sized rock nearby that appeared to have traces of blood on it, not that finding it gets me any closer to knowing who might have used it to bash in the blacksmith's head. I also got a good description of the body from Hank and Oren, although with youngsters their age it's possible they embellished things a bit by the time they got around to giving me the gory details."

"They talked about finding the body when they came to school the next morning. Things were fresh in their minds then." Bianca related, as exactly as she could recall, what the boys had told the class.

Tyler nodded. "That's pretty much the way they told it to me. Something else troubles me, though. The boys said Nolan was lying on his back in a little gully. When an Indian kills an enemy, I've heard he usually turns the body face down. I don't know exactly why."

"Then you think Joanna is right——it wasn't an Indian who killed Daniel Nolan?"

"I'm not sure what I believe at this point. I've talked to everybody in Oakfield, and nobody seems willing to be completely forthright. Hank and Oren were open enough about how they found the body, but when I quizzed them about their whereabouts on the evening when the shot was fired at you, they hemmed and hawed a lot.

"Cap offered to go out and help me shoot Indians, but if his brain isn't clear pickled in alcohol he's covering up something. I suspect Frenchy Blauchet is supplying Ed Fowler with bootleg liquor, but making sure the government gets its tax money isn't part of my job. Maybe that's why they clam up when I come around, but I think there's something else going on. Cushing Pangston is so afraid he'll offend somebody he wouldn't say boo to a goose. Lars Larson built the coffin, and he might be able to answer some of my questions about the wounds to the blacksmith's body, but his English isn't up to describing anything in much detail. So, here I am—"

"Turning to me as a last resort."

"You know, Miss Stratton, I've talked to the Pangston girls and the Fowler youngsters. They all say you expect them to work hard, but they also say you're fair. I could use a little fairness about now."

The sheriff was right. He was trying to do his job, and the least she could do was offer her cooperation.

"What can I do?" she asked contritely. "To help you, I mean."

"Talk to your students. See if you can find out what Hank and Oren are covering up. Maybe the Fowler boys know what's going on with Ed Fowler and Frenchy."

"Well, I'll talk to Hank and Oren, but it wouldn't be proper to encourage any of my students to tell tales on their parents."

"You're right. But think carefully about where you've been and what you've seen since you came to Oakfield. If somebody was shooting at you on purpose, there must be a reason."

"I'll do that, of course. And I'll talk some more to Joanna. I'll let you know if I come up with anything new."

"I appreciate your help, especially after we seemed to start off on the wrong foot."

"I'm sorry, Sheriff Wells. Sharp words fly out of my mouth sometimes."

"Yes, they do. I was beginning to think whoever liked Mr. Shakespeare's plays well enough to name you picked the right play but the wrong sister."

"I admit I often wish my name were Katherine," she said. "Of the two sisters, she is the more interesting."

"Well, my English professor said Kate's shrewishness was her way of keeping men at arm's length."

"Really, Mr. Wells, this conversation seems to be taking an unwarranted turn. It's time I closed the schoolhouse and went home."

"That sheriff!" Cushing sputtered indignantly and helped himself to seconds of lumpy mashed potatoes. "You'd think I've got nothing better to do than answer his questions all afternoon. No wonder I'm behind on my chores. He even asked me to account for my whereabouts on . . . er . . . several occasions."

"I'm sure the sheriff was only doing his job." Bianca didn't volunteer the information that his investigation had included a lengthy visit to the schoolhouse.

"That's right, Cushing," Mattie agreed. "He probably knows how everyone in Oakfield relies on you for advice, and he thought you might have information that would help him."

"True, True." The little preacher seemed mollified, but Bianca wondered if he really believed it. Or if Mattie did, for that matter.

"Edna Fowler says the sheriff was a Reb in the war," Cora said.

"How would she know?" Katie asked.

"Reb, Reb." Tina pounded her spoon for emphasis.

"Tina, it's very impolite to bang your spoon on the table," Gertrude admonished.

"Reb, Reb." Tina kept pounding. "What's a Reb?"

"Somebody who fought on the wrong side in the war," said Cora.

"What's the wrong side?" Tina asked.

"The side that lost," said Gertrude. "The losing side is always the wrong side."

"Well, the war is over." Mattie passed the undercooked venison stew around for the second time with no takers. "So I don't believe Edna Fowler's information is important however she came by it."

"She heard her mom talking to some of the other customers in the store. Somebody knows somebody who lives over at Wesleyville who knows the sheriff's uncle." Cora wasn't about to be denied spreading the latest bit of gossip. "His uncle is a lawyer, not that there's much call for a lawyer in Wesleyville, and his uncle talks real southern. That's what Edna said."

"Some people need lawyers. Mrs. Nolan needs a lawyer," said Katie. "Lenny was fishing with Aiden Saturday morning, and Aiden told him his mom was taking him to Wesleyville to talk to a lawyer and buy a horse."

"Well, Aiden won't be going anywhere for a few days, anyway," Mattie said. "The poor little fellow looks absolutely pale, and he hasn't been able to make a sound."

Mattie and Bianca's account of their visit to the ranch took considerable time due to the frequent questions and interruptions from the four girls.

Bianca was relieved when the conversation turned away from the sheriff's past. All the professors at the academy had been staunch abolitionists, and the whole community around Wesleyville had gone into mourning at the news of President Lincoln's assassination. Some of the girls at the academy said their parents left Kentucky because of family disagreements over slavery, but Bianca had never actually met anyone who fought on the Confederate side.

She'd begun to feel the young sheriff was someone she might be able to trust, but now, as she looked around the table, she realized again how really alone she was here in Oakfield. She'd hoped Mattie and she might become friends, but underneath Mattie's cheerful demeanor lay a bundle of narrow-minded prejudices. Cushing—well, how could anybody know what Cushing really thought about anything?

Nora Donovan had invited her to come back to the ranch to see Aiden, and she intended to do so as soon as she could find a way to get there. Bianca considered asking to take the wagon, but she was afraid Mattie would insist on going along. She'd started enough tongues wagging in Oakfield with her visits to the Nolans, so it wouldn't be wise to be seen riding in a buggy with Jesse Landry.

Lately it seemed she had to keep reminding herself of her total disinterest in men entirely too often. And no number of reminders helped during the night, when Jesse's face unaccountably persisted on invading her dreams. She tried to dismiss the dreams as romantic nonsense born of reading too many of Mr. Shakespeare's sonnets and Sir Walter Scott's fanciful tales, but the fluttery feeling in her throat when her eyes met Jesse's at the ranch earlier had been entirely too real.

When the last of the scorched bread pudding had been eaten, Bianca helped clear the table and headed gratefully upstairs to her little garret. Sleep was slow in coming. Her thoughts kept returning to the questions the sheriff raised when he stopped by the schoolhouse. He'd said she seemed to be right in the middle of everything, but the Nolans were the real focus of all the tragedy. Daniel Nolan's body had been discovered after Bianca began teaching in Oakfield, but nobody knew for sure when the murder had taken place. She tried to remember if Joanna had said exactly when she last saw Daniel alive. That might be important.

Still, the gunshot that narrowly missed her in the woods wasn't aimed at the Nolans. She believed a hunter's shell had simply gone astray, but Tyler Wells disagreed. Her insistence on Aiden being allowed to attend school upset people, and her friendship with Joanna made things worse. But was that a reason for anyone to harm her?

She'd promised the sheriff she'd think carefully about where she'd been and what she'd seen since she arrived in Oakfield, and she let her mind drift back. Most of the time she'd been either at school or here at the house. She'd overheard a lot of chatter among her students, but she could recall nothing that could be considered sinister in any way.

She sighed, fluffed the feather pillow and tucked it back under her head, urging her tired body to relax. Finally she drifted into a restless sleep. A series of troubled dreams began with Jesse Landry pulling up in front of the schoolhouse saying, "I knew you'd let me take you for a buggy ride today."

CHAPTER 25

Keeping well away from the road, Running Fox guided his pinto through the trees fringing the property where his sister and nephew lived. He'd grown accustomed to hearing his sister called Joanna, but in his mind she still bore the beautiful name that recalled a shy girl with luminous eyes. Even translated into the pale people's language, "She-Who-Keeps-the-Stories-of-Our-People-in-Her Heart" depicted his sister much more faithfully than the harsh-sounding Joanna.

The white men not only took his people's land and way of life, but they also stole the poetry from their names. Those who had gone to the reservation bore names like Henry and George.

While Joanna was in the service of the Methodist minister, Running Fox stayed at the mission briefly. The missionary couldn't, or wouldn't, pronounce the name he'd been given at his tribal ceremony and dubbed him Elmer Running Fox. He'd never accepted himself as Elmer. On the rare occasions when he was forced to come into contact with the pale people, he identified himself as Running Fox.

Except for a few who'd been lured by the white men's promises of a better life, their tribe avoided the pale people. Some dissolved into the secret places in the hills and forests rather than be marched to reservations. For the most part they escaped the terrible diseases the pale people brought with them, but they suffered greatly from the loss of their hunting and gathering places. Each year their numbers decreased.

Even before his people were forced onto reservations, a number of native women married white men. By the time they reached marriageable age, women in most villages outnumbered men, and in those difficult times two or three wives were a luxury few men, even chiefs, could afford. Pale women seemed to be in short supply, so there was little concern, especially if the marriage included a fair number of horses or guns as part of the exchange.

Joanna, however, was a different matter. Not only was she his sister, but her move into the white man's world meant a great loss to his people. She was gifted with the tongue that told ancient stories. Her hands understood which leaves, roots, barks and berries could be collected and transformed into poultices and broths for healing injuries and warding off illness.

And the blacksmith beat her, of this Running Fox was certain. He understood why men found it necessary to discipline their women on occasion, especially those who had been purchased from other tribes and were slow to learn the ways of their husband's people. But Running Fox had disliked the squint-eyed blacksmith from the start, and he was sure gentle Joanna had never given her husband provocation.

If she'd stayed with her own people, Joanna would have been accorded status as an honored storyteller and healer. Moreover, Running Fox would have been beside her to see that she was protected and treated with respect. Still, there was no point in dwelling on the past.

The blacksmith was dead—murdered and scalped. The information had come, as did most news these days, in round-about fashion. Running Fox traded beaver skins with a trapper who relayed a conversation overheard at a trading post. News, especially bad news concerning native people, spread quickly.

Now enough time had passed that he believed he could slip in unobserved and persuade his sister to return to her family.

The boy, though a half-breed, seemed unusually alert. He, too, could be an asset now that his drunken father was out of the way.

Running Fox slipped off the pinto's back and tossed the reins lightly onto the ground. The mare would graze quietly until summoned by his special breathy whistle. He moved to the edge of the clearing and surveyed his sister's home, noting the scorched earth and newly repaired rooftop with alarm. Still, all appeared quiet, and smoke curled from the front chimney.

Moving silently through the small orchard behind the house, he slipped through the screen door and into the chilly kitchen. He shook his head in amusement at the sight of the unlit iron stove the pale people favored for cooking their food. It was a squat, black monstrosity with heavy doors in front and a large pipe to the ceiling. He wondered why anybody would want such a contraption. The warmth of a hearth provided a gathering place for the family, and the pleasing aroma of venison stew simmering in a kettle welcomed a tired hunter. A separate room for the cooking of food was simply another incomprehensible pale people's notion.

He crossed the small kitchen and put his ear to the door that led into the rest of the house. Hearing no voices, he eased the door ajar. Joanna, kneeling to add a fresh log to the fire, looked up, her eyes wide with surprise. Then she sprang to her feet, embraced him warmly, and greeted him in their native tongue.

"Oh, my brother, I have been wondering when you would come. I have much to tell you."

He glanced around the large room, noting with satisfaction that the beautiful willow baskets hanging from hooks on the walls bore evidence his sister had not totally abandoned the ways of her people.

"I know of the death of your husband," he said. "And with my own eyes I have seen signs of a fire. Now I must hear everything from your lips." He crouched by the hearth and listened attentively as Joanna recounted the events of the past weeks.

"You have entrusted the boy to the care of a white woman you don't even know? How could you do such a thing?"

"She is kind. She has opened her home to Aiden," Joanna replied quietly. "She is a powerful woman, but she does not look at me with fear or disdain but only with warmth in her eyes."

"Warmth is something I have yet to see in the eyes of any pale person. Your husband—did he have warmth in his eyes when he gave you the bruises I see on your face? You are well rid of that man, Joanna. Now you must get the boy and come with me before your warm-eyed white friends march you to the reservation with a gun at your back."

"Calm yourself, brother." Joanna poured him a cup of hot mint tea from a cast iron kettle that simmered on the hearth. "Daniel left papers—important papers—papers that mean nobody can move us off this land. As soon as Aiden is stronger I will see a lawyer, and everything will be taken care of legally."

Running Fox shook his head in frustration. "Do you really believe a piece of paper can protect you from the pale people if they want your land? Look at what's happening to our brothers who were marched north to the reservation against their will. The white men considered the reservation land worthless, but now they've changed their minds and are moving to take back what was never theirs in the first place. Do you think our people had no important papers to prove the land was theirs? You are a fool, Joanna, to put your faith in the promises of these people."

"But the papers—"

"The papers are as worthless as the promises!" Running Fox drained his cup and slammed it onto the table. "Come to your senses, woman!"

He was gratified to see his sister bite her lip and remain silent as he stood and paced back and forth in front of the hearth. He knew it was best to contain his anger and leave her to ponder the wisdom of his words, but keeping his temper in check was a lesson he had never learned easily.

"I'll prepare a place for you in the mountains," he said firmly.

"But, brother," Joanna objected, "Aiden isn't well, and I'm not sure—"

"The village is well hidden. Game is plentiful, and a clear stream provides fresh water as well as fish for our table. The forest abounds with berries and the other plants you know so well. The boy will recover there. You are needed by your people."

He moved quickly to the kitchen door. "Pack up what you and the boy need to take with you. I'll be back in a few days."

Joanna sighed and shook her head as she followed Running Fox into the kitchen and watched him disappear into the orchard. Anger seemed to consume her brother, but she suspected it was also the fuel that kept him alive in these precarious times. She knew her people had ample reason for mistrust, but she was irritated that Running Fox believed he could simply turn up in her house and dictate her future.

It was a good thing she hadn't told him about her friendship with Miss Stratton or her talks with the sheriff. Running Fox was furious about Aiden staying at the Donovan ranch. She couldn't bear to think of his reaction if he'd known Aiden was attending school in Oakfield.

Although her brother never accepted her marriage, she was surprised at the hate in his eyes when he spoke of Daniel. Running Fox couldn't have . . . She banished the unthinkable possibility from her mind. But her brother's intolerance of all white people and their ways frightened her. She was certain Running Fox knew in his heart, as she did, that there were kind, generous people among the white people just as there were in their native family.

She recalled the story, well known to her people, of how animals and humans once lived as brothers. They shared land in the shadow of the great mountain, Mazama, and talked to one another. But an evil chief proclaimed himself stronger than the Great Spirit and began killing the animals unless they did his bidding. Finally, the Great Spirit sent the animals to safety. Then he brought down smoke and fire until the entire top of the mountain rose in the air, leaving only a deep hole filled with the water white people called Crater Lake. Native people never went there. They knew evil spirits were buried under the water.

When the first settlers arrived with their plows and their cattle, Joanna's family had traded and co-existed peaceably with the newcomers. It seemed there was room for all. But now everything had changed. There had been no explosion, no top of a mountain blown away, but the native people and the white men seemed to be as alien to one another as humans were to the animals who had once been their brothers.

Now Joanna was forced to choose, not only for herself, but also for her son who had thus far been raised in the white man's ways. True, he knew the language of his people, and she had taken him with her into the forest and shared with him the secrets of the plants growing there. He loved her stories and asked for them far more often than the tales Daniel had read him from the worn missionary Bible. But now Aiden was going to school—a real school where white children went, not a missionary school where native children only learned about the white people's God and were trained to be household servants or field hands.

If only there were someone she could truly trust and confide in, but that was impossible. Nobody in Oakfield must learn of the hidden mountain village. Not even Miss Stratton could be entrusted with the safety and future of what little remained of her family. And Running Fox had demonstrated there was no way she could discuss the future with him rationally. It was devastating to feel so alone, but she would simply have to endure it until she had Aiden safe beside her.

Joanna had never been away from Aiden before, and his absence depressed and frightened her. She hadn't realized how much she'd come to depend on him to serve as a buffer between herself and the white people she lived among. She banked the fire, went to the barn and saddled the gentle buckskin horse. She secured her willow basket to the saddle horn and shook her head in amusement at the sidesaddle, a strange invention.

She followed the river road toward the ranch and reflected that Running Fox was wrong about many things, but he was right to chastise her for leaving Aiden in the care of others. She would thank Mrs. Donovan for her kindness and bring Aiden home today. It was time.

CHAPTER 26

Cap Mackay emptied his jug and passed out as soon as the pesky sheriff left. The day was more than half gone when he finally came around, feeling queasy in the stomach and worse in the head. After a wake-up nip from the bottle of good bourbon he kept under his mattress for emergencies, he stirred himself to bring in some kindling and get a fire going. Then he made the effort to roast and grind some coffee beans. As the aroma of brewing coffee freshened the stale inside air, his spirits rose considerably.

He poured coffee into a battered tin cup, added a little whiskey, and nursed the brew while he waited for the pounding in his temples to ease up. After a second cup of coffee, he stirred up a batch of hominy gruel, which usually set easy on his stomach after he'd had a mite too much to drink.

He wished he could remember exactly what he and the sheriff had talked about, but he hadn't really been thinking straight when Tyler Wells barged in. Still, he knew he wouldn't have said anything incriminating no matter how drunk he was. They'd talked some about Injuns, he remembered that much.

He didn't think anybody'd seen him hanging around Nolan's place, and he was sure he hadn't brought that up when the sheriff was hollering at him. He wanted to talk to the squaw woman, but every time he got near her the nosy schoolmarm or the sheriff turned up. He wasn't sure what they were up to, but his gut told him trouble was brewing.

After filling his hip flask he tossed the empty bourbon bottle into a pile of rags near the foot of his bed. He often bragged how the silver flask had saved his life by stopping an arrow. The truth of the matter was he'd been scurrying out of danger. The arrow wouldn't have killed him, but it would have been some time before he'd have been able to ride his horse in any comfort. Anyway, the flask was his good luck charm. He took a swig and reflected that maybe things were starting to go his way.

Although the fire at the Nolan's place hadn't done much damage, the squaw got a taste of how dangerous it was with no man to protect her. A woman needed a man, no question about that. And men, he reflected, were never cut out to do women's work. All that cooking and cleaning ate into a feller's hunting and fishing and drinking time.

Batching was hard on a man, but getting hold of a woman was damn near impossible in these parts. Back a few years he'd tried to cozy up to Nora Donovan, but she'd sent him packing in a hurry. Guess she figured he was too old when there was young bucks like Jesse around. Cap knew he was way past his prime, but Nora Donovan was no spring chicken either.

Well, no matter how desperate he was for female companionship, he'd never stoop to taking up with one of them red savages. Some men around these parts weren't so picky, though, and a young squaw like the blacksmith's widow wasn't likely to let her bed stay empty for long. He'd need to make his next move soon.

Ed Fowler reached under the counter, pulled out a jug of Frenchy's white lightning, took a swig, and scowled. Who in tarnation did Tyler Wells think he was, anyway? The sheriff said Daniel Nolan was killed sometime between Wednesday, when the squaw last saw him, and the following Tuesday, when the teenagers found the body. And then Wells had the nerve to ask what Ed had been doing during that time. He'd explained that he'd been up north buying stock for the store, but that didn't seem to cut any ice as far as the sheriff was concerned. Wells kept pestering him for details, asking exactly where he'd been and what he'd done every damn day. Ed didn't appreciate it one little bit and said so loud and clear.

Tyler Wells ought to be out running down renegade Injuns instead of poking his nose into the business of hard-working white folks. There was a lot about Ed's business dealings even Agnes didn't know, and he sure as hell wasn't likely to talk about it to a young whippersnapper of a sheriff.

Probably Tyler Wells was questioning everybody, but that notion didn't make Ed feel any better. He hoped Frenchy had sense enough to clam up if the sheriff got to him. Ed knew he never should have gotten mixed up in that business with Frenchy. Still, he was making a tidy bit of change off the deal. Every month he was closer to his dream—a real saloon, and later a real hotel.

When the railroad came through, there'd be no stopping him. Hell, he'd own the whole town, and everybody would know Ed Fowler was the most important man in the county. Agnes wouldn't approve, but Agnes would never stand in his way as long as she could wear fancy clothes and be looked up to. Maybe they'd even change the name of the place to Fowlerstown or Fowlersburg. Agnes would like that all right. It was amazing how respectable Agnes had become.

Of course, he'd come a ways himself considering his pa was an itinerant peddler who overcharged for shoddy wares and never went back to the same area twice. Their family of five lived jammed into the back of a squeaky lynchpin wagon that had seen better days crossing the plains.

It had been a miserable life, but he'd learned a thing or two about peddling before he'd sneaked off one night and headed to the goldfields. He hadn't had much luck panning gold, but peddling supplies to the miners was another matter.

Storekeeping, horse-trading, saloon keeping—it was all peddling when you came down to it. Talking up the merchandise, buttering up the customer when he started looking too close at the goods and, in the end, convincing him that he'd got the best of you. That was pretty much it.

Of course, running a store where you had to deal with the same people day in and day out was a mite harder. Most of the goods anybody was willing to pay cash money for arrived on the packets that sailed up the coast from San Francisco. Now that the train linked San Francisco with the east coast, farm implements and yardage were cheaper and easier to come by than when everything came around the Horn. Still, there was lots of competition at the Oregon docks for merchandise. Most of his trade nowadays was barter, and that didn't pay worth beans.

The booze he sold in the back room was the only part of the store operation that was in the black. The womenfolk had their quilting bees and Bible reading, but they couldn't seem to get it through their heads that men needed a place to drink and play cards. Agnes had turned into one of them holier-than-thou Methodists, which was quite a switch considering that he'd met her in a Sacramento saloon.

She'd been a pretty little thing once you got past her beaky nose. Hell, she was still a fine-looking woman, and she'd kept her figure even after popping out five babies. She'd had a hard life before he met up with her, and he'd never been much of a hand with women. He considered himself lucky she picked him even though he knew she had a loaf in the oven when he married her. Two identical loaves, as it turned out, but hell, it was as likely as not he was the father, wasn't it?

Sometimes it was hard to put up with her prissy ways these days, but he knew putting down roots was as important to Agnes as breathing. She'd look the other way no matter what went on in the back room or on his trips out of town as long as she had a solid roof over her head and the folks hereabouts treated her like she was really somebody.

No, he didn't have to worry about Agnes. What he had to worry about was the meddling sheriff. Without saying it in so many words, Ed had tried to let on that Cap probably knew more about things than anybody else, which was true as far as it went. The old fool had as much as admitted shooting off his rifle to put a scare into the schoolteacher.

Maybe the sheriff would put two and two together and they'd be rid of Cap Mackay permanently. Cap and Frenchy had gotten way too friendly of late, and if the old sot figured things out there was no telling where he'd start blabbing once he had a snootful. Meanwhile, Ed determined to hedge his bets by having a serious talk with Frenchy.

Tyler felt rejuvenated after an honest-to-goodness bath and a sleep in his own bed. He poured a second cup of coffee and finished off the scrambled eggs and sourdough biscuits Clayton had prepared.

He'd given his uncle a brief rundown on his trip to Oakfield and was waiting for Clayton's reaction and the inevitable advice that would accompany it. Clayton could no more help giving advice than he could help sweating. More often than not, his counsel was right on the mark.

"So you're heading back this afternoon to see the Indian woman and check in with the intriguing Miss Stratton?" Clayton peered over the top of his spectacles. "I notice you polished your boots and put on a clean shirt for the occasion. I'd like to know more about this schoolteacher, unless it's the blacksmith's widow you're trying to impress."

"I don't know what gave you the notion I'm interested in impressing anybody in Oakfield." Tyler knew his tone was defensive, which probably meant Clayton's remarks had hit home. "I've got a murder investigation to wrap up, and the schoolmarm is a nosy busybody who's got no business getting mixed up in it. The sooner she goes back to wherever she came from and marries her Norwegian farmer, the better off everybody will be."

"I declare, Tyler, you do get riled up sometimes. In these parts even an old maid schoolteacher has to be mud ugly to stay single for long. Is she really so hard on the eyes?"

Tyler felt a telltale flush creeping up the back of his neck as he pictured Bianca Stratton in his mind—the direct, no-nonsense gaze, the flyaway hair. Then there was her mouth, a bit generous, true, but with lips so full and soft he'd fantasized more than once about how they would respond to his kiss.

"She's as tall as I am, and bossy and over-educated to boot," he snapped.

Clayton raised a bushy eyebrow. "There's a lot to be said for an intelligent woman," he said. "Now tell me about this widow. I don't think I've ever had an Indian as a client before."

As usual, the discussion with Clayton helped clarify things in Tyler's mind. Of course, his uncle was way off in suggesting he was smitten with Bianca Stratton, but it was true she'd been in his thoughts more than a little. He was worried about her—that was all. She got people pretty upset when she pushed the minister into letting the young half-breed attend school. Cushing Pangston hadn't any backbone about him, and Tyler was sure the schoolteacher had no idea how strong people's feelings were when it came to Indians.

Joe Red Deer, the frightened boy he had in custody, had confessed to stealing chickens, but there was no evidence whatsoever to charge him with murder. The sad-eyed little fellow had already done enough jail time to pay for his petty crime. The circuit judge, due to arrive tomorrow, was not known as an Indian hater, so Tyler expected the lad would be sent back to the reservation as soon as his foot healed a bit.

Which brought Tyler back to the troubles at Oakfield. Even though the ragged little chicken thief hadn't killed Nolan, another redskin might have done the job. The widow protested, but maybe she was trying to shield somebody. Maybe she had relatives who weren't too happy about her marrying a white man. Or maybe Joanna grabbed something like a poker to defend herself, and managed to haul the body into the woods.

Anything was possible, and clearly Bianca Stratton had no idea how serious the situation was. If the shot in the woods was meant to scare her off and she kept right on with whatever was making somebody nervous, what might happen next? The longer he puzzled, the more worried he got.

He shouldn't have enlisted her help. Anything she said to her pupils was likely to get right back to the adults in the community, which could put her in even greater jeopardy. She needed to back off and leave the investigating to him. That would be the first thing he'd tell her when he met her at the blacksmith's house this afternoon. Despite what he'd told Uncle Clayton, he couldn't help looking forward to seeing her.

CHAPTER 27

Mindful of her talk with Sheriff Wells, Bianca encouraged more conversation than usual among her students. However, their chatter provided no new insights. She recalled the sheriff saying he thought Hank and Oren were being evasive, so during the noon recess she took her lunch basket to the grassy spot where they were sitting.

"You know," she said, "I've been thinking about the shot that buzzed by my head when I was walking home from the Nolan's place."

"We don't know nothing about no shot." Hank's response was immediate and defensive. "I don't know why everybody keeps pestering us about it. We never even left the ranch that evening. Ain't that right, Oren?"

Oren was quick to corroborate Hank's protestations of innocence. "That's right. We never did. We never hunt by the Nolan's place anyway. There's plenty of game in the woods north of our own pasture."

"I wasn't accusing you of anything," Bianca said mildly. "But you boys are known to be out with your guns in the evening, and—"

"So are lots of folks. Twilight's a good time for hunting rabbits. Everybody knows that." Hank extracted a piece of jerky from his knapsack and chewed noisily.

"First it was Aunt Nora, and then the sheriff treated us like a couple of outlaws. We never left the ranch. That's what we said the first time Aunt Nora asked us, and that's what we keep saying, because it's the truth. Right, Hank?"

"Right, Oren. Just 'cause nobody seen us for a couple of hours don't mean we wasn't at the ranch."

Bianca winced and made a mental note to have Hank spend more time parsing sentences. "Maybe that's the problem," she said.

"What do you mean?" Oren blinked and tried to look unconcerned.

"Seems like it'd be easy to clear things up. I mean, if folks knew exactly where you were during those evening hours when nobody saw you . . . "

Hank frowned at Oren.

"Unless, of course, you were getting into some other kind of trouble." Bianca could tell from the stricken expression on Hank's face that she'd hit a nerve.

"I guess we better tell, Oren. We're in for it either way." Hank ran a hand through his untidy hair.

"Be quiet." Oren shot Hank an angry look. "We never lied, Miss Stratton."

"I ain't getting in no more trouble," Hank protested.

"Well . . . "

Bianca sensed Oren wavering. "Of course, if you've broken a law or put some innocent person in danger—"

"We never broke no law." Hank was obviously anxious to get something off his chest. "We was out behind the horse barn the whole time."

"Aunt Nora will have my hide if she finds out," Oren protested, but his tone was less vehement than before.

Bianca waited.

Oren finally broke the silence. "What it was, Miss Stratton, well—we was smoking."

"We both signed the pledge when the traveling priest was here." Hank said. "We promised not to touch tobacco or hard spirits until we was eighteen."

"And we never did until Hank found a corncob pipe lying on the floor of the bunkhouse."

"But Oren—he dared me."

"And then Hank got sick and started throwing up."

"Well, you was all green and sweaty looking."

"Yeah, but I never threw up."

"Oren, I'm sure your aunt will forgive you," Bianca said. "Especially since it seems you're not likely to try tobacco again soon."

"It ain't really the smokin' part that worries us," Hank explained. "It's the fire part."

"When Hank started throwing up, he dropped the pipe in a patch of dry brush near the barn. I never even noticed, being as how I wasn't feeling so good myself. Anyway, as soon as I saw the blaze, I grabbed a bucket and filled it from the horse trough."

"So you put out the fire before it did any damage?"

Oren nodded. "Well, almost. There's a scorched place on the corner of the barn, but nothing really bad. I was pretty scared there for a few minutes, and afterward I was going to own up to Aunt Nora before Jesse or somebody went out behind the barn and noticed. But then there was the fire over at the blacksmith's place, and—"

"Seems like anything bad happens around here, everybody starts blaming me and Oren."

"The fire at the Nolan's house started on the roof," Bianca said. "Nobody would believe you had anything to do with it."

"I guess you're right. I know we ought to own up about the barn, but I hate to think what Aunt Nora's going to do when I tell her."

"When we tipped over the outhouse last Halloween, she locked up Oren's rifle for a whole month, and my uncle, he tanned my hide."

"Sometimes when you admit you're wrong, folks realize you're growing up and getting to be more responsible." Bianca said.

"You think so?" Oren asked hopefully.

"It's a possibility." Bianca stood, brushing the crumbs from Mattie's leaden sourdough biscuit off her lap. "I hope you'll let me know what you decide to do. But now it's time to get back to our lessons."

The rest of the school day flew by. Bianca was sure Oren and Hank's story was the truth. Of course, Tyler Wells would say she was making an assumption before all the facts were at hand. She couldn't help feeling frustrated at the sheriff's painstaking deliberations. Maybe when she convinced him Oren and Hank weren't involved he'd be closer to finding out who was really responsible. She'd tell him so when she met him at Nolan's place later in the afternoon.

CHAPTER 28

Running Fox kept well out of sight as he threaded his sure-footed pinto through an ancient path, paralleling the road that ran from east to west at the north end of Oakfield. The wagon track they called Stage Road ran from north to south, and he crossed it cautiously, dismounting, retracing his steps and obliterating the mare's hoof prints. He disappeared behind a thicket of olallie berry bushes when he heard footsteps. Peering out, he saw an old man in a filthy buckskin jacket, a rifle slung over his shoulder.

Running Fox figured from Joanna's description of the settlers that this must be the old soldier they called Cap. The man stopped, pulled a battered metal flask from his pocket and took a swig. Then, with whiskey dribbling down his already matted beard, he headed purposefully on. Curious, Running Fox followed, leading the mare and staying among the trees where a carpet of cedar and pine needles muffled any sound.

Before long he caught a whiff of smoke in the air. Minutes later he spotted a small cabin only a few hundred feet from the road but tucked so snugly into the woods that a traveler could easily pass by without knowing it was there.

He slipped off his horse and waited until he heard Cap holler, "Hey there, Frenchy. Open up."

Huge trees surrounding the cabin made concealment a simple matter, and Running Fox quickly found a vantage point for observing the front of the cabin. Cap stood on the porch and pounded his rifle on the door. Running Fox remembered Aiden talking about a trapper who lived in the woods and liked to fish. No doubt the boy had been describing this Frenchy person who opened the door and motioned Cap inside.

Instinctively, Running Fox felt he should eavesdrop. Such hunches had served him well in the past. He slipped to a corner of the cabin where the broken pane of a small window was covered with yellowed newspaper. He couldn't see inside the cabin, but neither could they see him, and by putting his ear close to the window, he could hear their voices clearly.

Although it was sometimes useful to act as if he didn't understand, Running Fox had spent enough time at the missionary school to become fluent in the white man's language. They were talking about a sheriff who had been questioning everyone about the murder of the blacksmith. The hoarse voice, like the call of a crow, was the one he'd heard hollering. That would be Cap. The low, musical voice, which must be Frenchy, was saying he'd been out checking his traps and hadn't seen the sheriff or anybody else. Running Fox cursed silently, wondering why his sister hadn't said anything about a sheriff nosing around.

"The sooner the squaw and her boy go back to where they belong, the better," Cap was saying.

"Aiden's a good boy. He likes to fish with me. It's too bad he was hurt. I don't suppose you know anything about the fire."

The voices grew loud, and Running Fox no longer had to keep his ear close to the broken window. Frenchy was saying he knew Cap had fired the shot at the teacher and he'd probably set the fire too. Then both men started talking at once, and it was difficult to understand. It was obvious, though, that Cap was angrily denying all Frenchy's accusations and Frenchy didn't believe Cap's alibis.

"That's the truth, Frenchy," Cap's voice was almost a whine.

"Truth! You wouldn't know the truth if it bit you on the ass! Hell, for all I know you murdered Daniel Nolan, too."

"Maybe Daniel Nolan stumbled onto something you and Ed Fowler didn't want him to see, and you—"

"Don't be an idiot! Nolan was harmless, even when he drank too much."

"I don't think his squaw would agree with you there. The way I hear it, he knocked her around pretty good."

"Well, I guess that's true. Aiden did tell me his father was mean to his mother sometimes, and he wished his uncle would come and make his father stop. He said his uncle was a big, powerful chief who could lick his dad with one hand tied behind his back."

"I never heard of the squaw woman having no relatives, much less some Injun chief," Cap was saying. "Probably that was just a tall tale."

"Aiden's quite a talker, but I never knew him to lie."

Running Fox suppressed a chuckle at hearing himself described as a fierce, powerful chief. Despite what he had told Joanna, survival at his mountain hideaway was a precarious day-to-day matter. Still, it was a shock that these men knew of his existence. Aiden needed to learn not to speak of family matters. He was dismayed that Joanna hadn't instilled more caution in the boy, but that was what came of her disastrous marriage.

"I wonder if the sheriff knows about this Injun. Maybe I oughta make sure he does."

"If Tyler Wells is asking questions all over Oakfield, maybe he's thinking the murderer's no Indian," Frenchy said.

"The man was scalped, for Christ sake. Nobody but a savage would do that."

"There are plenty of tales about white soldiers taking scalps during the Indian wars. Funny you never heard about it."

"Well, I never. I shot Injuns, plenty of them, but I never cut on one, if that's what you're getting at. Still, I ain't going to pretend I'm sorry they'll be packing the squaw and the little half-breed off to the reservation."

"If she's got papers, she won't have to go to the reservation."

"Papers or no papers, if she's got any sense at all she'll get out of Oakfield. Folks around here only put up with her because they thought we needed a blacksmith. Once the pity wears off she'll be in for a rough go."

"I don't know. Aiden's mighty excited about getting to go to school like a white kid, and she sets a lot of store by the boy."

"The school thing ain't going to last. If somebody's willing to take the squaw's place off her hands and give her some cash, she should be grateful. After all, she's lucky to have a roof over her head. Next time there's a fire in the neighborhood things could be a lot worse."

Running Fox's fist clenched in anger. Then he slipped back into the forest, his mind struggling to assimilate everything he'd overheard. So Aiden was attending a white man's school, another detail his sister had neglected to mention. After a moment's reflection he was forced to concede he hadn't given her much chance to talk. If he hadn't lost his temper and started issuing orders, she might have spoken more freely.

Even as children he and his sister had squabbled constantly, and it was hard for him to remember she was no longer the little girl he could boss around. For the first time he considered that she might think he was responsible for Daniel's death. Everyone in his mountain hideaway would swear to his whereabouts. Even though such reassurance would mean nothing where white law was concerned, it might put his sister's mind at ease.

The men in the cabin were right about his dislike of Daniel Nolan and all he represented, but he was greatly disturbed to hear himself accused of the murder. If those men knew about his sister's renegade brother, it only a matter of time before the sheriff knew it too. Maybe it was time to change his plans.

Etienne "Frenchy" Blauchet breathed a sigh of relief when Cap Mackay finally left. The old man's offhand remarks about Ed Fowler set Frenchy's teeth on edge. He'd been worried since Cap caught up with him and Ed heading out with that loaded wagon. Cap was no fool. Even with more liquor in him than the average man could handle, he might put two and two together.

Today when Cap said he was going to talk to the widow Nolan, Frenchy had refilled the old man's well-worn flask. Between booze and preoccupation with getting hold of Nolan's land, maybe Mackay would lose interest in what Ed and Frenchy were up to. For a little extra insurance, Frenchy thought he'd stop by Fowler's store and mention that Nolan's widow had a brother who might have had a grudge against the blacksmith. That should start Agnes Fowler's tongue wagging.

Frenchy was amused at Agnes Fowler's pretensions of Christian piety while she turned a blind eye to Ed's activities. Ed Fowler was quietly piling up cash by selling Frenchy's booze to a greedy Indian agent whose reservation trading post was poorly stocked with foodstuffs and tools but amply supplied with bad whiskey. Meanwhile Ed ranted about his motley brood having to attend school with a half-breed.

Frenchy's attitude was purely pragmatic. The bible-thumping Protestants who carried on about the evils of alcohol were among his best customers. Even Cushing Pangston had been known to pay a surreptitious visit to Frenchy's cabin for a bottle, ostensibly for the disinfecting of cuts and abrasions. Frenchy winked, nodded and obliged. And if the poor redskins wanted a few drinks to ease the misery of their existence on the reservation, what right did the government have to deny them? He and Ed were providing a public service, when you came right down to it.

As a youngster Frenchy had chafed at the restrictions of life at his parents' estate outside Quebec City. He spent hours trapped in a chilly drawing room while he ached to run free outdoors. He hated his velvet suits and lace collars. The violin lessons weren't so bad, but he longed for lively tunes rather than endless etudes and finger exercises. His English tutor coughed incessantly and smelled of camphor, but when young Etienne stole gold pieces from his father's safe, it was the tutor who accepted a bribe and helped him escape. Frenchy was fourteen when he saddled a horse from the family stable and joined a group of ruffians heading west. He never looked back.

Trapping for the Hudson Bay Company throughout the Pacific Northwest, he discovered the natives were pretty much like everybody else, some good, some bad, some hostile, some peaceable, some simple, some clever. Many of his fellow trappers had taken up with native women and raised large broods of youngsters who all seemed to be larger, healthier and smarter than either of their parents.

Frenchy himself had tied up with a Yakima girl and even had the union blessed by Father Jacques, who had also taught him the rudiments of distilling hard spirits. His young wife had carried their first child only a few months when she came down with measles and died. More than thirty years later he still looked back on the brief span before her death as the happiest time of his life.

He'd done a lot of wandering after that, logging, prospecting, and trapping. These days an old hip injury plagued him mightily in the winter, so he'd meandered southward. Lately he'd been thinking about California, and if things around here got too sticky he was ready to pull up stakes at a moment's notice.

Cushing Pangston hung his dirt-spattered overalls on the hook near the screen door and changed into the starched shirt and soft twill pants Mattie had set out before she left to do her marketing.

Tuesday was his day to call on the sick and the elderly, and anybody else who'd been missing church for more than a Sunday or two. The latter group, he thought ruefully, pretty much outnumbered those who attended regularly. Today his first stop would be a visit to an elderly couple who hadn't been to services since Easter and probably wouldn't turn up again until Christmas, but who, thank the Lord, were conscientious about their tithing.

He hitched up the wagon and headed out of the barnyard when something fluttering on the front gatepost caught his eye.

He reined in Flossie, the aging plow horse who seemed to perk up considerably on Tuesdays when she got to leave the farm, and retrieved a piece of paper that had been nailed to the post.

The message was printed in uneven, block letters on copybook paper like his girls used for their homework. He could feel an angry flush creep up his neck as he read the words.

WE DONT NEED NO INJUN LOVRS TEECHIN ARE CHILDRN YOU BETTR GIT RID OF THAT WOMN BFOR ENNYTHIN ELS BAD HAPPNS OR IS SHE YOUR LOVR TO ?

Reflexively Cushing's hand crumpled the paper into a ball, and he reached into his pants pocket for a box of matches. He'd known Bianca Stratton was going to be trouble, but he hadn't expected her to get the whole village in an uproar. He struck a match, relishing the acrid sulfur fumes that seemed to mirror his state of mind. Then, after staring a moment at the flame, he blew it out and crammed the note into his pocket with the matchbox.

Acting impulsively had brought him grief in the past, and he could always destroy the note after he thought things through. Who would write such garbage, anyway? How could anyone even hint that he would break his sacred marriage vows? Mattie was the greatest blessing the Lord had bestowed upon him. He'd feel better after he talked to her. Maybe he'd even show Mattie the note when he got back from his rounds. He didn't like keeping secrets from her. She had a sixth sense about that sort of thing and generally wormed the truth out of him anyway.

He flicked the reins and Flossie plodded forward. Bianca his lover? The notion was ludicrous. He'd as soon try to bed a porcupine.

CHAPTER 29

As she walked up the path to Joanna's house, Bianca noted that no smoke rose from the chimney. Joanna was probably at the ranch with Aiden, and there was no sign of the sheriff. Not really expecting a response, she walked to the door, gave a perfunctory knock and stepped back in surprise when the door swung open at her touch. Then, seeing Joanna's precious box lying open with papers scattered over the table and the floor, she froze.

Everything was quiet except for the pounding in her temples. She commanded herself to be cautious, to think things through. The box, sitting in plain view, had obviously survived the fire. But the unlatched door and scattered papers meant someone had been inside. Maybe an intruder was still hiding in the house, someone who heard her footsteps and was even now watching through a crack in the kitchen door. Sheriff Wells will be here soon, she thought. I'll be safe out by the gate.

She stepped off the porch, silently commending herself for her prudence, when a new thought halted her. What if Joanna hadn't gone to the ranch? If an intruder had found Joanna at home, she could be lying inside, hurt. Or worse. A heavy rake was propped against the wall near the front stoop. Bianca grabbed it and headed for the open door, brandishing her makeshift weapon.

"What the devil are you up to now?"

At Tyler's shout she whirled and lowered the rake, her knees weak with relief. A smartly outfitted buggy pulled by a sleek roan stallion wheeled up to the gate. Moments later the sheriff was at her side.

"Better hand me the rake before you hurt somebody." His jocular expression turned grave as she explained. Then he drew his six-shooter and started for the door. "Don't take one step until I've searched the place."

No sounds came from inside the house. Apparently Tyler Wells could move as silently as a thief when he chose. She waited, impressed by the way he'd taken charge so competently. Minutes later he was back on the porch, his pistol back in its leather holster, his Stetson pushed back on his head.

"There's nobody inside and no sign of Mrs. Nolan," he said, "but somebody has been here, somebody wearing boots. I found fresh footprints around back at the edge of the garden."

"When I first got here I thought Joanna had probably gone over to the Donovan place. Then I saw those papers scattered around, and—"

"The little buckskin mare is gone, and there's no sign of a struggle. She probably left before the intruder got here."

"I hope you're right," Bianca said.

"Come inside and help me check things out."

Bianca nodded and started up the path.

"You can put the rake down now."

"I'd have used it if I'd had to." Bianca's tone was defiant, but her hands were still shaking as she unclenched her fingers and replaced the tool where she'd found it.

"I don't doubt it for a minute." He grinned down at her from the porch, and she noticed that his eyes now seemed to be a smoky blue. "Still, I'm glad I got here when I did."

So am I, Bianca thought, but she wasn't about to admit it aloud.

Inside, Tyler gathered up the scattered papers while Bianca sorted and replaced them in the wooden box.

"The will and deed aren't here, and neither is the marriage certificate, but I'm not sure about anything else," she said. The letters—they're from Daniel's first wife—they were tied with this bit of blue ribbon when I saw them before. And the clippings and photographs—I didn't pay close enough attention to be able tell you if they're all here."

"I'll take the box along and head over toward the Donovan ranch. I seem to do a better job talking to Mrs. Nolan when you're there, so I'd be pleased if you'd come with me. I'll get you back home by suppertime."

Bianca assured him that missing supper at Mattie's would be no loss and climbed into the buggy. "Maybe Joanna kept those papers with her. She knew how important they were," she said.

"Well, I hope that's the case. But somebody else was in the black-smith's house, and my money's on that old scoundrel, Cap Mackay."

"He could cause a lot of trouble for Joanna and Aiden if he destroyed those papers."

"I think trouble must be Mackay's middle name."

Bianca stole a look at the sheriff, who was sitting properly beside her and handling the rig with the same easy competence she'd observed earlier. She forced herself to put Joanna and her troubles out of her mind. After all, there was nothing she could do at the moment, and it was, she noted with surprise, a lovely autumn day. When she'd made this trip with Mattie the trees by the river had been lush and green, but a sharp frost had turned them into a riot of crimson and honey.

"Beautiful, isn't it?" Tyler Wells waved his free hand at the panorama of color.

"Incredible. This is such a charming little valley. It almost seems unreal that such terrible things could be happening here. Which reminds me—I haven't told you about wringing a confession from Oren and Hank."

By the time Bianca finished relating the smoking episode, both she and Tyler were laughing out loud. In fact, the distance to the ranch seemed considerably shorter than when she'd traveled it with Mattie, and the buggy was a great deal more comfortable than the minister's creaky farm wagon.

"This is a fine rig," she remarked as they started through the gate to the ranch. "I seem to remember you were on horseback before."

"The horse and buggy belong to my uncle," he said. "My bay threw a shoe yesterday, and he was due for a rest anyway. If I spend the night at the ranch I plan to offer Mrs. Nolan and Aiden a ride home tomorrow if he's ready to travel."

Nora Donovan greeted Bianca and Tyler warmly. Bianca recalled the wounded look that had followed Mattie's curt refusal to stay for tea. She'd make sure Mrs. Donovan understood she didn't share Mattie's prejudices.

"Joanna came early today," Nora said. "She was determined to take Aiden home, but, with some assistance from Doc Schneider, I've persuaded her to stay for a few days."

Tyler said, "Oh, then Doc's been here."

"Early this afternoon. He says Aiden's doing well, but he wants to give those vocal cords more rest."

"I've heard smoke damage is tricky," Tyler said.

"But Aiden's going to be all right? He'll be able to speak?" Bianca couldn't keep the anxiety out of her voice.

"The doctor is hopeful," Nora said. "He was really interested in Joanna's herbs."

"Herbs?" asked Bianca.

"She's got a kettle steaming on the hearth in Aiden's room. You'll see. In fact, you'll smell it long before you get there. Mr. Wells and I will wait here."

The aroma that greeted Bianca as she stepped onto the veranda was a mix of cedar, juniper and some other less familiar scents, spicy and not altogether pleasant, but also somehow soothing. As she reached the door, she almost collided with Oren, who was carrying a leather-bound history book she'd loaned him.

"Oh, Miss Stratton. Wasn't expecting to run into you until school tomorrow," he said with a grin.

"Good afternoon, Oren. I see you've been reading."

"Well, Aiden seems to like me to stop by and read out loud some." Oren was clearly embarrassed at being caught in an act of kindness. "I'm stuck in the house anyway."

"I'm sure Aiden appreciates your company."

"I guess. Seeing as how I'm not allowed to get together with Hank unless Aunt Nora or Jesse is with us."

"I gather you're being punished."

"It's not too bad. It's only for a month, and I guess I do feel better now that we owned up. Hank and I still get to help Jesse work with the horses. Jesse got Aunt Nora to agree on counting it as one of our chores."

"Well, I'm glad things are working out."

"Yes, Ma'am." Oren headed back toward the parlor, whistling between his teeth.

Inside the bedroom Bianca found Aiden bundled into a comfortable chair by the hearth, a patchwork comforter tucked around his legs. An iron kettle simmered beside him, sending ribbons of steam into air already thick with scent.

Joanna, smoothing the bedcovers, greeted Bianca with a broad smile. Aiden held out his arms for a hug, and Bianca happily complied. His skin, almost the same olive shade as her own, had lost most of the pallor she'd noted on her previous visit.

"Mrs. Donovan tells me the doctor says you're much better, but I could tell by looking at you."

Aiden nodded.

"He still must not speak," Joanna said.

"Yes, you need to take care of your throat," Bianca agreed. "But I have an idea. Do you remember the game we sometimes play at school—the game called Twenty Questions?"

Aiden nodded.

"I think we should show your mother how much fun it is. Only you'll have to be the teacher."

Aiden's response was a puzzled frown.

"When we play at school, I think of an object, you children ask questions, and I answer yes or no. So now, you think of something. I'll ask the questions, and you can answer by nodding or shaking your head. All right?"

Aiden nodded, his dark eyes shining.

The game continued until Bianca had used all twenty questions without guessing that the object was the slingshot he retrieved from the folds of the comforter.

"That was a hard one! But now I need to talk to your mother for a few minutes." She handed him the primer she'd brought. "You're getting to be such a good reader, I bet you can read silently now. You sound out the words inside your head instead of saying them aloud. That's the way grown-ups read, and you're really growing up fast."

Aiden opened the book eagerly, and Joanna followed Bianca back onto the veranda. Bianca explained why she'd stopped by the house and described what she and the sheriff had found there.

"You worry for us. You kind lady." Joanna said. Then she slipped back into the steamy room and reappeared carrying one of the colorful baskets Bianca remembered. Joanna reached into the basket and pulled out the deed, the will and the marriage certificate.

"Aiden run into fire. Save papers," Joanna said. "I keep close now."

"We brought your box and the rest of the papers with us," Bianca said. "Was there anything else—-anything valuable—that someone would want to steal?"

Joanna glanced down at the basket and hesitated. "All important papers here," she said. "Papers in box are Daniel's. Most from years before Aiden and me."

"Well, I'm relieved you've kept everything safe," Bianca said, following Joanna back into the bedroom. Then, recalling her first visit, she said, "Aiden, do you remember when I came and brought you the copybook the children made?"

Aiden nodded and smiled.

"You were pretty sick then, but I thought there was something you wanted to say. We could play twenty questions again, only this time it won't really be a game. Do you want to do that?"

Aiden nodded, his eyes dark and solemn.

"So there was something you wanted to tell me?"

Aiden's eyes darted toward where Joanna was standing beside his chair.

"Do you want your mother to leave?"

Aiden shook his head and took hold of his mother's hand. Joanna smiled.

"What you wanted to tell me—was it about school?"

Aiden shook his head.

"About the fire?"

An emphatic nod.

"Is it about how you got hurt?"

Another no.

"Something that happened later?"

He shook his head again.

"Something that happened before you went inside to get the box?"

A tentative nod.

"Would it help me to know where you were?"

Another nod. More emphatic.

"He is in the house with me when we smell the smoke," Joanna said.

Aiden waved his hands impatiently at his mother and turned back to Bianca.

"Is this something that happened before you and your mother saw the smoke?"

Aiden nodded.

"Did you see something, Aiden?"

A vehement nod.

"Was it a person? Did you see somebody?"

Aiden nodded and knotted his little face into a fierce scowl. Then he pantomimed a long beard.

"Cap!" Bianca exclaimed. "Was it Cap?"

A solemn nod.

"Did he start the fire? Did you see him start the fire?"

Aiden shook his head and slumped back into the chair, clearly exhausted by the game.

"That's enough for now," Bianca said, brushing back the lock of shiny black hair that had fallen across his forehead. "You did a good job, Aiden. I know this has all been scary for you, but you and your mother are both safe here."

She prayed it was true.

Leaving Joanna with Aiden, Bianca returned to the large front room where Nora Donovan and Tyler Wells were seated on massive leather chairs flanking the fireplace. Nora poured tea from a silver pot into a paper-thin china cup and motioned Bianca into a chair beside Tyler.

"I won't take no for an answer this afternoon," she said, passing a plate filled with an assortment of tiny pastries.

"Oh, these look delicious!" Bianca helped herself to a square of rich chocolate cake topped with walnuts and whipped cream. It had been so long since she had tasted anything really edible that it was difficult to nibble delicately as etiquette demanded.

"I'll send a few home with you," Nora Donovan said.

"Oh, I'm sure the Pangston girls will be delighted," Bianca said. The tea was full-bodied and smelled of oranges. She added a dollop of thick cream, sipped and sighed with contentment.

"Rolf Knudsen mentioned staying for supper at the Pangston's." Nora's dark eyes danced. "He seemed to appreciate the snack I fixed him later."

"Is Mattie Pangston's cooking really as terrible as everybody says?" Tyler asked.

"Don't put Miss Stratton on the spot, Sheriff," Nora said.

Bianca searched for a change of subject. "Aiden doesn't look nearly so peaked today," she said. "I'm pleased he's feeling better."

"I really think Joanna's herbs are helping," Nora said. "Doc Schneider thinks so too. He says some of the native remedies are better than the ones he learned about in medical school."

"Well, I'm sure they're better than those patent medicines they sell at Fowler's store," Bianca said.

"Lots of those patent medicines are mostly alcohol," Tyler said. "I don't know how anybody expects me to enforce temperance laws when the people who holler the loudest about Demon Rum are the ones nodding off into their soup after dosing themselves with some miracle elixir."

"So you look the other way while Ed Fowler sells whiskey." Nora refilled his cup. "What else can you do? It's a bad law."

"Still," Bianca said, "it is the law. People can't pick and choose which laws they'll obey."

"Our earnest Miss Stratton isn't one to compromise on principles," said Tyler. "When I was seventeen I guess I saw everything as black and white, too. Now I only seem to see shades of gray."

"Sounds like a pretty serious discussion for afternoon tea."

At the sound of Jesse Landry's gravelly voice, Bianca looked up to see the foreman filling the large doorway.

"Join us." Nora Donovan motioned him to the empty chair.

Bianca found herself seated opposite Jesse, looking directly into his eyes and holding the gaze much longer than she intended. She looked away, helped herself to a tart, and felt her face flushing as she noted that the blueberries were the exact shade of Jesse's eyes.

"It's time for me to be getting back." She stood and crossed the room to where Joanna's wooden box sat on a table near the terrace door. "I'll stop in and say goodbye to Aiden."

"I'd be happy to see Miss Stratton home," Jesse said. "I'm sure you've already had a long, busy day, Sheriff."

"My buggy's all hitched up and ready to roll," Tyler said, "so you needn't trouble yourself."

"No trouble. No trouble at all. I'd consider it a pleasure."

"I still have some business to take care of in Oakfield, so I'll be heading that direction anyway."

"No need for you to go out of your way to drop Miss Stratton off."

Bianca stood in the doorway, Joanna's box in her hand, not sure whether she felt embarrassed or flattered at the banter.

Nora Donovan smiled and poured herself another cup of tea. "It might be a good idea to ask Miss Stratton," she said.

Being escorted home by Jesse Landry would cause talk, and it simply wouldn't do to encourage his attentions. There was no room in her life for that sort of thing. Bianca knew only too well where it led. Tyler Wells, on the other hand, presented no problem. True, she found his company pleasant, but he was simply doing a job. Besides, she needed to tell him about Cap lurking near the Nolan place before the fire.

"Thank you for your kind offer, Mr. Landry," she said primly, "but I think it's best I return with the sheriff. I shall only be a moment, Mr. Wells, but do take time to finish your tea."

She found Aiden back in bed, sleeping soundly.

"His face is cool, and he breathes well," Joanna said.

"I'm glad you and Aiden are going to stay at the ranch for a few days. We don't know for sure Cap started the fire, but you're much safer here until the sheriff gets to the bottom of things."

"Yes. Aiden must be safe."

Bianca handed over the box. "You might want to look through the papers in case something is missing."

"All papers look alike to my eyes. Aiden look in box many times. Aiden try read everything."

"Well, the box will be safe here, and Aiden can look at the papers again when he's feeling up to it."

"Thank you, Miss Stratton. You good to us."

Bianca brushed Aiden's forehead with a kiss, blinking back tears at the sight of his bandaged hands and his small, vulnerable body.

"I'll be back soon," she whispered.

CHAPTER 30

As soon as she settled into the buggy, Bianca told the sheriff about the game she'd played with Aiden. "Cap was there," she concluded. "Aiden saw him just before the fire started."

"I'm glad you didn't say anything about this while we were inside," he said.

"Well, it seemed better to wait."

"Not that I think anybody at the ranch is involved, but news has a way of traveling around here. I don't want Cap to get wind of what we know."

"Are you going to arrest him?"

"Not until I've got more to go on."

"But if Aiden saw him—"

"Now, don't go jumping to conclusions, Bianca." Tyler bit his lip. "Sorry, Miss Stratton. It just slipped out. I don't mean to be taking liberties."

"I think we know one another well enough to be on a first-name basis," she said. "And you're right—about jumping to conclusions. It's a habit I'm trying to break."

"Cap may well have been near the Nolan's place when the fire started, but that doesn't mean he was responsible."

"That's true. Aiden didn't say he saw Cap actually start the fire."

"Aiden didn't really *say* anything. When he can finally talk and tell me in his own words what happened, I'll know more."

Bianca frowned. "Are you implying I put words in his mouth?"

"Of course not. Not intentionally, anyway. But he's a small boy, and you're his teacher. You probably have more influence than you realize."

"If you'd seen Aiden's face, if you'd been there—"

"Well, I wasn't."

"Tyler Wells, you are the most exasperating man!"

"And you, Bianca Stratton, are enough to test the patience of a saint."

"Well, a sheriff who doesn't enforce the temperance laws is hardly a candidate for sainthood."

Tyler snapped the whip, and the stallion picked up the pace. Bianca regretted getting involved in yet another argument when it had seemed she and the difficult Mr. Wells—she wouldn't dream of calling him Tyler—were beginning to understand each other. The set of his jaw convinced her anything she said now would only make matters worse, so they completed the trip in stony silence.

Tyler helped Bianca out of the buggy. Then, instead of getting back in the rig and driving away, as she had assumed he would, he kept a courtly hand on her elbow and escorted her to the door.

Cushing was waiting on the front porch. "Good evening, Sheriff," he called. "I'm glad to see you have Miss Stratton with you. We were beginning to worry. Supper's on the table."

"There was a break-in at the Nolan's house," Tyler said. "Miss Stratton was kind enough to accompany me to the Donovan ranch and help with my investigation. I'm sure she didn't intend to cause you concern."

Cushing stood at the doorway clearing his throat. Mattie appeared behind him, her blue gingham apron splattered with grease.

"Come in, come in!" she said. "Supper's waiting, and Mr. Wells, you simply must join us."

"Why, that's very kind of you, Ma'am."

"I'm afraid the sheriff has pressing business in town," Bianca said.

"Nothing that can't wait until after supper." Tyler shot Bianca an irritated look, removed his hat, and followed the Pangstons into the house where the reek of hot fatback overpowered any aroma of whatever else Mattie had piled into the skillet.

The girls were already seated at the table, and Cushing favored them with a simple grace and a minimum of stammers.

"Help yourself to the fried chicken, Sheriff Wells," Mattie said, passing a platter of lumps the color of burnt toast.

Bianca watched with amusement as Tyler speared the smallest piece. Fried potatoes swimming in grease followed, along with a bowl of succotash boiled to mush. Bianca helped herself to applesauce, which looked harmless enough, but was so tart it puckered her mouth. She gave Tyler an I-told-you-so look as she watched him struggle to extract a chewable piece of chicken from the charred remains on his plate.

"I heard you say you were at the Donovan place," Katie said, adding salt and pepper to the succotash.

"Did you see Aiden?" Gertrude asked.

"Can he talk yet?" Cora chimed in.

"He's feeling better, but the doctor doesn't want him to try to speak yet," Bianca said.

"I didn't know doctors treated Indians," Gertrude said. "Don't they have medicine men?"

"Aiden's only half Indian," Katie pointed out.

"And I bet whenever Mrs. Donovan calls the doctor, he comes." Cora said. "Oren says she's really rich, and everybody does what she says."

"That will do," Mattie said. "You know we don't gossip."

Tina regarded Tyler curiously. "Are you the Reb?" she asked, banging her spoon on the table for emphasis.

"Tina!" Cushing scowled. "We don't ask rude questions of guests in this house."

Tina's lower lip trembled at her father's surprisingly harsh tone. Then she began to wail, which effectively ended table conversation for the remainder of the meal.

By the time the three older girls cleared the table, Tina had subsided into muffled sobs and hiccups. While Mattie poured anemic brew from the coffeepot, Bianca brought out the basket Nora Donovan had pressed into her hands as she was leaving the ranch.

After everyone consumed the pastries with obvious enjoyment, Cushing stood and placed his folded napkin on the table. "Before you . . . er . . . leave us, Sheriff," he said, "there's something—"

"Perhaps it would be best if we all step into the parlor," Mattie suggested. "Away from little ears."

Bianca and Tyler followed Mattie, with Cushing trailing behind.

"I suppose you want to know more about the break-in at the Nolan's house," Tyler said. "Actually, nothing was—"

"Actually," Mattie interrupted, "we want to show you what Cushing found nailed to the gatepost when he left on his rounds this morning." She handed the note to Tyler, who read it silently and passed it to Bianca.

Bianca felt a flush flood her face, whether from anger or humiliation she couldn't be sure. She seemed to be feeling both emotions in full measure.

"I don't think you realize, Bianca, how much trouble you've stirred up around here," Mattie said.

"I'm sure Miss Stratton has only acted from the best of intentions," Tyler said.

"And we all know where the road paved with good intentions leads," Cushing snapped without the slightest hesitation.

"And we all know an anonymous note is the work of a small-minded coward," Tyler retorted. "In this case, apparently, a badly educated one as well. The question is, what's to be done about it?"

"We could . . . simply . . . ignore the entire business." The suggestion that some kind of action on Cushing's part might be required brought the stammers back in force.

"Unless you're seriously considering finding a way to terminate Miss Stratton's teaching position, that's probably the wisest course," Tyler said.

"But that writing—it's disgusting." Mattie said. "Not that anyone who really knows Cushing would believe for a minute that—"

"It's the threat of something else bad happening that worries me," Tyler said. "I suspect our anonymous writer didn't think anyone but Mr. Pangston would see this scurrilous bit of prose."

"I almost destroyed it the minute I read it," Cushing admitted.

"Well, I'm glad you didn't," Tyler said. "May I hang onto it for a spell?"

"Of course," Cushing said. "It may well be part of all the other trouble we've been having."

"Then, again, it may not be," Tyler said.

"You'll never catch Sheriff Wells leaping to conclusions," Bianca said. "Even obvious ones."

"Miss Stratton believes I'm overly cautious," Tyler said with a smile.

"A little prudence wouldn't be amiss where you're concerned, Bianca," Mattie said tartly.

Bianca bit back a retort. Mattie's attitude about many things might be totally incomprehensible, but in this case she was saying exactly what Viola would have said. Instead of needling the sheriff for doing his job conscientiously, Bianca knew she should be doing everything possible to assist him. She vowed anew to curb her tongue and think before she spoke. Of course, that would be easier said than done, considering that Tyler Wells was an impossibly irritating man.

"I'd best be on my way. I intend to stop by Fowler's before I head on back to the ranch for the night." Tyler clapped his

Stetson on his head and started for the door. "Thanks for your hospitality, Mrs. Pangston."

"You'll look into that awful note business, won't you?" Mattie's forehead furrowed in concern.

"Yes, ma'am. There's plenty around here needs looking into."

Bianca followed the sheriff outside. Somehow she felt she ought to make amends for the disastrous evening. "I'm sorry about everything," she said, flapping her hand self-consciously.

Tyler stopped at the gate and turned to face her. "I can't say I wasn't forewarned about the food."

"Yes. You did bring that on yourself, but I needn't have—"

"I'm getting used to your barbs. In fact, I'd have to say I'm starting to look forward to seeing where the next one's going to land."

She shook her head. "Saying the first thing that comes to mind is a terrible flaw. I know it, but I can't seem to——"

"Don't be so hard on yourself. I've been around far too many women who are all riddles and innuendo. Your directness is refreshing. It's part of your charm, Bianca."

She stiffened at the use of her given name, but she'd given permission in a weak moment, and there seemed no way of turning the clock back. "Well, it's been an interesting day, anyway," she said lamely.

"No disagreement there. But from now on you'd better stick to your teaching. No more trying to get information from your students. No more drop-in visits to the Nolan widow. You're in danger, Bianca. That nasty note only underscores the fact."

Tyler's hand brushed her shoulder, his touch so feather light she almost wondered if she imagined it. Then he jumped into the buggy and drove off, leaving her standing alone in the chill, moonless night.

Upstairs in her attic room, Bianca put on her flannel nightgown and gave her hair the required hundred brush strokes. Then she stretched out on the creaky bed and puzzled over the day's events. Her stomach knotted as she acknowledged that someone in Oakfield disliked her enough to scribble a vitriolic note.

Tyler Wells had admonished her to stick to teaching school, but the note was written on paper that appeared to have been torn from a copybook belonging to one of her students. How could she fail to track down the source? The copybooks her pupils used were among the supplies she'd brought with her from Wesleyville. She marked each student's work daily while she discussed individual progress. Copybooks went home at the end of each day along with homework assignments.

She couldn't recall any copybook with a missing page, but of course she hadn't been looking for missing pages. She would check carefully tomorrow. Paper was a scarce commodity, and the children were careful not to waste it. She doubted Cap or Frenchy would have access to copybook paper, if they owned any paper at all. Which meant one of her students, or someone in their households, had written the note.

Bianca was well acquainted with the peculiarities and limitations of her students' writing. Even with its dreadful grammar and spelling, the note was clearly beyond the present capabilities of Hank or Junior. The twins were studying hard and passing each spelling test with flying colors. Oren's copybook was so meticulous she couldn't imagine him producing such a sloppy piece of work, even if he were trying to disguise his identity. The message was anything but childlike, so she was certain that none of her younger students was responsible. That left the adults. But which adults?

The Fowlers had made no secret of their displeasure at Aiden's schooling. Bjorn and Elke Larson had befriended Aiden immediately, but Bianca realized she had no idea what Mr. and Mrs. Larson's attitude toward native people might be. Jesse Landry had certainly given Bianca no reason to think he'd be happier if she left Oakfield. She had no idea, however, how he felt about Indians. Nora Donovan was kind to Joanna, but there were others at the ranch—people Bianca had never even seen. Although Hank often talked about his Uncle Charlie, Bianca hadn't met him.

Something else about the note troubled her, something she couldn't quite put her finger on. It was as if a small bell was tinkling somewhere in the recesses of her brain, and she couldn't identify its source. I'll keep thinking about it, she decided. However, concentration didn't come easily after such a long day, and minutes later she had drifted into a dreamless sleep.

Cap Mackay lurked in the shadows across from the preacher's house. He'd been in the orchard behind the blacksmith's place when he first spotted the strange horse and buggy. Later he'd watched the schoolteacher and the sheriff ride off together. Tyler Wells had been toting the box Cap had left on the table when the nosy schoolmarm had almost barged in on him. Cap figured they were headed for the Donovan ranch, and he kept an eye out for their return.

He'd arrived at the Nolan place all primed to make the squaw a serious offer for the property. When nobody answered the door, he'd gone around back to see if she was in the barn or the orchard, but there was no sign of her. Hell, the house was practically his, so he was entitled to have a look inside. The door wasn't even locked. He'd have tidied up the papers, too, if he hadn't had to skedaddle out the back when he spotted the meddling Stratton woman heading up the path.

The flicker of a candle in the upstairs window of the preacher's house meant the busybody schoolteacher was settling down for the night, and about time too. Cap headed back to his cabin wondering how she and the sheriff had managed to get so cozy. The damnable woman popped up everywhere, and Cap knew he'd better steer clear of the sheriff. What he needed to do now was spend a little time mapping out his next move.

Maybe he ought to get Frenchy to go along when he made his next visit. He hadn't realized Frenchy and the half-breed boy were so friendly. He'd have to patch things up a little, but he didn't think Frenchy was one to hold a grudge. The little row they'd had earlier didn't amount to a hill of beans when you came down to it.

Even though he hadn't gotten what he came for, his visit to the Nolan place wasn't a total loss. He fingered the clipping in his pocket, wishing he knew exactly how to make use of it. Well, he'd figure it out. In the meantime another nip or two from his flask would warm him up on the way home.

CHAPTER 31

The schoolhouse door was open. As Jesse had hoped, none of the youngsters were in sight. He called out a cheery, "Good morning, Ma'am," as he went inside. When Bianca looked up from her desk, her smile actually made his knees go weak. No question about it, this tall woman had gotten under his skin.

"Well, Mr. Landry, you're out and about early." She looked behind him as if she expected Oren and Hank to follow.

"The boys will be along later." Jesse had planned to arrive at the schoolhouse before anybody else showed up. He wanted to see Bianca alone, but every time he tried to talk to her she took off like a skittish colt. The schoolroom seemed like a likely spot to corner her.

"That was a good thing you did," he said. "Getting the boys to own up about smoking and nearly burning down the barn."

"Confessing was their decision. I just gave them a nudge in the right direction."

"Nora's worried about Oren. She's even been talking about sending him down to California so her father can whip some sense into him."

"Oren's very bright."

"Oh, he's got smarts. It's common sense he's lacking. Having Hank ready and willing to go along with any harebrained scheme he cooks up only makes things worse."

"At least we know the boys weren't responsible for firing the shot in the woods."

"True enough. That's why I stopped by. Nora asked me to tell you she appreciated your help."

"You needn't have gone out of your way to—"

"Not out of the way at all, Ma'am. Matter of fact, I'm off to Wesleyville with one of Nora's lists. She's got a lot of odd jobs for me lately what with the Nolan boy there and the big shindig coming up."

"Shindig?"

"It's a big party she throws every year. Nora was sorry you couldn't stick around longer yesterday afternoon. She wanted to invite you personally, not that you need an invitation."

"The Fowler twins have been talking about a party, but I—"

"It's a celebration for Oren's birthday. Oren's mother, the first Mrs. Donovan, started it right after Oren was born, and it's been going on ever since. We roast a whole steer in the outdoor fire pit. There's more food than you've ever seen in your life, and music and dancing. Nora calls it a fiesta. She says they have them all the time on the ranchos down in California."

"It's kind of Mrs. Donovan to invite me, but—"

"Now, don't even think of saying no. Everybody in Oakfield turns out. Even the prudes who think dancing's a sin wouldn't miss Nora Donovan's fiesta."

"But I shouldn't—"

"Now don't go all prim and proper on me, Miss Stratton. Nobody expects you to spend every minute cleaning erasers and grading papers."

She laughed, a low musical chuckle even more irresistible than her smile. "That does sound pretty dull."

"Seems like you've been missing out on a lot of fun in your life, Ma'am. There's music and dancing and hayrides and spooning and—"

"How I choose to spend my time is my affair."

The ice was back in her voice, but Jesse wasn't ready to back off yet. Gentling a wild filly was touchy business. You dangled a carrot, you talked softly, you didn't spook her. You kept moving in.

"I'd be pleased if you'd spend some of that time with me," he said. "But you always run off or freeze up like you're doing now. Why is that, Bianca?"

"I don't know what you're talking about."

"Oh, yes you do." At least she hadn't cringed when he'd taken the liberty of using her given name. "There are sparks between us, Bianca. You feel them. I know you do, but you're always there with a bucket of cold water. I want to know why."

"It wouldn't be fair to encourage your attentions," she said softly.

"Nobody could accuse you of encouraging me. This is the first time we've exchanged more than a few words. Don't keep running away. At least say you'll come to the fiesta."

"I'll think about it, Mr. Landry." Another smile flickered at the corners of her mouth.

"Well, that's a start I guess. And, if you should call me Jesse, that would be—"

"That would be unduly familiar." She looked at the clock, stood, and went to the window. "The children are starting to arrive."

"My cue to leave, I know." He jammed on the Stetson and strode to the door. Then he stopped and turned. "Even though she's at the ranch a good deal, Mrs. Nolan still hasn't taken Mrs. Donovan up on buying the blacksmith's paraphernalia. It's a generous offer. Maybe you could talk to her."

"I've no idea when I will see Aiden or his mother again, and I'm sure Joanna is quite capable of making her own decisions."

"It was just a thought." He headed out the door and down the steps where the Fowler twins intercepted him.

"Good morning, Mr. Landry," they chorused, each executing a little twirl. Brown curls bobbed and yellow skirts flounced.

Jesse gave them a perfunctory smile and hurried to the wagon while they scurried behind him chattering. Feeling as if he was being pursued by a couple of chickadees, he made his getaway. Too bad he didn't have the same effect on Bianca Stratton.

It was good that Nora trusted him to make the bank deposit and pick out a new saddle for Oren's birthday, but he didn't exactly enjoy being an errand boy. Every time she embarked on one of her Good Samaritan projects, it meant extra work. When the boy and his mother cleared out, things could get back to normal. With them gone, maybe the sheriff would stop hanging around pestering everybody. Tyler Wells couldn't get out of Oakfield too soon, as far as Jesse was concerned. Yesterday the sheriff and Bianca looked entirely too comfortable riding off together in that fancy buggy.

Still it wasn't long until Saturday, and after that things would start looking up. Some good fiddle music and a glass or two of Nora's special punch should help. Providing, of course, Bianca showed up at the fiesta at all.

CHAPTER 32

Tyler Wells washed up at the pump outside the Donovan's bunkhouse. He needed a change of clothes and a decent night's sleep in his own bed, but he meant to track down Cap Mackay before heading back to town.

He tended to Clayton's prize stallion, gulped down a cup of Nora Donovan's strong coffee and hitched up the buggy. Even if he couldn't get Mackay to confess to Daniel Nolan's murder, Tyler figured he had plenty of cause to haul him in.

Tyler had gotten a good look at the old man's boots when he'd routed him out of bed Monday afternoon. He was sure the print outside Nolan's back door was Mackay's as soon as saw it. Even if nothing was missing, Cap had broken into Nolan's house. Probably an arson charge would stick, too. He'd told Bianca he needed proof, but he didn't doubt Aiden's story for a minute. Something about Bianca Stratton brought out his contrary streak.

Last night when she'd followed him out to the buggy she'd seemed different, less prickly somehow. He hoped he'd convinced her to butt out of his investigation. Stubborn as she was, she'd probably keep right on stirring up trouble. He shook his head and flicked the reins.

When Tyler pulled up in front of the dilapidated pile of logs Cap called home, he thought the place looked deserted. Nobody answered when he pounded on the door, so he scouted around the cabin, rubbed the grime off a small paned window and peered inside.

The cabin had only one room, and there was no sign of Cap. Moth-eaten blankets had been thrown to the foot of the bed, and the table was cluttered with food scraps, bottles and dirty dishes. Behind the house Tyler found a lean-to stall with straw on the floor and a feedbag hanging from a rusty nail. Nobody had mentioned that Cap had a horse, but the strong smell of horse sweat and fresh manure left no doubt.

If the old man had taken off on horseback, he could be anyplace, and there was no telling when he'd get back. Still, it was probably worthwhile to drop by Fowler's store. The way news traveled in Oakfield, it was likely somebody could fill him in.

At the store Tyler found Agnes Fowler busy with a feather duster.

"Ed's in back," she said.

Tyler nodded and pushed his way through the swinging door. The little storekeeper was shoving some heavy barrels around, but he was more than willing to settle into one of the cane-backed rocking chairs by the pot-bellied stove.

"Well, Sheriff, you're out and about early this morning." Ed was wearing his snake-oil salesman smile. "It's a little early for a drink, but I'd be happy to oblige if you're—"

"This isn't a social visit, Ed."

The smile vanished. "If you've a mind to keep pestering me about—"

"I'm looking for Cap Mackay." Tyler took a seat in an adjoining chair. "I just came from his cabin, but there's no sign of him."

"Well, now, I can't say as I can be much help to you there, Tyler." Ed relaxed visibly, but he hadn't managed to recover his amiable host face.

"You could start by telling me when you saw him last."

"Let's see, now. Hard to say. You know how folks come and go around here."

"Let's start with last night."

"Well, Mackay usually stops by for a nightcap, but he didn't turn up last night. We had a nice crowd, too. Bunch of the ranch hands played some poker."

"What about earlier in the day?"

"Earlier?"

"You know. Morning. Afternoon. Did you see Cap yesterday at all?"

"Now that you mention it, I believe he did stop by. Around noon as I recall. Bought some shells for his rifle."

"Did he say anything about heading out?"

"Nope. Wanted to gab, though. Hell, he always wants to gab. You'd think I didn't have anything else to do the way people hang around here talking."

Tyler suppressed a smile. If anybody liked to talk more than Agnes Fowler, it was Ed. "So what did he have to say?"

"Can't say as I paid him much mind."

"Try to remember. It might be important."

"Nothing that old drunk says is important. He's always yammering about the past. If it's not war stories, it's logging or prospecting. Come to think of it, that's what he was carrying on about yesterday."

"Prospecting?"

"Yep. Rehashing all the gold strikes clear back to forty-nine. Asking did I remember who went where and all. Hell, every man and boy in Oregon caught gold fever at one time or another."

"But Cap didn't say anything about where he was going next?"

"Nope. Didn't even try to cadge a drink. Bought some rifle shells and left."

"Did you notice if he was on horseback?"

"Horseback? Cap?"

"There's a shed behind his cabin, and I could tell—"

Ed laughed. "That's old Smoky."

"Smoky?"

"The scrawny old nag he keeps in the shed. Says it was his Army horse. Can't even guess how old the critter must be. I never knowed Cap to saddle him up, though. Hell, I don't know if he even owns a saddle."

"Well, the horse was there recently, but it's gone now."

"If that's the case, I guess when you locate Smoky you'll find Cap. Though it seems to me your time would be better spent tracking down that squaw's renegade brother."

"Joanna Nolan has a brother? Funny you never told me about him."

"Oh, I would have, Sheriff." The fake smile was back. "Only, you see, I never knew nothing about it until this morning when Frenchy happened to bring it up."

Worming the whole story out of Ed took all the patience Tyler could muster. By the time he left the store he could barely control his boiling anger. What else had Bianca Stratton and the inscrutable Indian woman neglected to mention? Nobody in the whole damn village ever gave him a straight answer. As for the meddlesome schoolteacher—well, he should have known better than to trust her in the first place. Which only proved how little he knew about women.

Paperwork was piling up on his desk back at the office, and he headed the buggy toward Wesleyville. Writing up briefs and filling out forms were chores he'd hated when he studied law. Still, as sheriff he was meticulous about keeping case files up-to-date.

If only he could write a final report on the miserable business of Daniel Nolan's murder. But the file kept getting thicker, and he was no closer to solving it than he had been on the first day he rode into Oakfield—the first day he saw Bianca Stratton. Well, when he saw her again, she'd get a piece of his mind.

CHAPTER 33

While Bianca conducted spelling drills and checked homework assignments, her thoughts veered off in all directions. She met with her students and leafed through their copybooks, but at first glance the pages seemed to be intact. Junior had left everything at home, but he assured her his homework was done and promised to bring it the next morning.

Mainly, however, she had difficultly focusing on geography lessons and penmanship samples because Jesse Landry's face kept appearing and reappearing in her head like an uninvited visitor. Their early morning encounter had thrown her off balance. She overheard the twins whispering about the fiesta and silenced them with a stern look, but she couldn't help thinking about it too.

Jesse was right—there had been little joy in her life. When Rolf and Viola were first married they entertained frequent guests at the ranch, but over the years Viola's failing health and Rolf's gloomy attitude kept folks away.

Jesse talked about music, dancing, hayrides and spooning. At the academy music consisted of singing hymns at morning chapel, and dancing wasn't allowed. Bianca had never been on a hayride. The closest she'd come to what Jesse called spooning was a box social where the high bidder for her basket, a pimply boy with bad teeth, nuzzled her neck before she shoved him clean off the bench they were sharing. What would her reaction have been if Jesse had been doing the nuzzling? It didn't bear thinking about, but she couldn't seem to control her foolish thoughts.

Bianca collected the copybooks before the noon hour, determined to remain at her desk during lunchtime and look at them more closely. She'd just sent the children outdoors when Mattie arrived, smiling and offering an orange, a rare treat.

"Lars Larson picked up a shipment at the wharf yesterday," Mattie said, "and he managed to get a whole crate of oranges from California. I was lucky to be at Fowler's when he brought them in. Agnes appropriated most of them for marmalade, and the rest will be gone by now."

"It's been years since I've eaten an orange." Bianca said, caressing the pebbly surface and inhaling its pungent fragrance. "I think I'll save it until after school when I'll have time to really enjoy it. Thank you, Mattie."

"Well, I feel bad about snapping at you last night." Mattie settled onto the student bench closest to Bianca's desk.

"That note put everybody on edge," Bianca said.

"Have you given any thought as to who wrote it?"

"I've gone over and over it in my mind, but I simply can't conceive of anyone doing something so hurtful."

"Well, you're young and trusting, Bianca. People aren't always what they seem to be. Even after three years in Oakfield, I don't know a lot about most of the people, even the regular churchgoers. It's not like Connecticut where we knew everybody's family history."

"Maybe that's a good thing. Maybe coming west gives people a chance at a fresh start."

"That's one way to look at it," Mattie said. "But it doesn't feel like a good thing when somebody nails a hateful note on your gatepost."

Bianca fingered the copybooks. "I didn't notice any missing pages when I was checking homework this morning, but the note certainly appeared to be written on copybook paper."

"Well, a missing page wouldn't necessarily mean it was used for the note."

"You're right, of course. A page could be torn out because of an inkblot or because somebody needed paper for a grocery list. Still, the copybooks seemed like a good place to start."

"But you didn't find any missing pages?"

"I couldn't really examine them closely while I was working with the children. I was about to go through them again when you arrived."

"Don't let me interrupt. I have to get home and finish hemming the dresses I'm making for the girls to wear to the party on Saturday. You're coming, of course."

"I really hadn't considered it."

"Well, I meant to tell you, but you've been gone so much, running around the countryside with the sheriff and all."

Bianca ignored the implied criticism, and she wasn't about to mention Jesse Landry's visit. Mattie might tell the girls that gossiping was improper, but she could give Agnes a run for her money as a news source.

"It's all quite outlandish, you know." Mattie said. "Roasting a whole steer and rolling up the rugs and pushing the furniture to the wall for dancing. It's some sort of California style celebration."

"It sounds exciting."

"We don't commemorate birthdays that way in Connecticut, but from what I hear California is like part of Mexico anyway. Not very civilized, if you know what I mean."

Bianca realized it was pointless to respond. In Mattie's view, civilization probably ended at the Connecticut state line.

"Everybody goes to the party—fiesta, they call it," Mattie rattled on. "And I must say Nora Donovan isn't one to scrimp on food. By the way, those pastries you brought home yesterday were heavenly."

"I'm sure Mrs. Donovan will be pleased when you tell her so."

"In a way, I can't help feeling sorry for Nora Donovan. I mean, she can't help being Mexican and all. Running a ranch with no husband has got to be hard. A woman needs a husband. You know, Bianca, you'd make somebody a good wife. It's none of my business, but your brother-in-law, Rolf seems like a fine, solid man. And a nice big farm near Wesleyville would be a sight more comfortable than a little attic room here in the sticks."

"I want to see more of the world than a little corner in the south of Oregon." Bianca refrained from adding that Mattie was right, it was none of her business. "I don't intend to marry."

"But you're so good with children."

Some women seemed to take childbearing in stride. Mattie would never understand that in the Stratton family marriage led to stillborn babies and early death.

"I need to be on my own," Bianca said, picking up one of the copybooks and scrutinizing the pages.

"Well, I know you're busy. I'd better be going." Mattie stood, started toward the door, and then turned. "You never did tell me about your visit to the ranch."

"There's really not much to tell."

"Did somebody really break into Nolan's house?"

"Yes, but as far as we know nothing was missing."

"And Doc Schneider—what did he have to say about the little boy?"

"I didn't see the doctor." Bianca was determined to provide no additional fodder for the Oakfield rumor mill.

"I hear the Indian woman brewed up some kind of potion to drive away the evil spirits. I bet Doc Schneider raised the roof."

Bianca took another copybook from the stack on her desk and pointedly began turning the pages.

"Well, I'll run along."

"Thanks so much for the orange!" she called as Mattie made her reluctant way through the coatroom.

Bianca thumbed through the copybooks as she pondered Mattie's visit. She kept hoping the minister's wife would prove to be a real friend, but Mattie was quite beyond understanding. One minute she was doing something thoughtful, and the next she was glibly condemning everyone whose views differed from her own.

Mattie had come from the store, which meant she and Agnes Fowler had plenty of opportunity to pool information. But Mattie wouldn't have told Agnes about the note unless she wanted everybody in Oregon to know about it. Still, bringing the orange might simply have been an excuse to stop in, do a little snooping and chatter.

Was it possible Mattie had written the note herself? Putting it on the gatepost on her way to the store in the morning would have posed no problem, and Mattie had been only too eager to point out that there could be many reasons for a missing copy-book page. Bianca couldn't believe Mattie would accuse her own husband of immoral behavior. Unless, of course, it was a test to see what Cushing would do. Could she possibly be so hateful, so devious? Bianca dismissed the notion. Neither venom nor duplicity seemed part of Mattie's makeup. And Mattie certainly had nothing to do with the break-in at Joanna's house. A man's boot had left that telltale footprint.

Glancing at the clock, Bianca realized the lunch hour was ending. She'd examined the copybooks and discovered pages carefully torn out from Cora's, Edna's and Edwina's. During the afternoon she pulled the girls aside.

"Tina spilled soup on my copybook. See. There are still some spots I couldn't get out." Cora sounded puzzled. "Did I do something wrong?"

The twins, after much blushing and giggling, whispered that Edwina was doing a watercolor rendition of the schoolhouse with everyone sitting under the oak tree. She'd needed to paste two pages together in order to make the picture large enough so all the faces would show. It was a surprise for Oren's birthday, and Lars Larson was even making a frame in exchange for a new bonnet for his wife.

Bianca promised to keep the secret, but at dismissal she was no closer to answering any of the questions that plagued her.

CHAPTER 34

Rolf Knudsen walked into the sheriff's office in Wesleyville, hat in hand. "I'm not really sure what I'm doing here," he said. "I guess I need some information."

Tyler Wells looked up from his desk. "It's Knudsen, isn't it? I believe we crossed paths at the Donovan ranch."

Rolf shook the extended hand, noting the sheriff's good, firm grip. "I'm really worried about my sister-in-law," he said. "She's the new schoolteacher down in Oakfield."

"Miss Stratton and I are acquainted. Have a seat." The sheriff waved a hand at a scarred rocker near his desk.

Rolf sat down, leaned forward and frowned. "I shouldn't be poking my nose into things that aren't my affair, but Bianca's never been away from home before, and there's been way too much trouble in Oakfield lately."

"I understand your concern."

"She's been pretty sheltered. She's determined to be on her own, but she does have a way of stirring up trouble."

"I've noticed."

"Sending her to Wesley Academy was my wife's notion. A big mistake as far as I can tell. Well, that's water under the bridge.

I really stopped by to see if you've managed to get to the bottom of things down in Oakfield."

"I wish I could reassure you, but the truth is that the blacksmith's murder still has me baffled."

"I thought you had an Indian in custody."

"Joe Red Deer? He's a chicken thief, but I'm certain he's never been as far south as Oakfield. And I'm not so sure it's an Indian we're looking for."

"I've tried to talk Bianca into coming back to the farm with me. My sister is here, so there wouldn't be talk. But Bianca's stubborn."

"She seems to be doing a good job with her students."

"I'm not surprised. She was wonderful with my boys. They miss her. Am I worrying too much, or is she really in danger?" Rolf hoped to hear that Bianca was perfectly safe, but the sheriff's sober expression and the lengthy pause before he replied were less than reassuring.

"Miss Stratton put the fat in the fire when she took up the cause for Mrs. Nolan and her son. I'm afraid she had no idea how much fear and outright hatred there is where Indians are concerned."

"That's Bianca—jump in feet first and worry about it later," Rolf said. "I wish I could get her to listen to reason and come home where she belongs."

"She's not a child, Mr. Knudsen. Many young women her age are married and caring for youngsters of their own."

"I know. If she hadn't been so tall I expect we'd have had suitors lining up at the door, but she got her growth early. By the time she was thirteen she was a head taller than most of the boys her age."

"But some of the boys must have caught up in a year or so."

"Well, yes, but by then she was at the academy and my wife was ailing. Now she says she's never going to marry."

"Could be she's going through a phase."

"I know it's a woman's privilege to change her mind, but Bianca's different. She turned me down in no uncertain terms.

And she's not getting any younger. No, I think she means to remain an old maid."

"I wouldn't be too sure about that. Yesterday the foreman out at the Donovan ranch seemed more than a little interested, and he appears to be quite a hand with the ladies."

"Landry? I met him at the ranch. Too handsome if you ask me."

"I guess you can't blame him for that. I wouldn't mind having the kind of looks that turn a woman's head. Even though she rode back to the preacher's place with me, I knew it was Landry she was thinking about."

Rolf eyed the sheriff critically. "It sounds like you and Bianca are more than acquainted."

"The widow and the boy trust Miss Stratton. Without her help I'd know even less about the blacksmith's murder than I do now. But every time we talk, she ends up on her high horse for one reason or another."

"Those professors at the academy encouraged her willful nonsense. Well, I've taken up enough of your time." Rolf stood stiffly, hat in hand.

"No problem. I only wish I could offer more in the way of reassurance."

"It sounds like you're doing what you can. I'd be glad to ride down to Oakfield and give you a hand if you think of any way I can help out."

"Thanks. I may take you up on that offer later, but there's some trouble up at the north end of the county. I won't be spending much time around Oakfield for the next day or so."

"I thought maybe you'd be turning up at that party they're having at the Donovan ranch on Saturday."

"I hear it's a real wing-ding, but I'm not sure I'll be able to make it."

On the way back to the farm Rolf stopped at the mill. His sister, Berta, had said they were getting low on flour, which was his excuse for going into town in the first place. He'd spent the morning puttering around the milk house and fussing at Berta about the boys' rowdy behavior, while the situation at Oakfield nagged at him like a loose tooth.

Nothing the sheriff said made his mind easier. If the Indian in custody wasn't the murderer, there was even more cause for alarm. Rolf had been stewing about Bianca since his last visit, but she showed no sign of coming to her senses and leaving Oakfield. She'd be furious if he turned up again, but there was nothing to prevent him taking Nora Donovan up on her invitation to Saturday's fiesta.

CHAPTER 35

After supper Bianca went to her room and mulled over everything that had happened since she came to Oakfield. Then she took an old copybook out of the chest and began making notes. Writing information down and reviewing it had helped her organize her thoughts when she prepared for essay tests at the academy. Maybe it would clarify things now.

She thought of the Twenty Questions game she'd taught Aiden. Bianca and Viola had played the game with their father. She was always better at it than her sister. Her father said she had a knack for getting to the heart of a problem by asking the right questions. That was an idea. She'd write questions. If she knew the answer, she'd write that too. And when she saw what information was lacking, maybe she'd know what she ought to do next.

Tyler wouldn't be pleased. He'd said she was in danger—that she should leave the investigating to him. But it wasn't as if she was actually *doing* anything. Simply sorting things out in her mind couldn't put her in harm's way. She caught her lower lip between her teeth and began writing.

When was Daniel Nolan killed? Joanna had last seen him on Wednesday, and the boys had discovered the body the following

Tuesday. Unless it was possible to pinpoint the time of the murder, there was no way to tell whether anybody had an alibi.

Who fired the shot in the woods? The boys were in the clear, and a bullet from a careless hunter was still a possibility. Tyler suspected Cap. But why would Cap shoot at her?

What about the fire? An accident? Fires were common enough. Even though Tyler still wanted proof, she was certain Cap was responsible. He wanted Nolan's land. Maybe that was reason enough for him.

Who put the note on the Pangston's gatepost? Cowards liked to hide behind anonymity. Everything that had happened in Oakfield had a cowardly smell, and Cap's behavior seemed to fit. But writing a poisonous note? That seemed totally out of character. She'd be willing to bet he signed his name with an X. There was something else about the note—-something she'd tucked away somewhere in her head. What was it?

Why was Daniel Nolan killed? That was the big question. When she knew the answer, everything else would fall into place. She stared at the page in frustration. Questions. Only questions. And no real answers at all.

What was she missing? Everything circled around the Nolans. Maybe Joanna held the key. Maybe she knew more than she had let on. Joanna had little reason to trust anyone in Oakfield. Bianca wiped her pen and pushed the copybook aside, wishing she could talk to Joanna. But she was way out at Donovan's ranch, which made a drop-in visit impossible.

She thought of Patches, the docile mare that had given her so many hours of pleasure and freedom until her accident two years ago. Patches had been a marvelous present for her twelfth birthday. If Bianca went back to the farm, would Patches still race to the corral gate and find the carrot poking out of her pocket? When it was obvious Bianca's riding days were over, Rolf had complained that Patches was nothing more than a pet. In Rolf's view, animals that didn't earn their keep had no place on a farm. She didn't believe Rolf would sell Patches without consulting her. Still, she could have brought the horse with her to Oakfield. Maybe there was still hope. Maybe now that more time had passed she could somehow conquer her panic and ride again.

Even if that miracle occurred, it wouldn't take her to Donovan's ranch tomorrow. But Saturday was the fiesta. She could see Joanna then. The rest of the time she'd enjoy the party and stick close to Mattie and the girls. And she needn't even speak to Jesse Landry.

CHAPTER 36

Joanna prayed that the dark cloud which hovered over them was finally dispersing. She believed Aiden's recovery was a good omen. His hands were still bandaged, but they were healing well. Dressed in his faded blue overalls and favorite plaid shirt, he seemed almost his old self. Reading was fast becoming his favorite pastime, and she left him sitting at a plank table near the fireplace, once again shuffling through the papers in the oaken box and sounding out the words as he read each letter and clipping.

Joanna found Nora Donovan in the spacious kitchen where the Chang, the Chinese cook, presided. Joanna seldom used her own kitchen, but she loved this huge room with its hearth crafted of native stone and its aroma of baking bread.

Mrs. Donovan emerged from the pantry carrying several jars of preserves. "It was lovely having Aiden join us at breakfast this morning," she said.

"Yes, Aiden well now. We go home and he go back to school."

"Of course. I'll have one of the men hitch up the wagon and drive you whenever you're ready."

"You very kind. I want to thank, give you something, but I—"

"It's been a treat getting to know you and Aiden. Chang tells me you've been helping out in the kitchen, too."

"I love to bake." She lowered her eyes, hoping she had not done anything to displease this generous woman. "Missionary show me white people cooking. You have fine, big ovens."

"Well, I don't know how you managed it. I've tried to talk Chang into getting help, but he doesn't even let me get near his precious stove unless I shove him out of the way. He says you made those scrumptious blackberry pies we had for desert last night, and the pastries I served to my guests the other afternoon too."

"I help more, but not want be in the way."

"Joanna, you've been an ideal houseguest. I know you want to take Aiden home, but it would be wonderful if you could stay on and give us a hand with the preparations for the fiesta."

"Chang say he make food for many people. I like to help."

"Then it's settled. We'll arrange for you and Aiden to go home on Sunday."

"But I think young Mr. Oren want room back."

"I'm afraid Oren is badly spoiled, and I have only myself to blame."

"He read for Aiden and give slingshot. He promise teach Aiden to ride horse. Oren is good boy, Mrs. Donovan."

"Please call me Nora. I've been calling you Joanna ever since you came. I hope we have become friends."

"Friends, Yes." Joanna smiled. "But, Mrs. Donovan——"

"Nora."

"Nora, I need go home. Short time only. Water garden. Gather eggs."

"Of course. Take the little buckskin mare. I'll look in on Aiden. And, Joanna, while you're riding back and forth, give some thought to my offer to buy Mr. Nolan's blacksmith equipment. The sheriff told me he suggested you see the lawyer in Wesleyville. I'd be happy to drive you in on Monday. If you decide to sell me the tools we can open an account for you at the bank as well. Three hundred dollars is too much cash to have lying around, especially after that break-in."

"Yes, Nora. I think on it. You kind friend."

Back in Oren's spacious bedroom, Joanna reverted comfortably to her native tongue and told Aiden of her plans.

"Mrs. Donovan has been very kind to us, and I want to repay her by staying to help with the fiesta."

"It's nice here, but I'd rather go home." Aiden's voice had been hoarse and breathy yesterday when Doctor Schneider allowed him to say his first few words. This morning he sounded almost normal.

"We'll leave on Sunday. Monday you can go to school, and Mrs. Donovan will take me to Wesleyville to speak to the lawyer."

"But I want to go with you. We talked about getting me a horse, and——"

"You are not yet strong enough for riding a horse."

"But you still need me to help with your English."

"I depend on you too much, Aiden. I understand English well enough, and most people understand me, even though my speech is not perfect. What is important is for you to be in school every day."

"I like school a lot, and if we're not going to get a horse——"

"Not right away. But you will have your horse when you are ready."

"You promise?"

"Yes, Aiden. I promise."

"All right, then!" His smile lightened her heart. "When you promise, I know it's really going to happen."

"There are two other things I need to tell you." Joanna retrieved the willow basket from its hook on the wall. "Mrs. Donovan wants to buy your father's forge and all of his tools and supplies. I haven't agreed because everything of mine is also yours."

"I don't think I want to be a blacksmith when I grow up."

"So, is it all right if I accept Mrs. Donovan's offer of $300?"

"That's a lot of money! I bet we could get a horse and a rig and still have some left over."

"Mrs. Donovan says there's a bank in Wesleyville where they will keep the money until we need it.

"Mrs. Donovan has lots of money, so I guess she knows about keeping it safe. But you said there were two things you wanted to talk to me about."

Joanna reached into the willow basket, took out the leather pouch and placed it in Aiden's hand.

"It's heavy!"

"Open it carefully and look inside."

"Gold!" His eyes widened. "Is it real? Where did you get it?"

"Yes, I believe it is real. Your father kept it hidden under a floor board in the bedroom." She didn't explain she'd spied on Daniel to learn of the pouch's existence.

"Lenny Fowler told me there's a place in Wesleyville where people take gold and get money for it. I don't remember what it's called. I bet Mrs. Donovan would know, though."

"Should I show the gold to Mrs. Donovan and ask her advice? I think I trust her, Aiden."

"I think I do too. She looks right at me when she talks, not over my shoulder like some grownups do. Are we rich then?"

"I'm not sure if there's enough gold in the pouch to make us rich. But I hope we will have enough to keep sending you to school. Maybe, when you are older, you can even attend an academy such as the one Miss Stratton speaks of."

"I don't know if I'm smart enough for that."

"Oh, yes, Aiden." Joanna took back the pouch and covered his olive-skinned hand with her darker one. "I believe you are smart enough to do anything you set your heart on."

"Well, I am getting to be a good reader. You know, it's funny about the papers in the box. The letters from Elizabeth—Pa's wife who died—they were all mixed up. And some things are gone, too."

"Are you sure?"

He nodded. "The will, and the paper saying you and Pa were married, and—"

"Those papers I have kept with me ever since the fire." She reached into the willow basket and held the documents up for him to see. "But somebody broke into our house after the fire. Miss Stratton found the papers scattered around."

"You didn't tell me."

"I didn't want you to worry when you were so sick."

"Well, if the important papers are safe I guess the clipping doesn't matter."

"There is a clipping missing?"

Another nod. "I remember because Pa's name was in it. There were lots of big words in it, too, and I wasn't reading so well then. It was about a man who died, and I didn't understand how he could find gold in a frozen river. Maybe I got it mixed up."

"It's probably not important. Maybe the clipping slipped out of sight and Miss Stratton didn't notice. I'll look for it when I sweep up today."

"You're going home?"

"I'll be back before supper. Mrs. Donovan said she would look in on you, and Chang said to tell you he's fixing something special for your lunch. All you have to do is be a good boy."

"Can I go into the kitchen and talk to Chang? He tells good stories."

Joanna smiled. "Don't be in the way. He's busy getting ready for the party on Saturday."

"It's called a fiesta. Oren says it's the best day of the year. If we're staying, does that mean we get to go to the party too?"

"I think it does. Now, I've answered enough questions."

CHAPTER 37

Bianca hadn't planned on measurement being the topic for Thursday's arithmetic lesson, but the twins brought a tape measure to class and asked to stay after school to get help understanding inches, feet and yards. Bianca had discovered her students remembered better when a lesson was about something they were really interested in, so she agreed to put off the work on borrowing and carrying.

"The boys grow out of their shirts so fast we're always making new ones." Edna measured Junior's arms. "And they hate to stand around while we fit things on them."

"She always pokes me with those pins," Junior complained.

"Junior's hand-me-downs are still too big for Lloyd, so we have to cut them down and—"

"Edwina got this idea that writing down the inches would make our sewing a lot easier." The twins habitually finished each other's sentences.

Bianca brought out a yardstick and several rulers from her box of supplies. Soon everyone was involved in measuring copybooks, desks, lunch buckets and one another. Bianca had the older students record the measurements on the blackboard, and the follow-up discussion comparing sizes was lively.

While the class copied the information from the blackboard for penmanship practice, Bianca made it a point to check on Junior. He'd remembered to bring his copybook, which, unlike most of the others, was badly smudged and wrinkled. Conspicuous ragged edges showed where several pages had been ripped out.

"I can't seem to get the hang of this." Junior scratched away at the page, dipped the pen in the inkwell and produced an ink-blot which rapidly evolved into a smear covering half the paper. "See. That always happens!"

"Dip the tip, and then use your pen-wiper." Bianca demonstrated the procedure as she had done several times.

"He never remembers." Edna was always eager to reprimand Junior.

"Is that why you have so many missing pages in your copybook, Junior? Because of the inkblots?" Bianca asked.

"I guess I did rip out a page or two." Junior shook his head in self-reproach. "I'm sorry."

"Everybody makes mistakes, and learning new skills isn't easy." Bianca said. "You don't need to tear pages out of your copybook when you make an inkblot. Copybooks are for practice. I don't expect them to be perfect."

It was pointless to try to pin down exactly how many pages Junior had ripped out. The anonymous note had been wrinkled, but Cushing said he'd crammed it into his pocket. Had one of the edges been ragged? She couldn't remember. When she'd read the note, the clumsy printing and crude message were foremost in her mind.

At lunchtime Bianca carried her basket to the grassy area under the oak tree where the children were gathered. Oren reported that Aiden had joined everybody at the ranch for breakfast.

Hank said, "He's got his voice working, too."

"Aunt Nora's making me wait until after my birthday to get my room back because Aiden and his mother are going to stay so she can help with the fiesta."

"Chang—he's the Chinaman cook—he lets her work right along beside him," Hank added, "and Chang don't never let nobody help in his kitchen."

"Aiden's mother is some good cook," Oren said. "The black-berry pie we had for dessert last night is the best I ever ate. Jesse said so too."

"I'm glad Aiden is so much better," Bianca said. "I hope he'll be back in school soon."

"On Monday, I think," Oren said. "He was in the kitchen talking with Chang when I left for school. Aiden sure does like to talk."

"Yes, he does," Bianca agreed. "It must have been awful for him not to be able to use his voice."

"He said his Ma was going over to their place today, and on Monday she's going to Wesleyville with Aunt Nora to see a law-yer, but he couldn't go along because he'd be back in school."

Bianca was pleased that Joanna seemed to have found an ally in Nora Donovan. She admired Mrs. Donovan's independence and generosity, and she was surprised to discover how much she was anticipating Saturday's fiesta. She was anxious to see for her-self that Aiden was truly well, and she'd decided that her father's leather-bound copy of *Ivanhoe* would be a perfect birthday gift for Oren. She'd never learned to dance, but still she'd enjoy watching and listening to the music.

Afternoon lessons proceeded smoothly, and at dismissal every-one hurried off, chattering about the fiesta. Even Junior left with-out offering to sweep the floor. Bianca tidied up quickly, humming to herself and trying to decide what she should wear on Saturday.

She hadn't many clothes. The skirts and shirtwaists she wore for teaching were the same utilitarian garments she'd worn to class at the academy. Her black Sunday dress was too somber for a festive occasion, but with the addition of a bright scarf, it would have to do.

Bianca put on her bonnet, closed the door, and was almost at the schoolyard gate when she heard hoof beats. Moments later the sheriff's bay horse appeared. Tyler Wells dismounted and stalked toward her, his eyes a stormy gray.

"I need to have a word with you, Miss Stratton." The after-noon sun glinted off his badge, and his Stetson remained firmly on his head.

"I'm glad you're here. About that note—"

"The note is the least of my concerns at the moment." His tone was harsh. "What I need is a few straight answers."

Speechless, Bianca stared at his clenched jaw.

"When you and Nolan's widow were busy convincing me no Indian had murdered her husband, was it to throw me off the trail of her renegade brother?"

"Renegade brother?"

"Don't tell me little chatterbox Aiden never got around to mentioning his big chief uncle."

"I honestly have no idea what you're talking about."

"You and Joanna Nolan were so chummy she even had you read her private papers. But she never told you about her brother?"

"Believe me. I had no idea Joanna had any living relatives."

"Well, you must be the only one who hasn't heard by now." He removed his hat and scratched the back of his neck.

"I thought you prided yourself on never leaping to conclusions. You can't believe I'd deliberately mislead you about something so important."

"No, I guess you wouldn't." His tone wasn't quite so belligerent. "But your friend, Mrs. Nolan, has some explaining to do."

"Where did you hear about this so-called brother?"

"I stopped by Fowler's. I've been looking for Cap, but he seems to have made himself scarce. Apparently Frenchy Blauchet lets Aiden fish with him, and Aiden bragged about his uncle, a big chief who wasn't afraid of anybody."

"Well, if there is such a person, I guess it would be natural for Joanna to try to protect him."

"I suppose that's true. She'd figure, and rightly too, that I'd consider him a suspect. I guess I'd better ride out to Donovan's ranch and have another talk with her."

"Oren said she went home this morning. She may still be there. I'll go with you if you like."

"I'd appreciate it. The widow doesn't clam up quite so much with you around." His eyes had returned to their neutral hazel hue. "I shouldn't have snarled at you."

Bianca closed the gate and headed down the road. Tyler sauntered beside her, leading the bay gelding.

"We'd get there a lot faster on horseback," he said, "but I guess it wouldn't be seemly for you to jump on behind me."

"It certainly wouldn't. Anyway, I don't ride."

"Too bad. It would make your stay here a sight more enjoyable if you weren't stuck so close to the preacher's place and the schoolhouse."

"I know." She found herself telling him about her horse, Patches, the fall and the subsequent panic she couldn't overcome.

"Those things take time," he said. "Back in Georgia, after the war, I swore I'd never touch a gun again."

"Well, I noticed you had that six-shooter drawn with no hesitation when you thought there was somebody lurking inside the Nolan's house."

"I finally realized the problem was in my head. When they offered me a job as Deputy, I knew I had to face up to it. My horse is a gentle creature. Does walking near him bother you?"

She forced a smile. "Not unless I have to ride him later."

"Don't worry. I'm a mite short of sidesaddles. Now there's a misbegotten contraption. I'm not sure I'd be much of a horseman if I had to ride off balance the way ladies do."

Bianca cast a sidelong glance at Tyler from under the shade of her bonnet as she walked beside him with the bay horse following obediently behind. He'd mentioned Georgia. That was in the South, so if he'd been in the war, the rumors about his being a Rebel must be true. A dozen questions sprang into her head, but she felt too awkward to pursue them. Talking about horses seemed a safer course.

"I've been thinking about Patches a lot lately. I guess my brother-in-law would bring her over if I asked—if he hasn't sold her."

"Speaking of your brother-in-law, he stopped by my office in town yesterday."

"Rolf went to see you? Whatever for?"

"He worries about you."

Bianca sighed. "Rolf worries about everything."

When the Nolan's house came into view Bianca was surprised to see three horses tethered outside. "It looks like we're not Joanna's only visitors this afternoon," she said, "but I don't recognize any of those horses."

Tyler surveyed the scene. "That buckskin mare is probably the one Nora Donovan loaned Joanna. I don't know about the brown one, but—"

"The other horse—the gray one—looks like he can hardly stand up."

Tyler nodded. "That's old Smoky, unless I miss my guess. Seems we've finally tracked down Cap."

CHAPTER 38

Running Fox peered through the bushes, saw three horses tied outside Joanna's house, and swore under his breath. He slipped back into the woods and whistled. When his obedient pinto appeared, he retrieved his rifle. Then he edged his way to the back of the house and slipped through the screen door and into Joanna's chilly kitchen.

He heard voices in the next room, nudged the door ajar, and peeked through the crack. Joanna's back was to the hearth, and two men stood in the middle of the room facing her.

"It's a fair offer." Running Fox recognized the old one with a beard who was talking.

Joanna shook her head.

"Hell, it's more than fair. I know what Nolan paid for this place."

"I not sell."

"Well, you're being foolish. Folks don't want you here." The menace in the man's voice was unmistakable. Running Fox gripped his rifle.

"What Cap means is that by selling this place you and Aiden could go anywhere—make a fresh start."

The man called Frenchy was trying to smooth things over, but Running Fox wasn't fooled. These people were here to make trouble for Joanna. Still, the idea that Joanna might have money—quite a lot of money—was something he hadn't considered. He'd simply planned on Joanna and Aiden leaving Oakfield with what few possessions they could carry. White men's money could make life in the mountain hideaway easier for his people. Buying guns and supplies was risky, but it could be done.

"You go now." Joanna waved her hand toward the door, but Cap stood his ground.

"I guess you don't get it, squaw woman," he said. "You and the little half-breed ain't safe here."

Frenchy put out a cautionary hand, but Cap shrugged him away.

"Bad things happen to folks who stay where they ain't welcome. Could be another fire. Or your boy might have an accident. He might even fall in the river."

The old man took a step toward Joanna, and the alarm on her face unleashed Running Fox's rage. He cocked his rifle, kicked the door open and leveled the gun.

"Anything happens to Joanna or the boy—you die, old man," he snarled. "Now get out."

"Please, brother. No more trouble." For a minute Running Fox was afraid Joanna would try to shield the white men, but she remained motionless. Only her twisting hands betrayed her anxiety.

"We're leaving. We're leaving." Frenchy's black moustache quivered as he gave the older man a shove.

"I ain't afraid of no Injun," Cap protested.

Running Fox moved closer. The old man reeked of liquor and sweat. "Don't think I won't shoot," he said. "Even white man's law would understand I need to protect my sister."

"Come on, Cap. Let's get out of here." Frenchy swung the door open.

Keeping the rifle trained, Running Fox glanced outside. A tall woman and a man leading a bay horse were on the road.

"Are you expecting more visitors, sister?" he asked.

Joanna's eyes followed his gaze. "Is sheriff," she said. "Teacher, Miss Stratton, with him."

The old man stopped at the door. "I guess you ain't about to shoot nobody with the sheriff heading this way."

"I hear the sheriff figures you're the renegade Injun who scalped the blacksmith," Frenchy added.

"I think sheriff looks for Cap," Joanna said. "Sheriff smart man. He know Indian not kill Daniel."

"I ain't anxious to meet up with Tyler Wells right now," Cap said.

"Well, then, let's go." Frenchy gave him a final shove, and the front door slammed behind them.

"I'd better clear out myself," Running Fox said, switching to his native tongue. "I'll come back after dark when things aren't so busy around here."

"I was leaving when those men showed up. Aiden is still at Donovan's ranch, and I'll be staying there too for a few more days."

"Selling this place might not be such a bad idea," he said. "Not to him, of course. But if he is willing to buy it, there are no doubt others as well. The pale people's money can be put to good use in our village."

"I will think about it, brother." Her lowered eyes gave her away. He had always been able to tell when his sister was trying to deceive him. Joanna was a very bad liar.

Bianca watched, astonished, as Cap and Frenchy dashed out the door, jumped on their horses and headed down the lane toward the river.

"Aren't you going after them?" she asked.

Tyler shook his head. "It's Mrs. Nolan I need to see right now. I'll track down Cap and Frenchy later."

"I didn't think those two men could move so fast," Bianca said. "And that old horse really high-tailed it out of here."

"Goes to prove that appearances can be deceiving."

"So you keep telling me."

While Tyler tethered his horse next to the buckskin mare, Joanna greeted them from the front stoop. "I see you coming," she said.

"Looks like Cap and Frenchy spotted us too," Tyler said. "But you're the one I was looking for."

Joanna motioned them inside.

"Cap make—how you say—offer for land. I say no."

"So that's why he was here. Brought Frenchy along to help soften you up, did he?"

Joanna shook her head. "Soften? I not understand."

"It's not important. I'm here to ask about your brother."

Joanna's eyes darted toward the kitchen door. "My brother?" Her voice was almost a whisper.

"Aiden talked about him to Frenchy," Bianca said. "Now, I think you need to tell us."

"My brother. Running Fox. I not know where he is." Joanna's eyes were downcast.

"How did he get along with your husband, Mrs. Nolan?" Tyler asked.

Joanna slumped into a chair and buried her face in her hands. "Sorry." Her words were muffled. "Running Fox not know Daniel. Not really."

"Mrs. Nolan, your husband was murdered, and I aim to find out who killed him. Right now your brother looks mighty guilty, and the more you clam up the more I've got to figure maybe you had a hand in it too."

Joanna cringed and shook her head. "Running Fox not like white people. Not happy I marry Daniel. But not kill. No, never kill."

"So when did you see him last?"

"Running Fox hide in mountains. I not know where." Joanna raised her head. "You find that man—Cap. He want hurt Aiden."

"But when—"

"Cap threatened Aiden?" Bianca ignored Tyler's look of irritation at her interruption. "What did he say?"

"I say I not sell. He say go away or bad things happen. Another fire. Aiden fall in river."

Bianca turned to Tyler. "That old man is a menace! Why don't you arrest him instead of badgering Joanna? Hasn't she been through enough?"

"Miss Stratton, I thought it would be helpful to have you along this afternoon. Obviously, I was mistaken." Tyler's controlled speech was icy.

"I apologize, Sheriff Wells." Bianca said through clenched teeth. "I'll leave so you can continue your interrogation without my interference." She turned and headed for the door.

"Please, Miss Stratton." Joanna stood and moved to put a restraining hand on Bianca's arm. "Aiden talk."

"Oren told me. I'm glad he has his voice back."

"But he talk about box, Miss Stratton—about missing paper."

"What's this about a missing paper?" Tyler asked. "What sort of paper? Missing from where?"

"Aiden like read. Look at papers in box many times. Try to read."

"Yes. You told me." Bianca moved to the table and sat down. "I know you're nervous and upset, Joanna, but try to remember exactly what Aiden said to you."

"This morning Aiden read papers in box. Say paper—clipping he call it—not there."

"There were a number of clippings as I recall," Tyler said. "It's not likely he'd notice if one was gone."

"He say he remember. Many hard words. Daniel name there too."

"All the newspaper stories I recall were about people who died," Bianca said.

"Yes. Clipping say man die. Man look for gold but river full of ice."

Bianca and Tyler exchanged puzzled looks.

"I didn't read all those clippings, but I scanned them," Bianca said. "I don't remember anything like that."

"I think we may have lost something in translation here." Tyler paced in front of the hearth. Then he turned to Joanna.

"Those papers were scattered all over the place when we found them. Maybe we missed a clipping when we gathered them up."

Joanna shook her head. "This morning I look. I sweep. I move everything. Clipping not here."

"Looks like I've got another reason to track down Cap." Tyler started for the door.

"I need to be on my way too," Bianca said. Following Tyler out, she turned to Joanna. "Tell Aiden I'll see him at the fiesta on Saturday."

Joanna nodded and smiled, but her eyes remained guarded.

Bianca followed Tyler to where the bay gelding stood quietly near the buckskin mare. "I hope you lock that old man up and throw away the key," she said. "The idea! Threatening that poor woman after all she's been through."

"That 'poor woman' changed the subject in a hurry when I started asking when she last saw her brother." Tyler swung his lanky frame into the saddle. "And you jumped right in and let her off the hook. So now Cap's taken off for God knows where on that old nag of his, and I haven't learned anything useful about Running Fox either."

"I was only trying to help."

"Any more help from you and I'll never get to the bottom of things around here."

The sheriff rode off in the direction Cap and Frenchy had gone, and Bianca trudged down the road. She supposed Tyler had good reason to be angry with her. But keeping Aiden safe was more important than finding out all about Joanna's brother. Obviously Cap was the real danger. Tyler Wells might be a smart man with a fancy education, but his methodical, plodding way of doing things was simply maddening.

CHAPTER 39

After class on Friday Edna and Edwina appeared from the coatroom carrying a large parcel wrapped in brown paper. Giggling even more than usual, they placed it on Bianca's desk.

"It's for you," Edna said.

"We made it," Edwina added.

Bianca stared at the package and ran her fingers tentatively over the brown wrapping.

"Open it," Edna urged.

"Really, girls. You shouldn't have—"

"Please, Miss Stratton," Edwina said, "open it now." .

The crackle of paper gave way to a rustle of taffeta as Bianca uncovered a rose-colored blouse, meticulously fashioned in the latest style. A ruffle of sheer lace outlined the V neckline and edged the long, flared sleeves.

"It's simply beautiful!"

"I hope it fits." Edna scooped up the blouse and held it up to measure across Bianca's shoulders. "We put the final seams in last night after we knew your size. Getting you to teach us about measuring was Edwina's idea."

"You tricked me," Bianca said with a smile. "But, honestly, I can't accept such an expensive gift."

"You have to, Miss Stratton. It's all made, and it wouldn't fit anyone else."

"At least let me pay you for the material," Bianca insisted. "I've never had anything made of taffeta, but I know it costs a lot."

"It was the end of a bolt, and there wasn't enough for a whole dress, so Mama said we could have it." Edna folded the garment expertly and put it back on the paper on Bianca's desk.

"We knew the color would be perfect with your hair." Edwina rewrapped the brown paper into a neat parcel.

Bianca didn't know what to say. The tiny stitches, fine darts, tucks and gathers must have involved hours of work. There was no way she could refuse this present without hurting the twins' feelings.

"It's for the fiesta," Edna was saying. "It's too bad you don't have a really nice skirt, but the black one you wear to school will look all right."

"It's beautiful! I'd be proud to wear it anywhere."

Twin smiles greeted her remark.

"What you really need to go with the black skirt is a bit of black velvet ribbon around your neck," Edna said.

"That's what the picture in *Godey's Ladys Book* showed with this neckline," Edwina chimed in. "A black velvet neckband fastened with a brooch. I don't suppose you've got a brooch."

The girls' enthusiasm must be contagious, Bianca thought. Getting all gussied up for a party was totally foreign to her, but she was surprised to discover she was actually looking forward to it.

"As a matter of fact, I have a very pretty pin," she said. "But I guess I'll have to pay a visit to your parents' store to get a bit of ribbon."

"Why don't you walk home with us?" Edna suggested.

"We sent Junior on so he wouldn't spoil the surprise," Edwina said, "but we'll help you tidy up."

A short time later Bianca headed for Fowler's store with a twin on either side. The girls prattled happily of hem braids, box pleats, gimp embroidery and bonnet casings. Bianca didn't have the least notion what they were talking about, so she simply relaxed and enjoyed feeling like a seventeen-year-old girl instead of a proper schoolmarm.

Inside Fowler's store Bianca experienced the mixed reactions she'd felt on her first visit. Mingled aromas of licorice, pickle brine, tobacco and peppermint brought forth welcome memories of the happy hours she'd spent in her father's store. The chilly atmosphere and shadowy corners, however, were mute reminders that this was a different time and place. Her light-hearted mood faded in the gloom.

She noticed a canvas bag labeled US Mail on a hook by the door and wondered if Leandra Stratton, whoever she was, had received her letter. If so, would she write back? Mail service was faster and more reliable now that the railroad connected California with the East, but it might still be months before a reply reached her. She sighed.

The twins, apparently immune to the depressing atmosphere, chorused, "We're home from school, Mama," and were acknowledged by a muffled reply from behind the partition.

Bianca scanned the cluttered counters. Something had changed since her previous visit.

"The ribbons are over here," Edna called, and Bianca followed the bubbly pair to the dry goods counter. Edwina carefully measured and cut velvet ribbon while Edna demonstrated how to loop it into the fashionable flat bow that would show off Bianca's brooch.

"If you put your hair up into a chignon, another piece of ribbon would really set it off," Edna was saying.

"Oh, yes!" Edwina measured and cut a second piece of ribbon. "A chignon would be perfect."

Bianca nodded absently, looking from one counter to another. "Something about the store seems different," she remarked, "but I can't put my finger on what it is."

Edna shook her head. "Everything's right where it's always been. We're always suggesting new ways to display merchandise, but papa doesn't like change."

"Well, there's the signs," Edwina said.

"That's right," Edna said. "I forgot. Mama saw us practicing our letters and said we might as well save her some work and put our schooling to good use."

"Of course." Bianca wandered to the section where the food was displayed and paused in front of a carefully printed sign, "Beef liver—fresh today."

"Edwina made that one," Edna said. "Her printing is better than mine."

"The printing is very neat, and your spelling is perfect," Bianca said. Then she stopped short as she recalled the sign, "Frsh beef livr," that had greeted her on her first visit to Fowler's.

When Tyler first handed her the anonymous note, she knew she'd seen the crude printing and dreadful spelling somewhere before. Until this moment she hadn't been able to make the connection. The twins were rattling on cheerfully, and she realized she hadn't heard a word.

"I'm sorry, girls. I must have been woolgathering." Bianca moved to the counter and paid for her purchase.

"I was saying I bet Cora would do a chignon for you. She's really good with hair." Edna tucked the ribbons into the parcel with the Bianca's new blouse.

"Not that your hair doesn't look lovely the way you usually wear it."

"You're just being kind, Edwina," Bianca said, forcing a smile. "I've always been hopeless about fixing my hair, and it never stays put anyway. Since you've gone to so much trouble to be sure I look my best for the fiesta, the least I can do is see if Cora will help with my hairdo."

She thanked the girls again and started for the door. Then she turned and cast a final glance toward the back of the store. Undoubtedly Agnes Fowler knew she was here, but it was just as well the storekeeper's wife stayed out of sight. Bianca's sharp tongue had gotten her into trouble all her life, and sure as anything she'd have lit into Agnes about the note.

She headed down the road trying once again to sort things out. She was certain the anonymous note was Agnes' work. Still, it was hard to believe the tiny woman could have accumulated so much dislike in so short a time. Had writing the note been her own idea, or had Ed put her up to it?

Bianca was truly fond of all the Fowler children, and it was hard to reconcile those feelings with her new suspicions about their parents. And what about Mattie and Cushing? Mattie considered Agnes a close friend. Should she even tell Mattie she believed Agnes was the anonymous letter writer? When had life become so complicated anyway?

CHAPTER 40

"Don't do anything too fancy," Bianca protested. "I feel foolish the way you're fussing over me." She sat at the kitchen table with a towel draped over her shoulders while Cora wielded the hairbrush. An audience of Pangston girls hovered, adding to her discomfort.

Cora laughed. "I declare, Miss Stratton, you make almost as much fuss as Katie. You've got wonderful, thick hair, but it needs a bit of taming."

"Like the shrew lady you told us about." Katie stirred a concoction of sugar and water in a large glass, sloshing a fair amount on the table.

Gertrude grabbed a dishrag and mopped up the puddles. Then she sat across the table from Bianca and began arranging a pile of hairpins in neat rows. "Cora does Mama's hair every Sunday," she said. "She does Tina's curls, too."

"A chignon isn't difficult." Cora dipped the comb into the sugar water. "I'll leave a front curl on each side. The twins say it's the latest style."

Controlling Bianca's unruly mop seemed to require endless applications of sugar water and countless hairpins. Finally Cora stepped back and regarded her handiwork. Then she handed Bianca the mirror.

The flyaway mane with a carelessly pinned bun at the back of her neck had been transformed into a sleek chignon set high on her head and secured with black velvet ribbon. Her natural waves softened the center part, and curls trailed provocatively from her temples to the jaw line.

"I don't even recognize myself! I've always been hopeless about fixing my hair, and I never tried to put it up—I'm tall enough already."

"You look like a queen," Katie said. "A really, truly queen, not the storybook kind."

Mattie bustled in from the parlor.

"It's not too fussy?" Bianca asked. "I mean, are those curls a bit—"

"You look lovely. The curls are perfect." Mattie nodded and gave Cora an approving pat on the shoulder. "Now run along and change into your new dresses, everybody. We'll be leaving soon."

Upstairs Bianca put on several extra petticoats to add fullness to her old black skirt. Then she slipped the rose taffeta blouse over her chemise and fastened the row of tiny covered buttons up the front to the frill of lace. The top was a perfect fit, skimming her body and hugging her waist. She noted with dismay that the neckline was much lower than any of her other blouses, and the swell of her breasts was unmistakable under the lace.

"Five minutes!" Mattie's voice floated up the stairwell.

Bianca fastened the narrow black velvet ribbon at her throat, adding the amethyst brooch as a finishing touch. Then, at the last minute, she flung on her black cloak.

CHAPTER 41

Rolf wheeled to a stop at the end of Nora Donovan's circular drive. Charlie Mollers, the bandy-legged hand he'd run into when he stayed at the bunkhouse, met him as he got out of the surrey.

"I'll see to them fancy trotters of yours, Mr. Knudsen." Charlie took the reins and ran an appreciative hand over the nearest horse's chestnut flank. You're early, but this place will be crawlin' with folks before long. I'd best take the rig around back too and get it out of harm's way."

Rolf frowned. "Harm? What kind of harm?"

"Manner of speaking, you know. Folks can get a mite rowdy as the day wears on. Mrs. Donovan's punchbowl packs a pretty good wallop." Charlie grinned and led the trotters toward a cluster of outbuildings.

Rolf shook his head and climbed the broad steps of the front veranda. Before he lifted the heavy iron knocker, the door flew open. Nora Donovan clasped his outstretched hand with both of hers, and the touch of her cool fingers sent a shiver of pleasure up his arm.

"Rolf! What a nice surprise! I was afraid you'd decide that driving so far for a party wasn't worth the effort. I'm so glad you decided to come."

Her welcoming smile lessened his misgivings, and he followed her inside. Logs blazed in the enormous fireplace, infusing the air with the scent of cedar. The massive furniture had been shoved to the edges of the room.

"One of the nice things about this place is that I can always make plenty of space for dancing." Nora fingered the fringe on a mantilla draped over the ornate square piano.

"Well—dancing, drinking hard spirits—I've never had much use for that sort of thing. And with all the trouble you folks have had in these parts—"

"All the more reason to make time for some pleasure." She tilted her head to meet his eyes and flashed a disarming smile. "Some folks seem to think enjoying life is a sin. I've never been able to understand that."

"I'm beginning to suspect you enjoy leading people astray." Rolf meant the words to sound serious, but for some reason he ended up grinning.

"There will be two punch bowls. You can choose." She whirled and led him away from the piano. "We'll talk about the dancing later. Now come back into the kitchen where the real preparations are under way."

"Get busy on that saddle, Oren." Jesse circled the tack-room where Oren and Hank, along with several ranch hands, were cleaning and polishing the ranch's working gear into fiesta condition. "You've still got to put a shine on your spurs so you can do your Aunt Nora proud this afternoon."

"I don't see why we can't have a regular rodeo instead of this Mexican charade thing," Hank grumbled.

"It's not a charade—it's a charreada," Oren said. "Aunt Nora says the charros—that's what they call cowboys on Grandfather's ranch—do a lot more fancy roping than we do."

"Right." Hank sighed. "We do Oregon mishmash. No bucking broncos, no bull riding—a bunch of tame stuff."

"Mrs. Donovan doesn't see any sense in torturing animals just so folks can have a little amusement," Jesse said. "Roping and riding are honest-to-God useful ranch chores."

"Still, it would be fun to at least have bronc riding," Oren said. "Breaking wild horses—that's important ranch stuff."

"We're fresh out of bucking broncos in these parts." Jesse whacked the dust off a saddle blanket.

"Oren wants to get on some mustang so he can show off for Edna Fowler." Hank dipped a soft rag into a tin of linseed oil and rubbed it into the reins he was holding. "Edwina's just as pretty, and I think she's nicer."

"Edna's got more spunk." Oren studiously polished the leather pommel on his saddle. "I like a gal with spunk."

"You think Miss Stratton's got spunk, Jesse?" Hank flicked the reins in Jesse's direction.

"You got your eye on Miss Stratton, Jesse?" Oren shot Hank a wink.

"Uncle Charlie says her brother-in-law got here bright and early." Hank grinned. "Guess he wants to keep tabs on her."

"I've got better things to do than jaw with you boys," Jesse said. "Get finished here and wash up before any more folks arrive."

He stopped at the pump and sloshed cold water over his hands and arms. What was Knudsen doing here, anyway? Probably Nora had invited him when he was bunking here after the fire. Hell, she invited everybody. Most likely the boys were right and Knudsen was doing his best to keep a tight rein on Bianca Stratton—as if she wasn't already way too much of a goody-goody. Well, Jesse had plans, and there was no way some hick farmer was going to stand in his way.

CHAPTER 42

"We're never going to get there," Katie complained as yet another horse and buggy wheeled around to pass the Pangston's farm wagon.

"And I've already got dust all over my new bonnet." Gertrude held a handkerchief over her mouth with one hand and waved the other to ward off a persistent blowfly.

Tina whined while the others bickered, but Bianca resisted the urge to comment on the girls' behavior. Cushing Pangston's poor old farm horse was undoubtedly the slowest animal in Oregon. Probably everybody for miles around would arrive at the Donovan ranch long before they did. However, Bianca didn't share the girls' impatience. She fingered the back of her neck where her bun should be.

Getting all dressed up seemed like a lark when Cora was fixing her hair, but soon everybody would be looking at her. Still, it would be a treat to relax and enjoy the outing, and she did want to see for herself that Aiden was recovering from the fire. Now that Aiden could talk, she was anxious to ask him about the missing clipping. If Tyler was right and Cap had left the footprint outside the Nolan's back door, then Cap must have taken the clipping. But why? She wondered if Tyler had managed to catch up with Cap. Even though Mattie said everybody for miles around turned up at Nora's fiesta, she was willing to bet Cap wouldn't be there. Would Tyler? She really needed to talk to him about Agnes Fowler and the anonymous note.

At last the creaky wagon rumbled through the gate and down the tree-shaded road. Bianca was surprised at the number of wagons and buggies lining the circular drive. People she'd never seen before gathered on the front veranda, and even more folks milled around by the corrals.

"Come on." Cora jumped down and smoothed the wrinkles from her skirt. "It looks like they've already started the calf roping." She hurtled down a gravel path with Gertrude and Katie trailing in her wake.

Bianca climbed off the wagon and followed the girls. People were shouting, and the air was thick with the smell of horse-sweat and sawdust. She found a spot by the high wooden fence that circled the large corral. A man on horseback was chasing a half-grown brindle calf. His lasso circled in the air and landed in the dirt near the calf's hind legs. A chorus of boos and catcalls greeted him as the calf escaped.

"Oren's next. He's been practicing for months."

Bianca turned at the sound of Nora Donovan's voice. Rolf stood at Nora's elbow. Bianca blinked in surprise. What in the world was Rolf doing here?

A cheer from the crowd forced her attention back to the corral. Oren's lasso caught a brown calf squarely around its neck. Within seconds Oren was off his horse and securing the rope around all four of the struggling animal's feet. Then, almost as quickly, he untied the rope. The calf got to its feet and raced to the far gate amid whistles and cheers from the crowd.

"Nice roping, Oren!" Jesse tipped his hat in salute, and an errant breeze ruffled his hair. He was on the far side of an adjoining pen, mounted on a black stallion. Bianca watched in admiration as horse and rider moved effortlessly among the milling herd, separating the next calf and guiding it smoothly into the chute.

"Jesse on horseback is quite something, isn't he?" Nora said.

Bianca flushed. "Doesn't he compete in the roping contest?" she asked.

"It's Jesse's job to see that the whole charreada goes off smoothly. But before I made him foreman, he won every event. Everybody knows he's the best roper around, so we decided the others ought to have a chance." Nora moved closer and patted Bianca's shoulder. "I must say, Bianca, your new hairdo is charming. Don't you think so, Rolf?"

Rolf mumbled something unintelligible.

Bianca wrapped herself more snugly in her cloak. "The children say Aiden is feeling much better," she said. "I hope I'll get to talk to him."

"He's here somewhere. He's been helping Chang and Joanna carry food out to the patio."

"Then he's really all right?"

Nora nodded. "Children recuperate in a hurry." She waved as Oren's horse cantered past them and left the corral.

"Oren sits his horse like a champion." Rolf observed.

"He's been riding all his life," Nora said. "Come to think of it, Bianca, you should have a horse while you're here in Oakfield. Spending all your time at school or with the Pangstons can't be too lively. Riding would give you some freedom."

"Bianca used to be a reckless rider, and she had a bad fall. She doesn't ride anymore." Rolf turned back to the corral as another calf left the chute, this time with Hank in pursuit.

Bianca watched as Hank's rope found its mark. His dismount and skill at tying the calf's feet left room for improvement, but he managed to do the job. Bianca joined in the applause as he doffed his hat and waved.

"Maybe I gave up riding too soon."

"On horseback it's not far from Oakfield out here to the ranch," Nora said. "You could drop in any time."

Bianca turned to Rolf. "I've been thinking about Patches. If she were here, I could at least be sure she hasn't forgotten me."

"I suppose I could bring her along the next time I'm out this way." Rolf frowned. "But you tried to ride her after your accident and always ended up all pale and shaking. I don't know what makes you think things will be any different now."

"I believe I'm ready to try again."

"Well, even if you could ride, you shouldn't be gallivanting through the woods."

"Really, Rolf. I'm quite capable of looking after myself."

"Well, I can't help worrying. From what the sheriff says, he's not even close to catching up with whoever murdered that blacksmith fellow."

Nora scanned the crowd. "Now that you mention the sheriff, I was hoping he'd join us, but I haven't seen him."

Jesse remained on the fringe of the activities, but he was clearly in charge of everything. He edged riders into position and signaled the ranch hands manning the gates, calling out each event and announcing the winners. Oren's time was fastest for calf roping, and one of the hands from a ranch up river walked off with the grand prize, a tooled leather belt with a silver buckle. But Jesse's gravelly voice and ready smile kept Bianca's eyes riveted on the tall man riding the black stallion.

After the final applause at the corral died down, Bianca joined the crowd and followed the tantalizing aroma to the rear of the ranch house. A side of beef roasted over a pit filled with glowing coals. Planks laid across large barrels formed trestle tables loaded with roast duck, pheasant, mashed potatoes, corn on the cob, sauerkraut, and sourdough biscuits. Smaller tables held crocks of butter, bowls of berry and peach preserves and dozens of pies and cakes.

Aiden emerged from the kitchen carrying a large platter which he deposited on one of the tables. A moment later he dashed toward her, and she greeted him with a hug.

"My goodness, you really are all better," she said. Except for the bandages on his hands, Aiden didn't look at all like the sickly child she'd visited after the fire.

"Yes, Ma'am. We'd be back home now, but my ma is helping with the vittles. I never seen so much food before."

"I don't believe I have either. And your voice is fine, too."

He scuffed the toe of his moccasin in the grass. "I sure didn't like it when I couldn't talk."

"It must have been terrible."

He nodded. "Having to stay in bed—I didn't like that neither. Oren came in and read to me. He reads real good, Oren does."

"And your mother says you've been reading a lot yourself. You know, I've been wanting to ask you—"

"I gotta go, Ma'am. Ma said to hurry back to the kitchen and fetch the turnips."

Aiden darted toward the kitchen door, and Bianca's eyes filled with tears as she watched him disappear inside the house. He'd been through a terrible ordeal, and she was afraid he was still in danger. Joanna was clearly frightened, and Tyler Wells seemed to take Cap's threats seriously. She glanced about her, but the only familiar faces were the Fowlers. They had spread a blanket under a tree on the far side of the patio. Bianca knew the twins would want to see her wearing the blouse they'd made, but she was in no mood to face Agnes.

People helped themselves and left the tables with plates piled high. Bianca started toward the kitchen to find Joanna when she spotted Tyler's lanky figure at the edge of the veranda. He was talking to Frenchy, who disappeared inside the house before she reached them.

Tyler turned and made a formal little bow. His dark gray frock coat with satin piping on the lapels erased any lawman image. "You're looking lovely, Miss Stratton," he said.

"Good evening, Sheriff Wells." The side-curls tickled her face, but she resisted the impulse to tuck them behind her ears.

"I'm not here officially."

"I see you're not wearing your badge. But I did want to talk to you about—"

"Frenchy and I were saying how fortunate it is that the fine weather held on for Nora's fiesta."

"Considering that the last time I saw Frenchy, you were chasing him into the woods, I'd think you'd have something more important than the weather to talk to him about."

"Oh, I have plenty to say to Frenchy. And to Ed Fowler too, but this is hardly the time or place for business."

"Ed Fowler? What's Ed Fowler got to do with—"

"The bit of velvet on your hair is most attractive." Tyler took her arm and steered her back toward the array of food.

Bianca tried to shrug loose, but his grasp was firm. "Really, Sheriff Wells, I need to—"

"I'd be honored if you'd join me for supper." They reached the trestle table, and he handed her a large plate. "I believe we're supposed to help ourselves and then find a shady spot."

Bianca pursed her lips in frustration. Tyler was clearly intent on playing the courtly southern gentleman. She had to admit he looked the part, right down to the gold watch chain looped across his vest. But she simply couldn't understand how everybody could be so cheerful in the face of threats and murder.

"This is a fiesta, Miss Stratton. You're supposed to relax and enjoy yourself. May I help you to some corn?"

"I'm afraid I've never had much time for parties."

"Well, then, it seems you're overdue. How about some pheasant?"

"Everything does look delicious." Her mouth was watering at the mingled aromas and the piles of food. She heaped mashed potatoes and succulent beef onto her plate.

"You're probably overdue for a hearty meal, too." He guided her to a stone bench near the tiled fountain. "Hunger pangs can make a young woman cantankerous—or so I've been told."

Bianca bit back a sharp retort. Laugh-lines crinkled the corners of the sheriff's eyes. She couldn't help smiling back. "Tyler Wells, are you poking fun at me?"

"I can't help joshing you. You're an easy target for teasing, Bianca."

"I suppose I am at that."

Tyler was right, of course. Everybody was here to have a good time. And the food was scrumptious. Bianca concentrated on savoring every morsel on her plate. After the last bite of corn she leaned back on the bench with a sigh of contentment.

"Want to go back and try the desserts? I spotted some mighty appealing bread pudding on one of those small tables."

"Really, Mr. Wells—"

"Tyler."

"I couldn't eat another bite right now. I know you don't want to spoil Nora's fiesta, but I have so many questions, and I need to talk to you about the anonymous note."

"Maybe after a little stroll you'll be ready for some pudding or, perhaps, a slice of pie." He pulled her to her feet. "While we walk, you can tell me what's so important it can't wait until tomorrow."

She told him about the missing pages in Junior's copybook and the signs she remembered seeing at Fowler's store. "The writing and the spelling were the same—I'm sure of it. Agnes Fowler wrote that note."

"You may well be right, Bianca."

"I'm really fond of all the young Fowlers. The twins even made me a beautiful new blouse and gave it to me as a surprise. But Agnes Fowler is another matter."

"Leaving a malicious note on somebody's gatepost isn't actually a crime."

"Maybe Ed put her up to it. Earlier when I asked you about Frenchy, you said something about Ed Fowler, and—"

"Leave the Fowlers to me, Bianca." He scraped corncobs into a barrel by the kitchen door and deposited dirty dishes into a large washtub nearby. Now about our stroll."

"Really, Tyler, I have no intention of—"

The screen door slammed. Aiden ambled toward them wearing a frosting moustache and carrying a half-eaten piece of spice cake. "Sorry I run off before, Miss Stratton, but—"

"You were helping your mother."

"Yes, Ma'am, I was. But she's got no more chores for me right now."

Tyler squatted to put himself at Aiden's eye-level. "We spoke to your mother when she was at home yesterday. She said something about a missing clipping."

Aiden nodded and took a bite of cake.

"We're not sure we understood everything your mother told us," Bianca said. "But somebody broke into your house, and—"

"My ma told me about it." Aiden wiped his mouth with his shirtsleeve.

"If someone took a clipping, he must have thought it was important." Tyler said. "We were hoping you could help us figure out what was so special about it."

Bianca echoed Tyler's calm voice and patient manner. "Why don't you tell us anything you remember about that particular clipping?"

"Well, it was old. The paper was kind of yellow."

Tyler nodded. "Now try to see the paper in your mind. What can you remember about the words?"

"It was about a man who died. All them newspaper pieces was like that—about folks dying, you know. Pa's name was in it, too."

"Your mother said something about an icy river." Bianca said.

Aiden sat down on the kitchen steps, elbows on knees and chin in his hands. "It said frozen river right there at the beginning of the story. Or maybe freezing river. Then there was something about gold. And some old man died when he hit his head on a rock. That's all I remember."

"You remembered a lot," Tyler said.

"Is it going to help you catch whoever killed my pa?"

"I can't say for sure, Aiden. But being a sheriff means getting little bits of information wherever I can until there's enough so I can see the whole picture. What you've told me may help me do that."

"That's good." Aiden jumped to his feet. "There's Oren over by the food tables. Did you see him rope that calf?" He dashed across the grass. "Hey, Oren!"

Bianca turned to Tyler. "I still can't make any sense of it."

"Aiden's a smart boy, but he's only beginning to read."

"The old man—maybe it said he was hit on the head with a rock. Maybe the clipping was about a murder. And if Cap took it, that means—"

"It means you're starting to jump to conclusions again."

"I can't help worrying. While Aiden and his mother were here at the ranch, I felt they were safe. Now they'll be going back home, and you agreed Cap's threat was a serious matter. And where is Cap, anyway? Did you ever catch up with him?"

He guided her across the veranda. "It's getting chilly out here, and I hear Frenchy tuning up inside. We better have a look."

"Frenchy?"

"Nora says he's the about the best fiddler she's ever heard."

"I'd have never guessed." Bianca allowed herself to be steered indoors. Tyler Wells was being his usual self—pleasant, polite and totally exasperating.

CHAPTER 43

People were gathering around the edges of the enormous room. Bianca spotted Rolf by the kitchen door where Joanna was ladling amber liquid from an enormous cut-glass punchbowl. An elderly Chinese gentleman emerged from the kitchen smiling broadly and carrying a silver punchbowl only slightly smaller than the glass one.

Bianca started across the room to speak to Joanna, but Tyler stepped into her path.

"Let me take your cloak," he said.

Bianca bit her lip. Cedar logs blazing in the fireplace warmed the room, and all of the ladies had shed their wraps. She'd counted on the black cloak to keep her from being noticed, but now it only made her more conspicuous. Reluctantly she untied the cord at her neckline as Tyler moved behind her and slipped the cloak off her shoulders.

"Well, if that's the blouse the twins made, I must say it does you proud."

Tyler took the cloak and moved toward a settee at the side of the room where wraps were being deposited. Bianca found herself standing alone. She glanced down at the swell of rose taffeta.

A flush of embarrassment flooded her cheeks and spread across her chest.

"I think we'll have time for a bit of punch before the dancing starts."

She whirled at the sound of Jesse's voice. The flush deepened as his glance, intimate as a caress, moved appraisingly over her.

"Good evening, Mr. Landry." What was wrong with her, anyway? She couldn't even speak to Jesse without the words coming out high-pitched and forced. She looked up and resisted a sudden urge to smooth the wayward swirl of dark eyebrow near the bridge of his nose.

"You're looking mighty nice this evening, Miss Stratton. Your hair looks fine all wound up on top."

"Thank you," she murmured. She glanced away from his face and found herself staring at his square, calloused hands. Cradled by his fingers, the cut-glass punch cups he carried seemed even more fragile.

He held out one of the cups, and she took it. The first sip of the fruity liquid warmed her mouth and slipped down her throat.

"Mmm. This is wonderful. It tastes of berries and apples and—I'm not quite sure what else."

"Nora says it's her secret recipe. Did you enjoy the charreada?"

"Oh—you mean the riding and all. I never heard it called char—what was that word?"

"It's a fancy Mexican kind of rodeo. Oren did a fine job of calf-roping."

"Yes, he did. I know you've been working with the boys."

Bianca started at the sound of Tyler's voice behind her. "Mr. Landry is a man of many talents."

"Good evening, Sheriff Wells." Jesse took a slow drink from his punch cup. "Figured you'd be off chasing outlaws."

"Even we intrepid lawmen get an hour to ourselves from time to time."

"Funny you'd want to spend your off time in a backwater like Oakfield."

"Oh, I'd say the area has its attractions." Tyler edged closer to Bianca.

"And more than its share of trouble lately." Jesse frowned.

"Of course, I intend to keep an eye out for anyone who might wish to harm Miss Stratton."

Jesse lifted an eyebrow. "I don't believe the lady needs a bodyguard."

"I'm afraid there's reason to think otherwise."

"In that case, I'll take extra good care of her as the evening wears on." Jesse cupped a protective hand on Bianca's elbow.

"I'm quite capable of looking after myself," Bianca said lightly.

She looked back and forth between the two men, each strong and capable in his own way. Jesse's casual cotton shirt with a bright blue kerchief knotted at the throat seemed somehow more festive than Tyler's elegant suit. How different they were, these two. Their verbal sparring match about her welfare sent a shiver of excitement down her back. She took another sip of punch, glanced across the room, and saw Rolf staring and scowling. She shot him an irritated frown and pulled free of Jesse's grasp.

"I really must go speak to Mrs. Nolan." She left Jesse and Tyler glaring at each other and moved toward the kitchen, edging her way through the people clustered around the punchbowls.

Joanna wore a lace-edged apron over a maroon calico dress. Her long braids were coiled around her head. She flashed a smile as Bianca drew near.

"Miss Stratton. Is fine party. Yes?"

"It's a wonderful party. So much food! Everything I tasted was simply delicious. You must have spent days getting ready."

"I like cook here. Mrs. Nora has fine, big kitchen. I learn new things from Mr. Chang, too."

"Still, I know you and Aiden will be glad to get home."

"Aiden happy at school. He like see other children. I—well, is nice here. Many people to talk to."

"I'm glad you and Nora Donovan have become friends." Until now Bianca hadn't realized how lonely Joanna's life must have been—isolated from her people and ostracized by the community. The time here on Donovan's ranch must have seemed like heaven once Aiden's recovery was certain.

She drained her cup and put it on a silver tray near the punch bowl. Another cup joined hers on the tray, and she turned and looked into Jesse's incredibly blue eyes.

"I'm not letting you get away so easy," he said. "They're about to start dancing, and I mean to claim you for the Virginia reel."

"Bianca oughtn't flaunt herself about in that skimpy outfit." Rolf shook his head. "I see nothing but trouble ahead if she keeps on—"

"Why, Rolf Knudsen, I do believe you're jealous." Nora nudged his arm. "You'd better have another cup of punch."

"Nora, you are the limit. Do you take anything seriously?"

"Absolutely. But never at a fiesta. Now I need to start the Virginia reel. How about being my partner?"

"I haven't danced in years."

"That's a poor excuse."

"Maybe later. Head couple in the Virginia reel is way beyond me."

"Well, I'll have to snag somebody else." She flounced away, turning back for a moment to waggle a forefinger and flash a beguiling smile.

Strong women fascinated Rolf, but he found them intimidating. Viola had been little more than a child when they were married, but she was an astute businesswoman whose advice he'd learned to value. She'd also been the leavening for his sober nature, and as the fiddler tuned up Rolf recalled how Viola had cajoled him into attending barn dances when they were courting.

Now he regarded Nora Donovan with a mixture of admiration and trepidation as she intercepted Tyler Wells before he reached the punchbowl and led him onto the dance floor. They took their place at the front as couples began forming a double line down the center of the room, the men on one side, ladies on the other. Then he saw Bianca looking up at the ranch foreman with a besotted grin on her face. Muttering under his breath, Rolf headed for the punchbowl.

Jesse took Bianca's arm and moved her to the side of the room. Frenchy, moustache gleaming with wax and lamp-black, sat in a straight-backed chair, a battered violin in his lap. A wiry, bow-legged man with a banjo stood beside him.

"The banjo player is Charlie Mollers—Hank's uncle," Jesse said. "He does the calling too."

The fiddle struck up "Turkey in the Straw." The banjo chimed in, accompanied by the rhythmic stamping of Charlie's booted foot.

"All right, everybody, grab a partner for the Virginia reel." Charlie's voice boomed over the music.

"We'd best join the line," Jesse said. "They'll start the music from the beginning when everybody's settled down."

"But I don't know what to do. I can't—"

"There's no real dancing to it. You kind of step in time to the music. Watch the other folks, and you'll see how easy it is. By the time it's our turn you'll have the hang of it."

Jesse took her hand and tugged her into position with the other couples. Tyler and Nora stood at the head of the line. Bianca noted that Tyler seemed completely at ease. No doubt southern gentlemen spent plenty of time at fancy cotillions. How in the world had she allowed Jesse to talk her into dancing? Her feet felt like blocks of wood.

"Head lady, foot man, forward and back!" Charlie's voice roared over the music.

Nora Donovan and a farmer from the end of the line moved diagonally down the open area between the couples, curtsied and bowed, and moved back to where they started. The flounces on Nora's crimson skirt contrasted with the man's baggy over-alls. Jesse grinned at Bianca across the space separating them, and she joined in when everybody began clapping in time to the catchy old tune.

"Head lady, foot man, right hand round!"

Nora and the farmer jogged forward again, joined hands and made a complete turn before going back to where they started. Bianca smiled. This didn't look too complicated, what with Charlie hollering out the moves. By the time Charlie called out, "Reel your partner, right to the center, left to the side," she simply ignored the puzzling directions and allowed herself to be whirled around and returned to her place.

The rest of the dance was like playing follow the leader. Then she and Jesse joined hands to form part of a long archway. The tempo of the music was contagious, and her heart raced as she felt his hands holding hers. By the time she and Jesse took their turn as head couple, Bianca felt as if she was floating on the music and the glow of Jesse's touch. When the dance was over, she stood breathless and laughing, her hands still clasped in his.

"I knew you were a born dancer," Jesse said.

"I had no idea it would be so much fun."

"Next one's a round dance. Are you game to try it?"

"Oh, I think I better catch my breath until they do the reel again."

"Another glass of punch, then, and a little fresh air."

"I'm really not a bit thirsty, but it does seem warm in here." She slid one hand free and fanned her fingers to cool her flushed cheeks

"Well, let's step outside."

The back veranda was tranquil and deserted. A shaft of moon-light filtered through a wispy cloud, setting the tiled fountain aglow. Bianca's hand was still enveloped in Jesse's grasp, and she felt as if all the nerve-ends in her body were concentrated there. Then he turned, his face only inches from hers. She stood looking up into his eyes. The sounds of music and dancing faded, and her breathing felt suddenly shallow.

"Bianca, I don't rightly know how to say this, but—"

"It's a wonderful party. Who'd have thought Frenchy could coax so much music out of a fiddle?" Now I'm babbling, she thought. "I can't help wondering—"

He placed his forefinger on her lips. "Let me have my say, Bianca, before I lose my nerve. This may seem sudden to you, but the first time I laid eyes on you, I knew. I've been on my own since I was younger than Oren, and I've been around some. But, Bianca, I never asked any gal to marry me. Not until now."

His arms circled her waist. The first brush of his lips against hers sent her pulse throbbing. Of their own volition her lips responded. She melted against him, overwhelmed by a host of sensations she had never even imagined. The kiss deepened, and she parted her lips to savor the tangy, warm taste of his mouth on hers.

"What's going on here?" Rolf's shout thundered in her ears.

She pulled back, but Jesse's powerful arms held her close.

"Not that it's any of your business, but I've asked Bianca to be my wife." Jesse's voice was calm.

Rolf stormed across the terrace. "My sister-in-law's future is very much my concern."

"Then I hope we'll have your blessing."

"I think it's a little early to ask for Rolf's blessing," Bianca said, trying to control her pounding pulse.

Jesse's arms fell to his sides, and he stepped back wearing a puzzled expression.

Bianca turned to Rolf. "Jesse asked me to marry him, but I haven't had a chance to give him my answer."

"I saw no sign you were resisting his advances," Rolf's voice rose ominously. "Quite the opposite, in fact."

"Actually, Rolf, Jesse was right when he said it wasn't any of your business. Go back inside and leave us alone."

"I'll do no such thing," he bellowed.

"Is everything all right?" Nora's words floated across the terrace. She moved swiftly to Bianca's side with Tyler close behind her.

Bianca stared at their anxious faces. Despite the evening chill, her cheeks were burning.

"We heard some commotion out here." Tyler had dropped the gallant southern gentleman tone. "What's the problem?"

"No problem, Sheriff." Jesse draped a protective arm across Bianca's shoulder. "Except that Knudsen here doesn't know when he's not wanted."

"Bianca?" Tyler's eyes had turned stormy gray.

"Rolf seems to think I'm a child who needs looking after."

Rolf stood clenching and unclenching his fists. Even in the dim light Bianca could see the distended veins in his neck.

"Come back inside, Rolf." Nora spoke softly, but she moved close to Rolf and put a tentative hand on his arm.

Tyler stepped to Rolf's other side. "Nora's right," he said. "I think it's obvious Bianca and Jesse want to be alone."

Suddenly Rolf's hands went slack, and he allowed himself to be steered back toward the house without a backward glance. Bianca watched the threesome proceed slowly down the gravel path. When they reached the door, Tyler turned and gave her a long, searching look. She averted her eyes and heard the door close behind him.

Jesse's arms enfolded her and she inhaled the scent of soap and hay that clung to him.

"I'm sorry about your brother-in-law," he said.

"It wasn't your fault."

"I know." His lips brushed her forehead. "Let's have that answer now. Will you marry me, Bianca?"

She caught her breath. "Oh, Jesse, I don't know what to say."

"I won't rush you, Bianca, but I intend to do some serious courting until you say yes. Is that all right with you?" His mouth ranged slowly across her temple and cheekbone.

Bianca caught her breath at the sweet warmth of his touch. "Oh, yes, Jesse. Serious courting sounds wonderful!"

CHAPTER 44

"Aren't you the sly one, Bianca!" Mattie crossed the parlor, brandishing a feather duster at everything in her path. "Why, every unmarried lady for miles around has set her cap for Jesse Landry. We'd pretty much concluded he wasn't the marrying kind."

Bianca aligned the last row of chairs and plopped a worn leather hymnal on each one. Last night, after the festivities ended, Jesse had driven her home, a proprietary arm around her waist. She'd nestled beside him and gazed dreamily at the stars overhead.

This morning dark clouds scudded across the valley and bunched against the Cascades like bundles of dirty laundry. A dull ache throbbed in Bianca's temples, and Mattie had been rattling on ever since they'd left the breakfast table.

"Of course, there aren't many single women in these parts." Mattie flicked the duster over the melodeon and straightened the *Praise the Lord* cross-stitch sampler on the wall behind it. "Have you set a date?"

Bianca shook her head. "Really, Mattie. I haven't even given him my answer."

"I was wondering how long we'd have you here."

Was there a hopeful note in Mattie's voice? Would everybody in Oakfield be relieved if she packed up and moved away—even Mattie?

"I had no idea Jesse was about to propose." Seeing the world, making something of herself—were those mere daydreams of a foolish girl she was about to leave behind without a backward glance? "I told him I needed time to think it over, but . . ."

"Let's face it, Bianca. You're not getting any younger." Mattie placed a hymnal on the melodeon and flipped the pages to *Blest Be the Tie That Binds*. "Jesse Landry is as good a catch as you're likely to find."

Bianca bristled. "It's not as if I came here to trap a husband."

"I didn't mean it that way."

"And marriage is—well, it's a risk, you know."

"Life is a risk. Having a big, handsome man who wants to look after you is no risk at all. Think of it as security. And if you love each other. . ."

Of course they loved each other. His kisses said so much more than mere words. "Everything's happening so fast, Mattie. I can't help wondering if . . ."

"I know. I was jumpy as a grasshopper before Cushing and I tied the knot."

"But you were sure, weren't you?"

"Ever since he kissed me behind the lilac bush when I was nine." Mattie giggled. "But I still wondered if I was making a mistake. It's only natural, I guess. Setting the course for the rest of your life is a big step."

"When I'm near Jesse I can't see anybody or anything else. When we're apart, he's all I think about. When I go to sleep, I dream about him." She turned away, blushing at the memory of the wanton images that kept her tossing and turning at night. "But, really, we don't know each other at all."

"Well, take your time." Mattie picked a piece of lint off the worn carpet and sighed. "Being spoken for is the best part. Once you get married and the babies start coming, things change in a hurry." She patted her bulging belly. "Of course, the little ones make everything worthwhile."

A sudden image of Viola tucking the boys into bed and listening to their prayers brought tears to Bianca's eyes. Had Viola thought giving life to her sons made everything worthwhile as she lay bleeding to death beside her stillborn daughter?

"Agnes says Ed always thinks about money, but she knows it's her children who are the real treasures."

Bianca pressed her hands against her temples. If only Mattie would stop talking.

"Agnes says she loves her boys, but it's the twins who'll be a comfort in her old age."

Would Mattie be so eager to quote Agnes if she knew who had nailed the anonymous note to the fencepost? Bianca knew it was time to confide her suspicions.

"Agnes says I'm lucky to have daughters because—"

"I know you consider Agnes Fowler your friend, Mattie, but I'm almost certain she wrote that spiteful letter."

"Agnes? What a terrible thing for you to say!"

Bianca hesitated. Even if she told the whole story, Mattie might simply refuse to believe it. Despite her shortcomings, Mattie was warmhearted and patient. Bianca hadn't made many friends in Oakfield, and she didn't want to alienate Mattie.

"Maybe I'm mistaken."

Mattie sniffed. "You can't accuse Agnes and let it go at that."

Bianca took a deep breath and described the signs, the missing pages from Junior's copybook, and the sheriff's agreement that Agnes was the culprit. At the end of Bianca's explanation, Mattie waved the feather duster aimlessly and slumped onto the organ bench.

"I'm sorry," Bianca said. "But I really thought I should tell you."

"Agnes is the only person in Oakfield I can really talk to. I mean, until you came here. Why would she—"

"Maybe the note was Ed's idea. You know how angry he was about Aiden coming to school. Sheriff Wells is going to talk to them both."

"Mama, I picked some roses." Gertrude minced into the room carrying a bouquet. "I'll fix them nice and turn the vase so the chip doesn't show."

Bianca wondered how long Gertrude had been lurking in the shadows on the front stoop. If Oakfield ever held an eavesdropping bee, Gertrude would win hands down.

"That's fine, dear." Mattie waved a hand toward the door. "Put the flowers on the table by the door so folks will see them when they come in."

Cushing bustled in from the kitchen, sermon notes clutched in his hands. He picked up a cracked dish from the shelf inside the podium and shoved it at Mattie.

"You know I want the collection plate by the door. Some folks like to make their offering when they come in so everybody can see how charitable they are."

"Everything's ready, Cushing," Mattie said, placing the plate near the roses. "Bianca helped me set up the chairs."

"Well, take off your apron and get the girls ready for the service." He scowled and began shuffling papers. When he smoothed a scraggly strand of hair across his balding forehead, Bianca wondered if Mattie could still look at him and see the boy who kissed her behind the lilac bush.

CHAPTER 45

"This morning's sermon was the worst Cushing's dished out yet."
Ed Fowler stomped out the door with Agnes and the children
trailing behind him. "Carrying on about bearing false witness—
what a bunch of hogwash!"

"What's a false witness anyway?" Junior scratched his
forehead.

"I think it means it's a sin to tell lies about people." Lenny
opened his Bible to the page he'd marked with a piece of red
satin ribbon. "Right here in Exodus, it says you shouldn't bear
false witness against your neighbor."

"Lenny's getting to be a real good reader," Edna said.

Ed gave Lenny an approving pat on the shoulder. At least
one of his boys had some smarts. And Lloyd might amount to
something if he ever stopped clowning around. Junior meant
well, but he took after Agnes in the brains department.

"You mean if I tell a lie, I'll go to Hell?" Junior looked worried.

"I don't think a little white lie sends you to Hell." Lenny
closed the Bible carefully, keeping the ribbon tucked in as a
place marker. "Just big mean ones you tell on purpose to hurt
somebody."

"Still, lying is a sin," Edwina pointed out.

"I guess there are big sins and little sins," Lloyd said. "Oren says Catholics can confess, pay the priest some money and get rid of their sins. I don't rightly know how we get rid of ours."

"We pray for forgiveness, I guess." Edna smoothed the maroon grosgrain bow on the back of her new Sunday bonnet.

Junior said, "Murder—that's a big sin. I don't guess you'd get forgiven for that, even if you was Catholic."

"Injuns ain't Catholic, so when the sheriff catches the redskin that killed Aiden's pa, he'll get strung up and go straight to Hell." Lloyd noosed his hands around his neck, flopped his head to one side, gurgled, and stuck out his tongue.

"Aiden and his Ma don't think it was an Injun." Lenny fingered the Bible thoughtfully.

"Of course, the squaw would stick up for her own kind." Ed climbed onto the driver's seat of the wagon, and Agnes settled in beside him.

Most Sundays the womenfolk fluttered around the yard after service like a bunch of clucking hens, with Agnes right in the middle of the flock. "You're mighty quiet this morning, Agnes," he said. "I figured all you womenfolk would have so much to chew over this morning I'd be lucky to ever get you in the wagon."

"I don't feel much like visiting." Agnes sat stiffly, arms folded across her chest.

"Are you ailing?" Ed regarded her curiously.

Agnes shook her head, and Ed shrugged. He'd long since given up trying to understand what made Agnes tick. "Come on, young 'uns," he hollered. "Time to head for home."

"I want to stay and talk to Miss Stratton," Edwina said. "Isn't it exciting about Mr. Landry asking her to marry him? I wonder why he didn't come to church this morning."

"Probably there's a lot to do out at the ranch." Ed shrugged. "Some folks didn't even start for home until this morning. Come on. You can talk to the teacher woman at school tomorrow."

The boys clambered into the wagon, and the twins followed reluctantly. Ed flicked the reins, and the wagon lurched forward.

"I wonder why old Pangston decided to talk about bearing false witness today," Junior said. "Seems like there's lots of more important sins."

"Seems peculiar to me, too," Ed agreed. "And Mattie Pangston looked a mite peaked this morning. Never said a word to you, did she, Agnes? Usually she talks your arm off after service."

Agnes pulled a handkerchief out of her reticule and dabbed at her nose. Then she pursed her lips and stared silently at the threatening clouds overhead.

Ed blocked out the children's chatter and rubbed the back of his neck. Too much of Nora's punch had left him with a throbbing head, and he'd thrashed around most of the night. He sure as hell hadn't figured on the sheriff turning up at Nora's fiesta and talking to Frenchy. Ed hadn't been able to get hold of Frenchy, what with him front and center sawing away at his infernal squawk box. The wagon lurched over a rough patch of road. Ed steadied the team with a firm tug of the reins and scowled at the road ahead.

CHAPTER 46

When Bianca glanced out the window and saw Rolf's surrey pulling up with her mare trotting behind, she hiked up her Sunday skirt and dashed out the front door.

"Oh, Rolf! You brought Patches!"

Before Rolf let go of the reins, Bianca had untied the rope from the back of the surrey. The mare eyed Bianca warily.

"Oh, Patches, don't you even remember me?"

"She's only a horse, Bianca." Rolf jumped down and looped the reins around a fencepost.

The mare's silky tail swished away a fly. Then, ears perked, she nuzzled at Bianca's pocket.

"Look, Rolf! She does remember! I always hid a carrot in my pocket before we went for a ride." Bianca gently scratched the soft hollow at the base of the mare's ear. "Sorry, girl. I didn't know you were coming. But there'll be plenty of carrots from now on."

Rolf reached into the back of the surrey and hauled out the scuffed sidesaddle Bianca had saved egg money to buy. "Now show me where to put this."

All the Pangstons trooped out the back door, following Bianca as she led the mare to the barn. Rolf marched stiffly beside her, the sidesaddle balanced on one broad shoulder.

"You might have . . . er . . . mentioned you were bringing . . . Another animal means another mouth to feed, and we can hardly . . ." Cushing's stammer trailed into a strangled cough.

"I only talked to Rolf about my horse at the fiesta yesterday. I had no idea he'd bring her. Of course, I'll pay for—"

"Don't be ridiculous." Mattie moved ahead to swing open the barn door. "Your board and room is our contribution to the school. Of course, that includes your horse."

Katie danced through the door and gestured at an empty stall. "There's plenty of room. I'll help you brush her, too."

Cora regarded the mare critically. "She looks tame enough," she said, "but I thought you were scared of horses."

Gertrude, holding her little sister by the hand, wrinkled her nose. "I hate it out here. It smells of manure. Come on, Tina. Let's go back inside."

"Wanna see the pony." Tina's lower lip quivered.

Rolf deposited the sidesaddle on a sawhorse near the barn door and turned to Bianca. "If you're really determined to ride again, don't try to do it all at once. A horse can sense it when you're afraid."

"I'm not scared of horses." Katie fingered the sidesaddle. "I could ride her for you if you're not ready to—"

"You'll do no such thing." Cushing waved the girls away from the stall. "Now, go back in the house, all of you." He scooped Tina into his arms and herded his brood toward the back stoop.

Tina was still wailing, "Wanna see the pony," when the screen door slammed behind them.

"Does that child cry all the time?" Rolf shook his head and began spreading fresh straw in the empty stall next to the Pangston's farm horse.

"It's not quite that bad," Bianca said. "Rolf, I really do appreciate your bringing Patches."

"She's your horse, and you've got a right to have her with you. You've got a right to live where you want and marry who you choose. I know I made a fool of myself last night, but I've been worried ever since you came out here."

Bianca waited, expecting more of Rolf's gloomy pronouncements.

"Once I knew Landry's intentions were honorable, I guess I finally realized you're a grown woman and not my responsibility. But I still don't want you galloping around the countryside and breaking your neck the next time this critter bucks you off."

"She didn't buck me off. She shied when I tried to jump her across that flooded stream. She's gentle as a lamb and probably has better sense than I do." Bianca picked a currycomb off the shelf near the stalls and went to work on the mare's tangled mane.

"Don't do anything foolish." Rolf paced the length of the barn. "I know it's useless to give you advice, Bianca, but it's better to be safe than sorry."

Bianca smiled. "I'll be careful, Rolf. I promise."

"Well, then, I'd best be heading back." Rolf stopped at the barn door. "And, Bianca, I promised the boys I'd talk you into coming home for a visit."

"Give them all a big hug for me. Tell them I miss them."

"Maybe your Mr. Landry could drive you over next weekend."

"I don't know why not. I'll talk to him about it."

Rolf waved a hand and disappeared from her sight. Bianca busied herself with the once familiar routine of brushing the mare's gray coat until it gleamed like freshly polished silver.

"Well, Patches, what do you think? Rolf says it may take weeks, but I think I'm ready to give it a try right now."

The mare nickered, and Bianca was sure Patches was encouraging her. She smoothed a blanket over the horse's broad back, hoisted the sidesaddle into place, tightened the girth, and adjusted the stirrups. Once the bit and reins were in place, she patted the mare's warm flank. Then she led Patches out of the barn and into the fenced section of the barnyard, stopping to gently scratch the two white rectangular splotches below the mare's forelock.

Bianca felt beads of sweat break out on her upper lip. Sheltered inside the barn everything had seemed simple. Now, looking at her trembling hands, she realized her confident words to Rolf were mere bravado. She recalled Rolf's admonition that a horse could sense fear, but Patches waited placidly. She clenched her jaw, opened the barnyard gate, and led the mare onto the dusty road.

Patches tossed her head as if to say, "Well, what are we waiting for?"

"I'm doing the best I can, girl," Bianca murmured. She stood uncertainly, one hand on the pommel. Maybe she wouldn't be able to ride today, but at least she could force herself to mount. Taking a deep, slow breath, she put her foot in the stirrup and hoisted herself onto the saddle.

She sat motionless, dreading the moment the old terror would strike, but her breathing remained normal. She settled more comfortably in the saddle and felt the reassurance of her foot fitting solidly in the stirrup.

An old white hen pecking at the side of the road clucked a warning, and Bianca grinned. "You're as bad as Rolf," she said. "But I'm going to fool you both."

She flicked the reins, and Patches ambled down the road. Red sumac and yellow alder leaves played contrasting notes against the deep greens of cedar, fir and hemlock. Bianca had forgotten how different everything looked from the heightened perspective of horseback, and she was astonished to discover she could actually relax and enjoy the ride. She breathed in the aroma of fresh pine and frost-touched autumn leaves. How foolish she'd been to let fear rob her of such pure pleasure.

They plodded down the road, and Bianca nudged the mare into an easy trot. As they rounded the curve that brought the schoolhouse into view, the horse swerved to avoid a fallen branch. Bianca lurched precariously, and her exhilaration vanished. She struggled to keep her balance as dizziness engulfed her. The reins slipped free of her clammy hands.

"Whoa, Patches, whoa!" Her voice, a panicky squeak, seemed to come from far away. The mare slowed and came to a gentle stop near the schoolyard gate. Bianca slid to the ground and leaned against the fence, gasping for breath. After a few minutes she tottered down the path and collapsed on the schoolhouse steps. She sat, head in her hands, until the vertigo passed. Then, still shaken, she walked to where Patches stood.

"I'm afraid that's all the riding I can manage today," she said, picking up the reins. "Rolf warned me and, as usual, I didn't listen."

The mare whinnied softly and swished her tail.

"Come on, girl. I'll lead you back to the barn. We'll try again tomorrow."

After a few paces, Bianca stopped. Why would anything be different tomorrow? Earlier today she'd been sure she couldn't even get herself into the saddle, but she had. She wasn't sure of the exact words, but she could almost hear her father quoting something about cowards dying many times before their death.

She placed a sweaty hand on the pommel and swung herself back into the saddle. Blood pounded in her temples, but she was determined not to give in to the panic. She braced her feet firmly against the stirrups and snapped the reins.

The horse moved slowly into the middle of the road. Bianca looked down at her hands clenching the reins. You've got to relax, she told herself. Feel the horse's rhythm and lean into it. Remember how it used to be when you and Patches raced through the fields, relishing the freedom.

Gradually her death-grip on the reins lessened, and she held the leather in a firm, comfortable grasp as the horse moved into a steady trot. Suddenly it was as if a gentle hand swept away something deep inside that had held her captive for years.

"Let's go, girl!" She felt the power beneath her and, at the same time, an incredible sensation of release as horse and rider, moving as one, galloped down the dusty road past the Nolan's house and came to an easy stop at the river's edge.

Along the river the road narrowed into a rutted wagon track through cottonwoods and berry vines. She eased Patches into a leisurely pace and inhaled the damp, mossy scent of the slow-moving stream. Somehow the colors of the trees and brambles seemed even more vivid than before. She breathed it all in—the earthy aroma, the play of light and shadow on the river, the fresh breeze cooling her cheeks.

Then the path curved away from the water's edge, and she found herself in a small clearing. In summer it would be a grassy glade sprinkled with wildflowers, a perfect spot for a picnic. Now, however, dark clouds overhead cast threatening shadows, and dead leaves crackled as she passed. The trail skirted an aged fir tree that had fallen at the far edge of the open space. As Patches approached the log, her nostrils flared and her ears flattened. A squirrel chattered and disappeared into the branches of a yellow-bark pine at the edge of a shallow ravine.

The mare whinnied and pawed the ground, and a chill wind whipped at Bianca's skirt. For a fearful moment she was sure the old panic was returning, but her head was clear, her breathing normal. Still, she was gripped with a sense of foreboding, as if invisible insects were crawling up her arms. She shuddered and turned the horse around.

"Let's head home, girl," she said. "I don't like this place."

As if in reply, a flash of lightning lit the sky. Within seconds a roll of thunder followed. Patches shied, and Bianca gripped the pommel to hold on. She urged the horse forward, steadying her with murmurs of reassurance. By the time they reached the riverbank, scattered drops of rain moistened her face.

She recalled Rolf's warnings, but somehow she knew she'd stored all of his gloomy pronouncements away in a far corner of her mind along with her irrational terror. She held the mare to a steady trot as the shower changed to a cloudburst. Tilting her face toward the sky to welcome the downpour, Bianca let the rain wash away the last vestiges of her fear. She laughed aloud as Patches, pewter coat splotched with mud, plodded for home.

CHAPTER 47

"Wait up, there!" Cap Mackay nudged his horse off the deer trail and onto the road. He'd been tracking his prey, staying out of sight until he was sure nobody else was around.

"Well, Cap. Haven't seen much of you lately."

"I been hoping to talk to you." Cap edged closer, smiling and waving friendly like. No point in spooking the feller. No point in getting too close, neither. He'd been careful asking around, steering the talk to the old days. Hell, everybody had gold fever after the big strike down by Sacramento. And stories—they all had stories. Once you got folks talking about them rip-roaring mining camps, all you had to do was sit back and listen and put two and two together. "I've got a little something I think might interest you."

"I'm pretty busy right now, Mackay."

"Not too busy to read an old piece from a newspaper up north." Cap leaned across his saddle and spewed a stream of tobacco juice on the ground.

"Can't imagine why I'd give a hoot about some old newspaper story."

"Seems an old miner and his nephew struck it lucky on their claim."

"Must have been an awful big strike to rate a story in some newspaper."

The feller was a cool customer, no doubt about that, but his eyes narrowed for a split second. In Cap's poker-playing days, he'd learned to read a man's face. There was no doubt in his mind. He'd struck pay dirt.

"Murder was what the story was about. Seems the old man got his head caved in, and they never found hide nor hair of the boy or the gold. Benobia Lewison, the old man was called. Hard to forget a name like Benobia. Nephew went by Jimmy."

"Can't say those names ring a bell with me." There it was again. The telltale narrowing of the eyes.

"Whoever wrote up the story must have spent some time talking to the other miners. A man who'd staked his claim right next to Lewison's said Benobia was a mean old cuss. Them was his exact words right there in the paper—quoted, I think is what they calls it." He pulled his flask out of his saddlebag and took a swig. "And the feller the reporter talked to—his name was there too. That's probably why he clipped the piece out and kept it. Ain't often a man gets his name in the paper. Daniel Nolan—now there's a name should ring a bell."

"Well, I guess that does interest me a bit. Let's see that clipping."

Cap put a little more distance between them. "I ain't fool enough to carry something like that around with me. It's in a good, safe place. Maybe we could work out a little trade."

"What did you have in mind?"

"I figure a thousand dollars ought to cover it."

"You've got to be plumb loco, Cap. There's no way I can lay my hands on that kind of money."

Cap's hands were starting to sweat. He knew he was playing a dangerous game, and he really needed another nip to steady his nerves. "All things considered, I sorta think you can scrape it up."

"Supposing I can. How do I know that'll be the end of it?"

"Frenchy's been talking about heading for California. You know he's about the only friend I've got in these parts. With the extra cash, I could go south too."

"You'd clear out?"

Cap nodded and reached for his flask. Things were finally starting to go his way.

CHAPTER 48

Tyler spent Sunday in a foul temper, moping around the house and snapping at Uncle Clayton's good-humored questions about the fiesta. He went outside and chopped firewood until his arms and back throbbed, but the image of Bianca in Jesse's arms persisted. When the rain drove him back indoors, he attacked his backlog of paperwork, staring gloomily at the notes that led him no closer to solving Daniel Nolan's murder.

After a fitful sleep, he hitched up the buckboard and left for Oakfield at dawn amid glowering skies and drizzling rain. Monday morning he stalked into Fowler's store.

"Sheriff Wells." Agnes Fowler's smile almost erased the worry lines in her forehead. "You're out and about early. Ed's in the back."

"First, I'd like a word with you, Mrs. Fowler."

"Me?" The box of buttons Agnes was sorting clattered to the floor.

Tyler fished the note out of his shirt pocket, watching her eyes widen as he unfolded it carefully. "Would you like to tell me about this note?"

"Note?" Tyler knew Agnes was trying to sound unconcerned, but there was a telltale quaver in her voice.

"The reverend found it nailed to his front fencepost. But I think you already know that."

He held the paper out for her to take, but she averted her eyes, picked up a broom that had been leaning against the counter and began sweeping up the buttons.

"I got no idea what you're talking about, Sheriff."

Tyler smiled. Bianca's suspicions about Agnes being the author were right on target. An innocent Agnes Fowler would have drooled with curiosity and snatched the paper from his hand.

"It's unsigned, of course. A nasty piece of business, Mrs. Fowler. I guess you figured the reverend would burn it, but he didn't. He showed it to his wife, and then they brought it to me."

By then the buttons were in a neat pile at her feet, but Agnes kept sweeping furiously.

"Miss Stratton has seen it, too. In fact, she's the one who recognized your spelling and printing."

"It's all her fault," Agnes hissed. "Things were fine until she came—bringing that devil's spawn of a half-breed into the schoolhouse and putting notions into the young 'uns."

"Notions?" Tyler waited for the confession he sensed would be forthcoming.

"It's 'Miss Stratton says this and Miss Stratton says that' until I swear I want to puke. Lloyd talks about her like she's some sort of high mucky-muck. Lenny's always got his nose in a book so's I can't get a lick of work out of him. She's got my girls sewing up pretties for her, and Junior hangs around the schoolhouse like a moonstruck calf."

"So, it's Miss Stratton who's got your dander up. But the note was to the minister."

"Getting her here was his doing. She's living in his house. If he boots her out, she's got no place to go but back to wherever she came from." She plucked a dustpan from a nail on the wall and stooped to brush up the last of the buttons.

"That's not going to happen, Mrs. Fowler. By all accounts Miss Stratton is doing a fine job. What you've done with your meddling is get the reverend's back up and upset his wife in the bargain. I had the idea Mrs. Pangston was your friend."

"I never thought he'd show it to Mattie." Agnes poured the buttons back into the box and turned to face him. A hint of moisture gathered in the corners of her eyes.

"And then, of course, there may be legal consequences as well." Tyler refolded the note and slipped it back into his pocket.

"I only wanted the schoolmarm to go away." She put the button box on the counter and swiped her nose with the back of her hand. "Ed's been on a regular rampage ever since that half-breed started school and the blacksmith turned up dead. I never meant to break no law, Sheriff."

"I've heard Ed carry on about Aiden attending school. I can't help wondering if the note was his idea."

The tiny woman's face crumpled and the tears began to flow in earnest. "Ed don't know nothing about the note, and he'll be fit to be tied if he thinks I got myself on the wrong side of some law." Her voice rose to a wail. "Please, Sheriff. Don't say nothing to Ed."

As if on cue the storekeeper burst through the swinging door from the back room, wiping his hands on his canvas apron. His face wore a mixture of consternation and confusion as he took in Agnes's teary eyes and turned to Tyler. "What's going on here?"

Tyler felt a flash of pity for Agnes. She wasn't the swiftest goose in the flock. Even so, it was time she faced up to what she'd done. He retrieved the paper from his pocket and handed it to Ed.

"I was asking Mrs. Fowler about an anonymous note stuck on Reverend Pangston's gatepost. Maybe you ought to take a look at it." He watched as Ed unfolded the paper and reached into the apron pocket for his wire-rimmed spectacles. A crimson flush started at his ears and slowly diffused over his face as he read. Then he crumpled the note, threw it on the floor, and stormed over to Agnes.

"My God, woman! What were you thinking?"

"I never meant no harm, Ed." Agnes cringed against the counter. "You're always saying how the teacher woman ain't nothing but trouble, and I was only trying to—"

"Trying to what? Get the sheriff nosing around more'n he is already?"

"I'm not surprised that my nosing around, as you put it, has you worried, Ed." Tyler picked up the crumpled note from the floor and smoothed it out. "After all, you've had a lot on your mind lately, haven't you?"

"Now I don't know why you'd say that, Sheriff. Of course, running a store's no easy job, but I manage." Ed put his glasses back in his pocket and rubbed his hands together.

"I was thinking of your little sideline. Actually, I guess it's more than a sideline, isn't it? Probably you've made more money smuggling Frenchy's white lightning onto the reservation than you ever have from the store."

Agnes gasped. "You and Frenchy been selling booze to the Injuns? And you're mad at me about writing a silly note? Oh, Ed, how could you—"

"Hush, woman!" Ed snarled. Then, wearing an expression of outraged innocence, he turned to Tyler. "Sheriff, I don't know where you got such a crazy notion. Sure, I've been known to dispense a little whiskey out of the back of the store, but—"

"Save it, Ed." Tyler refolded the note and returned it to his shirt pocket. "Last Saturday I had a mighty interesting discussion with a sheriff up north. Seems a goodly amount of liquor has been finding its way onto the reservation, and he's had his eye on a certain Indian agent for some time. Friday he arrested the fellow. We're talking federal law here, Ed."

Agnes's wailing resumed. "Oh, Lordy! What will become of me and the young-uns if they put you in prison?"

Ed's normally ruddy complexion paled. "Now, let's be reasonable, Tyler. You know I'm just a poor storekeeper—"

"Tell it to the Marshall, Ed. You're in way over your head. Unless, of course—"

"What, Sheriff? Unless what?" Agnes was wringing her hands.

"The sheriff up north seemed to think the government was mainly interested in convicting the crooked agent. I can't say for sure, but if you'd be willing to testify against him—"

"The whole thing was the agent fella's idea, Tyler. Me and Frenchy, we ran into him at the dock up north when we was meeting the packet ship from San Francisco. He was picking up supplies for his trading post, and we got to talking, you know."

Words tumbled out of the storekeeper's mouth. Apparently Ed Fowler believed he could talk his way out of anything.

"He said it was a damn shame them poor Injuns wasn't allowed to buy liquor, because they had a great hankering for it. But he said it was no matter anyways seeing as how them Redskins couldn't afford the good stuff from Canada. Then Frenchy, he piped up about his still, and—well, one thing led to another."

"And you'd be willing to testify—put it in writing first, and then stand up in court and swear—"

"Oh, you bet, Sheriff. And Frenchy will back me up, too." Some color had returned to Ed's face, but his cheeks and forehead were beaded with sweat.

"I wouldn't count too much on Frenchy."

"He'll tell you it happened like I said." Ed pulled a checkered bandana from his hip pocket and mopped his brow.

"I had quite a talk with Frenchy at Nora's fiesta. His rheumatism's been acting up, and he's not looking forward to the winter cold."

"He's been using *Doctor Greene's Miracle Liniment*." Agnes hopped over to the medicine counter and held up an amber bottle.

"Well, I guess it hasn't helped much because he said he was heading south. Unless I miss my guess he's already well on his way to California."

"You mean you let him get away, and he don't have to testify or nothing?" Ed shook his head in disbelief.

"The Indian agent said you delivered the goods, and it was you who took the money. The way he told it, Frenchy didn't much come into it."

"But Frenchy's the one made the liquor, same as he's been making it all along." Agnes waved the liniment bottle for emphasis. "Ed, if I told you once, I told you a hundred times that selling whiskey in the back room was gonna get you into trouble. But would you listen?"

"I need to take you back to town with me, Ed." Tyler put a hand on the storekeeper's shoulder. "We better get your statement written up and witnessed all legal and proper."

"You ain't gonna put him in jail are you, Sheriff?"

"I can't make any promises, Mrs. Fowler."

"But you said if he testified . . ." Agnes fluttered between the two men.

"That's true as far as the liquor business goes. But I've still got me a murder to clear up, and Ed's jumped himself up to the top of my list of suspects."

"I'm ready to write everything down about the booze, like you said, Sheriff. But there's no way you think I killed Daniel Nolan. What reason would I have? I hardly knew the fella."

"I admit that had me concerned, but once I learned about your little smuggling operation, it all seemed pretty clear."

"Honest, Sheriff. I ain't no killer. I don't even carry a gun. You know that."

For a minute Tyler almost believed he was telling the truth. But lies fell out of Ed Fowler's mouth faster than water out of a well-primed pump.

"In case you've forgotten, Daniel Nolan's head was smashed in. You didn't need a gun for that job. I figure Daniel was out in the woods on one of his drinking sprees, and he came across you and Frenchy heading off with a load of booze. Then, after he sobered up some, maybe he started asking questions. Too many questions. So you fixed him up with a fresh bottle and trailed him back into the woods. It's no secret you're an Indian-hater. Scalping him to pin the job on a renegade redskin probably seemed like a fine idea."

"You got it all wrong, Sheriff."

"Well, you'll have plenty of time to convince me on the way to town."

Tyler gave Fowler a final push out the door. Agnes's wails were still ringing in his ears as they headed off in the buckboard.

CHAPTER 49

"So you let Ed Fowler off the hook, did you?" Clayton Wells peered quizzically over the top of his wire-rimmed glasses.

Tyler inhaled the rich aroma of freshly ground coffee beans that filled the small room behind his uncle's law office. Life with Clayton was a series of interrogations, but the man was a marvel in the kitchen. "I wouldn't say I let him off the hook."

Clayton spooned dollops of sourdough into a muffin pan. "You turned him loose about daybreak, didn't you?" He slid the pan into the oven of the cast iron stove that dominated their crowded quarters.

"Didn't see any need to keep him locked up. I've got his statement, and Agnes will make sure he comes back when the Marshall gets here."

"Guess you don't think he's the one that scalped the blacksmith fellow?" Clayton slapped six slices of bacon into a heavy skillet and joined Tyler at the table.

"Let's say he was a lot more willing to talk about the liquor business when he was trying to convince me he was no murderer."

Tyler retrieved two pewter mugs from the pantry and filled them with coffee. The last packet ship from San Francisco had brought real coffee beans—a rare treat after bran and molasses brew. Roasting and grinding coffee beans was Tyler's one culinary talent, but Clayton never trusted him with the actual brewing.

Clayton poured thick cream into his coffee, stirred and sipped appreciatively. "So where are you on the murder business?" he asked.

Tyler sighed. "Nowhere, really. I haven't written Ed Fowler off completely, but Cap Mackay's at the top of my list. Still, I'd like to smoke out Joanna Nolan's brother."

"The renegade?"

"I think he's hiding out in the mountains, but I never really got to question her about him."

"She dropped in to see me yesterday." Clayton hopped up, grabbed a long-handled fork, and began turning slices of sizzling bacon. "Brought her will and marriage certificate and the deed to their property. Seems like everything's in order."

"You have any trouble understanding her?"

"She didn't say much. Mrs. Donovan did most of the talking."

"Nora brought her?"

Clayton nodded and speared another slice of bacon. "Now that woman's got more charm than I've seen since I left Savannah. Mighty good-looking, too. How come you never got around to mentioning that?"

Tyler laughed. "You know, uncle, your southern accent's nearly disappeared except when you start carrying on about the ladies."

The aroma of baking biscuits mingled with the scent of frying bacon and coffee. Tyler's stomach rumbled in anticipation.

"Speaking of ladies, have you seen your pretty schoolmarm since she got all cozy with that ranch foreman?"

Tyler's mouth went dry. He stood and headed for the back door. "Those biscuits must be nearly done. I'll get the butter."

Outside, he stood for a moment breathing in the crisp morning air. He'd managed to get through a whole day without thinking about Bianca Stratton. Nights were another matter, but he kept telling himself it was only a matter of time before her image faded from his dreams.

He walked to the north side of the house and swung open the door to the milk room. Leaving the door open to provide light, he stepped into the windowless room and. retrieved a crock of butter. Then he plodded back to the kitchen where Clayton was shoveling scrambled eggs onto plates already heaped with bacon and biscuits.

They ate quietly for several minutes until Clayton broke the silence. "I guess Mrs. Nolan and the boy aren't going to have any financial problems."

"Oh?" Tyler was relieved that Clayton was back on the subject of Joanna Nolan.

"Before they got to my place, they'd already stopped by the assay office and the bank."

"The assay office?"

"Mrs. Nolan said her husband salted away a pouch of gold. Apparently Mrs. Donovan convinced her that it would be safer converted to currency and stashed in the Farmer's Mercantile."

"I'm not surprised Daniel Nolan did some mining. I guess you and I are the only two men in Oregon who didn't get here in time to catch gold fever. The clipping Aiden says has gone missing—that was about mining. Only he keeps talking about a frozen river."

"The boy—Aiden's his name?" Clayton refilled the coffee cups.

Tyler, mouth full of biscuit, nodded.

"Pretty young, isn't he?"

"Seven or eight, I guess."

"Can't have been reading too long. Maybe he got some words wrong. Could be instead of a frozen river, it mentioned the name of a river, or maybe the name of a town near a river"

"You could be right," Tyler said.

"Seems like I heard mention of a big gold strike up north of the border—place called Frazier River. That would be an easy mistake for a little tyke."

"Frazier River. Of course! Maybe Cap was mining up there in Frazier River and killed somebody in a squabble over a claim, and Nolan was there too. It would have been quite a shock to have Daniel Nolan turn up practically on his doorstep after all these years."

"If it was Cap, that is." Clayton stirred his coffee.

"I know for a fact that Cap did some mining up north. Maybe he killed Nolan and then started worrying about what Daniel had told Joanna or the boy. Or wondering if maybe Daniel kept some kind of journal. Lots of men did. That would explain why he set the fire."

Tyler stood up and drained the last of the coffee from his cup. His leather vest with the star attached hung on a peg near the back door along with his Stetson and gun belt.

"Looks like you're getting yourself rigged up to arrest somebody." Clayton munched a piece of bacon. "Oakfield's a pretty small place. You keep going down there and arresting folks, pretty soon there won't be anybody left."

"Very funny." Tyler put on the vest and adjusted his holster.

"You sure this Cap fella is the one you're looking for?"

"I should have brought him in days ago. I knew right away he was the one who broke into Nolan's place. I can't believe I didn't make the connection—frozen river, Frazier River. But now I'm worried about Bianca Stratton doing something foolish."

"You don't think she'd try to—"

"No telling what that crazy woman might do. You should have seen her marching into Nolan's house armed with a garden rake."

Clayton laughed. "No wonder you're taken with the lady."

"Bianca Stratton means nothing to me. Nothing at all."

Tyler jammed the Stetson on his head and stomped out the back door. Clayton might be an extraordinary cook and a fine lawyer, but sometimes he was a real pain in the ass.

CHAPTER 50

The killer honed his razor until the edge gleamed. Shaving was a damn nuisance, but a man had to keep up appearances. He lathered his face and noted with satisfaction that his hand was steady. He didn't rattle easily, a good thing considering what he had to do later.

Damn that blacksmith! Even six feet under, Nolan kept causing trouble. Just when it began to look like things were working out, Cap Mackay had to get hold of some newspaper clipping and put two and two together. Hell. He hadn't known anything about a newspaper article, much less figured on Daniel Nolan reading it and squirreling it away. What were the chances of that?

Mackay stunk of booze and flop sweat, but his rheumy eyes still glinted with animal cunning. For a minute he'd been ready to finish the old fool off when he made his blackmail pitch, but there was still the chance of the clipping turning up. And lots of folks traveled that particular stretch of road, so close to town. Still, he had to admit hearing the name Benobia Lewison had given him quite a turn.

He peered into the mirror and wondered for the hundredth time if Nolan had recognized him when he'd turned up at the blacksmith shop. He'd grown up and changed a lot more than

Nolan over the years, but the blacksmith stared too long. He couldn't chance Nolan's memory improving after he sobered up.

He dipped his razor in the water, finished shaving his jaw line and moved to the chin. Damn! He nicked himself in the tender spot below his lower lip. A few drops of blood spattered into the basin. Red splotches against white. That was how it all started. Only there had been more blood then—blood splashed on white snow.

The events of that miserable Canadian winter came flooding back. His worthless uncle huddled by the fire, giving him the short end of their meager rations and beating him for no reason. He'd done all the digging while the old man limped around and complained about his rheumatism. Then, when they hit a lucky strike, his uncle said he was too young to be trusted with so much money.

"I'll take care of your share. You can't be a real miner when you're still a minor. That's a joke, Jimmy," he cackled.

That was the last time anybody called him Jimmy.

The law never paid much attention to what went on in mining camps, and he high-tailed it south across the border that same night. Now he had to deal with Cap Mackay—not that the old drunk would be much of a problem.

A final glance in the mirror told him the nick on his chin had clotted. He rubbed a hand over his clean-shaven jaw and freshened his face with a splash of water. In a way, it was a stroke of luck Cap was the one who'd stumbled onto the clipping. Mackay was a secretive sort. It was a safe bet he hadn't shown that scrap of newspaper around while he was figuring out how to make use of it. Cap had as much as admitted he'd broken into the Nolan place after setting fire to it. No, Mackay wasn't the sort to go running to the sheriff.

The old fool wanted money and said he'd leave Oregon. As if that was likely to happen. The pay-off was set for late this afternoon. He chuckled. With Mackay out of the way he'd be in the clear once and for all.

CHAPTER 51

Bianca hummed *Paper of Pins* as she groomed Patches and stowed copybooks into the saddlebags. Finally, the rain was over. Nature's scrub brush had polished everything in its path. Pine needles and cedar branches sparkled in bright morning sunshine.

As she rode toward the schoolhouse she burst into song with the pure wonder of being alive and in love. I'm happy, really happy, she thought. She left Patches free to graze along the fence and started for the schoolhouse door. At the sound of hoof-beats, she turned.

"Miss Stratton! Ain't she a beauty?" Aiden, riding a sorrel mare, wore a smile bright enough to light up the forest on a moonless night. "Aunt Nora—she said I should call her Aunt Nora—picked her out, and Ma bought her for me yesterday."

"An absolute beauty!" Bianca ran an appreciative hand over the horse's reddish-brown flank and held the reins while Aiden bounced to the ground.

"I got to ride her home from the ranch last night. We're at our own place now, me and Ma. Oren said I could have his old saddle, but Ma don't like to be beholden to anybody, so we bought it off him. Ma said we got it too cheap, but I think—"

"Slow down, Aiden. You're making me dizzy!"

"Ma, she says I talk too much. I guess maybe she's right."

Bianca smiled. "It's wonderful to hear you after all those days when you couldn't say a word. But right now, you'd better hitch your horse to the fence and loosen her girth so she'll be comfortable."

"I guess if I turned her loose, she'd head right back to where we got her."

"She'll be fine after a few days. Horses learn their way around in a hurry."

Bianca strolled up the path to the schoolhouse door, still smiling. She stepped to the blackboard and used her best penmanship to write, "Thought for the day: To thine own self be true. William Shakespeare."

Quoting words of wisdom was easy, but finding her own true self wasn't nearly so simple as it had seemed even a month ago. She'd been so sure she wanted to be independent, to travel to new, exciting places. Now everything had changed, and she only wanted to fly to Jesse's side.

She brushed the chalky residue from her hands and looked out the window. Hank and Oren were retrieving books and lunch buckets from a ranch wagon. Then the door creaked. She whirled and ran into Jesse's waiting arms.

"Oh, when I saw Oren and Hank outside, I was hoping you would—"

His kiss smothered her words, and she twined her arms around his neck, leaning into the warmth of his embrace.

"I've been thinking about you," he said, nuzzling her ear.

Reluctantly she pulled back and tucked a flyaway lock of hair back into the bun at the nape her neck. "Someone might come in."

His rough hand traced the line of her jaw. "It's no secret I'm courting you."

"I know, but—"

"You're right. There's better times and places. In the buggy after dark when the horse knows the way—now that's a better time and place for serious kissing."

"Tonight?" She was astonished at her own boldness.

Jesse raised an eyebrow and grinned broadly. "Tuesday's when Nora and I go over accounts. You and I'll make up for lost time tomorrow."

"And, Jesse . . . " She started to tell him they needed to talk, but the words dissolved in the surge of heat she felt just being close to him.

"Yes, sweetheart?"

Her knees turned to jelly. Nobody had ever called her sweetheart. "I can't wait for tomorrow."

"Nora wants you to come to supper, so I'll pick you up about five. We'll have two buggy rides—one at sunset, and one after dark. Does that suit you?"

"Oh yes, Jesse. That suits me fine."

He glanced out the window, and she followed his gaze. The playground was empty. She looked at the clock and gasped. "I should have started class five minutes ago." She raced through the coatroom and flung open the door. Jesse followed, gave her hand a final squeeze, strolled past the waiting children, and flashed a goodbye wave of his Stetson at the gate.

The whole class was gathered at the foot of the schoolhouse steps. There were no welcoming smiles on their faces, and the unnatural quiet told Bianca something was terribly wrong.

Everyone shuffled into the classroom with none of the usual noisy banter. Bianca scanned the children's faces as she marked the attendance roster.

"Sister not here." Bjorn pointed at the empty space on the bench beside him.

The Larsons missed church on Sunday, and Elke had been absent from school Monday. A case of croup, Mattie had reported. But maybe it was something really serious like diphtheria. That would account for the somber atmosphere. However, Bjorn's next words dispelled her fear.

"Better now. But still cough." He wheezed in imitation and glanced around the room with a puzzled frown when nobody laughed.

"I'm sorry she's still too sick to be in school, but I'm glad she's feeling better."

Whatever was happening, Bjorn apparently wasn't in on it, or his English wasn't yet good enough to understand. Bianca passed back the children's copybooks. Moments later the scratching of quill pens vied with the ticking of the clock as they copied the thought for the day from the blackboard.

"All right." Her voice echoed in the still classroom. "I'm sorry I was late starting class, but there's something else the matter here. Until somebody tells me what's going on, I don't know how I can help."

"We don't need none of your kind of help." Lloyd's words came out through clenched teeth. "The sheriff arrested my pa, and you're the one put him up to it."

Bianca blinked in astonishment. She thought back to the evening at the fiesta when she'd told Tyler she suspected Agnes Fowler of writing the anonymous note. Tyler said she should leave the Fowlers to him, but she was sure there'd been no mention of an arrest. It all seemed so long ago. She'd scarcely given a thought to anything but Jesse from the moment he'd taken her hand in the Virginia reel.

"We knew something was wrong when we got home from school yesterday," Edna said.

"Mama's eyes were all red and puffy." Edwina bit her lip and swiped a sleeve across her own eyes. "But she wouldn't tell us anything."

"I'm sure there's been some mistake," Bianca said.

Lenny looked up from his primer. "That's what Ma told the folks at the store."

"I'm sorry, Lenny, but I don't understand."

"Last night some folks came in to buy flour. I was on a stool behind the dry-goods, reading. Nobody noticed me, so I stayed and listened. One of the farmers said he was in town and saw Pa in jail. Mama said it was all a mistake and we didn't need any help. Only after they left, she started crying."

"Mama saw you talking to Sheriff Wells at the fiesta." Edna said. "She told me you was saying mean things about her."

"Sunday before church you said bad things about Mrs. Fowler, too," Gertrude chimed in. "I heard you talking to my mother."

Bianca didn't know what to say. She couldn't tell the children about the venomous note, and now wasn't the time to scold Gertrude about eavesdropping. She turned away from the angry, accusing faces and began writing subtraction problems on the chalkboard.

The anonymous note was Agnes's doing. Even if Ed had been the instigator, that wouldn't lead to his arrest. If Tyler had Ed Fowler in jail, it had to be something serious. Like murder? The storekeeper was such a little bantam rooster of a man. She couldn't conceive of him killing anyone. But then, it was almost impossible to imagine anyone she knew taking a life in cold blood. For the children's sake, she hoped it was all a dreadful mistake.

The morning dragged on, everyone going through the motions. No hands were raised to ask questions or volunteer responses. The ground was too wet for eating outdoors, so at noon Bianca checked papers at her desk while lunch buckets rattled. After cold chicken, sausages and apples had been consumed amid whispered remarks and glum expressions, she sent the class outside for a few minutes of exercise.

She'd started the day in such a euphoric mood, and now she felt completely defeated. She paced the floor. Why had she ever thought she could be a teacher? She opened a window to dispel the lingering odors of warm bodies and leftover food. Junior was at the far corner of the schoolyard pelting the outhouse with dirt clods. She knew just how he felt.

CHAPTER 52

"This here little bit of paper don't look like much, Smoky, but it's our ticket to easy street." Cap tightened the girth and patted the horse's bony flank. He wrapped the yellowed piece of newsprint in a tattered blue bandana and tucked it deep into the saddlebag.

The position of the sun and the shadow of his cabin told him it was well past noon, but still early enough that he didn't need to hurry. There'd been two jugs of Frenchy's special bran mash whiskey on his front stoop Sunday morning. That was a surprise. He'd thought maybe Frenchy was riled at him for some reason. Cap had been laying low and hadn't seen a living soul all day Monday. He was mighty glad he could count on his flask being full without having to go to Fowler's.

He climbed on his horse and headed for Frenchy's cabin. Plenty of time to stop by, thank him for the booze. Ask him where he'd been keeping himself.

The padlock on the front door took him aback. He peered through the window and shook his head. Looked like the whole place had been cleaned out. No clothes hung from the pegs on the wall. Even more puzzled, Cap walked around back. The traps that usually hung from a wire stretched across the back stoop were gone.

Frenchy was always complaining about how cold weather made his joints ache. He'd been talking about heading for California, but he'd been saying that for the last year or two. And he sure as hell hadn't breathed a word lately. After a couple of trips around the house, Cap gave up, shook his head, and got back on his horse.

It sure looked like Frenchy had pulled up stakes, without even saying goodbye. As soon as Cap had his thousand dollars tucked away, he'd been planning to talk to Frenchy. Tell him he'd come into a bit of luck. Suggest they head south together. He'd had his mind set on the widow Nolan's property, but with a thousand cash in hand he could move to where the winters were warm. Buy a nice little place and live out his days in comfort without having to wait for the railroad to come through. Hell, with a thousand dollars in his pocket, he didn't care if the railroad never connected Oregon with the rest of the civilized world.

It was still early, but being a little ahead of schedule was probably a good idea. It'd give him a chance to get the lay of the land, be sure everything was on the up and up before he turned over the clipping.

Cap headed down the road and took the trail leading to the river, like they'd agreed on. The passing storm had left the ground oozing mud. He'd never seen it so bad. Streams of water seemed to have sprung up everywhere. He needed to backtrack more than once before he made his way to the clearing. He eased himself out of the saddle and freed his horse to graze near a thicket of berry bushes. Then he settled down on a fallen log, propped Sweet Betsy against his knee and uncorked his flask.

"Are you ready?"

Joanna Nolan whirled at the words spoken in her native tongue. The long-handled spoon she was holding clattered to the floor in front of the hearth. Her brother's muscular frame filled the doorway.

"You startled me. I keep forgetting how skilled you are at moving silently."

He looked around the room and scowled. "Why aren't your belongings packed?"

She motioned to the table. "Let me fix you something to eat."

She had always been able to soothe her brother with food. Their mother said Running Fox had been born hungry and never eaten his fill. Now she hoped the aroma of the herb-rich chicken soup that had been simmering since daybreak would work its magic.

"Get your things together," he snarled.

She ladled the soup, thick with carrots, noodles and chunks of chicken, into an earthenware bowl and put it on the table. "Sit down, brother. Fill your stomach, and then we can talk."

"The time for talk has passed." His tone was harsh, but he lurched into a chair, snatched a biscuit from the basket she placed beside him, and dipped it into the steaming bowl.

Watching him wolf down all the biscuits and gulp a second bowl of soup, Joanna wondered how long it had been since he'd last eaten. His face was so thin that his cheekbones looked as if they were about to pierce the taut flesh. How could he expect her and Aiden to join him when his own existence was so precarious? But Running Fox fed on anger. This she knew. Reasoning with him would lead nowhere.

"Where's the boy? You're still sending him to the pale people's school, aren't you?"

"Aiden's teacher says he's very bright. He's already reading."

"Much good that will do him. Get busy now. We need to get into the mountains before nightfall. You can fetch Aiden on the way."

"My life is here now, brother." Her lips trembled as she formed the words. "I cannot go with you."

For a long moment he simply stared. Then he stood, shoved the chair aside and moved quickly toward her, his clenched fist inches from her face. "You dare defy me?"

"Your life is yours to live as you choose, brother. I must do what I know is best for myself and my child." She didn't believe he would strike her, but she had suffered Daniel's blows and survived. She waited, unflinching, her heart hammering in her chest.

"You turn your back on your own people." His thin lips curled in scorn. "You are no longer my sister." Then his fist dropped to his side and he slipped away as silently as he had come.

CHAPTER 53

Finally the hands on the schoolroom clock crawled to dismissal time. As the children gathered their belongings, Oren slammed a copy of the *Oregon Statesman* on Bianca's desk.

"Aunt Nora picked up the paper in town yesterday." He was out the door before she could offer thanks.

Usually Bianca hungered for news of the outside world, but at the moment she was too distracted to do more than glance at a couple of articles. She collected the paper along with the children's copybooks and trudged outside to where Patches was waiting.

She headed for home, mentally rehashing the dreadful day and wondering how a competent, experienced schoolmarm would have handled it. Scattered clouds over the mountains to the west warned of more stormy days ahead, but bright afternoon sunshine filtered through the fir and cedar trees. At the turnoff for home Patches stopped, waiting for Bianca to open the gate to the Pangstons' farmyard and the barn beyond. Inside Bianca would no doubt face more accusations from the Pangston girls. If Mattie had been to the store and seen Agnes, there was no telling what her frame of mind might be.

Taking advantage of what might be the last spell of good weather suddenly seemed infinitely more appealing than Tina's screams and the other girls' scowling faces. Any trouble brewing inside the Pangston's house would keep. Bianca turned the mare around and flicked the reins. Patches tossed her mane and trotted briskly down the road.

"You didn't want to go home either, did you, girl?"

The forest was unusually quiet. Soft earth and layers of mushy leaves muffled the sound of the mare's hoofs. As she rode, Bianca mulled things over in her mind. Was it possible that, in some way, she was responsible for Ed Fowler's arrest? She remembered Tyler saying she seemed to be right in the middle of everything. If she could talk to Tyler, she'd know exactly what was going on. But that wasn't going to happen. He was over at Wesleyville, doing whatever it was sheriffs did when they weren't out arresting people.

She shook her head, wishing there was somebody she could talk to, somebody who would reassure her. She remembered Aiden saying his mother had been to town with Nora yesterday. If Joanna had seen the lawyer about Daniel's will, she might have heard about Ed Fowler's arrest. Such news had a way of spreading quickly, and the lawyer was Tyler's uncle. A visit with Joanna would lift her spirits in any case.

Bianca guided Patches off the main road and onto the river trail. The ground was soggy, and as they got closer to the river an odor of decay permeated the air. The forest was dense here. Shining pools of rainwater lingered in rocky outcroppings. A red squirrel scolded her for interrupting his bath and disappeared among the branches of a myrtle tree.

"See, Patches, even the squirrels are upset with me today."

The horse slowed and stopped. A mudslide blocked the trail ahead.

"It's all right, girl," she said. "We'll turn around and head back to the road. We shouldn't have taken the river trail after all the rain we've had lately."

The mare picked her way around puddles and rain-soaked clumps of thimbleberry bushes. When they were back on the trail, Bianca patted the horse's withers.

"I know you're not happy about all the mud, Patches, but you're doing fine. Probably we should head for home after all."

She didn't have to talk to the Pangstons when she got back. She could head upstairs and correct papers until suppertime. And she had the copy of *The Statesman* to look forward to. Newspapers, hard to come by, were passed around and discussed endlessly. She was lucky to have a copy less than a week old. She'd only glanced at the issue before leaving the schoolhouse, briefly noting a couple of headlines. Flooding in Willamette Valley. Governor Warns of Cholera Outbreak.

But something else about the paper had caught her eye. Something she should have noticed. What was it? The paper, published in Salem, carried national news as well as stories from all around Oregon, but she hadn't seen any articles datelined Oakfield or Wesleyville. So what was that pesky voice in her head trying to tell her?

It couldn't be about the clipping Aiden said was missing. This morning he hadn't even mentioned the clipping. He'd been too excited about his new horse to think of anything else. And at the fiesta, when Aiden had talked to Tyler, he'd kept talking about a frozen river.

"It was about a river, Miss Stratton. I remember that for sure. Right there at the beginning of the story. Frozen river, it said—or maybe freezing river—but that wouldn't make any sense, would it?"

That was it! Of course! Why hadn't she seen it before? Why hadn't Tyler? Right at the front, Aiden had said. Something about a river. Maybe it was a place—the name of a place, like Rogue River or Red River. But Aiden said frozen river or maybe freezing river.

Then it hit her. Frazier River. The first day of school, when the children had been finding places on the map, they looked for Frazier River. Somebody had been there panning for gold. Daniel Nolan must have been there—his name in the clipping was what had drawn Aiden's attention when he was learning to read. But Aiden couldn't have been the one who'd brought up Frazier River. Aiden hadn't been at school the first day.

The mare pulled up short. The trail stopped abruptly at a swift-flowing stream. Bianca was sure she hadn't crossed it earlier. In fact, she couldn't remember ever seeing a stream when she'd taken the river trail. Patches must have veered off onto some other trail when they'd gone around the mudslide.

"I should have been paying attention, Patches. Now I don't know where we are, but if we follow this brook downstream we're sure to come to the river. Let's go, girl."

CHAPTER 54

Even before he pounded on the door, Tyler sensed that the place was empty. No smoke rose from the chimney, and the woods were eerily quiet.

"Mackay!"

Tall trees surrounding the cabin muffled his shout. He banged on the door again and lifted the latch. The wooden door creaked open. The cabin looked and smelled as bad as on his last visit. He grabbed a poker propped against the fireplace and stirred the ashes. A few coals smoldered in the hearth.

Outside, the smell of manure was strong, and there were fresh droppings on the dirt floor of the horse stall. Hoof prints in the muddy earth led to the road. There the tracks headed toward the river, but wagon ruts and the hard-packed roadbed made it impossible to follow further. Cap had been here earlier, but there was no telling where he'd gone. Tyler shook his head in frustration.

He'd intended to leave for Oakfield right after breakfast, but Wallace Bigelow, who owned the livery stable, waylaid him on his way out of town to report a couple of missing horses. Bigelow was pushing eighty and more than a tad forgetful, but he was sure he'd closed the corral gate. By the time Tyler located the horses grazing in a nearby alfalfa field, it was nearly noon. Fallen branches and mudslides made the eighteen miles to Oakfield seem more like fifty. Tyler checked his watch. A few minutes after three.

Back on his horse, he headed for the schoolhouse. Bianca Stratton was an exasperating woman, but aside from Clayton she was the first person he'd really been able to talk to since he got to Oakfield. He missed her conversation. He even missed her sharp tongue. Damn it! He missed her. Period.

He hadn't seen her since the fiesta when he'd been too much of an idiot to hang onto her when he had the chance. She'd been with him when they'd talked to Aiden about the missing clipping. He'd stop by and see what she thought of Clayton's Frazier River theory. And he'd warn her to steer clear of Cap. Not that she'd listen.

The schoolyard was empty, which didn't surprise him. Class would have been dismissed at least a half hour ago, but he figured Bianca would still be inside tidying up and correcting papers. He pushed open the door and walked through the coatroom, calling her name. Then, at the classroom door, he froze.

The room was a shambles. Bianca's beloved books were scattered on the floor near the stove amid a welter of firewood, broken chalk and the tattered remains of a map. On the blackboard in crude capital letters someone had scrawled BICH.

CHAPTER 55

Patches threaded her way through rocky debris that edged the water. Suddenly she lifted her head and whinnied. Almost like an echo, an answering whinny floated back. The mare, ears pricked, followed the sound. Another horse, Bianca thought, meant somebody was nearby. Probably she'd wandered in a circle and come back to the main road. Several small streams joined the one she was following, and the sound of rushing water seemed to engulf her.

The mare stepped cautiously around a gnarled sycamore tree, and Bianca found herself in a clearing. Rain had altered the landscape, but from the fallen log and the gooseflesh on her arms she knew she'd been there before. What had been a shallow ravine was now an angry river carrying branches, rocks and mud in its wake.

A mud-splattered horse peered out from a thicket of wild grapevines. His stringy mane was matted and snarled. Bones protruded sharply beneath a scabrous hide. She'd have taken him for an aged mustang abandoned by his herd, but he wore a saddle and bridle—leather relics that looked as abused as the horse. Bianca was sure the creature was the one she'd seen outside Joanna's house. Cap Mackay was the last person she wanted to meet up with.

Something was moving on the other side of the glade. Bianca edged Patches back into the shadows of the sycamore and peered out cautiously. She breathed a sigh of relief. She couldn't see his face, but she knew those broad shoulders. She started to call out, but her voice died in her throat. Jesse was dragging Cap feet first into the open space near the fallen log. The old man must have fallen. The horse was on the opposite side of the clearing, but it could have bolted.

She started to dismount, to run to Jesse and offer help, but something about the angle of Mackay's head told her he was beyond help. Blood oozed from behind the old man's ear and seeped into his grimy beard.

Jesse dropped Cap's feet and began foraging through the dead man's pockets. "Where in hell did he put the damn thing?" he muttered.

Bianca squeezed her eyes together, desperately willing the horror before her to somehow disappear. Instead, something clicked inside her head. As clearly as if it had happened yesterday she heard Oren's words. "Jesse went to look for gold some place called Frazier River." She forced herself to look across the clearing. Then, as if he had sensed her presence, Jesse turned and regarded her through hooded eyes.

Somehow Bianca subdued the emotions warring within her. "Jesse?" she called. Even to her own ears, her voice sounded hollow.

He straightened up and swiped muddy hands across his leather chaps. Moving across the clearing, he stopped a few feet from her. "Looks like his old horse slipped on the muddy bank, and Cap lost his balance."

Bianca willed herself to stay calm. She must be mistaken. Maybe it was somebody else who'd been mining at Frazier River. And even if Jesse had been there, probably hundreds of others had gone north for that big gold strike. Tyler had warned her about jumping to conclusions.

"Is Cap—-I mean, is there anything to be done for him?"

Jesse shook his head. "Appears he hit his head when he fell. I knew he was a goner as soon as I came across him."

Bianca struggled to blot out the images that flashed through her mind—Jesse armed with a heavy rock, smashing the old man's skull. Just as he'd stuck down another old man so many years ago in a place called Frazier River. And poor Daniel Nolan, murdered and scalped, had died of a blow to the head. No! It wasn't possible. Not the Jesse she knew.

"I was figuring on laying the body across his horse and taking him into town."

Bianca nodded. "I saw a decrepit old horse across over near that grape thicket. I could help you . . . "

Why hadn't he rounded up the horse first instead of dragging the body into the clearing? And why was he going through Cap's pockets? The nagging voice inside her head whispered the answer.

"You better get on home. I'll take care of this." Jesse scanned the darkening sky. "Looks like there's more rain coming. You shouldn't be out alone in the woods in this weather."

"I—I'm afraid I got turned around and lost my way." She kept her voice steady. Jesse couldn't know she'd learned about the clipping. Even if the voice in her head was right, she was safe as long as he didn't think she knew the truth. He'd held her in his arms, asked her to marry him. No matter what he'd done, he'd never harm her.

"Easy to get turned around after those storms. The road's on the other side of this fallen log." He sounded so—so normal, so concerned for her safety.

"Are you sure you don't want me to—"

"Just go, Bianca."

Was the road really so close? Could she believe Jesse at this point? Behind her the white water in the rain-swollen stream churned. If the road, her only hope for safety, was nearby, she had to cross the clearing and ride toward Jesse and past Cap's battered corpse. She flicked the reins, and Patches took a few tentative steps into the glade.

"You don't like this place, do you, girl," Bianca whispered, placing a reassuring hand on the mare's neck. "Well, neither do I, but we don't have a lot of choices here."

As they drew closer to the body, the mare balked and pawed the ground.

"It's the blood," Jesse said. "Horses can smell it. Hand me the reins, and I'll lead you out of here." He reached toward her, and Bianca couldn't help herself. She cringed from his touch.

He pulled his hand away, stepped back and gave her a long look that sent a shudder down her spine. "What's the matter, sweetheart?"

"Seeing Cap's body—up close like this—I guess I—"

"You never struck me as the sort who'd swoon at the sight of a little blood." He studied her face, and she fought back the wave of revulsion that swept through her.

"It was a shock—coming across you out here in the woods. I mean—"

"I don't know how much you saw, but I'm afraid I know what you mean." His eyes narrowed, and there was a grim set to his mouth she'd never seen before.

"I don't understand, Jesse."

"I think you do. I always knew you were smart. That's one of the things I liked about you. I thought about it a lot—-the kind of life we could have together."

"But nothing has changed." Her hands on the reins were clammy, her voice a quavery whisper.

"I wish I could believe that. Everybody warned me about you—how you were always snooping around. I should have listened."

"Cap was a terrible old man. Nobody will be sorry he's dead. It was an accident, and—"

"We both know that's not true, Bianca. I'm real sorry things turned out this way, but I can't have you running to the sheriff, now can I?"

"Are you going to kill me, too? You'll never get away with it."

"I always get away with it, Bianca." He smiled, a malicious flash of teeth. "And this time it will be simple. Everybody's been complaining how you're always poking your nose where it doesn't belong. You figured out how Cap killed Daniel Nolan, and he shot you before you could go running to the sheriff. I saw you go riding off into the woods, and I was worried about you, knowing how easy it would be for you to get lost after the storm. I heard the shot, but I didn't get there in time. Cap turned on me, and I shot him. Too bad I was too late to save you."

"But Cap wasn't shot. The sheriff will know—"

"No problem." Jesse made a low, clucking sound deep in his throat. The black stallion pushed its way through the vines edging the clearing and trotted obediently forward. Jesse untied the rifle that was slung on the saddle, sighted down the barrel and fired into the old man's corpse. "Now he's been shot. Must have hit his head on a rock when he went down."

CHAPTER 56

Tyler had broken up domestic fights and barroom brawls, but the classroom didn't have the look of a place where there'd been a struggle. No, this was deliberate destruction. He stared at the wreckage in dismay. Who had done this? Why? Where was Bianca? Had Cap come to the schoolhouse assuming, as Tyler had, that she'd be there? Had he ransacked the place in a drunken rage? Tyler hoped to God Bianca had already left when it happened.

The classroom was silent, but he checked under the desks and behind the stove to be sure nobody was there. Then he went outside and made a quick survey of the empty playground and outhouse. On the road a single set of hoof prints led toward the preacher's place. Minutes later Tyler was pounding on Pangston's front door.

"Oh, Sheriff Wells." One of the preacher's daughters—the plain mousy-haired one—opened the door. "Papa's out back someplace. I'll call Mama."

"I'm looking for Miss Stratton."

"Oh, she's not here, Sheriff."

"Who's at the door, Gertrude?" Mattie Pangston's voice came from somewhere in the back of the house.

"It's Sheriff Wells, Mama. He's looking for Miss Stratton."

"Gertrude, where are your manners? Invite the sheriff in." Mattie, a smudge of flour on her nose, appeared behind the child. "Bianca's probably still at school."

"I've come straight from the classroom. She's not there." Inside, Tyler found himself surrounded as the three other Pangston girls clattered down the stairs into the parlor.

"Oh, dear. I have no idea where she might have gone. To the store, maybe." Mattie wiped her hands on her apron and turned to the oldest girl. "Cora, did Miss Stratton say anything about stopping by Fowler's?"

Cora shook her head. "I don't think she'd go near the store today. Not after causing so much trouble for poor Mrs. Fowler."

"Trouble? What kind of trouble?" Tyler managed to keep his voice calm.

"You know. Getting poor Mr. Fowler sent to jail."

"Ed Fowler's been arrested? Good Lord, Sheriff, how can that be?" Mattie grabbed the feather duster and began brushing invisible specks of dust from the keys of the melodeon.

"It was Miss Stratton's doing. Lloyd told me his mother said so." Red-haired Katie's pigtails bobbed in emphasis. "We were all pretty mad at her."

Tyler hadn't planned to say anything about the vandalized classroom. Now he suspected the children were involved. "After school. Tell me what happened after school," he said.

"I went straight home, like I always do. Lenny and Aiden walked with me a ways." Gertrude said. "Cora and the twins think they're too grown-up to walk with us."

"Oren and Hank rode off, and I walked with the twins as far as the fork in the road," Cora said. "Sometimes Junior stays and helps Miss Stratton tidy up, but I bet he didn't today."

"Junior's sweet on Miss Stratton," Katie said. "The twins are always teasing him about it."

"I don't tease him. Teasing is mean, and I try never to be mean." Gertrude straightened a pile of hymnals on the table near the door.

"About Ed Fowler, Sheriff. Is he really in jail?" Agnes asked.

"It's true, Mama," said Katie. "Some folks who'd been to town came into the store. They told Agnes they saw him locked up. Lenny heard them talking."

"And the twins said Mrs. Fowler was crying all night," Cora added.

Three-year-old Tina began to wail.

"Miss Stratton had nothing to do with the Fowler family's problems." Tyler's patience had run out, and trying to make himself heard above Tina's screams wasn't helping.

"Hush, Tina. Don't be such a crybaby." Cora scooped the three-year-old into her arms and nuzzled her neck. The howls stopped as abruptly as they had begun.

"I'm not a baby. I'm three." She held up four chubby fingers to illustrate.

All the girls started talking at once. Tyler paced the floor in frustration. The damage to the classroom was done. Finding the culprits could wait. The important thing was to locate Bianca and make sure she was safe. Then he needed to find Cap. He raised his hand and scowled, and everybody stopped talking.

"Mr. Fowler was released early this morning," he said. "It's true he was in custody, but Miss Stratton was in no way involved. Now, do any of you have any idea where she might be?"

"Well, Sheriff, I did happen to be looking out the window after I got back from school." Gertrude retrieved a stray hymnal from a chair and added it to the stack. "She was on her horse, you know, and I thought she was coming home. I mean, she sort of stopped at the gate."

"Oh, Gertrude," Mattie exclaimed. "Why didn't you say so right away?"

"I was going to, but everybody started talking about the Fowlers, and—"

"Never mind all that," Tyler interrupted. "She stopped at the gate, and then what?"

"Well, all of a sudden she galloped off toward the river."

Back on his horse, Tyler cursed himself for wasting time at the Pangston's place. He'd assumed Bianca had gone home. Assumed. He knew better than to make assumptions, but he didn't seem to be able to think straight where Bianca Stratton was concerned.

As he neared the river, puddles and mudslides made the going more difficult. Then the hoof prints he was following disappeared completely as the trail deteriorated into muddy ooze. Streams swollen from the heavy rain carried rocks and debris in their wake. He was about to turn back when, above the noise of rushing water, he heard the sharp crack of a rifle shot.

CHAPTER 57

"Nobody will mourn Cap Mackay." Unable to look at Jesse, Bianca focused her eyes on the shining hairs of her horse's mane. "I'll back up your story-—tell everybody how you saved my life."

"You're a bad liar, Bianca. I'm sorry. I thought we could have a proper life, you and me. I really wanted that, you know."

He pulled a shell out of his cartridge belt. "Damn nuisance, reloading a rifle, but this old Springfield shoots as true as the day I bought it."

Bianca watched his hands-—those square, capable hands—fingering the bullet that would end her life. Tears stung her eyes. In desperation she dug her heel into the mare's flank and cracked the reins. The horse lunged forward. Bianca clutched the saddle horn and struggled to keep her balance as they raced across the clearing, splattering mud as they went.

Jesse's startled black stallion reared. As Bianca sped past, she saw Jesse struggle to load the rifle while dodging the stallion's flailing hoofs. Patches plunged through thorny underbrush, and Bianca hunkered down in the saddle, searching for the road or at least a trail leading to it. Jesse would be after them in a matter of minutes. Her little horse was no match for the stallion's speed.

Ahead, another newly swollen stream blocked her path. The same rushing stream she'd seen in nightmares since her disastrous fall. Only now, the stream was real and the sound of the stallion's hooves thudding behind her more frightening than any nightmare.

Desperately she dug her heels into the mare's flank. "Jump, Patches. Jump, girl!"

Her cry echoed in her ears as they approached the rocky bank. Patches lurched forward, and Bianca felt herself sailing through the air. She closed her eyes, waiting for the blow when she struck the ground.

But there was no blow. Her hands were still gripping the saddle horn, and she could feel the mare's warm body beneath her. They landed with a splash, and Bianca opened her eyes as Patches scrambled up the bank and onto the road beyond.

She glanced over her shoulder as she urged her horse forward. In the middle of the stream the black stallion, surrounded by debris and rushing water, struggled to maintain its footing. Then a swift eddy swept the terrified animal downstream and out of sight. There was no sign of Jesse.

At the sound of hoof-beats on the road, Bianca jerked the reins in confusion. Had Jesse somehow recovered the stallion and doubled back? Then, around a curve in the muddy road, a familiar bay horse came into view.

"Bianca! Are you all right?" Tyler guided his horse close beside her.

Still trying to catch her breath, she nodded.

"I heard a shot."

"Cap," she gasped, waving a hand toward the stream behind her.

"Are you hurt? By God, Bianca, I warned you about—"

"Dead." She breathed a long sigh and forced her hands to loosen their grip on the reins. "Cap's dead."

Rocks clattered and branches snapped. Tyler turned toward the stream. He stiffened as he watched the black stallion clamber up the bank and shake water off its coat.

"That horse, Bianca. That's—"

"Jesse's horse."

And she told him everything.

CHAPTER 58

Bianca sat cross-legged on the braided rag rug in her attic room and tried to concentrate on the stack of copybooks in her lap. Even checking spelling lists seemed beyond her. Finally she shoved the copybooks unto the floor, stood, and stared out the small paned window. Sudden tears blurred her vision.

Reaching into the pocket of her gingham skirt, she pulled out a handkerchief and dabbed at her eyes. She knew she had to get herself together somehow, but doing it seemed to be another matter. In the classroom she managed to function pretty well. It was as if another Bianca—Bianca the schoolmarm—was alive doing her job. Not doing it really well, but at least going through the motions. She muddled through the days and hibernated in her room at night.

Jesse's lifeless body had been found on the riverbank downstream. The following day Bianca watched dry-eyed as his casket was lowered into the ground. Now her stomach churned at the memory of Jesse's kisses and the even more vivid image of him dragging Cap's lifeless body across the clearing. She'd always been so sure of herself. Suddenly she wasn't sure of anything.

Stuffing the handkerchief back in her pocket, she peered through the window. The noise of hammers and saws had been so constant over the past week that she really didn't hear it any more unless she stopped to listen. Between the house and road a building was nearing completion. Cushing was finally getting his church. It was ironic that he had Agnes Fowler to thank.

Ed's testimony had sent the dishonest government agent to prison, and Ed had gotten off with only a hefty fine. But Agnes, humiliated by the whole affair, had demanded that every cent he'd put aside be used to build a church. It was a simple rectangular building about the size of the schoolhouse. Cushing wanted a steeple, but Agnes hadn't been that embarrassed.

"Bianca, are you up there?"

"Yes, Mattie." Of course. Where else would she be on a Saturday morning? Mattie, who knew exactly where she was, probably was going to insist she come downstairs and have some gingerbread.

"May I come up?" The footsteps on the stairs told her the question was rhetorical, but Bianca was surprised. Mattie never came to the attic uninvited, and she'd been emphatic with the girls about Bianca's right to privacy. Now she stood in the doorway, round face flushed and eyes bright with excitement.

"Come in, Mattie. Sit down. Goodness, you're all out of breath."

Mattie sank onto the edge of the bed and fanned herself with the envelope she held in her hand. "I took the extra eggs to the store this morning to trade for some lace to finish that petticoat I'm making for Tina. Ed went to Wesleyville yesterday to meet the stage, and some mail came through. This letter's for you. It's from Boston. It took a long time getting here, so I knew you'd want to have it right away."

Bianca took the envelope. It was smudged, wrinkled and postmarked more than a month ago.

Mattie waited. A letter, especially a letter from back east, was an event. This was the only letter Bianca had received in the nearly three months she'd been in Oakfield. She knew Mattie hoped she'd open it and share whatever news it contained, but she simply stared at the tidy script and the return address.

Leandra Stratton, whoever she was, had answered Bianca's letter. Probably a distant cousin had replied out of a sense of duty. Still, the letter might contain answers to some of the questions plaguing her.

"Thanks, Mattie." Bianca pushed the envelope into her pocket, snatched her everyday bonnet from the hook by the door and plopped it on her head. "I think I'll go down to the barn. Patches needs a good grooming. I'm afraid I've been neglecting her."

"Of course, you want to read your mail in private. I understand. Letters so often bring bad news, don't they?" Mattie stood up, smoothed her skirt and patted her belly. "I really think it's a boy this time. He never stops kicking."

Finding Katie at the barn was hardly a surprise. Bianca wasn't sure how the eight-year-old had persuaded Cushing to let her adopt Cap's horse. Katie practically lived in the stall, and already Smoky bore little resemblance to the woebegone creature Bianca had seen in the forest.

Katie waved a currycomb in welcome. "I'm almost finished here, Miss Stratton. Doesn't he look handsome?"

"He does, indeed. You're taking wonderful care of the old fellow."

"Cap fought for the Union, and Smoky was his horse. So that makes him kind of a war veteran, too, you know. Papa says it's a waste because he's so old he's not going to live long, but President Grant says we should honor those who served our country."

Bianca smiled. "He's very lucky you're looking after him."

"I can help you groom Patches, too, if you want."

Bianca fingered the envelope in her pocket. "Thanks, Katie, but I'm not really in the mood for company."

"I don't blame you for still being mad at me."

"Angry? At you?"

"About the classroom. I knew Junior was gonna do something really bad. Lloyd said not to tell, but I should have said something. I'm awful sorry."

"That's all past, Katie. All of you pitched in and helped clean up. You run along now and tend to your Saturday chores."

Katie fed Smoky a carrot, gave him a final pat on the nose and scampered toward the house.

Bianca sank down on a bale of hay, opened the envelope and took out a sheet of creamy vellum paper. Her eyes jumped to the signature at the bottom of the page. Her heart began to pound as she read the signature, "Your grandmother, Leandra Stratton."

Her grandmother! For a moment she sat absorbing the astonishing news. Then she smoothed the paper and read the entire letter.

My dear Bianca,

You cannot imagine the joy your letter brought me. How delighted I am to discover a granddaughter I have never met! As much as it grieved me to learn of your father's untimely passing, I think I knew somehow that he was gone. Perhaps mothers have a sixth sense about those things.

Until your letter arrived this morning I'd had no news of Charles since he and your mother left to be married over the strenuous objections of both of their fathers. So many years have passed, and much that seemed important at the time seems almost trivial now.

How difficult it must have been to suffer so many losses in your young life. And now your beloved sister, too, is gone and you are making your own way in the wilderness. It is admirable, but it breaks my heart.

I am an old woman now, widowed nearly twenty years. I've become accustomed to taking matters into my own hands, a skill I regret not having learned earlier. My holdings include shares in a number of sailing vessels, one of which, Resourceful, is carrying this letter. By the time it reaches you, the ship will be on her way north to Granville where she will take on supplies and a cargo of wheat.

It is presumptuous of me, but I pray you will grant an old woman's prayer and board Resourceful for the journey back to Boston. Captain MacDonald is a trustworthy gentleman and an excellent seaman. Accommodations for passengers aboard the vessel are somewhat Spartan, but he assures me that should you find it possible to make the voyage, a spacious cabin will be put at your disposal.

I know I have not answered all the questions your letter posed, but there is much to be said that is best imparted in person.

Whatever your decision, I hope you will find a way to meet with Captain MacDonald when the ship puts in at Scott's Landing. I have entrusted him with funds with which you may purchase any necessities for making the voyage, or, if you are determined to remain in Oregon, please use this small gift to relieve the burdens of pioneer life.

I shall be at the dock to meet Resourceful when she returns, with the fervent hope that I shall have the joy of embracing you at last.

Your grandmother,
Leandra Stratton

After reading the letter several times, Bianca carefully replaced it in the envelope and tucked it back in her pocket. She stood, brushed wisps of hay off her skirt, and began the familiar task of grooming her horse.

"I can't take it all in, Patches. A grandmother. A real, live grandmother. Can you believe it?"

"Mattie told me you'd been acting strange. But, really? Talking to a horse?"

At the sound of Tyler's voice, Bianca whirled.

"Tyler! You startled me. And I've always talked to Patches. She's a good listener."

"I'm a good listener." Tyler perched on a sawhorse outside the stall.

"You must have more important things to do." Bianca sank back on the bale of hay and faced him.

"Actually, the sheriff's office is pretty quiet right now. Just the way I like it. I was out at the Donovan place. Nora asked me to go through Jesse's cabin before she disposed of his belongings. I'm sorry I haven't seen you since—"

"I know you've been busy tying up all the loose ends. Between Mattie and the children at school, I seem to keep up on things." She pulled the envelope out of her pocket. "But today I got some surprising news."

"Mattie said you received a letter."

"When I came to Oakfield, I wasn't sure I had any family left except for my nephews. Then I found a name and address in the bottom of a box of Viola's things Rolf brought me. I wrote a letter that same night. It seems so long ago I'd almost forgotten about it." She opened the envelope, took out the letter and handed it to him. "The reply came today. I'd like you to read it."

"Are you sure?"

She nodded. "That's what I was talking to Patches about. I need some help, Tyler. Patches isn't much good at giving advice."

He pushed the gray Stetson to the back of his head as he read and re-read the letter. Then he folded it and handed it back to her, his face solemn. "That's a lot to digest all at once."

"Of course, sailing around the Horn to Boston is totally out of the question, and—"

"I thought you wanted advice." He picked up at piece of straw and broke it in half.

"My teaching contract is almost up, but Cushing says the job is mine for as long as I want it, so you see—"

He tossed the straw aside and stood. "You might as well go back to talking to your horse."

She moved toward him and put her hand on his arm as he turned to leave. "Please, Tyler. I really do want to know what you think."

He covered her hand with his and stood silent for a long moment. "You must know by now, Bianca, that I care about you. I care about you a lot."

She took a step back, but his hand held her fast. "Tyler, I—"

"Let me finish, Bianca. How can I tell you that you should leave Oregon when, more than anything in the world, I'd like to have you close by?" He dropped her hand and sank back on the bale of hay.

"Tyler, I don't know what to say. I really didn't—"

"It's all right. From the first time you laid eyes on Jesse, it was all over. I saw how you looked at him, and I knew I didn't have a chance."

"That's what's making me crazy. How could I have been so blind? A cold-blooded murderer. I'll never be able to trust my feelings again."

"You've grown up a lot in the last few months, Bianca. But you're still very young."

"I'm seventeen. Already an old maid," she objected.

"Out here, perhaps. But in New England young ladies don't routinely marry at thirteen. They wear stylish clothes and go to cotillions. In Boston there are wonderful libraries and opera houses. You can't even imagine what opportunities you would have." He leaned toward her, took the currycomb out of her hand and hung it on a nail in the stall.

"I've always dreamed of traveling, but—"

"Bianca, your grandmother sounds like an amazing woman. If you don't go to her, I'm afraid you'll regret it all your life."

"Rolf would have a fit."

He chuckled. "Then that's another point in favor of Boston."

"You're serious. You really think I should go."

"And when you come back, I'll be waiting."

"It's a long way, Tyler. Another world, really. If I leave, I may never come back."

He leaned toward her and brushed his lips across her forehead. "In that case, Bianca, I'll have to come to Boston and find you."

ACKNOWLEDGEMENTS

Many thanks to all those whose unstinting gifts of time, expertise and encouragement kept me writing, revising and rewriting. Jane Weyhrauch, Richard Miller, Kristen Taylor, BB Hill, Amy Fanning, Jack Havlina, Ruthe Price, Jean-Robert Bayard, Jacqueline Grossman, Barbara Staton, Larry Miller, Nancy Klann, Judth Klausner, Myra Posert and Raymond Obstfeld all critiqued my work and made it better. I never could have written this book without their support.

Finally, I must pay tribute to my maternal grandmother, Hortense Reed Applegate, whose stories about teaching in a one-room schoolhouse in the 1870's kept me enthralled as a young child and whose memoirs inspired me to use Southern Oregon as the setting for *The Deadly Glade*.

www.ingramcontent.com/pod-product-compliance
Lightning Source LLC
Chambersburg PA
CBHW062015170626
46813CB00001B/167